W9-ALX-292

Critics rave about Miranda Jarrett and her marvelous tales of sea-swept romance . . .

MOONLIGHT

Winner of the 1999 Golden Leaf Award for best historical romance

"Five stars! Miranda Jarrett is one of the genre's best, and her newest eighteenth-century American tale, *Moonlight,* will only enhance her high esteem with readers. . . . Fast-paced and delightful!"

—amazon.com

"What a touching, heartfelt story! . . . Every detail will keep you wanting more. Beautifully written."

—*Rendezvous*

"Wonderful. . . . The magic of *Moonlight* lies in the characters, and Miranda Jarrett has given her readers a beautiful relationship with lovers who will clearly spend their lives living happily ever after."

—booksquare.com

WISHING

A *Romantic Times* "Top Pick" and a "Pick of the Month" for January 1999 by barnesandnoble.com

"Readers are sure to find themselves swept off their feet by this utterly enchanting and imaginative romance by the mistress of the seafaring love story. Delightfully charming and fun, yet poignant, exciting, and romantic, this is Miranda Jarrett at her finest!"

—*Romantic Times*

"Vivid and enjoyable. . . . Believable characters and an engrossing, heartwarming story set in a true historical background."

—*Cape Cod Journal*

"Wonderful, heartwarming. . . . The [Fairbourne] stories keep getting better, and harder to put down."

—*Old Book Barn Gazette*

"Wonderful. . . . The early eighteenth century come[s] alive for the reader."

—*Under the Covers*

CRANBERRY POINT

Named amazon.com's #1 Best New Romance Paperback for June 1998 and a "Pick of the Month" for July 1998 by barnesandnoble.com

"A vivid and exciting portrait of colonial America. . . . A memorable tale of trust and love, of healing and passion, and most of all the magic of romance."

—*Romantic Times*

"[A] passionate love story rich in history and characterization. She takes the reader back in time and place to an era where men are strong and caring and extremely possessive and defensive of their women. . . . This is an award-winning saga from a sensational author."

—*Rendezvous*

"No author . . . brings to life the early eighteenth century better than Miranda Jarrett. . . . [The] fast-paced story line is exciting and the lead protagonists are thrilling and real. . . . Everything Jarrett does is magic."

—*Affaire de Coeur*

THE CAPTAIN'S BRIDE

"As always, Ms. Jarrett takes the high seas by storm, creating one of her liveliest heroines and a hero to be her match. Readers are sure to delight in Annabelle's sometimes outrageous schemes and fall in love with Joshua, hoping to see them return in another book in the Fairbourne chronicles. Hurrah for a new series!"

—*Romantic Times*

"The queen of colonial romances has another winner. . . . Miranda Jarrett is the admiral of the historical sailing romance and *The Captain's Bride* is at her usual level of excellence. The story line is superb and filled with nonstop action, and the lead protagonists are a delightful, intrepid couple."

—Amazon Books

"A fabulous colonial sailing romance that is loaded with action and high-seas adventure. The lead characters make a classy couple as they passionately duel with each other and fight to survive their ruthless enemies. Miranda Jarrett continues to be top sea dog of the historical romance."

—*Affaire de Coeur*

"A well-written book that is a joy to read. As usual, Ms. Jarrett's heroes raise your blood pressure and make you want to claim them for your very own!"

—Suzanne Coleburn, *The Belles and Beaux of Romance*

Books by Miranda Jarrett

The Captain's Bride
Cranberry Point
Wishing
Moonlight
Sunrise

Published by POCKET BOOKS

For orders other than by individual consumers, Pocket Books grants a discount on the purchase of **10 or more** copies of single titles for special markets or premium use. For further details, please write to the Vice President of Special Markets, Pocket Books, 1230 Avenue of the Americas, 9th Floor, New York, NY 10020-1586.

For information on how individual consumers can place orders, please write to Mail Order Department, Simon & Schuster Inc., 100 Front Street, Riverside, NJ 08075.

MIRANDA JARRETT

Sunrise

SONNET BOOKS
New York London Toronto Sydney Singapore

The sale of this book without its cover is unauthorized. If you purchased this book without a cover, you should be aware that it was reported to the publisher as "unsold and destroyed." Neither the author nor the publisher has received payment for the sale of this "stripped book."

This book is a work of fiction. Names, characters, places and incidents are products of the author's imagination or are used fictitiously. Any resemblance to actual events or locales or persons, living or dead, is entirely coincidental.

An *Original* Publication of POCKET BOOKS

A Sonnet Book published by
POCKET BOOKS, a division of Simon & Schuster Inc.
1230 Avenue of the Americas, New York, NY 10020

Copyright © 2000 by Miranda Jarrett

All rights reserved, including the right to reproduce this book or portions thereof in any form whatsoever. For information address Pocket Books, 1230 Avenue of the Americas, New York, NY 10020

ISBN: 0-671-03262-3

First Sonnet Books printing January 2000

10 9 8 7 6 5 4 3 2 1

SONNET BOOKS and colophon are trademarks of Simon & Schuster Inc.

Front cover illustration by Fredericka Ribes

Printed in the U.S.A.

For Meg, of course,
who knows better than anyone
how to steer a career
while piloting the Plushmobile
straight to Altar Rock.

With affection, regards,
and two pounds of fudge!

Sunrise

Chapter 1

Nantucket Island
September 1727

He could not keep away.

It was the season for hurricanes and nor'easters, cruel winds and devil-driven seas, for weather so wicked that any sane man would huddle close to his fire and thank the good Lord that he'd no need to move. But Daniel Fairbourne had long ago lost the blessing of an easy, reasonable mind, and on this black and howling night he once again bent his shoulders into the wind and walked the beach with all the grim purpose of a man driven by desperation.

Desperation, and guilt. He would never forget what had happened five years ago. Five years, three months, seventeen days, a handful of uncounted hours and minutes, yet still the pain of his loss was as keen and sharp as it should be. As it *must* be.

No, he thought with every step, he would never forget.

He walked close to the water, his boots leaving deep prints in the wet, packed sand until the next wave curled and hissed his marks away, bits of foam clinging to the worn leather toes. He'd come this way so many times before that his feet knew the way, and his gaze stayed focused on the sea itself, searching the waves and moonless horizon with the glass-sided lantern in his hand.

He was a large man in his prime, a blacksmith whose trade had made him the strongest man on the island. He realized that if he must labor so against this storm, then any poor unfortunate cast into the sea on such a night would surely perish before he could help. No one else would fault him if he turned back now. The wind sliced through his heavy coat, the cold cutting deep to his bones, and the driven spray peppered his face like shards of salty ice, yet still he walked, still he searched.

Without a growl of complaint Daniel's dog Sachem followed close at his heels across the sand and rocks. Sachem understood this kind of hunt, and its importance, too, for three winters ago he himself had been rescued by Daniel on this same coast, a scrawny spotted pup tossed to drown over the side of some long-past boat.

For a moment Daniel paused, bending to ruffle the dog's pointed ears while he still continued to scan the churning horizon.

"A dirty night to be about, eh, Sachem?" he said as they began again, the dog swinging his tail in loyal agreement. "Not fit for any but sorry fools like us."

Curving to the west, the beach grew rougher now, the waves breaking over great granite rocks. It was here, too, that ships and sailors most often came to grief, confounded by the twisting currents of the shoals, and as Daniel climbed to the crest of the rocks, he held his lantern high, sweeping the flickering light over the shallow pebbled beach before him. Rocks, more rocks, a shattered cask, a limp mass of wrack-weed, and a tangled knot of tarred rope.

And the lifeless body of a woman.

As Sachem bounded ahead, Daniel clambered down the rocks after him. He wondered if he'd imagined it, his grief playing cruel, false games with his conscience, but the closer he came the more he could see, and the heavier his own heart became in his chest.

The woman lay on her side on the stony beach where the waves had left her, her face turned away from him and her long tangled hair streaming out behind. She was wrapped in a cloak of sodden red wool that clung to her like the shroud it had become, covering her, hiding her, except for one leg that lay bent at the knee, curled behind her. One small, pretty leg in a white stocking with three hearts embroidered in pink over the ankle and a half-tied striped garter trailing forlornly down the calf, a red-heeled shoe buckled high with a pinchbeck buckle that glittered in the lantern light.

A brave, saucy show for one small, still leg to make, thought Daniel sadly, and far too brave to find death on a rocky Nantucket beach. Gently he pulled the cloak over the woman's leg, giving her back her decency as he murmured a little prayer for her soul.

Sachem whimpered, ducking his head, as if in sympathy with Daniel's sorrow.

"Not what we'd hoped for, was it, pup?" said Daniel softly. He'd found sailors before, men like himself, but never had he come across a woman, and he hesitated before he turned her over. A woman was different, her suffering worse. No woman should have to know the terrors of drowning like this, and he dreaded seeing the face of one who had. He struggled to remind himself how he'd be sure that this lady would have a Christian burial, that her friends and family would know what had happened to her, that she wouldn't vanish into nothingness as if she'd never lived, the way his own wife had done.

His wife: his fair angel, his dearest love, his sweet, lovely Catherine, who had gone away forever and would never return from her sister's house in Bridgetown, not to him, not to anyone.

With a strangled sound deep in his throat, Daniel gently eased the woman onto her back. Her delicate hands were bruised, her fingers scratched and her nails torn; clearly she'd fought to save herself, and he wondered what had become of the others on her ship.

He set the lantern beside her head and, pulling off his glove, he carefully, almost tenderly, swept the tangle of wet hair from her face. Her skin was icy beneath his fingertips, bluish pale except for the angry bruises left from the stones, and he swore softly when he saw how young she was. Twenty, he guessed, twenty-two at most, and far, far too young to die. Her face belonged with that fancy stocking and striped garter, a merry face fashioned for beguiling rather than pure beauty, with full cheeks that he'd wager would have dimpled when she'd smiled and a generous mouth with a tiny mole near one corner, as if pointing the way for a kiss, a kiss that, now, would never come.

"Poor little lady," said Daniel softly, bending close to shield her from the wind. "What was your name, I wonder?"

He thought it was a trick of the lantern's flicker across her face, the way she seemed to shudder, her brows twitching as if she were waking from a dream. Then suddenly her eyes fluttered open, blue eyes that were large and bright and very much alive, and very much startled to find him so close.

"Juliette," she gasped, her voice raw and breathless enough to make Sachem back away. "My name is Juliette. But oh, *mon Dieu,* who are *you?*"

"Daniel," he answered, startled himself, "not that it matters now. All you need know is that I'm a friend who wishes to help you. Can you recall the name of your ship, or her captain, or where you were bound? I'll want to send word to your people as soon as I can that you're safe."

But she didn't answer, only staring at him with pale eyes so wide he wondered if she'd struck her head when washed ashore. More likely when the vessel she'd been in had foundered or wrecked, she'd witnessed sights no woman should, horrors so great her poor wits had fled in defense. He'd seen it happen to grown men, to sailors and fishermen, but the shock that a gentle young creature like this must have felt was unimaginable.

Though he'd imagined Catherine's suffering often enough, hadn't he, each time praying from the depth of his miserable soul that her end had at least been quick and merciful. As if his prayers could bring her any comfort now, or ease the pain that would always haunt him. . . .

"Don't worry, lass," he said gruffly as he pulled off his coat, tugging his arms free of the sleeves. "You'll be well enough in time."

Gently he raised the girl to her feet to wrap his coat around her shoulders and over her own sodden clothing. His hand brushed against the mottled skin of her forearm, as chilled as that of the corpse he'd mistaken her for.

"Can you walk?" he asked. "My house isn't far."

She stared at him with the same empty eyes before she swayed unsteadily against him, his heavy coat flapping around her narrow shoulders in the wind.

"Aye, that's answer enough, isn't it?" he said as he caught her to stop her fall. "Come then, we'll manage together."

He slipped his arm beneath her knees and lifted her up. She didn't protest or fight him, settling instead against his chest with her head upon his shoulder with a little fluttering sigh of acceptance. Juliette, she'd said her name was. She *was* a Juliette, too delicate to be a sturdy Nantucket Ruth or Betsey. Even soaking wet she was a little bit of a thing to hold, so small boned and fragile he marvelled that she'd survived this long.

"Sachem!" he shouted into the wind, and the dog came bounding up to him again. "Sachem, here! Handsomely now, you rascal. High time we got this poor lady home."

Home and a fire and dry clothes for them both. That was enough to deal with for now. And tomorrow—if there was a tomorrow for her—he'd worry about the rest.

Chapter 2

She felt as if her body were on fire, the very flames licking at her skin, yet she had neither the will nor the energy to move clear of their heat. Her arms and legs were too heavy, too weak, to shift from where she lay, and in her misery the only sound her parched throat could make was a low moan of painful despair.

"Here now, lass," said the man's voice. "Can you hear me?"

Somehow she forced her eyes open, just wide enough to make out the large face that was so close over hers. It could have been handsome; she couldn't tell for certain, not now. In the haze of her fever, only the most important things registered: that his eyes were a deep, clear blue like the ocean, that his hair was black and shaggy and fell around his unshaven jaw, that though his mouth was awkwardly curved into a coaxing smile, the rest of his face seemed burdened with such deeply etched sadness that, even as sick as she was, she could not miss it, not in Daniel's face.

Daniel. She squinted, striving to see more of him. He was a large man, thick with muscles and big bones that made the little stool he sat upon look like a child's by comparison. He was dressed simply, in a homespun shirt open at the throat beneath an unbuttoned red wool waistcoat, and well-worn leather breeches with horn buttons at the sides of his knees.

Of course it was Daniel. She knew that much for sure, if nothing else.

"Daniel?" she whispered, scarcely better than a croak. "Daniel, I—"

"Hush, now, you've no business talking just yet." She felt him slip his arm gently beneath the back of her head to lift it from the pillow, up to the rim of the pewter cup he held to her lips. "Drink this first."

The broth he tipped into her mouth was warm and salty but best of all wet, and she swallowed so eagerly that she almost gulped, welcoming the liquid that slid along her parched throat.

"Ah, that's better," he said. His voice was deep and rough, almost gruff, as if unaccustomed to much conversational use, and now that she was awake his awkward smile had vanished as well. "First time you've taken it in two days. Drink up, Juliette."

She frowned as she swallowed, concentrating hard on what he was saying. If his voice sounded rusty from disuse, then her own wits were a perfect match, for she couldn't begin to sort out even the simplest facts about herself. Her name, for one. Daniel had called her Juliette, and so it must be, for he didn't seem like the sort of man who'd playfully call her another.

She was Juliette, then. But Juliette what? As hard as

she tried, she couldn't remember anything else of who she was or even what Daniel meant to her, and tears of misery now stung behind her fever-burned eyelids.

"Daniel, please, I—"

"Hush now, and drink," Daniel ordered again, and without any choice she unhappily obeyed.

Her name was Juliette, and she was lying in clean, rough, linen sheets beneath a woolen coverlet on a low bed without curtains in the corner of a room lit only by the hearth fire. She'd been here for at least two days, maybe more. She looked down, and realized that she wore not a woman's shift or night-rail, but a man's coarse shirt, so much beyond her size that even with the sleeves pushed in thick rolls over her forearms she still seemed swallowed up and dwarfed by yards of extra cloth.

With a great effort she pushed the cup away from her mouth. "Where are my clothes?"

Daniel frowned, cradling the battered cup in his hand with his thumb through the handle. "Near the fire, where I put them to dry."

"Then this shirt," she whispered, "this shirt is yours?"

He nodded, his frown deepening. "I could not leave you in your own things."

She couldn't remember this happening, either, but she could imagine it now all too well. "You undressed me while I've been ill?"

He took a long moment before answering. "If I hadn't," he said finally, "you would have died."

She couldn't see how he'd used her fever as an excuse for such freedom. What other liberties might he have taken at the same time, liberties that she couldn't remember, let alone have resisted?

Unless, of course, there was one other thing she couldn't recall.

"Daniel," she whispered, her voice no more than an urgent, painful croak as she struggled with her rising panic. "May God forgive me for asking such a question, Daniel, but I swear I do not know. Are you my—my husband?"

He drew back as sharply as if she'd struck him with her fist. With the battered cup clutched tight in his hand he lurched to his feet, looming over the low bed so that his shadow blocked the light from the fire.

"I have no wife," he said with harsh finality, "and if you've a husband anywhere, it's not me. Now sleep, and leave us both in peace."

Juliette slept, but found no peace. In restless, repetitive dreams, blue-faced demons chased her across fields and waves that had neither beginning nor end, and the harder she tried to escape the more the demons laughed and mocked her pleas for mercy. And when at last she woke, it was with a final disjointed cry that jolted her upright in the rumpled bed, her heart still pounding from the nightmares.

She felt weak and exhausted, her hair a matted tangle around her shoulders and the shirt clammy and damp on her back. But the fever was gone, broken in her sleep, and with it the heated murkiness that had so tangled her thoughts.

Or had it? With a disconsolate sigh she settled back against the pillow, for this room looked no more familiar now than it had last night. It was, she realized now, not so much a room as the entirety of a spare little house, a single, square space that served as kitchen and parlor and bedchamber combined. The walls were crudely plastered and unpainted, the windows shuttered instead of curtained, and the few pieces of furniture—a long trestle table, a bench, two tall-backed chairs, a chest for clothes, and a cupboard for food—were sturdy and without ornament. Yet though everything was as well swept and tidy as the best housewife would wish, there was still a spartan quality that marked it as a man's domain, and one man at that.

Daniel. At least there was no sign of him here now, and she shuddered with relief. Dear God, why could she remember this ill-mannered, black-haired bear of a man, the scent of wood smoke on his shirt as he'd bent over her and the sound of his gruff, growly voice, and yet recall nothing of herself?

She frowned, rubbing her arm against the chill. He'd told her he'd set her own clothes to dry near the fire. There, folded neatly on the bench near the hearth, those must be hers, just as the heavy red cloak still drying on a peg by the fire must be hers, too. Trying not to consider again how Daniel must have undressed her, she shoved back the coverlet and swung her legs off the bed. Lord, but she was weak! Cautiously she rose, her legs unsteady beneath her, and made her way to the bench. She wanted to change now, before he returned, so he wouldn't catch her still shamefully wearing nothing but his shirt.

But what pretty clothes these were, she marvelled as she slipped the Holland linen shift over her head, what fine, elegant things! Even her pocket was beautifully worked in shaded blue Irish stitch, with two gold guineas and a handful of other coins still tucked inside. Two guineas! That could hardly be commonplace. Even though every piece of the clothing was badly wrinkled and blotched with white salt stains, it was still clear that the fabrics and the fashionable handiwork were of the best quality, bespoke clothing made for gentry.

Could she be a lady herself, then? Was that why Daniel had grown so defensive when she'd asked if he were her husband? She'd never intended to insult him, but no woman who wore clothing as fine as this would live in a cottage as simple as this one.

Lightly she traced the initials cross-stitched below the neckline, tiny pink letters, a *J* and an *L*. *J* for Juliette, and *L* for—for what? Daniel had known her given name; perhaps he could tell her the other, along with his own. Even in her thoughts, she didn't feel proper calling him only by his first name.

She frowned, lacing her stays up tight over the top of her petticoat. It was as if all the important bits and pieces of her memory had been plucked clean from her head, and the harder she tried to remember, the more elusive those same thoughts seemed to become, like tufts of milkweed floss tossed into the wind. Her only connection to her past seemed to be this man Daniel, and she still wasn't sure how much he'd be willing to share. But perhaps now that she was feeling better, she'd be able to persuade him to tell her more.

And if he didn't know who she was, either . . . but no, she didn't want to consider that, not yet.

She slipped on her jacket and tied it closed, then with a little *umph* of weary resolution she pulled up her skirt to tie her garters. Who would have guessed that simply dressing herself could be so exhausting? As she bent forward, she heard the door open, felt the wind gusting clear across to her, and before she could sit upright again, a large brown and white dog with ears pointed like a fox's came bounding to her.

"Pretty boy," she crooned as the dog pressed his wet nose against her knee. His rough, wet fur feathered damply from his legs and belly, his tail a flopping plume wagging with delirious pleasure as Juliette ruffled his pointed ears. Here was another thing she could know of herself: she liked dogs, and dogs, at least this one, liked her in return. "Oh, what a lovely boy!"

"Sachem, down!" said the man sharply, and Juliette didn't have to look to know it was Daniel. "Come, I say, now!"

"Don't scold him." Juliette curled her fingers into Sachem's collar—braided of rope, and thick with sailor's fancy knots—to hold the dog next to her. In spite of the unwitting intimacy she'd already shared with this man, or more likely because of it, she felt reluctant to meet his eyes now, concentrating instead on Sachem's broad, shaggy back. "The poor animal's done nothing wrong."

"He's been in the marshes. He'll cover you with muck and wet."

"And do you think I'd care?"

"Aye," said the man irritably as he closed and barred the door behind him. "I did. Why else in thunder would I have told him to leave off bothering you?"

"Because you like giving orders," said Juliette defensively as she tightened her fingers around Sachem's collar. "Because you can't bear to see even your dog being agreeable when you are not."

He didn't answer, and at once she regretted her words.

She'd been forced to trust him up until now, while she'd been too ill to do anything else, but what happened, or didn't happen, next between them would be likely determined in the next minutes. She'd gain nothing by antagonizing him, and she could even be putting herself in danger.

"Pray forgive what I just said, sir," she said softly as she uncurled her fingers from Sachem's collar to set him free. "The dog *is* yours, and you are his master. You should expect him to obey you."

Sachem, however, did not choose to cooperate. Instead of going to his master, he remained pressed close against her skirts, gazing up at her in unabashed, panting adoration while he thumped his sandy tail against her knee. It wasn't that he was frightened of the man, or wary of returning to him; right now he simply, and perversely, preferred her company to his master's. Gently she put her palms against the dog's side and tried to push him away.

"Go, Sachem," she said firmly. "Be a good dog, and go away."

"He won't, not if he doesn't want to," said the man with gloomy satisfaction. "Look at him! He's too damned contrary for his own good, the wicked rascal."

"He's not a wicked rascal, sir," she said swiftly, "and I don't believe he's contrary, either."

"Sachem is both," he declared, "and a good deal worse besides. And blast it, stop calling me 'sir.' "

"I shall call you what's proper," she said warmly, rising to her feet, "and for me that is—that is—"

But whatever it is, or was, or wasn't, suddenly ceased to matter because for the first time she was standing before him. Before *him*: when she'd been so ill, tossing with fever, she'd no real sense of the man who'd tended her. He'd been only hazy bits and pieces, a strong forearm to raise her up to drink, a face leaning over hers, a growl of a voice telling her she'd be well soon enough if she'd do as he said. But there was nothing hazy about him now, and nothing vague about the whole of all those disjointed pieces.

He was so tall that he must have had to bow his head to enter the little house's low doorway, and still now he seemed to make the whole room too small, as if it couldn't quite contain him beneath its low beams. Even at ease his strength was obvious, as unhideable as the breadth of his shoulders and the bunch of his upper arms beneath his rough wool coat as he held the bundle of wood for the fire, and unmistakable, too, was the blatant maleness of that strength. His face was ruddy from the wind outside, his black hair wild and half-pulled from his queue, and his jaw dark and gleaming faintly from where he'd scraped away the morning's whiskers.

But what stopped her speech, stopped it cold, were his eyes. He could not be much older than herself, less than thirty, yet his eyes held the weariness of a man three times that, the emptiness and pain that came of having seen more than his soul could accept.

"And I say *sir* isn't proper for me," he answered without waiting for her to finish. "I'm a smith by trade, not some dandified ass of a gentleman that needs some damned *sir* to tell who he is. Plain Daniel Fairbourne is how I was christened, and plain Daniel Fairbourne's how I mean to be buried."

With a clatter he dropped the wood—gnarled twists of driftwood, flotsam from foundered ships, all of it culled from the beach instead of a forest—into the box beside the hearth, the shimmer of spray on his clothes turning to mist in the heat of the fire.

"*Sir*, hell," he muttered as he fanned the little fire back to brighter life. He held his hands over it to warm them and half turned to glower back over his shoulder at Juliette. "Are you better, then?"

"Yes, thank you," she murmured automatically, though the truth was very different. The longer she stood beside the table the weaker she realized she was. The room, and the man began slowly to blur before her eyes, while the only sound in her ears was a distant ringing, like church bells that drowned out everything else.

"Here, you're not well at all." His hand was steady at her waist, guiding her into a tall-backed chair. "You belong back in bed, missy. You're white as a winding-sheet."

"I'm quite well, thank you," she said weakly. Once she'd sat, the church bells faded and the room settled squarely back to where it belonged, and she felt more foolish than anything else. "It's only because I haven't eaten, that's all."

"Haven't eaten?" He was kneeling before her, his face disconcertingly level with hers. She didn't wish for such parity; she wanted distance between them, distance from the unsettling chill of those deep blue eyes. "Why the devil not? Look here, plain as day. Haven't I left you plenty to eat?"

Belatedly she noticed on the table before her the plate with the cut squares of cornbread and the little crock of honey beside it, and the empty cup waiting for the coffee in the kettle that hung over the coals. She felt double the fool now, and she dreaded having him point it out to her.

"I wished to dress first," she said quickly, before he could. "I wished to make myself decent."

"Oh, aye, even if you must keel over first for the sake of decency." He lifted the kettle from the trammel hook and filled her cup with coffee, the fragrant steam curling upward. "If I'd been tempted by your *in*-decency, then I would have acted on it long before this, wouldn't I? Go on, drink up."

She flushed as he slid the cup across the table toward her, but she didn't look away. "I don't know what you've done or haven't done. How can I, when I don't know anything about you, or what kind of man you are?"

"Then that makes a pair of us, doesn't it?" He dropped into the chair opposite hers, not taking his gaze from her even when Sachem finally padded over to rest his chin on his master's thigh. "For all I know of *you*, perhaps I should be counting my spoons to see what's gone missing while I was out."

Juliette gasped. "How dare you accuse me like that! I would never touch anything that didn't belong to me!"

"And neither would I," he said evenly, "so I'll thank you to stop saying I did."

"But I didn't—" she began, then broke off when she realized he was right, and worse, that she'd been wrong. If he'd been honest enough to leave her the gold in her pocket, odds were excellent that he'd left her virtue intact as well.

"Now go on, drink up," he said as he rested his hand on Sachem's head. "Then we'll talk."

She lifted the cup with both hands and sipped the hot liquid, watching him warily over the rim. He didn't seem smug, the way she'd expected, but he wasn't exactly playing the gracious host, either. Instead he sat sprawled in the other tall-backed chair, his thickly muscled legs with their sandy boots outstretched before him. He'd said he was a smith, so the strength she'd sensed about him would be real, real enough to be able to hammer and bend iron however he pleased. With one hand he gently caressed the big dog's ears while he watched her with the same unblinking concentration that a cat gives to a cornered mouse.

Juliette forced herself to swallow, feeling the coffee settle like a hot puddle in her chest. She had a great deal of sympathy for that little mouse right now. The man before her made her feel nearly as small, and nearly as helpless, too, and unconsciously her gaze flicked away from Daniel's face to the door behind him, the one way to escape from the house.

"You're not my prisoner, you know," he said softly. "You never have been."

But she wasn't as sure. "Then why did you bar the door?"

"To keep the wind out," he said, "not to keep you in. This is Nantucket, Juliette. If you don't stand firm, the wind will blow you and all you possess clear to China."

"Nantucket?" Her fingers tightened around the cup. She knew she'd heard the odd word before, but she couldn't say whether it was a city or a village, or worse, her own home. "And where, pray, is that?"

" 'That' is here," he said, tapping one finger on the table as if to mark the exact spot. "Twenty-six miles from the mainland, but far enough out to sea that it's as good as a hundred times twenty-six. A rolling, treeless, windblasted, God-forsaken blot of sand and sheep and righteousness in the middle of the ocean: aye, that's our fine island of Nantucket."

"Nantucket," she repeated unhappily, no wiser than before. "But how could I have come—"

"A few nights ago you were cast away, or adrift, or tumbled overboard from some ship or boat," he explained. "I have no notion of the details. I found you where the waves had left you, on the beach."

"Oh," she said softly. The sand had been hard and cold, the pebbles sharp where they'd pressed into her skin: she remembered that suddenly, the sticky taste of salt on her lips, the way her clammy, sodden clothes had clung and wound around her, how she'd been so wet and frozen she'd thought she'd never be warm again. "But why did you—"

"Nay, lass," he said as he rested his arms on the table to lean across toward her. " 'Tis my turn now to ask the questions. I know your given name is Juliette, but nothing else. Where's your home, Juliette, and where were you bound when you washed up on that beach?"

She stared down at the coffee, the shining dark surface quivering as her fingers trembled. "I cannot say," she whispered miserably. "I'd hoped you could tell me because I don't know."

He frowned, more perplexed than angry. "I thought you said you were better."

"I believe I am, yes," she said slowly, unsure how to explain what she didn't understand herself. "I don't feel ill any longer. Yet in my head, things aren't—aren't as they should be."

He leaned closer, folding one hand over his fist on the tabletop. "Very well, then. The ship you were in is not important, not now. Mark something else. Your family name, what you're called beyond Juliette. Surely you can remember that much."

She shook her head, her voice so low she hardly heard the words herself. "I can't remember anything before waking here."

"But you do," he insisted. "You remember how to walk and talk and say 'please' and 'thank-you,' and you remembered well enough how to get yourself rigged out in all that lady's frippery, and without the help of a lady's maid, either."

"But that doesn't mean I—"

"Comment dit-on cela en français?"

"Je ne peux pas faire ça," she answered impatiently, and without a thought for having slipped into the other language. *"Non, non, non!"*

"Seems to me you just did," he said. "Answered me in French, that is. So you remember that, too."

She stared at him in disbelief. "How did you know I could?"

"I guessed, that was all." Though he shrugged it off, the way his pale eyes gleamed showed he was pleased enough by her reaction. If only he'd let himself smile, too, then she might actually begin to feel less like that poor trapped mouse. "No real mystery to it. Juliette's a French name, so it seems likely your people might be French, too."

"But I don't *feel* French," she protested, considering the possibility. Until now she'd assumed she was English because that was what they'd spoken together. "That is, however being French would feel."

"Yet you've proved it yourself," he countered. "You

didn't just understand what I said. The way you answered quickly showed you were *thinking* in French as well."

But what she was thinking now would have been the same in English or in French. She was thinking that however gruff and blunt and outright rude he'd been to her, he still had saved her life, and for whatever reason, he still cared enough now to try to help her figure out who she was. He was behaving as honorably as she supposed a man like him could.

Warily she studied him again as she took another sip of the coffee. He *was* very large, and obviously very strong, but he'd never used that size against her. When she'd been ill, she'd trusted him because she'd been unable to do anything else. Now that her wits had returned, perhaps she should freely give him that trust again. She glanced down at Sachem, who'd fallen into a wheezy, blissful sleep with his head still resting on Daniel's thigh. If Sachem could trust him that much, wasn't it worth her trying it, too?

"You speak English so well," Daniel was saying, "that I'm also willing to guess that you've spent most of your life among us Britishers. Maybe you're from the north, up in the provinces where there's plenty of Frenchmen. That could explain—"

"Thank you," said Juliette softly, so softly that Daniel stopped, wondering if he'd heard her speak at all.

"Thank you, Daniel," she said again, her voice rising with a slight tremor of uncertainty. "For saving me, I mean. Thank you for saving my life."

So he hadn't been mistaken. She'd *thanked* him, for God's sake, thanked him for doing what he'd been driven by guilt and heartbreak to do. Didn't she understand he'd do the same for any poor creature that the sea had tried to claim?

Thank you, Daniel.

He stared at her, incapable of any sensible reply. She was waiting for it, he could tell. Her small, round chin was raised expectantly, her blue eyes full of anticipation. He doubted she'd found his looking glass, for with her concern for "decency" she'd be appalled to see how she looked: her long hair straggled, uncombed, and stiff with dried seawater, a purplish bruise swelling on her temple, and deep circles of fatigue and illness ringing her eyes. Yet somehow her sad, bedraggled appearance affected him more than if she'd been neat and spruce, the way he suspected she most usually was. Now she was just another stray, one more mongrel that had needed rescuing.

But she wasn't like Sachem, or any of the half-drowned fishermen and sailors he usually fished from the water. Not by half, she wasn't, and he scowled down at his clasped hands and away from her as he struggled with himself. When she'd been unconscious, he'd been able to be objective, even when he'd had to peel away the wet clothes from her lush, pale-skinned body and dress her in a shirt of his own. But not now. Now, with every passing second and every word she spoke to him, she was becoming more and more undeniably real, a flesh and blood woman here in his house, and he bit back an oath of despairing frustration.

How long had it been since he'd sat across from a woman, any woman, like this? How long since he'd heard a soft voice full of kindness that was meant for him alone?

And why in the name of God had this French-speaking fillip of a girl lived, and his Catherine died?

She cleared her throat, a *chirrup* better suited to an impatient robin. "I said *thank* you. Most people would grant me some sort of answer."

"Then don't go mistaking me for most people," he said sharply, "because I'm not."

Her eyes widened with bewilderment, and she flushed. "I never thought you were."

"Then you thought right." Abruptly he shoved his chair back from the table and stood, as furious with himself as with the fate that had tossed her into his life. "If you're done with your pretty show of manners, then I'm off for my shop. I've squandered enough of my day here already."

To his surprise, she pushed back her own chair and rose, too, her hands knotted into prim little fists at her sides.

"There is no 'pretty show' to my manners beyond common civility, *Mister* Fairbourne," she said heatedly, "and though I am most sorry if my gratitude has offended you, I won't take it back!"

"Did I ask you to?" he demanded, his voice rumbling deep enough to make Sachem whimper fretfully in response. "Did I ever ask you to do something as infernally foolish as that?"

"It doesn't matter if you did or not," she fumed, "because I've no intention of staying here with you another day to find out. You leave whenever you please because I'm leaving, too."

"You are not," he said with grim finality. "You'll stay here until I say so."

He thought she might have swayed on her feet, as gently as if blown by a breeze, but before he could reach for her she'd steadied herself on the back of her chair, her fingers tightening on the turned rail. Though she raised her chin in determination again, she was clearly too weak to keep the fire of her anger burning, and her cheeks had lost all their color. Damnation, why couldn't she understand how willfully foolish she was being?

"You—you promised I wasn't your prisoner," she protested. "You told me you kept the door barred against the wind, not to keep me inside."

"And I say it still," he answered as he reached for his hat. "You can recall no friends or family or home. You've only a handful of coins in your pocket and the clothes on your back, and you're so weak you can scarce stand upright. Hell, you don't even know your own name! I didn't save you from dying once to have you go founder again and perish on account of your own stubbornness."

She sniffed once, her eyes glistening with tears she wouldn't let herself shed. More stubbornness, he told himself sternly as he turned away and unlatched the door, more stubbornness of her own doing. He jammed his hat on his head, low so the wind wouldn't take it, and whistled for Sachem to join him.

"I didn't ask you to save me," she said behind him, her voice shaking with emotion. "I wish you'd left me there and—and let me die instead."

He stopped, holding the door, but he didn't turn back. "You might wish it, Juliette, but I wouldn't have left you. I couldn't have, even if I'd wished it, too. You're not my prisoner, but by God, you are my responsibility, and I'm not about to abandon you now."

Before she could protest again, he left, pulling the door tight behind him. Nothing would be gained by his staying, just as there was nothing more left to be said between them this morning. What was the point in them worrying over the same pitiful facts like Sachem with an old mutton bone? Better to leave her to rest and gather her scattered thoughts alone while he tended to his own matters. Aye, he told himself firmly, this way was better for them both.

Quickly he made his way down the narrow path away from his house, the tall, thin-bladed grasses on either side slashing at his legs while Sachem bounded on ahead. The sun had cleared the horizon behind his back, enough to cast his shadow on the path before him, and the wind came sharp and keen from the east, from the ocean, clear from Scotland for all he knew. A fine, fair day, and at last an end to the storminess.

So why, then, did his feet drag so slowly along the familiar sandy path to Sherburne? On a day of such promise, why should his conscience press as heavily on his chest as a bar of untempered iron?

And how long had it been since he'd turned his back on a woman and left her in tears, and told himself it was for her own good?

Oh, Catherine, forgive me. . . .

He didn't know what made him look back, and when he thought about it later he wondered if it had been the sound of the door opening again, or maybe a stray gust of wind that tickled his hair against his ear. But look back he did, and what he saw, he never forgot.

Juliette was standing beside the low pale fence that surrounded his house, her hands gripping the pointed tops as tightly as if her life again were in danger. She wasn't looking inland, toward him, but out to sea and the rising sun. The pink light of the dawn washed her in a luminous glow, her long, unbound hair streaming golden away from her shoulders in the wind. Yet all the glittering glory of dawn wasn't enough to mask the sad, lonely despair of her expression, or cheer the agonizing bleakness that shaded her eyes.

She'd said she wished she'd died instead, and in that moment, he realized how desperately she'd meant it. Who had she left to mourn her on shore, he wondered? Was there somewhere a lover or husband, lost in her memory but still locked in her heart, that now aimlessly walked another beach on the distant side of this same water, praying with every step for her safe return?

Daniel swallowed, swallowed hard, and shoved away the old grief like a friend who'd grown too familiar. This woman was his responsibilty only until she mended, or until he could find some other friend of hers to take her from his care. Of course she was sorrowful, of course she was lonely for what she'd lost. It would be an unnatural woman who wasn't.

But she wasn't Catherine, and she wasn't his.

And this time, when he turned back to the sandy path in front of him, he kept walking, and he did not stop.

Chapter 3

Carefully Daniel turned the broken link of the heavy boat chain, the ends glowing red from where they'd been heated, and nodded at John Robin Namis, who stood ready with the small hammer used for repair work like this. The short, stocky man with the braided hair had worked as Daniel's striker for so long that the single nod was all the communication needed between the two, and with a half dozen deft blows of the hammer the chain was once again whole.

Again Daniel nodded, this time with approval, and John Robin stood back to wait with the hammer against his shoulder while Daniel dipped the mended chain, hissing in protest, into the wide bucket of water to cool. The late summer light through the open windows of the blacksmith's shop was already beginning to fade with the afternoon, the shadows lengthening across the patch of sun where Sachem dozed and twitched and chased rabbits across the moors in his dreams.

"So what treasures did the storm bring you, John Robin?" called one of the men sitting on the bench by the shop's open door, lingering with a newly repaired bridle bit in his hand. "I saw your squaw down the beach, scooping something up into her basket. Rubies and pearls from the Orient, eh, John Robin?"

The man guffawed coarsely at his own wit, and the others loitering nearby joined in. But John Robin only smiled shyly to himself, the way he always did, and rubbed two fingers over the smallpox scars on the back of his neck, inside the collar of his worn linen shirt.

"There now, Abraham, none of that," warned Daniel softly, his voice deep and calm for all its authority. "None of that here."

Abraham's pie-round face went pink beneath his broad-brimmed hat. "I meant nothing ill, Fairbourne," he said, grinning with hasty contrition. " 'Twas only in jest, no harm meant."

Daniel didn't smile, and he didn't offer absolution, either. Abraham Greene was as foolish as his face, else he would have known better than to make such jests here at John Robin Namis' expense. His striker was a good, sober worker who suited Daniel in every way, but to braying asses like Greene he was next to nothing on this island, one of the island's few remaining Wampanoags, a red-skinned man that the English courts had sent into indentures to pay off the impossible debts of poverty. Only Daniel knew that he'd long ago dissolved the indenture and now paid John Robin a wage that was as fair as any other skilled worker earned. That was between him and John Robin, and certainly was no business of Abraham Greene.

"I meant no harm, Fairbourne," insisted Abraham uneasily. "I swear it!"

"No swearing, either, Abraham," said Daniel mildly, a mildness that no island man would trust. "Not in my shop."

Abraham shook his head vigorously while Daniel waited, watching, with his pale, unblinking gaze that was whispered to prove he had no soul.

There was, Daniel knew, a great deal whispered about him, none of it based on any fact. He'd overheard all sorts of stories about his life before he'd come to Nantucket—how he'd sailed with the pirate Blackbeard, how he'd killed a rich Virginian in a duel of dubious honor, even how when he rescued castaways he was saving lost souls only to give them to the devil—and while he'd smiled ruefully to himself at his neighbors' creativity, he hadn't bothered to deny the stories, either.

Why should he? The rumors served to keep others at a distance, which was the reason he'd come to Nantucket in the first place, and they let him run his shop exactly as he pleased, the same as he'd run his ship. He was probably the only blacksmith in all New England who could treat his customers with a deep-water captain's imperiousness and actually be obeyed.

And if in turn those customers believed that Daniel Fairbourne had no soul, well, let them. It wasn't so very far from the truth.

Deliberately he now turned back to his anvil, setting the mended boat chain aside to begin the next task. His work was more to him than merely a trade; he could lose himself in the intricacies of shaping and bending and coaxing the unyielding iron, and find a satisfaction that was otherwise so absent from his life. This morning he'd needed it to keep him from thinking about the girl he'd left in his house, and because there had been so many repairs after the recent storm, he'd been busy enough that he'd succeeded.

But that peace was shattered in the next moment, when Tom Kearny, Sherburne's best cooper and the man who'd brought in the broken boat chain, stepped to the counter to sign his account.

"I cannot speak for the rubies or pearls upon the beach, Daniel," he said as he bent over the book, "but there was much of value to be found on the sands for those with a sharp eye. There was enough timber and cordage floating in the tide off 'Sconset to outfit a new schooner."

"Or to mark the death of an old one," said Abraham quickly, eager to leave his own gaffe behind. "That's out your way, Fairbourne. Any sign of a vessel in distress the other night, eh? If anyone would spy it, it'd be you."

Daniel hesitated, at the same time as he prayed that no one noticed. Though Abraham's question was harmless enough—his house overlooked the southwestern shore where most wrecks washed up, and it was common knowledge that he searched for survivors—Daniel's heart was pounding as hard as if he'd rowed a heavy dory from the mainland.

Juliette must have been a passenger in this same foundered ship. It was often possible to discover the name or homeport of a wreck from the bits of wreckage washed ashore, and if he could learn that much, then finding Juliette's family and returning her to them should be easy. That was what he wanted, wasn't it?

So why, then, was he finding it so damned difficult to answer now?

"No ship, no," he said finally. "I saw no ship."

There, it wasn't a lie, though his unhappy conscience told him it wasn't the complete truth, either.

"Then most likely she sank on her own, off to sea," said Tom Kearny solemnly. "May God give peace to her poor crew lost with her."

Daniel nodded, unable to think of more to say. When Tom spoke of "she," Daniel knew he meant the wrecked ship, giving it the feminine gender that graced all vessels. But still Daniel's conscience jabbed at him all the harder with that deceptive pronoun, giving it the lovely, sorrowing face of the lost Juliette. For didn't she founder, too, and wash ashore for him to find?

To find, aye, but not to keep. Lord, what made him even think such a thing?

"Was there any marking on the timbers, Tom?" he said swiftly, before his wicked thoughts ran any deeper. "Could anyone guess from where the ship had come?"

There, he'd said the right thing, and made it easy to speak next of Juliette. Tom and his wife, Ruth, were known as good people on the island. More importantly, their home would be a far more respectable place for the girl to recover, crowded with children though it was. No one would fault him for offering Juliette shelter the last few nights, given the circumstances and her health, but keeping her there longer, alone with him in his remote little house, was another thing entirely. She was a lady, no easy slattern; she'd care about her good name, and what the world said of her.

But Tom, who knew none of this, only glanced at him curiously. "No name to the vessel that I've heard, Daniel, but then, without any survivors to answer to, no one's been asking questions like that, either. So far a dozen casks of good Newport rum have come floating in on the waves, and do you think anyone's daft enough to go looking for the shipowner to give them back?"

"No," admitted Daniel. Earning a living on Nantucket was too hard to waste much sympathy on the losses of any wealthy, faraway shipowner, especially when those same losses could be viewed as providential local gains by someone like Tom, who'd make a tidy profit by scavenging the cargo. "Not with rum."

"Not with rum, nor beer, nor wine, nor port, neither," declared Tom soundly. "Once it's slipped into the sea, by my lights it's as much mine as the next man's, and timbers and spars are always fair game. Especially when there's neither officers nor crew left about to dicker. May God rest 'em, and God keep 'em, too."

"Amen," said Daniel again, though more reluctantly. Given the quality of Juliette's clothing, she might well have been the captain's wife, or even the owner's daughter. Either would make her less than welcome in any Nantucket family that had already hauled away cargo or wreckage. He tried to picture her thrust into the Kearnys' noisy household, her poor confused mind trying to sort out another set of strangers, and strangers who wouldn't necessarily be wishing her the best. "I warrant no one will be asking after them."

But Tom had heard the hesitation in Daniel's voice this time, and as he did, the gleeful, predatory righteousness faded from his eyes. Instead he drew his sandy brows together with concern and puffed out his cheeks before he leaned across the ledger to speak more softly, nearly a whisper, for Daniel alone to hear.

"You're not playing me false here, Daniel, are you?" he asked anxiously. "Because I've already hauled a great deal of the flotsam ashore myself, me and my boys—that's how the chain was broke, truth to tell—and if there's some sailor man left alive from that wreck to make trouble for me, some poor bastard that you're not speaking of here, why, then I'll have to—"

"There's no man survived from the crew that I know," said Daniel softly. Juliette was so fragile, both in body and spirit, that to move her again to an inhospitable place too soon might cause her more harm than good. "None that I've heard, anyways. Besides, why would I've asked you if I'd already known for myself?"

Tom relaxed, his puffed out cheeks deflating with relief as he patted the front of his waistcoat. "Aye, that's so, that's so. And mark me, Daniel, it *is* the most prodigious Newport rum!"

Because he liked Tom, Daniel tried to smile with him over the rum, but instead his thoughts stayed firmly focused on Juliette. She was his responsibility, and the more he considered her situation, the more he realized she'd be better off for now staying with him.

"No castaways this time, then," Tom was saying. "Not that I'm surprised. This late in the season the water's turning cold enough to freeze the blood directly. You won't be finding any more strays until spring, Daniel, leastways not live ones."

But Daniel had, and he thought again of how Juliette's

pale cheeks had pinked and her fine-boned hands had twisted and turned in the firelight as she'd thanked him, shyly and sweetly, across his old pine table.

Thank you. For saving me, I mean. . . .

"Two days, then?" said Tom, his expression cheerfully expectant. "Mistress Kearny won't wait much longer."

Daniel stared at him blankly, long enough that Tom began to shift uneasily before him. What the devil had he promised, anyway? Had he lost his wits, too, and already babbled about bringing Juliette to Tom's wife?

" 'Tis only an old kettle with a broken handle, Daniel," said Tom, almost apologetically. "Ruth's favorite, aye, but she can make do with another until you've time to mend it."

Behind Tom, John Robin stood with the three-legged kettle in his hands as a belated reminder. It was a simple enough repair; cookery pots usually were.

"Tomorrow noon," he said, though he intended to do it now, before he forgot. "Send one of your boys if Ruth can't come herself."

That was, in his way, as much of a jest as Daniel ever made, and Tom recognized and honored it with an oversized chuckle that shook the buttons on his waistcoat. No island woman or girl with any sense of decency would dare venture into such a murky stronghold of maleness as Daniel Fairbourne's forge and blacksmith shop, and that included even outspoken Ruth Kearny.

"Someone will come fetch it, Daniel," promised Tom with a broad wink as he turned to leave, "though I won't swear to who it will be. And come sample that rum if you've half a moment after closing."

He waved as he stepped out into the sunshine, with Abraham following close behind him. Daniel lifted his hammer to his shoulder by way of salute, and silently thanked the heavens that they'd gone. He'd had enough of his customers' company for the day, and with relief he turned back to his work and his own thoughts.

With a sigh of relief he took the kettle from John Robin and hooked it over the horn of the bickern, the small anvil used for curved or hollow pieces. He pumped the heavy leather bellows to make the coals in his fire glow red again, then used tongs to thrust a narrow rod of iron into the coals until it, too, glowed white-hot. Instantly, before it cooled, he took the bar and hammered it into an arc over the thicker end of the bickern to make a new handle. In the very center of the arc he hammered a little dip, an extra refinement that would make the kettle sit level on the trammel hook over the kitchen fire, and keep Ruth's stews and chowders from tipping and spilling into the hearth. Again he held one end of the handle in the coals until he could hammer it into a curve, hooked it through the hole in the kettle's side, then repeated the process to finish the task.

It was a deceptively simple job, made easy only through skill, strength, and long practice, and as Daniel lifted the kettle from the bickern to cool and set up, he couldn't keep back the small smile of satisfaction. There would be plenty of people—his own brothers included—who'd swear that a perfectly crooked iron handle like this couldn't begin to match the rewards and responsibilities of his former life, but he knew better. His only regret was that the rest of his world wasn't nearly so malleable, or as easily mended, either, and he thought once again of the girl waiting at home.

"You and Sachem go along now, friend," said John Robin to break into Daniel's thoughts. "I'll finish here, and pack the fire for the night."

Daniel frowned, wiping his arm with the rolled-up sleeve across his forehead. It was always hot here near the forge's fire, and the sunny afternoon and his own labor had made the shop seem warmer still.

"For the night, John Robin? Doesn't look much like night to me yet."

John Robin nodded, his expression so set and determined that Daniel's own frown deepened in wary return. In general he trusted his striker more than he trusted most men, but when John Robin looked at him like this, his drooping black eyes so self-certain that it bordered on smugness, his thick forearms folded high across his chest above his worn leather apron, that trust evaporated as fast as dew on a summer morning.

"I say there's plenty of work left to do, John Robin," answered Daniel, ready to match the other man's determination. "That means for the both of us, mind?"

By way of example he pulled a squared bar of iron from the pile of scrap near the forge and plunged it into the coals, giving the bellows above a good wheezing pump for emphasis.

But the other man was undeterred. "Today's different," he said. "Today you'd best end your work now."

"The better for you to get your own sorry self into mischief?"

"No," said John Robin evenly. "Because, friend, you have a matter of importance waiting that calls you home."

Daniel glared at him, swearing softly to himself. *A matter of importance waiting.* Where in blazes had John Robin learned a phrase like that? There was no possible way he could know about Juliette, none at all. Yet what else could he mean? It was enough to make the hair stand up on the back of his neck, just like Sachem's did with things that frightened him.

This wasn't the first time he'd wondered if John Robin knew some sort of Wampanoag secret for reading an Englishman's thoughts, or at least the ones belonging to this particular Englishman. With every other white man on the island, John Robin was as shy as a new fawn, but when he got himself into a mood like this, with Daniel he could turn as high and mighty as old King Philip himself.

Now Daniel yanked the iron from the coals to the bickern, and began striking it forcefully with his hammer, more to drown out the other man's words than to shape the iron into anything useful.

But he and John Robin had worked together too long and had held too many other conversations punctuated by a hammer's ringing for this to stop what he wished to say.

"It's right that you go," he said, raising his voice. "You know it, too."

Daniel found another scrap of iron and thrust it in the coals. "If *you* want to quit early," he said, his voice louder, too, "then why the hell don't you just ask me outright?"

But the other man didn't flinch. "Is it the captain from the wreck you found the other night, the captain himself? He must be hurt bad for you not to tell Master Kearny. You should go to that castaway now. He'll be needing you, for sure."

"Blast it all, weren't you listening before?" demanded Daniel hoarsely. He supposed he should be grateful that John Robin didn't mean Juliette, but what he'd guessed still seemed too damned close to the truth. "I didn't find any damned sailor last night, and there isn't one waiting for me now at home!"

"You must go to him, friend," insisted John Robin. "A man who loses everything like that can go out of his mind. Same as a fox in a trap who'll chew his own leg off. This castaway, now, he might even try to kill himself if you let him."

Castaways and foxes and traps and Juliette all swirled around together in Daniel's head. Daniel didn't like this, any of it, and instead he tried to concentrate on his hammering.

But from the corner of his eye he still could see the well-worn tips of John Robin's moccasins, decorated with quillwork and purple shell beads, the only clothing he wore that wasn't English style.

Though Daniel had often railed about those moccasins in the shop—working around heavy tools and hot coals, they were just plain foolish, a hazardous invitation to lose a toe or two—now when he saw them all he could think about was John Robin's mysterious Wampanoag predictions. John Robin claimed to be a Christian, same as the others left of his tribe, but sometimes the old ways still won out. It had happened before, the last time when he'd accurately predicted the return of a whaling ship presumed lost, and he seemed to be doing it again now.

But damnation, not with Juliette, and not like this.

"If I leave," he said at last, "will you stop this heathen nonsense?"

"You are my master," said John Robin primly, as if he'd just remembered it. "You must decide what is right. But it surely would be a pity if the castaway you rescued dies because you left him alone."

She'd said she wished he'd left her to die, and today he'd left her, all right. What if she was like John Robin's fox in the trap? What if she'd decided to finish what the ocean had begun?

What if Juliette had died like Catherine, with his harsh words the last she'd heard?

Daniel's fingers tightened on the handle of the hammer in his hand. As he cursed himself he bowed his head over the iron he'd been working as he'd listened to John Robin, and swore again when he realized what he'd fashioned: a tiny sun, no bigger than his palm, the rays twisting outward with the glorious promise of daybreak.

The same sun, with the same promise, that he'd seen behind Juliette that morning.

He plunged the little sun into the cask of water to cool it with a hiss of steam before he wiped it dry. Then he tore off his leather apron and grabbed his coat and his ring of keys from the peg on the wall, tucking the little iron sun into the pocket.

"Here," he said as he thrust the keys into John Robin's hand. "You bank the fire and lock up. And by God, if you're wrong about any of this—"

"If *you* are wrong, Master Fairbourne," corrected John Robin. "Now go, friend, while you are still right."

* * *

Juliette sat high on the edge of the beach, nestled among the tall, shivering grasses with the woven woolen coverlet from the bed wrapped around her shoulders and over her head, a makeshift hood against the sun in place of her own still-damp cloak. She'd thought twice about bringing that coverlet, not sure what Daniel Fairbourne's reaction would be, before she'd told herself sternly that it shouldn't matter. She'd had to be stern with herself again about coming here at all, back to the place where she'd so nearly come to grief. Here, she reasoned, daring herself a bit, she might be able to remember more of the ship in which she'd sailed, and more, too, of her life.

What a bleak, lonely spot, she thought as she gazed about her. Though the view before her was far more agreeable this afternoon than it had been that night, now all glittering water that smiled the same blue as the sky overhead, the island itself was inhospitable enough to make her shudder. Surely she must live in some snug and close-packed city to find this emptiness so forbidding! As far as she'd been able to see from the little house, there was nothing but low hills of wild, windswept grass, golden green and heather rose, without any trees to soften the horizon. She'd discovered no other houses, not even a wisp of smoke from a distant chimney, and the only neighbors seemed to be the small herd of wild sheep she'd spotted grazing in the far distance. Though Daniel Fairbourne might claim otherwise, in a place as remote as this one she truly *was* as good as his prisoner.

That made her groan, and hug her knees to her chest for sad comfort, for Daniel Fairbourne, too, was one more puzzle without a solution. She couldn't deny that he'd been kind to her, or that he'd offered her more hospitality than any wayward stranger had a right to expect, and, of course, he had saved her life.

But when she thought of how rough and sharp he'd turned when she'd thanked him, she wondered why he'd even bothered, and the tears in her eyes once again made the sea before her grow blurry. What could she possibly have done to make him so angry? She tried to tell herself she didn't care, that as soon as she could, she would leave him and his temper behind. Once she was stronger, she would follow the same path that he'd taken away from his lonely little house, and find someone else that could help her. She would again become confident and independent, the shrewd, clever woman she felt sure she'd been before she'd landed here, with a wealth of loving friends and a home full of family.

But the miserable truth now was that she was still so weak from the fever that by the time she'd climbed this shallow dune from the house she'd been shaking and sweating with exertion, enough that she dreaded the trip back. And worse than that, until she could remember more, the only person she had to depend upon was a man who didn't want anything to do with her.

She sighed unhappily, and kicked her heels in the soft white sand before her. Though she welcomed the coverlet's warmth against the wind from the water, the heavy wool smelled of wood smoke and shaving soap and other unsettlingly distinctive male scents that belonged to Daniel. Being able to recognize them made her blush: what respectable lady could identify a man by how his bedclothes *smelled?* She might as well be Sachem, though from the brown and white dog hairs scattered across the coverlet, he, too, was familiar enough with Daniel's bed.

How much less complicated to be a castaway dog! Did Sachem ever pine for his former master or his littermates, she wondered, or did dogs simply accept each day as they found it, without looking back to regret yesterday's lost mutton bone?

She heard a rustling in the grasses behind her, and before she turned, Sachem himself came leaping over the top of the dune to her side with a happy little yip of greeting, his plumed tail whipping from side to side.

"Oh, good dog!" said Juliette with a chuckle as she reached out to rub his feathery ears in exchange for his panting adoration. "Who is the best dog, the very best dog in all Nantucket? Sachem is, isn't he?"

"What the devil are you doing out here?"

Her hand paused on the dog's ear. Of course she should have realized that if Sachem had come, his master would soon follow. She took an extra second to compose herself before she looked up, and up, toward the stern face towering above her.

"I am here because I wished it," she said, squinting up at him. He was silhouetted against the bright sky, his expression lost in the shadows and impossible to read. "Oh, and a pleasant day to you, too, Master Fairbourne."

But pleasantness didn't seem to be on his mind. "What are you trying to do to me, anyways?" he demanded, flinging one arm out as if to encompass every imagined wrong in the world. "I come back here, and the house is empty. You're gone, vanished. What the hell am I supposed to think?"

"That the day was mild," she said evenly, "and I wished to take the air."

She knew she shouldn't have been so flippant, but

having him thrash about like this over nothing was ridiculous.

Not that he saw it that way. "Oh, aye, as if *that* tells me anything! Hell, Juliette!"

"Hell has nothing to do with it," she said, lowering her gaze to stare out to sea instead of at him. At least the sea was calmer. "I thought perhaps if I came back to the beach, I might be able to remember how I'd come to be there that night, that's all."

He made some sort of deep growling sound of frustration that she suspected had begun as an oath, and she was most grateful that it had stopped there. But before she could feel too grateful, he dropped down on the sand beside her, his hands resting on his knees as he, too, stared out across the water.

Curiously and warily she glanced at him, even as she fought the impulse to wriggle farther away across the sand. In the bright sunlight, she could see that his skin was surprisingly weathered for a man who made his living indoors, his face browned and taut with the fanning lines that were more usually found on sailors. Another surprise were his lashes, so thick and black around his pale eyes that on any other face they would have seemed almost feminine. But his features were balanced and well cut in a manly way, she decided, and if he could only manage to smile more, she'd consider him comely. No, handsome. If he smiled, he'd be handsome.

Suddenly he caught her studying him and frowned, and she flushed as she quickly looked away, to his hands where they rested on the knees of his breeches. They were as large as the rest of him, and as strong, too, though right now they were grimy and black from his work, the nails oddly pale.

"Now what are you gaping at?" he asked suspiciously.

"Your hands," she said, deciding that the truth would be safest. "They're usually so clean, but you came home without washing them, didn't you?"

"Well, forgive *me*, my fine and dainty lady," he said. "The way I flew out of there, I'm lucky I remembered my head, let alone washed my hands."

"Why?" she asked, curiosity again leading her where perhaps she shouldn't go. "You said this morning you wouldn't be back until nightfall. What would have made you come home early instead?"

He drew his dark brows together, perhaps not quite into a frown but still a close cousin, full of incredulity. "You really don't know?"

"No, I do not," she said impatiently, sweeping back a bit of hair that had blown into her mouth. "I wouldn't ask if I did, would I?"

He cocked one brow to show he still didn't believe her, then sighed.

"Because of you, you ninny," he said without much gallantry. "I got to thinking about what you'd said this morning, about how you'd rather I'd left you to die. The more I thought about it, the more I worried that maybe you'd decide that dying was better than living. I came home to make sure you wouldn't."

"Ohhh," said Juliette, a bit incredulous herself. "That *is* very grand and good of you, wanting to save me again and all, but I would never have done such a thing."

"I didn't know that," he said gruffly. "And when I came home and found you gone, well, what else was I to think?"

She shook her head, eager to contradict him. "But if

you'd left me where you'd found me on the beach and I'd died, then that would have been fate. *My* fate, that is. But if today I'd gone and, oh, jumped from those rocks out there with the intention of drowning myself, then I would be killing myself, which is a grievous sin, and a disagreeable way to keep from going to heaven. So of course I wouldn't have done it, if you'd only stopped to think a bit."

As arguments went, this made perfect sense to her, but apparently not to him because he didn't agree, or even answer.

Instead he looked at her, simply looked, as if seeing her for the first time, and in a way that made Juliette acutely aware of how close they were sitting, and how his eyes weren't as icy pale as she'd thought, but really a warm blue, a nice blue that was more like the ocean than any ice, and how this late in the afternoon his whiskers had grown into a prickly little fringe around his lips, which by contrast seemed smooth and soft and, oh, *mon Dieu,* this was really not what she should be thinking about him, not at all!

Skittishly she looked away, curling her fingers inside the coverlet to pull it more tightly, and more completely, over her body until she was only a woolly lump on the sand. He might already have seen her without her clothes, but she didn't have to remind him of it.

Nor, for that matter, should she herself be thinking of it, either. Better to consider anything else than that, and the first thing she concentrated on was Sachem, bounding back and forth through the wavelets.

"If you woke up one morning to discover you'd become a dog," she began, her words racing nearly as fast as her heart, "what kind of dog would you be?"

"A dog?" he repeated, now regarding her as if she belonged in a cell in Bedlam. "Why should I think of such a thing?"

"Because I was, before you came," she said promptly, glad to have shifted the subject. "I think I should like to be a dog like Sachem, wouldn't you?"

"I cannot say," he answered cautiously. "I'm not given to fancying like that."

"I'm sorry," she said, and she meant it.

He shrugged self-consciously, his heavy shoulders shifting beneath his coat. "You don't have to be. It's just the way I am, not putting stock in dreams and other foolishness like that."

"Oh, but you must have dreams!" she exclaimed impulsively. "Everyone does!"

"I don't," he said, his voice going flat and his eyes shuttering against her. "Leastways not anymore."

She opened her mouth to continue, then stopped. His whole posture warned her to go no further, and this time she didn't. What right did she have to preach to him of the power of pretending and dreams when she'd no idea what was real or not in her own life?

"Did it work?" he asked finally.

She frowned, waiting for him to explain.

"Coming here to the beach," he continued. "You said you'd hoped it would help you remember more. Did it?"

"No." Abruptly she rose, the heavy coverlet swinging around her. For a handful of minutes while they'd sat together, she'd managed to forget her sorrows and loss, but now with his questions, they'd come crashing down upon her again. "It was a foolish notion, that was all."

Awkwardly she started down the dune back to the house, bunching her skirts in one hand to make it easier to walk across the sand. Of course he would want her to remember who she was so he could be rid of her.

"Juliette, wait!"

She heard him, but she didn't turn. He hadn't looked back at her this morning, and now she could do the same to him. Besides, what point would there be in letting him see her weep again?

"Juliette, please." He was at her side, gently taking her arm as if to guide her. "You didn't tell me your leg had been hurt, too. Here, lean upon me and I'll help you back to the house."

"Oh, no, you won't," she said as she shook away his hand, keeping her head bowed so he couldn't see her tears. "This happened years and years ago when I fell down the back stairs and broke my leg and my poor sister Amelie was blamed for not watching me. It's only when I'm tired that I limp now."

"Juliette, listen to yourself!" He seized her arm again, pulling her around so she couldn't help but face him. His eyes were so bright he looked almost fierce, his long black hair pulled free from its ribbon and whipping around his face in the wind. "Listen to what you just told me—you have a sister, Juliette, a sister named Amelie!"

But she was too overwhelmed to answer. Suddenly she could picture Amelie's dear face, so much like a darker version of her own beneath the white lace cap that she always wore. She could hear her sister's bubbling laughter and the lilting singsong of the French that they spoke together, and feel the cool touch of her fingers as she slipped her hand into Juliette's, and the cozy warmth of the big featherbed they shared since they'd been children.

Amelie, her older sister Amelie, kinder and more loving than their mother ever dreamed of being, Amelie who'd always been there to keep her safe.

And now when Juliette smiled up at Daniel, she didn't try to hide the tears that streamed down her cheeks. Why should she, when first he'd saved her life, and now he'd given her back her Amelie?

Chapter 4

With nightfall the wind from the water had died away, leaving an evening with only a hint of autumn's coming chill, and warm enough to keep the door propped open with an ocean-smoothed chunk of speckled granite. They ate by the flickering light of the same fire that had cooked their supper, while Sachem lay sprawled on the hearth-stones as close as he dared to the coals without being singed. Beyond the last pops and hisses of the dying fire came the muted, repetitive *shush* of the waves upon the beach, bringing in the new tide.

Silently Daniel leaned across the table to pour more tea into Juliette's cup. He felt unpracticed and odd playing the host like this, just as he'd felt ladling out chowder into two bowls instead of one, and cutting the cornbread into neat squares for sharing instead of eating it all himself directly from the pan.

It wasn't that he didn't know how to behave civilly—his mother had drilled that much into his head before she'd died, and Catherine had had her own set of expectations for a genteel table—but that it didn't seem *right*. He'd always had a strong sense of what was right and what wasn't, another legacy from his mother, and this wasn't right, not by half.

To be sitting across from a fair young woman like Juliette, making a grand celebration with her out of a hollow little nothing, being all snug and cozy like this: it simply was not as it should be, and pretending it was and that he, of all men, deserved such an evening was tempting the fates to snatch it all back the same way they had before.

Restlessly Daniel tapped his fingers on the edge of the table. John Robin would understand, not that Daniel was about to tell him. But he was equally certain that Juliette wouldn't, which was why he'd put off telling her so until now. Not only was he tempting fate, but he was also a pitiful coward in the bargain.

"Juliette," he began at last. "Juliette, all these things you're telling me about your sister, this green gown and that lacy pink petticoat and—"

"The gown is pink, a rose pink lutestring," she said, her eyes sparkling impishly in the firelight. "It's Amelie's favorite mantua on account of the color, and Amelie has the most excellent and elegant taste imaginable. But she does wear it over a green petticoat, which is likely what you heard me say."

Daniel sighed. As despicable as it was to admit, this would be much easier if Juliette were less attractive. Unfortunately, he was finding her very attractive indeed. While the afternoon on the beach hadn't brought back her strength or much of her memory, it had done marvels for her appearance. The flush and general dullness that came with fever had gone, and despite the ugly bruises that marred her face she'd become so shyly animated that she nearly glowed. She'd washed and combed her hair, too, ridding it of the salt water's sticky coating, and arranged it away from her face in a becomingly uncomplicated knot at the back of her neck.

Before his marriage, Daniel had been a great favorite with the ladies, and Juliette was exactly the kind of lady who had in turn been a favorite with him, small and well rounded and lively, with her blue eyes as bright as the sky and pale blond hair that shimmered like silver. Hell, there'd been a time when he would have written line after line of wretched poetical drivel simply to honor her dimples.

Not that dimples or any of the rest of her should matter now, and especially not after he said what needed saying. Once, in that faraway past, a young woman like Juliette would have been a challenge to be conquered, another feather to pluck and add to the gaudy array already in his cap.

But now, things were different. Now all a woman like her did was terrify him. What the devil was he going to do with her, anyway? He sighed again, and looked down at his hands to avoid the potential influence of those dimples.

"Then the rose silk mantua," he said, "if that was what it was."

"It was," she said firmly, "and still is."

"But you don't *know* that," he said quickly, "not as gospel. I'm not saying it's not good for you to remember Amelie, because it is, but so far all you're remembering is the frippery, what she wore or how she dressed your hair. Unless you're keeping it to yourself, you haven't said a blessed word about where you two were wearing all these gowns, what city or town or country it might have been that you called home."

He sighed. "You haven't said who's paying for all those gowns, either, whether it's your father with the deep pockets or your husband. Hell, Juliette, you haven't even told me your own last name."

He kept looking down at the table, waiting for her to answer. And waiting, and waiting, so long that he finally filled the silence himself.

"It's not that I'm trying to make more trouble for you," he said awkwardly. "It's only that—"

"I don't *know*," she said, her voice so brittle that he had to raise his gaze. "Is that what you wish me to say?"

"I don't wish you to say anything." Blast, she looked terrible again, with all that happy, charming rosiness gone and her mouth pinched and pale. "Only the truth."

"Or more precisely, only the truth that's useful to you."

"And to you as well!"

"Oh, yes, 'tis all for me." She swallowed visibly, and he prayed she wouldn't weep again, not on account of him. "The truth, then, is that all I appear to be able to recall of Amelie are good memories and happy times. I don't know why this is so, but it is. Our father's name, and the town where we lived, and all the other 'important' things you want to know, simply aren't there for me, not yet. But they'll come. They'll come, and then I'll be back with Amelie and you'll be rid of me, exactly how you wish."

"You're talking nonsense and folly now," he said automatically, but his own thoughts had already jumped ahead. If her head could only conjure the happiest memories of this sister of hers, then grim logic suggested that there were others far less pleasant that her confused mind wished desperately to avoid. He'd seen that, too, among other survivors.

And God help him for the greatest fool, he'd seen it happen in himself. . . .

"Juliette," he said carefully, unsure how either of them would respond. "It's possible that your sister was onboard the ship with you."

Her eyes widened, but the tears he'd dreaded still didn't spill over. "And that Amelie was lost with me?"

He nodded and looked back down at the plain planks of the table, his throat closing against saying anything more. No matter how hard this was for her, it was infinitely worse for him. Her pain would be based on shifting dread alone, while his was founded solidly on wickedly harsh experience.

How had he landed here, he thought with cynical despair? These were things he'd never shared with anyone. How had he begun speaking to a pretty stranger about the way he cut his corn bread, and ended up ripping up his old sorrows raw by the roots like they were weeds among the carrots and parsley?

"Amelie isn't dead," said Juliette, faith and conviction holding her voice steady. "She didn't drown. She's alive because I would know if she weren't."

"But you don't know for certain." He'd fallen into that self-blinding trap, too, and it had taken the coldest, cruelest proof of all to open his eyes and close his heart.

"Amelie *is* alive," she insisted, spreading the fingers of her right hand over her chest. "I know it here, in my heart, even if it's all still foggy and unsure in my head. Perhaps you don't believe in dreams, but you must have someone you love so much that you'd feel their suffering yourself, no matter where it happened."

He'd felt like that about Catherine, until he'd discovered that his love alone wasn't enough to keep her safe. And nothing, nothing that this silver-haired little lady could say would coax that bitter truth from him.

"I do not know how it is with men and their sisters, having never had a brother myself," she persisted. "At least I don't believe I do. But if you have a brother of your own, why, then isn't it as I say between the two of you?"

His first impulse was to deny it. Oh, he had brothers, two of them, and a younger sister as well, but once he'd been able to leave Appledore, the small town on the north shore of Cape Cod where they'd been born, he'd run and hadn't looked back. At first it had been ambition that had kept him away and silent; his older brother Joshua had found riches and success on his own, and Daniel had decided to return home only when he'd be able to better Joshua's achievement. But when he'd failed so spectacularly in every way that Joshua would value, he'd stayed away to protect himself, to try to let his wounds heal without his brother's critical scrutiny.

"Surely you have some sibling," she tried again. "On an island as unrewarding as this, I should think large families should be very much the rule."

That made him smile in spite of himself. "You would be right about Nantucket families, aye, but wrong about me, since I wasn't born here, but on the mainland. But considering my oldest brother is the toughest, most stubborn blue-water sailor in New England, I do not spare much time fussing over whether he's fallen into some trouble or not."

She tipped her head to one side, considering, as she idly traced one fingertip around the rim of her cup. "No fussing for *him,* then. I'll grant you that much. But you called him your oldest brother, which implies by right that there must be a middle one, too, and maybe a younger and youngest to complete the set."

"A clever little creature, aren't you?"

"When it serves to make my point, I am." She grinned, but in a kindly way, and without the gleam of triumph he'd expected. "So how many more fine Fairbourne brothers are there? Come, do you grace the world by the pair, the quartet, or the full gross?"

He nearly smiled again, balking at the last minute when he realized how unfamiliar such a simple motion felt. Oh, he smiled to be agreeable or to make a point, but he couldn't recall the last time it had happened spontaneously like this, not once, but almost twice.

"There are three of us, aye," he said, wishing, also for the first time in his memory, that he didn't sound so wretchedly *stolid.* "Joshua, Samson, and me."

"A trinity of Fairbourne men, then." She held up three fingers, one for each brother, and wiggled them like she was waving. "Is Samson as strong as his name?"

"Only between the ears." There, he'd smiled at something he'd said himself, and so, he marveled, had she. "When we were boys, we were so much alike some folk mistook us for twins, always plotting some mischief or another."

"So he's the one," said Juliette softly, resting her chin on her hand to listen. "You do have someone."

"More right to say I did." Absently he looked past her and out the open door to where a quarter moon had risen from the water. "That last summer, out on the big rock behind our house, Sam and I'd pledged to become pirate kings together. To make it stick we swore some sort of oath so awful that neither of us could sleep that night from fearing for our mortal souls, or worse, that Mam would find out and thrash us. Oh, we were a pair of wicked scoundrels, were't we?"

"I'm sure you were," she murmured gently. "How did he die?"

"Sam?" he asked, more surprised to be jolted back to the present than by her question. "Oh, Sam didn't die, at least not then. It was Father that died first, lost on his ship with all hands the winter I was six, and then Mam went soon after from missing him."

"Oh, Daniel, how awful!"

He shrugged, and kept looking out the door toward the moon. These were such old losses, old sorrows, that all the tears had long since been wrung from them.

"It wasn't the way any of us wished, that's true enough. The house had already been sold to pay Father's debts, and we didn't have any near family willing to take in four orphans. The magistrates sent Josh to sea, of course, him being oldest. Sam and I went to live in different houses, to earn our keep and learn a trade, as much as a boy that age can. I was put with the blacksmith to be his bellows boy, while they tried to make a carpenter out of poor Sam."

"But you still could see one another, couldn't you?"

"Only when our masters let us." Daniel shrugged again. "Not that it mattered, really. We both left that town as soon as we were of age, the way boys do. All I know of him now is that he's not a pirate king, leastways not one that's wicked enough to have a price upon his head."

"But you do think of him," she said. "You'd know if any harm came to him."

He frowned. The image of Samson as he'd been as a boy was suddenly so clear he almost blinked to make sure his brother wasn't standing there in the doorway. Which, of course, he wasn't. How could he be? No five-year-old Sam at all: no black hair falling in his eyes, nor eager-puppy smile, nor pockets that bulged with a score of collected treasures, and stockings always untied and puddling around his ankles.

He did blink, hard. That quarter moon must be rising faster than he'd realized; he couldn't possibly have yammered on so long about nothing.

"I think of Sam as he was, as we both were, aye," he said, choosing his words with care to try to make her understand. "I think of our old house on Cranberry Point, and the times when Father would take us out on the bay in a boat to fish, or how we'd lean over the edge of the loft at night when we were supposed to be asleep so we could hear Mam singing to our baby sister. But I don't squander my time imagining what Sam is doing now, whether he's married or prospering or even dead, any more than I worry over Josh or my sister, Serena."

"No, I suppose you wouldn't," she answered, surprising him again by agreeing. "If you are so practical, so serious minded as to not waste a single minute of the day or night upon dreaming, then why would you do the same for people you haven't seen since you were children?"

"I don't," he said, though he did glance warily her way just the same, wondering why she'd become so agreeable. The expression on her round face gave away nothing, little enough that he would hate to have her opposite him with a handful of playing cards.

"It shouldn't matter if they share the same blood and parents," she continued. "You have your own life and concerns here, as your brothers most likely have theirs, oh, anywhere else in the world."

"True enough," he had to admit, though to hear his argument phrased that way, in her voice with the musical hint of the French to it, made him sound more cold hearted than practical. He did not want her to think him cold hearted; he didn't think he was, not really.

But then why the devil had he told her any of this, about his parents and brothers and sister, and how their childhood in Appledore had come so abruptly to an end? She was still a stranger, even if she'd slept in his bed, and here he'd been rambling on like some inescapable town bore. And what had happened to his much-prized privacy? He wasn't even sure he'd shared that much with Catherine when they'd been married, and certainly not with any of those other sweet-faced girls in Boston and Bridgetown.

He pushed back his chair and rose, going to lean one arm against the frame of the open door. He peered up into the sky as if to gauge the weather, or the progress of the moon. He hoped Juliette would take it like that, anyway, while he tried to decide what the hell he was supposed to say next after such a damned fool *confession*.

He felt a bump against his leg, Sachem's nose, and he eased to one side to let the dog pass.

"Come along, Sachem," he muttered when the dog didn't come through. "You know we don't stand on ceremony here."

"No ceremony at all," said Juliette as she slipped into the spot left for Sachem. "Excepting, perhaps, this ritual for viewing the moon. Since I began this day seeing the sunrise and thanking you for the honor, it seems most fitting that I finish with the same homage to the moon. You will tell me if I am doing it incorrectly, yes?"

Oh, hell, yes, thought Daniel with despair. He'd tell her any damned thing she wanted to hear, and wonder later exactly how far into purgatory that moonlight could reach.

He glanced over his shoulder long enough to see Sachem still wheezing and snoring contentedly on the hearthstones. Some things, at least, didn't change.

But how the devil could he have mistaken Juliette for his *dog?*

Now she was being careful not to touch him, or take too much of his space on the doorstep. She'd even gathered her skirts in one hand to keep them from brushing against his legs, and she was determinedly gazing at the curving crescent moon as if he weren't standing less than a handsbreadth away.

Alas, the moonlight didn't flatter her tonight as the poets claimed it did to all women, and with concern Daniel saw how the merry glow he'd noted earlier had faded into the pallor and shadowed eyes of open exhaustion. Fevers often returned with nightfall, too. He'd be selfish indeed if he didn't send her back inside at once to sleep, which would also be a convenient way to end a most inconvenient conversation.

Except that, blast him for a fool, he didn't want to lose her company.

"It's a quarter moon," he said, and immediately felt

like an ass for saying something so blindingly obvious. "You can look at it anyway you please."

There, that was even worse. First he'd babbled on and on about his family, then this. He'd been right to find her so terrifying when this was the sorry result. He might as well just go toss himself in the waves now and be done with it.

"It's a most lovely moon, regardless," she said softly, bracing herself against the frame of the door with both hands behind her. "And though you are very good at saving pitiful lives such as mine, Daniel Fairbourne, you're an abysmal liar. You haven't stopped caring about your Samson and the others, not one bit. You may even care about them as much as I care about Amelie. But I think what worries you most is that those brothers of yours might not care about you as much as you do them."

"You're wrong," he said hoarsely. What right did she have to make such assumptions about his most private thoughts? What right did she have to be *right?* "Damnation, you're wrong."

She shook her head and smiled, a sad sort of smile even by moonlight. "Perhaps I am. It must be monstrously hard to accept any advice from a person who cannot even hazard her own last name. But wherever in the world your brothers have scattered, whatever their reasons are for keeping away from you, theirs is the greater loss."

"Loss, hah," he said roughly, falling back on the one sure way he knew to regain the distance between them. He didn't want these confidences and speculations from her. He didn't want anything. "What can you possibly know of loss?"

But she didn't back down or turn away. "I know what I

no longer have," she said wistfully. "Isn't that enough for you?"

He swung his arm out toward the vastness of the sea, as if to show how little her concern meant to him. "Why do you give a damn about me?" he demanded, his voice even harsher to mask his own pain. "What am I to you?"

Her wistful smile wilted, and as much as he hated himself for doing it, he felt sure he'd finally driven her away.

But for the second time, he was wrong.

"You saved my life," she said, her voice so small he barely heard it over the rush of the waves. "You won't let me thank you, but you must know I'll never forget what you did. You cared enough about me to save me, so now I care about you."

Before he could reject this, too, or even understand what she said, she'd closed the space between them in one hasty step, resting her hand lightly on his sleeve to steady herself before she reached up and kissed his cheek, right above his jaw.

"There," she said, breathless with her daring. "You cannot give *that* back!"

She slipped away, meaning to escape inside the house, but he caught her forearm and held her fast, pulling her back against his chest. It had only been the slightest possible kiss, her lips barely brushing over his stubbled skin, yet if she'd hit him with the blunt end of an axe he wouldn't have felt the impact more. He couldn't think straight, couldn't think of two words to string together to tell her how he felt because he didn't know himself.

"Wait," he ordered hoarsely, even though there was no chance she'd go anywhere with the hold he had on her arm. Her wrist was bare below the ruffle of her sleeve, her skin ridiculously soft, her pulse beating as crazily as his own. "You cannot do such a thing and then run away!"

"*Mon Dieu*, forgive me, I am never so bold!" she whispered wildly, and if there'd been more light he was sure her cheeks would be scarlet with shame. He could tell she wasn't by nature bold; she didn't have a true coquette's audacity. As it was, her eyes were enormous, and her breath was coming so fast with excitement that her lips were parted, moistened where she'd just licked them, inviting in a way he should never have noticed. "Forgive me, oh, forgive me!"

"There's nothing to forgive, lass." His voice had grown lower, more gruff. He'd loosened the hold on her wrist, and in return she'd swayed closer, not away, so her arm rested on his chest and her skirts fluttered between his legs and her fluttering breath was as insubstantial as a butterfly's wing on his cheek.

"But I—"

"Hush," he said softly. That was all, and that was enough, and then he kissed her.

Heaven, and hell.

He'd forgotten the magic of kissing a woman, of discovering how sweet and soft and welcoming her mouth could be. He curled his arm around her waist, lifting her up more tightly against him. Jesus, she seemed small, as light as a bit of cattail fluff, and as warm and supple to hold as a kitten. With a little moan of startled pleasure, her lips slipped apart for him, and hungrily he deepened the kiss, desire drumming deep in his belly with the taste of her. Her response was more rare for being unexpected and eager, and he could feel the bliss vibrate through them both like a live spark.

And it wasn't right, none of it.

With a groan of frustration, he broke the kiss, letting her slide down back to her feet, keeping his arm around her waist to steady her. Slowly she opened her eyes, dazed and heavy lidded, and touched her fingers to her lips in wondering disbelief.

"What have we done?" she whispered breathlessly. "Oh, Daniel, what have we done?"

He wished he knew the answer. For five long years, he'd shut away this part of him, letting it grow dry and parched and without feeling, and now, with this one kiss, he felt the sensation coming back, and it scared the hell out of him. He couldn't believe that a single kiss could do so much. No, there was more to it than that. It was *Juliette's* kiss that had this sort of power over him, enough to make him forget himself like this, and worse still, to remember everything else that was best forgotten.

He forced himself to look away from her, up at that blasted moon again instead. At least the moon was in its rightful place, there among the stars as it always had been. It was only him that had changed.

"You've done nothing," he said hoarsely. "I'm the one at fault. I've wronged you, taken advantage of you in a way that's unforgivable."

Forgive me, Catherine. . . .

"But Daniel, please, I didn't—"

"No, lass," he said, his voice leaden. "Don't try to make it better."

Juliette stared at him, more confused and bewildered by him now than she'd ever been. That kiss had been beyond all wonder, a heady experience that would have lifted her from the ground even if he hadn't, and it wasn't simply because she couldn't remember any other kisses for comparison. This one, she was sure, was unlike any other. She'd felt close to him when he'd spoken of his brother, realizing how rare such confidence was from a man like him, but even that couldn't compare to feeling his mouth move so tenderly, and so excitingly, across hers. She couldn't even say how she'd ended up in Daniel's arms, but she was glad—endlessly glad—that she had.

But how could it be that he hadn't felt the same? Why was it that when she'd felt joy beyond anything she'd known, all he'd found was shame and disgust? In her heart she believed she was a decent woman, not some coarse slattern, but maybe she'd been wrong, if she'd found pleasure where he hadn't.

Humiliated more by her own thoughts than anything he'd said, she stared down at her clasped hands, blinking hard so she wouldn't cry. If he hadn't liked kissing her, then surely he'd despise her more if she wept.

"If you please, I believe I shall retire now," she said without looking up. "To sleep, I mean. I find I am most weary."

She heard him take a deep breath. "That would be well. You need to rest."

"Good night, then." She gathered up her skirts in one hand, giving him the chance to say something more. He didn't, and with her head bowed as low as her heart, she slipped inside.

"Juliette!"

She paused before she turned, not wanting him to see

how much this meant to her. He stood silhouetted in the doorway, his strong-boned face in somber profile in the moonlight.

"You have my word I'll not disturb your rest, this night or any other," he said, and she felt her face grow hot as she realized his meaning. "You will be at peace in the bed. I'll sleep in the loft for as long as you are my guest."

She didn't dare ask how long, or how brief, that would be.

"Thank you, Daniel," she murmured automatically, before she remembered his dislike of gratitude. "You are a most kind gentleman."

"I am neither kind, nor a gentleman," he said roughly, "and the sooner you accept that, the better for us both."

He left then, striding off into the night toward the water with Sachem at his heels. For a long time she sat on the edge of the bed, and waited for them both to return. The fire died down to a shoveful of coals, and the moon rose so high that she could no longer see it in the rectangle of sky framed by the doorway. Finally she closed the door, leaving the latchstring out for when he returned, and curled up on the bed beneath the coverlet that smelled of him.

She was too exhausted to stay awake for long. If Daniel and his dog came back to the house in the night to sleep in the loft, she never knew it, for when she woke the next morning, she saw she would begin the day the same way she'd ended it.

Alone.

"You are here early, my friend," said John Robin as he made his way through the murkiness of Daniel's shop at dawn. Even though Daniel had already opened the wide front doors and unshuttered the windows, the pale early light had yet to penetrate the shop's habitual sooty gloom, nor had the fires come back enough yet to add their glow. "You're taking the food from my children's mouths, stealing my tasks like this."

Daniel tried to smile through his weariness. One of the reasons he'd come here so early was to speak with John Robin alone, before any customers were likely to appear.

"If you believe that building my fire is all you must do in this shop to earn your children's bread," he said, falling into their usual morning pattern of raillery, "then you are more daft than I thought, and lazy in the bargain."

"As long as we agree, friend." John Robin bent to ruffle Sachem's ears until the dog began sniffing at the canvas haversack that contained his dinner. With a grunt John Robin climbed up onto one of the workbenches and looped the haversack's strap on a peg high and safely out of canine reach, then took off his coat and hung it over his dinner for good measure. Then he hopped lightly back to the floor, his moccasins making no sound on the worn bricks, and as he tied on his leather apron to begin the day's work, he peered at Daniel through the gloom.

"Were you so eager to come do my work that you ignored your razor?" he asked curiously, and self-consciously Daniel's hand flew to his stubbled jaw.

"Isn't my fire worth more than my razor?" he asked, half hoping to bluff his way clear. The truth was that he always took care to begin the day with a clean shirt and a newly shaven face—an anomaly among blacksmiths, true, but not among Fairbourne shipmasters—and the fact that this morning he'd done neither must be as clear a sign to

John Robin that something was wrong as if he'd chalked an announcement on the front door.

So wrong, in fact, that John Robin decided to stop their banter and speak plainly. "You did not go home last night?"

Daniel sighed, and rubbed his eyes. He had spent the long night walking the beach, with only Sachem and the demons of his conscience for company. "Home, aye, but not to sleep. Have you heard anything more of that wreck?"

Thinking, John Robin touched two fingers to the back of his neck, not ready to volunteer what he knew without more first from Daniel. "Has your castaway offered you this trouble?"

"Trouble doesn't begin to tell the tale," said Daniel grimly. He'd no intention of sharing any more details with the other man; what had happened between him and Juliette wasn't something he was proud of, nor was it his to share. "Have you any notion if the ship was French?"

"French?" John Robin's dark eyes glittered with fresh interest. "I have not heard that, no. But it could have been French. Yes, it could have been French."

Daniel shook his head impatiently. "Damnation, John Robin, I need to know for certain! My, ah, castaway's a mite confused about the wreck, and I promised I'd find out what I could to help."

"He's a Frenchman, then." Thoughtfully John Robin rolled the sleeves of his checkered shirt over his forearms. "That Newport rum that Tom Kearny took came in casks with French branding. Your castaway captain is a French smuggler, friend?"

"No smuggler," said Daniel firmly, "and no captain, either."

"But trouble for you still." John Robin shook his head, his expression grave. "What if this castaway's friends are French, too? And what if they come to fetch him, to your house? You live too much alone, friend. You are a strong and brave man, but what are such against the desperate men of a smuggling ship?"

"Now you *are* talking daft," said Daniel, but his uneasiness grew.

"You have left your castaway alone in your house," continued John Robin, his imagination clearly warming to the possibilities. "What if he signals his friends to join him? What if they come to rob you and slit your throat while you sleep?"

"It will not happen," insisted Daniel, even as he remembered Juliette sitting alone on the dune, gazing out to sea, waiting, perhaps, for a sign from some vessel. "This is Nantucket, not the Caribbean."

John Robin pursed his lips and scowled, silently scolding him for a fool. "This is Nantucket, yes, and can you think of another place where the laws of your king are so little regarded?"

Daniel couldn't argue. The peace between the French king and the English had been a restless one in these years since the last war, and the lines between smuggling and pirating and privateering were blurry ones at best. His own brother Joshua had profited handsomely from such dubious trade, not worrying overmuch about either politics or legalities, and his French counterparts would not be any better.

Any French ship, so deep into English waters, would be sure to carry a particularly reckless and daring crew, quick to go to any desperate lengths to preserve themselves and their secrecy, the true thieves' honor.

Juliette had been the only one, alive or dead, to be found after the ship was lost. But what if the ship hadn't been lost at all? What if the rum and the rest of the cargo washing ashore on Nantucket beaches had been tossed overboard intentionally, a common precaution in a storm? What if Juliette were the French captain's petted daughter, or wife, or mistress, swept overboard in the confusion? How badly would that Frenchman want her back?

Daniel closed his eyes, trying to separate what he knew to be true, and what was only how he wished it. If these Frenchmen came to take Juliette back with them, would that be so dreadful? From the beginning, his one goal for her had been to return her to her people; it shouldn't matter who those people were, any more than it was his place to judge them. She belonged with them, her sister Amelie and the rest, and after she had left, all her pretty talk of caring for him would be worth exactly what it was: a handful of days out of her life, a passing bond of familiarity born from proximity alone, a few sweet-faced gratitudes and platitudes soon, and best, forgotten.

And one devastating kiss that had scorched his soul.

How much loss, how much betrayal could one man bear, and survive?

"Tell no one else of this," he warned, urgency and longing making his voice raw. "I don't need rumors starting that I'm harboring a Frenchman, mind?"

John Robin nodded, even though both knew the warning was unnecessary. Daniel was the only Englishman he ever spoke to, and in turn the only one who listened to him.

"If you need my help, Daniel Fairbourne," he said now, "you know you have it, in this or anything else."

Daniel clapped his hand on the smaller man's shoulder. "I know I do," he said, "and I thank you for it. But this is something I'd best handle myself."

"Then take care, friend," said John Robin softly. "Your good deeds and charity will earn you a place in heaven, but don't waste all that you have in this life for the sake of one poor castaway."

Except, of course, when the castaway was a silver-haired young woman named Juliette.

Chapter 5

Juliette had no notion when Daniel would return that afternoon, or even if he'd return at all. Though she concocted a dozen tasks for herself to try to keep her thoughts elsewhere, she still must have rushed to the window a hundred times as the sun dropped lower over the rolling hills and meadows, each time imagining she'd heard Daniel's whistle or Sachem's bark. Over and over she rehearsed what she'd say and how she'd act to make him forget that wretched, misguided kiss and instead remember the rest of the evening when he'd told her so much about his family. Another chance, that was all she wished, and she paused once again by the open door to gaze out over the path to town.

And yet when at last he did appear, he caught her by surprise. She was sitting beside the house in one of the tall-backed chairs she had dragged out from inside, her head bent over the white linen in her lap as she made use of the last of the sun.

"Juliette," he said softly, but still loud enough to make her start with a little gasp and look up from her handwork to find him standing there.

Her heart beating wildly, she wondered how long he'd been waiting there in rough-hewn, rumpled reality after all her watercolor imaginings. He stood leaning upon the whitewashed fence with Sachem panting at his side as he watched her, his jaw darkened with a stubble of beard and his shoulders bent with weariness, enough for her to realize that wherever he'd gone last night, he hadn't slept. But his blue eyes had lost that icy, agonizing distance they'd held last night, and what she found in his face now—could it really be bemused puzzlement?—was enough of an improvement to make her smile tentatively.

"Juliette," he said again, this time making a greeting from her name. "Juliette. What in blazes are you doing with my shirt?"

Hastily she looked down at the shirt in her lap, almost as if she'd forgotten it was there herself. This wasn't the picture she'd meant to present to him, with her perched on the edge of the tall-backed chair and her feet propped on the edge of the fence, the few pins she'd found conveniently bristling on a ribbon beside her arm and the threaded needle pinched tight in her fingertips. Though it seemed perfectly obvious to her what she was doing, it seemed she'd have to explain, anyway. And considering how many other explanations he could have expected of her, this one should be easy enough.

"I'm doing only good, I promise you." She gathered up the soft, white linen, spreading and smoothing it over her lap for him to see. "By my reckoning, you have four perfectly good shirts, more than most men in New England ever possess at a single time, and the linen is finer than most, too, good, fine-spun stuff that could almost be Holland."

"It is," he said blandly. "Good shirt linen is a weakness of mine. But you still haven't told me why you have this shirt here, or why you've seen fit to rummage through my clothing while I've been away."

"I did not 'rummage,' " she said indignantly, not pausing to consider why or how a blacksmith on a remote island like Nantucket would indulge in fine linen shirts. "I merely sought some way to be useful to you, and it's a good thing I did, too. I cannot fathom how you would own shirts of this quality and then let them fall into such disrepair! Look, look here. Every one of your shirts is peppered with these little holes."

He came around the fence and bent closer to inspect the shirt, close enough that she could smell the scent of the smoke from the charcoal fire of the forge clinging to his hair and clothes. He frowned a bit as he studied the spot she was pointing to.

"Oh," he said as if a great mystery had been resolved. "*Those* holes. The sparks from the fires do that, just as they burn holes in me, too, if I'm not careful. Every honest smith's shirts look like that."

"Well, now yours will not." She glanced up at him suspiciously. Though he'd always seemed too grim and serious for teasing, she had the uncomfortable feeling now that he was not treating this conversation with the same seriousness as she was herself. "It has taken me most of this day, but I've darned all those honest holes except the last few on the back of this shirt."

"Darned honest holes?" he repeated, striving to look innocent. "You, Juliette?"

She narrowed her eyes at him to prove she'd seen through his jest, but she couldn't be cross at him, not like this. It was too easy to see back to the boy he'd been with his brother Sam, two wicked little pirates afraid of what their mother would say.

"You can just judge the darned holes for yourself," she said primly, turning the shirt to the front to show him the patches of neatly woven darning that now dotted the linen where rough-edged holes had been. She had done good, neat work and she was proud of it, and though she didn't expect him or any man to appreciate such feminine craftsmanship, she rather hoped he'd see her efforts as a tiny gift to him in return for all he'd given her.

But she didn't expect him to lean over the shirt with such obvious interest, tracing his fingertips over her darning with an awareness that was unabashedly sensuous, moving across every tiny stitch. And today, she noticed suddenly, he'd taken the time to wash before he'd come home. It was almost as if by touching the threads that she'd labored upon, he was somehow touching her, too, and the thought made her shiver beneath her shift. His hands fascinated her, so broad and strong and so unlike her own. She caught herself imagining what it would be like to have those large male hands moving as carefully across her bare skin, learning it with the same curious concentration as he was showing the darns, and then, before she could stop, her imagination was once again racing back to that wild, shameful kiss they'd shared.

It was enough to make her duck her head and pray that, with the shifting light, he wouldn't see how flushed she'd become, or brush against her arm and feel the heat that he'd brought to her blood. If darning his shirts could reduce her to this, she thought miserably, what would happen if he asked her to do the same for his breeches?

"This isn't mending," he said, fortunately unaware of her thoughts as he smoothed the shirt's neck to better see the pattern of tiny crossed stitches worked beneath the opening. "A *D* and an *F*. For Daniel Fairbourne, I'll wager. I *hope*."

"Those were my reward," she said in a rush, now embarrassed that he'd noticed the monogram. "After the plain sewing to mend all those holes, I let myself do the fancywork of the letters. They're not in silk, of course, the way they should be—I had trouble enough finding sewing thread in your house, and I had to make do with linen threads drawn from inside the seams—but the style is proper for a gentleman, white thread on white."

He didn't answer as he traced the two stitched letters, each smaller than his fingertip.

"If you do not approve, I can rip them out," she said anxiously. "I know some gentlemen don't favor such fashions upon their linen."

"But I do," he said, his voice low. "I haven't had my shirts marked like this since I was a boy, and my mother made them."

"You are pleased, then?"

He then looked up to meet her gaze, and with a jolt she realized that their eyes were nearly level, and if their eyes were so close, then so, by logic, their lips must be as well. Last night she'd learned that this was not a proximity to encourage, but still she remained frozen there with the shirt bunched in her lap, his face near enough that she could, if she'd wished, count every one of his black lashes. So close like this, she was sure she saw something flicker through his eyes, some sort of internal warning or misgiving that he'd betrayed his thoughts, even if only for an instant. Then, with a sigh, he was the one who broke the spell between them, rocking back to lean against the fence, idly rubbing the ridge of white fur along Sachem's back.

"How could I be otherwise than pleased?" he asked lightly, but the teasing good humor he'd shown earlier was gone. "Your work shames my poor shirts by comparison. But now I'll scold you, lass. You were supposed to spend this day resting, not toiling over my clothing."

"I've rested enough," she protested, "and I didn't want to sit here idle the whole day. I wanted to be useful."

"I don't want you to be useful," he said firmly. "I want you to be well, so you can go home."

"But I still don't know where home is!"

"You will," he predicted, and the way he said it, with such unquestioning certainty, made her blood grow chill. "As soon as you're ready, or when your people come for you. You do wish to go back to your sister Amelie, don't you? Back where you can speak French again?"

"I do, of course," she said slowly, striving to make sense of whatever it was he was trying to tell her. "Have you heard something I should know, Daniel? About me, or how I came here?"

She didn't miss the slight wince when she'd asked, and she understood it, too, even as her heart sank with disappointment. She might not recall the details of her own life, but she certainly remembered how most English colonists distrusted everything and everyone French, including girls with French-sounding names. For all his kindness toward her to this point, Daniel might well feel the same way about harboring a Frenchwoman in his home any longer than he had to.

"I've reason to guess," he now said carefully, "that the ship you were on was French, smuggling rum to New England. Though they seem to have jettisoned you along with part of their cargo, I'm guessing now that they're still alive and still afloat. And once they figure you're here, I'm guessing they'll be coming directly to fetch you home."

"But why would I be onboard a French smuggler?" she asked, the panic in her voice rising. "I know I speak French with Amelie and that my name is French, but that doesn't make me a Frenchwoman. I don't *feel* like a Frenchwoman, Daniel, or at least how I'd believe a Frenchwoman should feel. I'm English. I *know* I'm English, just as I know I never would have sailed in a French smuggling ship!"

Daniel sighed. "But the pieces fit together, lass. 'Feeling' is all well and good, but you could just as well be 'feeling' English because you've landed here in an English colony."

"No, no, there's more!" she cried. She pressed her fingertips to her temples, striving to concentrate. "When I was mending your shirts, I could recall doing the same thing somewhere else, a place that must be my home. I was sitting beside a large front window, for light, of course, and through it I could see a city street in a genteel neighborhood with finely dressed ladies and gentlemen and children walking about. Diagonally across the street there was a church, too, whose spire cast a shadow over my work so that I had to shift my chair, and—and—oh, Daniel, it had to be an English city, I know it!"

"It could just have likely have been Ste. Pierre on

Martinique," he said, unconvinced, "or maybe Quebec. There's plenty of French cities in the French colonies."

"But this wasn't one of them! I could see shop signs from the window, and they were for English tradesmen, with English names, and there was a broadsheet on the table, and it was printed in English, too!"

He sighed again, more of a drawn out whistle of mixed feelings. "Wherever that city is, Juliette," he said, "that's where you belong. Not on Nantucket, and not here."

"I know," she said with a little gulp of frustration. "I *know.*"

In silence he watched her as she whipped the extra tail of the thread around a card and thrust it with the needle and pins into the center of the bundled shirt—jerky little motions as pointed as the needle that betrayed her agitation—and she was already on her feet before he spoke again.

"Last night," he said, "all you wanted was to escape me."

She glanced at him sharply. "Last night was different."

"Aye," he said, his expression carefully impassive. "Last night was last night, and today is . . . today. Here, I've brought you something."

He reached over the fence and brought up a hat he'd left tucked in the tall grasses, a plain, wide-brimmed straw hat with a shallow crown, the kind that ladies wore. Solemnly he placed the hat on Juliette's head, straightening it with his hands on each side of the sweeping brim.

"Why?" she asked, perplexed but still not moving as he looped the long, narrow ribbons beneath her chin.

"Because last night was last night," he said, his fingers brushed across her throat as he tied the ribbon loops into a neat bow, "and today is today. Because for now, I don't believe you're altogether French, either. Because you're more accustomed to sitting behind fine city windows than on the Nantucket sand in the sun and wind."

He stepped back to admire his handiwork and smiled. "There now. You look like the proper lady you are. An *English* lady."

She stood there for a moment without moving, her chin still lifted with the bow beneath it and the shirt clutched tightly in her hands at her waist. But only for a moment; then she grabbed the front of the hat and pulled it forward off her head.

"I cannot accept this from you," she said, holding the hat out for him to take back. "A hat is too personal, too private a gift for a man to give to a lady."

He frowned down at the hat, flopping awkwardly back and forth in her hand from the breeze, but he made no move to take it from her. "You can too accept it. You need it, don't you?"

"That is not the question." She knew perfectly well what the real question was, or rather the problem, not that she would tell him. She desperately wanted to keep the hat, unadorned though it was, for the inexcusable reason that it *was* a gift from him. She liked the idea that he'd chosen it specifically for her and with her needs in mind, and she liked the intimacy of having him tie the hat beneath her chin, enough that her heart had raced and her palms had grown damp. She liked it all far too much for any two people who were not man and wife and yet living beneath the same roof together, and far, far too much for any young woman with a claim toward being a lady.

"I thank you for your gift, sir," she said, "but I fear I cannot—*will* not—accept it."

" 'Sir,' hell." Lowering his chin like a challenging bull, he folded his hands behind his back to make extra sure they couldn't be tempted to take back the gift. "Who's to know I gave it to you anyway?"

"*I* would know. Any article that touches a lady's private person is not a suitable gift."

"Well, then, what about in reverse?" he countered, and she thought again of that bull. "What about you touching my private person? All those little stitches and darns and letters and such that you made on my shirt—those will touch my person, and damned privately, too, when I tuck the tails into my breeches."

That made her flush, and wonder how he'd backed her into such an unconscionable corner. "That is different."

"Oh, aye, exactly as last night was from today, and back we are again, at the same launching place." He took the hat from her, only to settle it back onto her head.

"No respectable English lady would wear a hat without a cap beneath it," she said realizing again, to her great distress, that he was teasing her again. Flustered, she abandoned her first argument for another with fewer pitfalls. "I should never be seen anywhere without covering my hair."

"I like your hair the way it is," he said, and the way he was studying her now showed that perhaps she'd traded one set of pitfalls for another. "I don't know why you'd want to cover it with some silly cap."

"I told you already," she said self-consciously. She hadn't dressed her hair in any special way, combing it straight back into a loose knot at the nape of her neck that the breezes from the water had done their best to pull apart into tiny, disheveled curls that couldn't possibly be attractive. But her pale hair had often drawn too much attention; "fairy hair," Amelie had called it.

"Because it's not safe to be near a fire with an uncovered head," she said. "Nor would any proper woman wish to do it."

"Not that anyone but us would know that, either." He sighed dramatically. "But if you wish a cap that badly, I'll find one in the shop for you tomorrow."

"In the shop?" she repeated, skeptical. Because all of what she'd seen of Nantucket was rough and wild, she assumed the rest of the island was like that, too. Even when she tried to imagine his blacksmith's shop, she saw it sitting alone in a sea of grass and sky, just like his house was. "A shop for ladies' things? I didn't think you had them here."

He chuckled. "Of course we have shops here. Why wouldn't Nantucket ladies crave the same sorts of frippery that you off-islanders do? Though I do doubt our shops are quite so fine, or costly, as the ones in that city of yours."

"Tomorrow, then!" she said gaily, eager for the adventure. "I've only a bit of money of my own, true, but if I spend only enough for half an ell of white linen—only half an ell, that is all!—then I could fashion a cap for myself in next to no time."

"And then would you deign to wear my hat with it?" he asked. "If I wear the shirts that you have mended to make me respectable, then you will wear the hat that I have brought to do the same for you?"

She nodded, and grinned shyly. Strange how she could

picture exactly the kind of cap she'd create, small and neat with a flourish of ruffles to frame her face beneath the hat's brim, and strange, too, how she already knew precisely how she'd make it, down to the hem stitching on the ruffles and the tiny cartridge pleats around the crown. "I'll come with you in the morning, so you can show me the way."

"Tomorrow?" He cocked his head, bemused in a way that she didn't understand. "The way is easy, along the single sorry rutted excuse for a cart path north across the island. But it's nearly four miles to Sherburne, and you're not strong enough for a journey such as that."

"It's because of my limp, isn't it?" she said wistfully, disappointed more than he'd know. "You've decided I'm a cripple, helpless to go anywhere on my own. But I can, you know. I could walk to your town with you, and I wouldn't slow you down one bit."

"Four miles on a rough path with plenty of hills tossed in for sport: that's why I'm not taking you," he said firmly, like a man who was accustomed to being obeyed. "Perhaps when you're stronger, I'll consider it, but not now."

She wasn't supposed to be his prisoner, and he swore that she wasn't. So why, then, did she feel so trapped here in the little house by the sea? "But if I promise I won't be a burden, or—"

"Promise whatever you please, lass, but you won't be walking to Sherburne with me tomorrow." He reached out and tugged one of the ribbons trailing from the hat, a playfulness she hadn't expected from him, especially not now. "Come, I've brought us a fine halibut for supper."

"Halibut?" Just as she'd known instantly how to repair

the holes in a gentleman's shirt, she was equally, instantly sure that she hadn't the faintest notion of how to turn a fine halibut into supper. "Daniel, I'm most sorry, but I am no cook."

"Then it's a good thing that I am," declared Daniel, reaching for the haversack with the fish from the other side of the fence. "So we won't starve, eh?"

He made certain of that, searing the halibut first in an iron skillet close to the coals, then covering it with thinly sliced wild onions to finish cooking more slowly. He liked to cook, which seemed much akin to working with iron, making useful things by way of fire. He'd also bought a small crock of Ruth Kearny's plum jam for them to vary the ever constant cornbread, and a customer just back from a trading trip to the mainland had traded a half bushel of new apples in exchange for a bit of welding.

It was a most agreeable meal, he'd thought, and if Juliette seemed quiet as they ate in front of the open door, well, likely she was still weary, more weary than she wanted to admit. He couldn't believe she'd actually thought she could walk with him clear to Sherburne and back, not as fragile as she so obviously still was. He wasn't certain she ever could make the trip; even people who'd lived here all their lives seldom came down to this lonely southern coast, which had been a large part of its attraction for him.

And even if through some miracle she'd walked that far, he could scarcely imagine the kind of reaction that would greet her in town. As in any seafaring town, men came and went, and strangers were nothing new. But women were a different story altogether, and a woman as young and beautiful as Juliette would be a rarity, a marvel, a dangerous interloper or suspicious foreigner, each possibility enough to spark gossip and speculation for weeks. Combined with the mystery of her appearance in connection with the wreck, and now her attachment to him—ah, he thought dryly, the entire island could quite possibly expire from its own excitement.

He watched her now across the table, taking delicate little nibbles from the apple slice in her hand. It was probably just as well she seemed so quiet and lost in her own thoughts this evening, and that their conversation had been limited to the weather and the tides. If she'd been more sociable and encouraging, the way she had last night, then he might have been tempted to spill more foolish personal confidences about his childhood, this time regaling her about why he'd never liked walnuts, say, or the misguided insults that Sam and he had tried out on one another. That was the kind of nonsense that had led him to stray so badly last night, and to make such a babbling ass of himself.

But most damaging of all, she'd made him realize how he'd accepted loneliness as being the same as being alone. And that—that he couldn't afford to let happen again.

Now that she was beginning to remember more and more, it was only a matter of time—perhaps as little as another day or two—before she'd disappear from his life forever, and he'd no intention of getting any more entangled with her than he'd already done. He had to stop now, when his interest in her was still based in kindness alone.

Mostly, that is, when he wasn't kissing her. Not even he could dissemble *that* into kindness, not when she'd been so warm and willing in his arms, her mouth such a sweet, soft invitation that he would have had to be dead and buried, too, to ignore it. He made a growling sound of frustration in the back of his throat and shifted in his chair, thankful that she wouldn't look beneath the table and see what effect she had on him.

No, it had to end here, now. Fate had tossed Juliette into his life, but the sooner he was able to toss her back, the better.

All he had to do now was find a way to do it.

He set his pewter plate down on the floor with a clatter for Sachem to lick clean. With an oversized yawn, he stretched his arms over his head.

"High time I found my bed," he announced to Juliette, in case he hadn't made it clear enough. "I can scarce keep my eyes open."

Or, he added mentally, my hands off you.

"Oh," she said, rising quickly with an anxious flurry of petticoats as she pushed her sleeves over her elbows. "I should have known you'd be tired! Here, here, let me finish with the dishes."

She swept his plate away from poor Sachem, who followed her, wagging his tail with hope, to the low kettle used for washing up. To Daniel's consternation, she bent over from the waist, her bottom rising upward as she sank her arms deep into the soapy water. Even covered by her petticoats, it was an exceptionally pleasing bottom, round in exactly the way he liked best. He remembered it, though he'd done his honorable best to forget.

Still waiting expectantly beside her for another chance at dinner scraps, Sachem whimpered up, then down, the canine scale, as he panted forlornly.

Daniel knew exactly how he felt.

"Are you still hungry, poor pup?" she asked, crooning to the dog over her shoulder. "I can't send you to bed hungry, can I?"

She turned, her white, bare arms glistening wet, and turned to give Sachem the rest of the cornbread—the cornbread that Daniel had set aside for his own midday dinner tomorrow. But he forgot that and everything else as he watched Juliette bend lower to pat the dog's head, low enough that he could see down her bodice, down the stiff cage of her stays to her shift and the bare skin of her breasts, glistening wet where she must have swiped them absently with the washing water. Temptation, temptation. . . .

"I'm going up the ladder now," he said, bolting upright from his chair in a way that was anything but sleepy. "To the loft. To sleep."

"As you wish." Mercifully she stood upright, wiping her hands on a towel as she dipped him a quick curtsey. No kiss tonight, then, and a good thing, too. "I hope you rest well, Daniel."

"And you, too, Juliette." In response to her curtsey, he bowed, woodenly, and fled up the narrow ladder to the loft overhead. In his haste he forgot to take a candle or lantern, and he forgot that the ceiling was low, slanting down sharply with the eaves. As soon as he'd pulled himself up through the narrow opening at the top of the ladder, he tried to stand upright, and promptly hit his head on the roof.

"Daniel?" asked Juliette, peering upward from the bottom of the ladder. "Are you in, ah, difficulty?"

By then he was sitting on the floor, rubbing the tender bump on the side of his head and mouthing furious silent oaths.

"No damned difficulty," he said in a strangled voice. "That is, no difficulty at all. Good night, Juliette."

"Good night, Daniel," she answered, though he would have wagered twenty gold guineas that that lovely lilting voice of hers was trying very hard not to laugh, and at his expense, too. With another, more audible oath, he felt about on the floor in the darkness until he found one of the wool-stuffed flock mattresses he kept there for his less genteel castaways. He tested it gingerly with his fingertips, feeling every plank of the floor beneath. Such was the comfort of the guilty conscience, he thought glumly, and took off his coat. With the brick chimney rising up to fill one wall and the shingled roof still holding some of the heat of the afternoon sun, the loft was warm and close, and he pulled off his shirt and stockings, too, though in case Juliette came up the ladder to survey his "difficulties," he decided to keep his breeches firmly buttoned. Cautiously he lay down on the mattress, rolling his coat into a makeshift pillow, and prepared to welcome sleep.

Which, of course, refused to come.

Instead he could hear Juliette's footsteps below as she put the pots and dishes away from supper, all the while making cheerful little asides to Sachem. Because that furry traitor couldn't manage the narrow ladder with his four clumsy paws, he hadn't even tried to follow Daniel, throwing him over for Juliette and her extra cornbread treats. Hell, the unfaithful animal would probably end up sleeping with her in *his* bed.

Her footsteps ended, and he realized she'd taken off her shoes. That was worse because then she must be undressing for the night, unpinning her hair and shrugging out of her bodice and untying her petticoat and undoing her garters and rolling down her stockings and unlacing her stays, pulling the cording through each eyelet one by one by one until her body in the thin linen shift was free and comfortably untrussed for the night. Finally she doused the last candle, and he heard the familiar creak and groan of the rope springs on the bed—*his* bed—as she snuggled into it, and the satisfied sigh as she settled into the soft mattress for the night, relaxed and drowsy and ready for sleep.

While he lay rigidly awake and painfully conscious of her lying in that bed beneath him.

Desperately he ordered himself to think of something, anything else to let himself sleep: the pair of horses he was scheduled to shoe tomorrow morning, or how much more Capaum Harbor had filled in during the last storm. He even tried counting sheep, an easy task on an island where sheep were rumored to outnumber people.

None of these ideas worked.

But to his surprise, the Juliette that filled his head wasn't the one bending over the wash kettle. Instead it was Juliette as he'd found her in the side yard this afternoon, her back nearly as straight as the ladderback chair, his shirt mounded like a cloud in her lap as her needle darted in and out of the white linen. He remembered his mother bringing her chair outside like that to sew, and the sunlight slanting across her head in the same way as it had done with Juliette today, making a soft halo of the wispy curls around her forehead. He'd thought of the comparison as soon as he'd spied Juliette today over the fence, and how oddly bittersweet a comparison it had been. His mother had been humbly born, a coasting fisherman's daughter from a tiny village, while he suspected

Juliette's background was considerably more complicated, but in that moment he'd realized that the two women would have liked each other enough to have become friends.

Which was, for better or worse, something he'd never been able to say of Catherine.

He never would have spied Catherine at her handwork because Catherine never did any, looking down her elegant small nose at any sort of laboring. Her father had owned four sugar plantations in the Caribbean, and he'd used his wealth to spoil his only daughter as royally as was possible. Catherine had grown up surrounded by house slaves who'd done everything for her, short of lifting her silver spoon to her lips. Impetuous and impulsive, she'd fallen wildly in love with Daniel because he'd been so independent, so different from the foppish gentlemen who'd courted her before that, and, of course, because a rough-edged Yankee sailor without property or fortune was the last thing her father had wanted as a son-in-law.

Daniel hadn't realized that, not at first. Instead he'd been so captivated by Catherine's beauty and wit, both as glittering and polished as the jewels she wore, that he'd been blinded to everything else as he'd let her lead him on a heady chase of passion and excitement. No wonder he'd fallen so instantly in love. She was exactly the sort of woman that young men dreamed of, and the fact that she was already carrying his child when they wed seemed to him to be all the blessing they needed. If in the short time they were married he'd never found the right time to tell her that he'd served his apprenticeship to a blacksmith, well then, that was because he'd loved her too much to destroy even that dream of hers.

In the dark he smiled sadly, thinking of how young and unworldly he'd been then. He'd thought he'd found paradise, and it hadn't even lasted a year. He hadn't missed the irony of having Juliette here now, trying so hard to remember her past, while he'd spent five years trying equally hard to forget so much of his.

But not Catherine. God forgive him, he'd never forget Catherine.

He sighed, thinking how the differences between Juliette and his wife could be distilled into the way each had accepted a gift from him. Catherine had loved any sort of present with the greedy exuberance of a child, pouncing on it, devouring the surprise, and then, the thrill of the new possession swiftly fading, looking expectantly for another.

But this afternoon Juliette had nearly refused the hat outright, finally deigning to accept his gift only after he'd bargained and cajoled her into it. She'd wanted it, too. He'd seen that in her eyes the moment he'd lifted it from behind the fence. But her principles had kept her from taking it, her tenuous position with him combined with her own sense of right and wrong. It wasn't even as if he'd meant the hat as part of a seduction; he'd intended it as a peace offering, pure and simple, a way to apologize for the bungled kiss.

Yet as maddening as her refusal had been at the time, he admired her for it now. He didn't expect women to have principles, especially where gifts from men were concerned. God knows Catherine hadn't had a single principled bone in her entire seductive body.

But Juliette—Juliette was different, and he smiled again as he thought of her round blue eyes anxiously peeking out from beneath the sweeping straw brim. Once she'd decided there was no sin in it, she'd kept it on until they'd sat down to dinner, stealing glances of herself in his looking glass, grinning happily as she tried tipping the brim this way, or tying the ivory ribbons to the side. His only regret now was that he hadn't brought her a more fashionable hat, one piled high with ribbons and silk roses and bits of lace. He would make it up to her tomorrow by buying her the most be-ruffled and be-ribboned cap to be found in a Sherburne shop, and he'd be be-damned before he let her pay him back for it, too.

His smile widened to a blissful grin at the prospect, and he realized he was finally sliding off to sleep. Sweet Juliette, he thought drowsily, sweet, sweet Juliette.

Even now he could imagine her dancing along the beach at Nobadeer, not far from where he'd first found her, her arms outstretched and her head tipped merrily to one side as the morning sun rose red behind her, the ribbons on her hat floating in the breeze. Sachem was there, too, the sly rogue, wearing a foolish bow of ivory ribbons that matched hers around his neck and barking as he trotted along the sand with her. She was laughing as if she hadn't a care in the world, her blue eyes crinkling in the sunshine, and as she crooked her finger to beckon to him, she called his name.

"Daniel, help me, oh, please, Daniel!"

It came as a terrified wail, not a greeting, cutting like a blade through the haze of half sleep. Instantly he was awake, and in another instant he was racing down the ladder to her. The house was dark, with only the faintest glow coming from the banked coals in the fireplace, but

Sachem's frantic barking and her own muffled cries led Daniel straight to the shadowy form tossing in the bed.

"Juliette, lass, wake up," he ordered softly as he sat on the side of the bed, not wanting to frighten her any more than she already was. "Juliette, I'm here. I'm *here.*"

Still she remained deep in the nightmare, twisting and thrashing in the bed as she struggled to escape whatever was terrifying her. Swiftly Daniel swept back the coverlet and gathered her into his arms and against his chest. Her shift was damp with her sweat, her hair torn from the neat braid and clinging moistly to her face and neck.

"You're safe, Juliette," he said as he rocked her gently back and forth. "Safe, mind?"

And with one last cry, she jerked in his arms, and woke.

She stared at him, wild eyed, her breath coming in rapid little gasps as she fought her way back to reality.

"It's all right now, sweetheart," he murmured, smoothing the damp hair back from her forehead. "It was only a dream."

"But it wasn't," she said, her voice still a terrified, trembling rush. "Oh, Daniel, it *wasn't!* I was in my cabin on the sloop and I had to get out, and the water was streaming down through the hatches, down the steps, and as hard as I tried I couldn't climb up to the deck. The water kept pushing me back, Daniel, pushing me down, so heavy and cold and I was sure this time I was going to drown, Daniel, and no matter how hard I shouted for you, you weren't *there!*"

"But I was," he said as she sobbed against his bare shoulder. "I'm here now, aren't I?"

She was crying too hard to answer, and he didn't make

her try, letting her find whatever relief she could in her tears. No wonder her poor consciousness had fought so hard against remembering the shipwreck, if it had happened as she'd dreamed and described. To be trapped belowdecks on a sinking ship as the waves poured down the companionways was a terror that he, mercifully, had never experienced himself. But for her sake he would have traded places in a second if he could have spared her this suffering now.

Gradually her sobs subsided, her exhausted body curling weakly into his for shelter and comfort. Gently he stroked her hair, feeling how soft and warm she was as she relaxed against him, and he smiled wryly to himself. When he'd dreamed of holding her in his bed, this wasn't quite the way he'd pictured it, but if he'd brought her peace, even if for this night alone, then he'd be grateful for that.

And, ah, Catherine, this time there'd be nothing to forgive. . . .

"There now, Juliette," he whispered, suspecting from the evenness of her breathing that she'd fallen back to sleep. He'd hold her as long as she needed him to, until dawn if it meant she could sleep. "It's done, sweetheart, over, and that's all that matters."

"*Non, non, mon cher,*" she murmured sleepily. "*Parce que je m'appelle Juliette Lacroix.*"

Chapter 6

With one hand on the crown of her hat to keep it from sliding from her head, Juliette leaned back to look up at the sun, trying to gauge from its height how long she'd been walking. She wasn't good at guessing the hour like this; she much preferred the more civilized way in town of looking at a clock, or asking the time of a gentleman with a watch in his pocket.

Had it been as long as an hour since she'd left the house, or did it only seem that way? She'd always been a good walker, but the fever had left her weaker than she'd wished to admit, especially to Daniel. Her shoes were stiff from having been soaked in the sea water when she'd been washed ashore, and the way the leather rubbed against her heels made it hard to be objective about passing time. And if it *had* been an hour that she'd been walking, how far did that mean that she'd walked? Again she longed for a city, with sensible landmarks like churches and shops and markets to help tell how far one had walked.

Here the scenery hadn't varied at all since she'd left the house, the same low rolling hills like land-locked waves or swells—moors, Daniel had called them—and the same treeless, waving green-gold grass scattered with patches of heathered wildflowers and small, marshy ponds shining silver in the sun, even the same flocks of grubby-gray sheep that watched her with unblinking yellow eyes as she passed by.

At least she knew she hadn't taken a wrong turn since, just as Daniel had said, this seemed to be the only road, running straight to the north across the island. With a grumbling sigh she lowered her gaze and began to trudge along again. She didn't expect Sherburne to be much of a town, not by her understanding of the word, but she had hoped that by now she'd have seen some other houses to show she was getting close. No, it was more than simply "getting close." She wanted to be there, at Daniel's shop, *now*.

Yesterday she'd decided to make this trip solely to prove to him that she could, but now, after last night, she was doing it because she needed to talk with him. She'd awakened uneasily this morning, with a distinct, disturbing memory of resting her head against his bare chest, of his arms around her and his fingers curled around her shoulders, holding her in the same bed.

She remembered feeling sheltered, protected, which she might have dreamed, but she also remembered undreamable things, the warm, sleek feel of his skin and the black hair that had curled across his chest and forearms and the regular drum of his heart beneath her ear.

She'd worried because she couldn't remember enough

to explain things to Daniel, but this was twisted the other way around, a memory that needed Daniel to explain it to her. But by the time she had wakened, he and Sachem had once again left; this time he'd left a note for her, written in pencil on the back of an old receipt and tucked into the curving handle of her teacup on the table where she'd find it at breakfast.

"Good day, lass," the note had said, his handwriting as forceful and without flourishes as he was himself. "I shall return by supper with your cap in my pocket. D.F."

A short note, hastily written, and no mention of whatever wrongness had happened in her bed, no mention of his arms around her so tenderly and his heart beating beneath her cheek. Like a lover, she thought, and her mouth turned dry.

Like *lovers*.

She lowered her head and with new determination she pushed ahead.

She saw the chimney smoke first, light gray puffs against the blue sky, and as she crested the last hill, she saw the rooftop that sat below those chimneys, roughly shingled like the one on Daniel's house. One house, then another, and another, set helter-skelter and apart, as if each were a tiny independent homestead with its own outbuildings and garden plots. These houses were much like larger versions of Daniel's, grown taller with a second row of windows and wider with another room or two, but not grander, for all were the same weathered gray clapboarding or shingle, without a fleck of paint to vary the scheme.

There were no pretty carvings over the doorways, no polished brass on the doors themselves, or bright-paneled shutters to frame the windows. Everything was so plain and gray and serviceable that the houses themselves might have sprung from the same grassy hills instead of having been built by Englishmen, and from the way the sand had been blown by the wind into drifts and banks around the houses' foundations, it was almost as if the dunes themselves were still striving to reclaim their lost ground.

Puzzled, Juliette slowed her pace. The houses were divided from the fields with the sheep by a low stone wall, interrupted only by a simple gate that let in the path she walked upon. In the distance, beyond the last houses, lay the sparkling sea with a handful of small boats and ships upon it. She'd crossed the island, and she must have walked the four miles that Daniel had warned. But could this disjointed cluster of houses possibly be Daniel's fine town of Sherburne?

She retied the bow beneath her chin, and walked through the gate, not sure where she'd go next to find the blacksmith's shop. From open windows and back steps she could see children and other women watching her with cautious interest. They dressed as plainly as their houses, these women, in sober colors and nondescript styles, and beneath their scrutiny Juliette found herself acutely aware of how fashionable, if rumpled, her own clothes were, how closely her bodice was tailored to fit over her stays and how many yards of costly fabric had been gathered into her petticoat, even how very red her heeled shoes appeared in the sunshine, the pinchbeck buckles glittering like the sea itself. To make everything even worse, her scarred leg was twinging with exhausted protest, and no matter how she concentrated on walking straight, she couldn't help limping.

Now she was doubly thankful for Daniel's hat, for not only had its wide brim kept that sun from burning her nose on the walk, but now it also sheltered her from the judgmental stares of those plain-dressed women inside their plain gray houses.

She was, as far as she could tell, the only person actually in the street at this time of day, and when a two-wheeled box cart, drawn by a single mule, came bouncing toward her along the sandy street, she hailed the driver with a wave of desperate heartiness.

"Good day, mistress," he called politely, though he studied her with the same unsettlingly open scrutiny of the women. "Have you had some trouble?"

"No, sir, thank you," she said with as graceful a small curtsey as she could manage. From his rough linen shirt and leather breeches and the raw new casks piled in the back of the cart, she guessed the man was some sort of laborer or farmer. Not the sort of man who'd ordinarily merit a curtsey, but she was too happy to have him speaking to her at all to care for such niceties now.

"Sir," she continued, "if you please, I should like to know if this is the town of Sherburne."

The man's rust-colored brows rose with surprise. " 'Course it is, mistress," he answered. "What other place would you be thinking it was? Boston, mayhap, or London itself?"

He laughed broadly, and Juliette smiled, too, to be agreeable, though she didn't think *he* was being particularly agreeable by laughing at a stranger's polite inquiry.

"I thank you," she said formally. "Now could you please direct me to Master Fairbourne's blacksmith shop?"

His laughter vanished, his expression turning guarded. "Now what would a pretty creature like you want with a man like Daniel Fairbourne?"

Juliette raised her chin, and one brow with it to show her disapproval. "I do not believe, sir, that such a question is any of your affair."

"And I say it is," the man answered. "If you knew Daniel Fairbourne the way we do here, then you'd agree, and thank me for it, too. He's a first-rate blacksmith, aye, the best we've ever had here, but that's not saying a thing about him as a man, not one thing. What I *am* saying, mistress, is for your own good. I wouldn't want any woman of mine, wife nor daughter, having aught to do with Daniel Fairbourne. A blacksmith and a black heart, that one!"

"And I say, sir, that if you believe that of Master Fairbourne, then you do not know him at all." She forgot her sore feet and her aching leg, and drew herself up tall as a queen. "Now shall you direct me to his blacksmith shop, or must I ask another?"

The man scowled. "Then you can go straightaways to the devil, you hussy, for if you go to Fairbourne, it will be much the same." He spat crossly into the grass for emphasis, and pointed back over his shoulder. "There, across Chester Street, after the sheep pens and before Master Folger's house, you'll find Fairbourne's shop."

"Thank you." She didn't curtsey to him this time, but she did hurry on her way, not wishing to have him next spit on her instead of the grass. She followed the sandy street as the man had explained, past the large empty pens of rough wood that must, in some season, hold the sheep that now roamed free. Yet as she neared the house that must belong to Master Folger, she slowed her steps, thinking of what else the man had said.

He'd warned her about Daniel, yet he hadn't given any details to explain why that warning was necessary. The Daniel she'd known these last days could be gruff and abrupt to the point of rudeness, but then from what she'd seen of the rest of these islanders, his behavior had been outright courteous. Otherwise he'd been, in his way, gentle and kind, and thoughtful of her needs. She'd seen nothing to mark him as the devil's own spawn, as the man with the cart had implied, or as a raging threat to virtuous women.

Instead she'd seen a man whose life had not been easy, yet who spoke regretfully and fondly of his lost family, a man who made a great show of living alone but who searched for unfortunates after every storm, a man who'd brought her a hat to keep her nose from peeling in the sun and who knew how to bake cornbread in an iron spider so it browned but never burned.

But the more she thought about Daniel Fairbourne, the more she realized there were dark corners about him as well, things he would not explain to her. Could her own need have blinded her to more about him? Kindness alone didn't drive him to walk the beaches at night with only Sachem for company, and a desire for solitude wasn't enough to have earned him the reputation he seemed to have in the town.

And last night, despite professing only the most honorable intentions toward her, he had found his way to her bed. . . .

She'd come far enough that she could see what must be

Daniel's shop, a long, low building on a hill overlooking the water, the uneven clapboarding nearly as black from smoke as its trade implied, with a thick chimney puffing smoke from the forge fire inside. She sighed, and tucked a few wayward curls up inside her hat. She could take the word of a malicious stranger and let it inflate her own misgivings, or she could trust what she already knew of Daniel, and ask him what she didn't.

Daniel won.

Yet as she walked the last paces to the shop, up the curving path to the entrance, she nearly faltered. This was, she sensed, not a place that welcomed women. Scraps of old iron—rusting broken bits of ship's hardware, old plows and wheels, cracked pots and sprung hoops—lay propped along the outside of the building, ready to be chosen and hammered into another useful life. A team of horses was tied to the fence, patiently waiting their turn for new shoes while their tails lazily brushed aside flies.

The main door was propped open and the three wide windows held no glass, their rough shutters hooked back to let in daylight and let out the heat from the inside. Heat, and tobacco smoke, and the clanging of the hammer mingled with sounds of laughter and deep voices from the men inside. Two more men sat idle on a bench outside, one likely the owner of the team, long-stemmed clay pipes in their mouths and nothing decent in their heads as they watched Juliette coming toward them.

Beneath their gazes, she had the same foreboding here as she did before a tavern or rumshop, that this was a distinctly male world where she had no place. What if the man in the cart had given her the wrong directions, just from spite? What if Daniel had gone somewhere else, and wasn't even here? If she'd more sense than pride, she would have turned now and run, and not stopped until she reached the other side of the island.

"You've climbed up here for naught, honey," said the heavier of the two men, dabbing at his forehead with a calico handkerchief. "No baubles and trinkets for you here, are there, Ethan? No baubles, and no bubs, either."

"I've not come for baubles," said Juliette, her voice shaking with anger as she tried to make herself heard over the men's laughter. "I am here to see—Sachem!"

The dog came racing through the open door to hurl himself at her, nearly knocking her into the sand in his exuberance. He wriggled with joy at seeing her here, licking her hands and yipping and dancing in a skittish, delirious circle, all by way of greeting.

"Sachem, come!" called Daniel from inside. "Damnation, you wicked rascal, come here now!"

With difficulty Juliette managed to hook her fingers into Sachem's rope collar, but once she did he nearly dragged her past the two men on the bench and through the open door with him.

With her fingers still in the dog's collar, she looked around the shop. The men who'd been talking had stopped as soon as she'd appeared, stopped frozen in place, while another man, dark and stocky with long black hair in two braids like a woman's, had stopped his work, too, a heavy hammer held tight in his two hands as he stood before an anvil. The whole scene seemed weirdly unreal, more of a tableau on a stage, with the men arranged like wooden figures, their stunned gazes all focused entirely on her inappropriate self. They looked so foolishly outraged that she would have laughed, except that controlling Sachem was taking so much of her concentration.

"Hell, John Robin, why did you quit now?" demanded Daniel as he ducked around the large brick forge. "We're right in the middle of—"

And then he saw Juliette.

She hadn't dreamed she'd be able to surprise him so thoroughly, but from the stunned expression on his face, she absolutely had, and it pleased her. He wore a heavy leather apron slung low on his waist, and his shirt was open at the throat with the sleeves rolled up high over his muscled arms, a heavy mallet in his hand. Clearly he'd been working hard, for his face and arms gleamed with sweat, and his black hair was damp along his temples and neck. The sunlight slanting in from one of the windows angled across his face, making his eyes seem as blue as the sky outside.

He had, she decided, never looked better.

"Good day, Daniel," she said as she beamed at him. "You didn't expect to see me here, did you?"

Daniel didn't answer.

He couldn't. How the devil did she expect him to answer a question like that, anyway? A simple "no," true though it might be, wouldn't be enough to satisfy her or the rest of their audience, and it *was* an audience now, no mistake. But some of the more wordy replies that came to his mind—such as "Not in this lifetime, no," or "No, and why the hell did you think this was something I'd enjoy?"—didn't seem appropriate, either, though equally honest. And the one that mattered the most—"No, and none of these other men did, either, but they most certainly will be happy to share the news with every other blasted soul on this island who hasn't heard it yet"—was going to become obvious enough whether he voiced it or not.

Yet still she waited expectantly, her round little face fairly glowing with delight at having surprised him. And the hardest part was that he truly *was* happy to see her, her slight, bright figure like a dream come to life there in the middle of his dark shop, especially after her nightmare last night. It was just that he wished all the other men weren't so damned happy to see her, too.

"The young woman is waiting for thy answer, Daniel Fairbourne," said Robert Ellis, as solemn as Father Time himself in his Quaker gray coat. "Thee should speak before the sun sets, or she'll take it amiss."

The other men laughed, and Daniel felt another half dozen unsavory and unsuitable answers bubbling up inside of him. What had become of his life when he let himself be taken to task by a Quaker worthy like Robert Ellis?

And still poor Juliette looked to him for an answer. She'd flushed when Ellis had spoken, and the longer he didn't answer, the faster her smile was losing its happy, eager luster. No matter how he felt himself, she didn't deserve that. He dropped the hammer beside the anvil, and in two long steps he was at her side.

"Good day, Juliette," he said softly, softly enough, he hoped, to reassure her. He considered taking her hand, but his own was so blackened from work that he couldn't imagine touching her pale white fingers with it. Besides, he didn't want the others jumping to any more unsavory conclusions than they already would. "You couldn't have surprised me more."

She blushed again, this time with pleasure. Plain as the hat he'd given her was, she'd found a way to bend the golden straw so it framed her face, making it charmingly her own, and that pleased him, too.

"You see, Daniel," she said confidentially, "I told you I could walk the whole way. I'm not nearly as fragile as you think."

He frowned with concern, searching for signs that she might have pushed herself too hard. "You're sure you're well?"

"Oh, perfectly. Excepting my feet, of course. My poor little red shoes did not appreciate swimming in the ocean, and they've paid me back royally today, the wicked things."

She looked down at her toes and delicately raised her petticoats just high enough so he could see the offending shoes, as well as the hearts embroidered at the ankles of her stockings. But if he could see them, then every other man in the shop could as well, and swiftly he put himself between them and Juliette.

"I know you came to go to the shop," he began. "I will take you there, but—"

"Oh, the shop." She sighed sheepishly. "I know you'd offered that to me, and you were most kind to do so, but I'd quite forgotten about that. Mostly I came today because I wished to see you."

That made him speechless all over again. It was one thing for her to walk clear across the island for the sake of a new cap—women did such foolish things all the time—but another entirely for her to have made the journey for the sake of seeing him alone. He'd see that she rode home in style if he had to pull the cart himself.

Behind him someone cleared his throat, a rumbling, blatant play for attention.

"You will introduce the lady to us, Fairbourne?" said the rumbler coyly. Abraham Greene: he should have known it, blast his interfering soul. "No lady deserves to be among strangers on Nantucket."

Juliette looked up at him, and from her expression it was clear she'd just realized what she'd done, and how difficult Abraham's simple introduction was going to be.

"Daniel," she whispered uneasily. "Daniel, I can't—"

"Don't worry," he said quickly, and turned to face Abraham and the others.

But before he could speak, he felt her hand slip into his from behind, her palm damp from nervousness and her fingers small as a child's, ignoring the soot and grease that blackened his hand in favor of the comfort his touch could offer. He closed his hand around hers, giving her fingers a quick squeeze of reassurance, marveling at the comfort that so simple a gesture could bring to them both.

But now he'd have to choose his words with extra care, for whatever he said would be repeated and scrutinized endlessly, and with endless repercussions, too.

"This lady," he began, adopting his most captainly voice. "This lady is my guest."

The men nodded, accepting this much but wanting a good deal more. Only John Robin didn't nod, a sure sign that he wasn't surprised, that he'd somehow already guessed the gender of Daniel's latest castaway.

"You all know I've done my share to help unfortunates after storms," he continued, and again they nodded, almost in unison. "Well, then. This lady is one of them. I found her washed ashore at Nobadeer after that blow the other night, and I thank God she survived where no others did."

There was a murmur of sympathy, of marveling, of more hosannas for her deliverance, but Daniel suspected this wouldn't be enough, and he was right.

"The lady's name, Fairbourne," said Abraham, masking his inquisitiveness with forced bonhomie. "Cannot we have her name, so we can congratulate her properly on her deliverance?"

Daniel felt a tremor of anxiety race through Juliette, her fingers clutching at his like they were her only lifeline.

"Her name is Juliette Lacroix," he said slowly, and heard her gasp beside him, a gasp echoed by the buzzing surprise of the others.

"Thee is French, child?" asked Robert Ellis, the first to voice the question in everyone else's minds. "Thee was sailing in a French vessel, this close to our shore?"

"She is English," answered Daniel firmly, and with a conviction that he hoped others would share. "She assures me she is, and I believe her. You've heard her speak; that's the voice of an Englishwoman, not French."

"Then how does she come by such a Frenchified name?" demanded Abraham. "No good daughter of King George has a name like that. What was the name of your vessel, girl? Who was her captain?"

"You will call her 'Miss Lacroix,' Abraham," said Daniel quietly, "else you will answer to me. She has given me her word that she is English, and that's enough."

The murmurs slowed, but didn't stop. "Miss Lacroix,

then," said Abraham. "But what about that French ship in our waters?"

"She doesn't owe you anything, Abraham," said Daniel sharply, and this time the others fell instantly silent. "A shipwreck is a terrible thing, and it doesn't matter to you or anyone else where she's from. This lady has suffered enough without you badgering her."

Robert Ellis stepped forward, his hand outstretched to Juliette. "Thee *has* suffered more than enough," he said kindly. "But if thee will come with me, my wife and I will offer thee a haven until thee is reunited with thy family."

Daniel stiffened, and fought the impulse to push the man away. What Robert offered was what Juliette needed, and what he himself couldn't provide, a safe, respectable sanctuary in the town. The Ellis house was large and comfortable, his wife and daughters of impeccable reputation, and because they were Friends, Robert and his family had no interest in the international squabbles between England and France.

There could not be a better place for Juliette on the island; so why, then, did he desperately wish that Robert had never spoken?

He swallowed hard, the words bitter in his throat as he looked down at Juliette's pale face.

"Robert's a good man, Juliette," he forced himself to say. "You'll like his wife, too. You'd do well to accept his offer."

She nodded once and looked away, but beneath the curve of the hat's brim Daniel still could see how she was biting her lower lip to keep from weeping.

"I know thee is distraught," said Robert, his hand still

open to her, "but thee will find peace in my home. Come, I'll take thee there now."

But as Robert reached to take her hand from Daniel's, she pulled back, shrinking against Daniel's side as she shook her head.

"No, sir," she said in a voice so tiny and brittle it nearly broke Daniel's heart. "No, thank you."

Robert smiled awkwardly, glancing to Daniel for support. "Then thee can come later today. Daniel here can bring thee, and stay for supper, too, if he pleases."

"No, sir," she said again. "Not now, and not for supper. I am grateful for your hospitality, but I cannot accept it. I prefer to stay with Master Fairbourne."

"Hold on now, Juliette," protested Daniel, even as he wanted to roar with joy. "Don't be hasty. What Robert here is offering you is a respectable home—"

"*Your* home is respectable, too," she said, for the first time looking back at him. "Until I can return to my own home, I prefer to stay with you and Sachem."

"Juliette, lass," he began, then broke off when he remembered the ring of eager listeners. "Here, come out back with me."

He hurried her outside, behind the shop and out of hearing of the others, and with both hands on her shoulders turned her to face him.

"Damnation, Juliette, why are you being so stubborn?" he said. "Robert there is giving you your last chance on this island at being a decent woman! Don't you know what will be said of you if you insist on staying with me? Don't you know what they'll call you?"

"Don't you want me to stay, Daniel?" she asked wistfully. "I rather thought you did."

"Hell, yes, I want you to stay," he said with an impatient sweep of his arm. "I like having you out there. I like it just fine. But my wanting you there doesn't make it right, not for either of us."

She smiled, a wobbly, loopy smile on the edge of tears. "It does for me, Daniel."

He shook his head, over and over. This wasn't right, none of it, but he'd be damned if he could find the words to make a convincing argument.

"It's not proper, Juliette," he continued doggedly, "and it's not right, not the two of us stowed together in that tiny old whaler-man's house, and—"

"But you knew my name," she said. "You *knew* I was Juliette Lacroix, even when I didn't know it myself."

"You did so know. You told me yourself last night, only you said it in French. '*M'appelle* something Juliette Lacroix.' "

She drew her brows together, perplexed. "*I* told you that? When?"

"When you had the nightmare," he said carefully. "You were dreaming about the wreck, and you called for me in your sleep, and when I came to wake you, you told me your name. No mystery in that."

"But then you held me," she said softly, and he watched her expression change as she connected what he said to her own thoughts. "I remember that now."

"Do you remember the dream?" There were some things he'd rather she didn't recall, and this was one of them.

"No," she said sadly. "I don't. But when you held me, you meant me no—no dishonor. I was frightened, and you held me until I'd stopped crying, and that was all."

"Here now, don't begin again," he said gruffly, but her tears had already begun, trickling down her cheeks as her nose grew red, and with a sigh he gave her his handkerchief. "Mind, I'm not going to hold you now, not here on the bluffs where the entire world could see."

"I wouldn't expect you to." She blew her nose loudly, and he sighed.

"You're not going to go with Robert, are you?"

She shook her head and sniffed. "Not unless you order me to. I'm accustomed to your ways, and I'd rather not have to become accustomed to anyone else's."

"I could give you orders from now until Judgment Day, and you still wouldn't obey me unless you wished to." He tried to sound exasperated, even angry, but the sorry truth was that he hadn't wanted to give her up, and now he didn't have to. He wasn't sure why this mattered so much. They weren't much better than strangers, not really, and for the sake of his own conscience and her good name, he didn't expect them to be much more before she left him for good.

The likelihood of which, for now, he didn't want to consider at all.

He turned away, ladling water from the cistern into a smaller pail.

"What are you doing now?" she asked curiously.

"I'm washing," he said, reaching for a scoop of the soap he kept out here for the purpose. "After this, my morning's as good as done. Once I tell Robert what you've decided, I expect you'll want to go find that linen I promised you for your cap, as long as your credit's good."

"It is." She waited while he scrubbed the soot from his face and arms. "Tell me, Daniel. If you know my name's

Juliette Lacroix, is that enough to find my home and Amelie?"

He splashed the water on his face. "Not really, no. As French names run, that one's about as common as a Jones or Smith to an Englishman."

"But I *am* English," she persisted. "Couldn't that make it easier? Juliette and Amelie Lacroix, two English women with French names who live in an English town?"

"An English town anywhere from Halifax to Barbados." He sleeked back his wet hair and began to roll down the cuffs of his shirt. "I'm sorry, sweetheart. If the two of you had been men in trade, names known to the world, then it might be possible, but two young women, no. I wouldn't begin to know where or how to look, not until you can give me a town, or at least a county, to start."

"I'm sorry, Daniel." Absently she gazed out across the sea, rubbing her hand across her arm. "But I know it will come back to me, all of it. It *will* come."

Aye, it would, he thought as he watched her. It *would* come.

And she, at last and too soon, would go.

"She didn't ask me what I would buy," whispered Juliette to Daniel as soon as the ruddy-cheeked shopgirl had left them alone. "That's what she's supposed to say—'What will you buy this day?'—and she didn't."

"What in blazes are you talking about?" asked Daniel, glancing down at her as if she were making no sense at all, which, in his defense, she probably wasn't. "If you don't see what you want here, why then, we'll leave."

"No, no, 'tis fine." But for some nagging reason, it didn't seem fine at all, and Juliette frowned, trying to decide why she *should* care how she was greeted by a girl in a shop. It wasn't even really much of a shop at all, not compared to the shops in that nebulous city of hers that she could only half remember. This one was so small that it only took the corner room of the owner's house, and though the doors to the rest of the rooms were closed, she and Daniel could still hear a baby crying and more children squabbling on the other side while their mother scolded. The ruddy-faced girl who'd greeted them, guessed Juliette, must be the shopkeeper's oldest daughter, drummed into serving behind the counter whether she wished to or not.

Ribbons and garterings were coiled tightly in plain baskets on the counter, hats and gloves were crowded on top of one another, and the folded lengths of fabric were piled on the open shelves with no regard to any display to tempt a customer. Not that Juliette saw much that would tempt most women to stray beyond what they'd come to buy: this shop's goods leaned toward the sturdy and serviceable, heavy woolens and linens in plain weaves. She supposed the owner knew her customers, and what would sell best here in Sherburne, but wistfully she wished there were a few fancy goods to admire, calimancos and camlets, silk sateens and damasks, Norwich broglios and Genoa velvets.

And then she wondered why the names of such luxurious goods should roll so easily off her tongue. Imported cloths like those were costly—and curiously she found she could quote the prices for each per ell, too—and some so rich that a finished gown for a lady could be worth more than twenty-five or thirty pounds, more than many laboring men earned in a year of toil. Could she herself really be such a grand lady like that, to dress herself with such extravagance?

"Here be our finest Holland, mistress." Awkwardly the girl spread the linen over her forearm, trying to show it to advantage without daring to raise her gaze from the counter. "You couldn't want better for caps."

In truth Juliette could, for she doubted this linen, full of slubs and bumps in the weave, had ever been near Holland. But because the shopgirl seemed so nervous, and because this likely was the best the shop had to offer, and most important of all, because she didn't wish to be difficult when Daniel was being so generous, Juliette merely smiled and nodded.

"It is very fine," she agreed. "I shall have an even ell, if you please."

Flustered, the girl cut the cloth with her shears, and as she folded it she finally stole a glance at Juliette.

"This be the lady you bought the hat for, Master Fairbourne?" she whispered loudly, as if Juliette weren't able to hear. "It does show most grand upon her."

"Yes, Betsey, it does," agreed Daniel, and that was all.

But the way he was looking at her when he said it made Juliette flush with delighted embarrassment, for that look promised more than all the words in the world. But it was also a look that didn't belong between two people in their situation, as he'd said, "stowed together in that tiny old whaler-man's house."

Swiftly she looked away, back to the shopgirl. "Your name is Betsey?"

"Aye, aye, mistress," said the girl, dropping a startled curtsey and betraying at least one sailor in her family. "Betsey Swain, mistress."

"I am honored, Betsey Swain. My name is Juliette Lacroix, and I'd be obliged if you'd call me so."

"Aye, aye, mistress," said Betsey, her ruddy cheeks nearly crimson. "That is, Juliette. Might I ask after your hat? How you made the brim curl so cunning?"

"Oh, there's no great secret to it." Juliette pulled the hat forward, off her head, to show the girl. "It's easy enough to shape it over the steam of a boiling teakettle. Just take care to hold it until it's cooled. Then look, here, I took a tiny stitch or two inside the crown for good measure. Usually the steaming is enough, but given the breeziness on this island, I added the stitches for good measure."

"Aye, aye, I ken that myself," said Betsey as she peered into the hat. "You're powerfully clever, to think of such—oh, good day, Mistress Greene!"

Betsey nodded quickly to Juliette by way of excusing herself, then hurried around the counter to curtsey low and clumsily before the short, stout woman of indeterminate age who'd just entered the shop. It was clear from the way she carried herself that Mistress Greene held herself in exceptionally high regard, and, with doubled ruffles on her cap and a bright yellow stomacher laced tightly across her prodigious bosom, that she also regarded herself as an arbiter of fashion and taste.

"Betsey, fetch me a pair of new gloves," she said imperiously, as if by noble blood she deserved to have poor Betsey groveling before her. "Cream kidskin, the best you keep."

But while Betsey scampered to obey, Juliette was not impressed, or intimidated, either. She had no patience with bullies and never had, and, to her mind, female bullies who exulted in their husband's position or power were the worst of the lot.

"That girl's done naught to deserve such treatment from you," she said, her head tipped to one side. "But how grand it must make you feel, ma'am, to be able to order little Betsey about."

The woman swept around, her jaw twitching and ready to reply until she saw Daniel. Or rather until she chose to notice him; Juliette didn't believe anyone could accidentally overlook a man like Daniel.

"Good day, Mrs. Greene," he said mildly, as if he, too, had just noticed her. "Or mayhap it's not, considering how choleric you seem to be."

"You have strong opinions for a blacksmith," said Mrs. Greene, her chins quivering. "As a customer of this shop, I'm entitled to be served."

"Oh, yes, ma'am, *served*," said Juliette, with a knowing nod. "Forgive me for forgetting! If you buy a pair of gloves, you've also purchased the right to flay the seller with your tongue."

"And you, hussy, are an impertinent little baggage!" sputtered the older woman, her eyes widening with triumph as she suddenly realized who Juliette was. "And worse! My husband was just telling me all about Daniel Fairbourne's new-found French whore!"

Juliette gasped, the word striking her like a blow. Hussy and baggage she could shrug off, but to be called Daniel's whore—his *French* whore—to hear his name linked so shamefully to hers like that, stunned her.

"How can you call me that?" she demanded. "You know nothing of me, and nothing of what I am to this man, or he to me!"

But Mrs. Greene smiled, realizing her words had found their target. "I know what I see with my own eyes, and what you said yourself, preferring to bide with a rogue like this instead of accepting Robert Ellis' offer."

"I'll hear none of that from you, Abigail," said Daniel, his voice vibrating with anger. "You've no right to call this lady any of your foul names."

"I've every right," purred Mrs. Greene, "because I'm speaking the truth. She *is* French, and she *is* your whore, for she as much as admitted it herself before my husband and a half dozen others. And since I've no wish to be tainted by your *whore,* Master Fairbourne, I'll leave, and wish you much pleasure of her."

It wasn't until after the shop door had slammed shut that Juliette realized how much she was shaking, her hands clenched in helpless fists at her side. She tried to tell herself it didn't matter, that she couldn't let herself be wounded by the cruelty of one vicious woman; but still the words hurt, each one ripping away at her fragile notion of herself.

"Wicked old jackal bitch," fumed Daniel. "I should never have let you stand in the same room with her, let alone have to listen to her venom, and I—"

"Please, Daniel," said Juliette, wrapping her arms across her chest as if to hug herself. Earlier she'd told him he didn't have to hold her, but now, though she wouldn't dare ask, she would have liked it very much indeed. "You warned me, didn't you? You said they—they would not be kind."

"But not this fast, blast the old cow." He took a deep breath, an obvious effort to calm himself for her sake. "I want you to consider it again, Juliette. I can take you to the Ellis house now, and you won't hear another word like that again as long as you're on this island."

"No." Her answer came instantly, and without hesitation. "I'm not a coward, Daniel. I've made up my mind, and I'm not changing it because someone's called me names."

"Wise lass," he said softly. Now he slipped his arm around her shoulders, and with a little sigh of longing for so many things, Juliette let him draw her close. "High time we went home."

Chapter 7

"Juliette!" shouted Daniel as he came over the crest of the dune, his hands cupped around his mouth. "Ju-li-ette!"

He called her name from habit, not necessity, for in this last week he'd always found her in the same place, sitting on the same clump of rocks overlooking the water. Coming to find her there had become part of the habit, too, striding across the fields with Sachem racing ahead, both of them so eager to see Juliette again that he'd come straight to the beach to sit with her until their shadows would stretch long over the sand and rocks toward the water.

Sometimes they'd talk, and tell each other how they'd passed the hours until this one, and other days they'd simply sit together, watching the gulls settle for the night as the moon rose before them and the sun set behind their backs. Then, when at last it was night, they'd slowly walk back to his house for supper.

Yet as pleasant and predictable as this routine had become, Daniel knew that not all of it was as happy as it seemed, and that for every confidence they exchanged, there was another held back or left unspoken.

Even the rocks where Juliette sat each evening, her skirts tucked neatly around her feet, had been chosen not for the view, but because of their proximity to where she'd been washed ashore during the wreck. Not that she'd explained this to Daniel—after that one nightmare of her fighting to escape the sinking sloop, she'd said nothing more to him about the accident that had brought her here—but even without her telling, he knew she felt drawn back to this spot.

He couldn't tell if this meant she'd remembered more that was too painful to discuss, or whether that night continued to remain as much a mystery to her as it was to him. She kept that secret bound tight inside herself, like so many others. But as he watched her scan the horizon in the fading light, her gaze intent and her hands clasped tightly together, he could not mistake the air of sorrow, of grief, that for all her cheerfulness and bright smiles, still clung to her like a mist on the surface of the water.

And he, really, was no better. Oh, he'd told her more of the misadventures of him and Sam as boys because the stories had made her laugh. He'd shared other, more recent stories of the rare sights he'd witnessed in his travels when he'd traded smithing for sailing, the grand plantations in the Caribbean he'd visited and the waters that he'd crossed that were filled with great ships and fleets from every country in Europe.

Yet he never told her that the town where he and Sam had caused so much mischief was Appledore, or that it lay less than two days away from Nantucket, on the north side of Cape Cod, or that for all he knew Sam himself could be living there now.

He hadn't explained why he'd turned his back on the sea right when he'd been made a captain and begun to prosper, or why he'd returned to the toil and lesser rewards of blacksmithing, or why he'd abandoned the lush, seductive beauty of the Caribbean for this sparse, unwelcoming island so much farther to the north.

And not once had he mentioned Catherine, or how much he'd loved her, or that she'd drowned and taken their unborn child with her, and that all of it, all of it, had been his fault.

His.

"Oh, Daniel, here you are," said Juliette excitedly, turning on her rock to smile his way. It was cool enough this late in the day for her to wear her red wool cloak, wrapped close and snug around her shoulders. "You're just in time. What is that ship, there?"

Daniel followed her pointing hand to the distant dark silhouette on the horizon. How fortuitous that this ship had chosen tonight to cruise by their beach, making what he had to tell her easier! "Some blue-water schooner, though from this distance I'd be hard pressed to tell you more. Could well be a packet, from Saybrook or New York bound for Boston."

"Ah." He could see her considering the possibilities, the likelihood that she'd been on a similar voyage. "Then why have I never seen one from here before?"

"Because every captain is different, and chooses the course that pleases him," he explained as he sat on the rock beside her—close enough for conversation, but not so close that they'd risk touching, even by accident. That, too, had become part of their habit. "Some captains like to cut out boldly across the open seas, while others will skitter along the coast, fearful of losing sight of land for even an hour."

She wrinkled her nose, considering. "Which is the better course?"

"The bolder captain will make a faster passage, and please his owners and passengers," he said, "but if he founders or runs afoul of weather, he could be too far at sea to make a run for safety."

"Then it's better to be cautious?"

"Not always. A too-cautious captain that creeps within sight of land can get caught on his lee shore with the wind driving him aground or onto rocks."

She sighed mightily. "I wish you'd been my captain, Daniel. You would've known what to do in that storm."

"Oh, no, I wouldn't. I've been land-locked so long I'd scarce know where to find the wheel." He set his haversack on the sand between his feet, and worked free a bulky, flat package wrapped in muslin while Sachem snuffled optimistically, hoping the surprise involved food. "Here, I've something for you."

She looked at him suspiciously, though she took the package. "I thought we'd agreed there'd be no more presents, not after the hat."

"This is different," he said. "This is useful."

"I don't care if it's useful or not," she said stubbornly. "You won't let me pay for anything on my own."

"That's because you'd be bankrupt in no time."

"Daniel, be reasonable. I eat your food, live in your house, warm myself by your fire, and sleep in your bed while you must lie on the floor of the loft. That is more than enough, and I *cannot* accept another thing from you."

He understood. For nearly two weeks now, since the afternoon he'd led her, trembling with shame, from the Swains' shop, Mrs. Greene's ugly accusation had hung unspoken between them, lingering like the stench of a piece of fish gone bad.

Your whore, your French whore. . . .

They had never mentioned it, never repeated it, but still it remained with a viable, painful presence. No matter how many times Daniel told Juliette she was his guest, entitled to his hospitality, the other word hovered there unavoidably between them, poisoning every small courtesy or accidental touch into an unfulfilled obligation.

"I tell you, lass, this is different," he insisted, as if insistence alone could change anything. "Now open it."

She frowned at him, trying to look stern and not succeeding, and at last opened the muslin-wrapped package.

"Oh," she breathed as her fingers stroked the yards of brilliant blue woolen cloth that spilled out. "Oh, Daniel. This isn't useful, not at all."

"Aye, it is," he said staunchly. "We're almost into October, and then it's nearly as good as winter. You've no notion how cold the wind can be on this island. I figured you needed to make yourself something warmer before then."

She smiled crookedly, smoothing the cloth over her knee with an obvious pleasure in the soft, finely woven wool. "You must worry that I'll be here all winter."

"You know you can stay as long as you need to." He cleared his throat self-consciously. "I chose the color because it reminded me of your eyes. But if you'd rather please yourself, you can come to town with me tomorrow and choose another."

"No!" she said quickly, looking down at the cloth. "That is, this is so beautiful, why would I want anything else?"

He understood that, too, why she'd no wish to return to town. He wouldn't call it cowardice because Juliette remained one of the bravest women he'd ever known. But if for now she preferred to hide herself away here, safe from the talk, then Daniel couldn't blame her.

And there had been talk, plenty of it, though little had slipped into his hearing. Men were always held to different standards, even on a pious place like Nantucket. In a perverse way having the island believe Juliette was his mistress had increased his stature, not hurt it, and the same scandal that could destroy a woman's reputation only added another layer of roguish gloss to a man's, no matter how much he denied it.

"Then it's settled," he said. "You'd best begin sewing tomorrow, so you'll be ready for those first winter winds."

"Daniel, please," she said, almost pleading. "You know I can't accept a gift as lavish as this from you."

"But it's not a gift," he said firmly. "I expect you to earn it."

"*Earn* it?" She gasped, her eyes widening with disbelief.

"Juliette, please—"

"*No!*" She scrambled off the rock and away from him. "*Mon Dieu*, Daniel, not you, too!"

He grabbed her wrist before she could escape. "Damnation, Juliette, do you really believe that of me?" he demanded. "Of *me*?"

She jerked against his grasp, struggling to free herself as her cloak tangled around her. "I don't know what to think anymore!"

"Hell, if all I wanted was to bed you, do you think I'd have waited until now?" Disgusted with himself as much as with her, he freed her wrist, letting her stumble backward on the sand. The tension simmering between them had been bound to spill over, he thought grimly, though this was hardly the way he'd wished it to happen.

He bent back over the haversack and yanked out another parcel. Quickly he tore away the muslin, standing with his legs as wide spread as if he still mastered his own quarterdeck, and raised his arm. Five yards of fine white linen rippled outward in the wind like a pennant of surrender in the late afternoon sun.

"There," he said, letting his voice boom across the empty beach. "There's your earning!"

She stared at him, wild eyed, clearly not sure whether to run or not.

"*There!*" he shouted again. "Isn't that enough for you?"

"*Sapristi*, you make no sense!"

"Haven't I?" He held the cloth higher. "There you are, *mademoiselle*, enough and more white linen for a gentleman's shirt! Since you judged my old shirts so tawdry, I thought I'd give you my custom for a new one instead of sending to a tailor in Boston. For his fee you could have had enough superfine wool for three petticoats, if you wished it. Which now, *mademoiselle*, I see you do not."

She stood without moving, listening, her silver-pale hair blew loose where her hood had fallen back, and the red cloak billowed away from her body, away from the strip of white he still held high in his hand. She raised her chin to meet his gaze, and impatiently swept back a stray lock of hair with her fingertips.

"Don't call me *mademoiselle*," she shouted back. "I am *English*!"

"Then stop swearing at me in French!"

"Not until you stop deciding what I will and will not do!" She reached up and grabbed the undulating end of the linen. "Give that to me, now! However am I to make a decent shirt if you treat the linen like one of your wretched sails?"

He'd won, he thought with surprise, he'd won, and she'd as much as admitted it. Yet nothing felt settled, and the tension that lay beneath the anger was still coiled there between them. With both hands she fought the wind for control of the cloth, striving to gather it back into neat folds. But drawing it toward her meant drawing closer to Daniel as well, and when no more than a foot remained between them, she stopped.

"Let it go," she said. "Now, Daniel. Please."

But he didn't. Instead he wrapped the end he held around his hand, reeling her closer to him, until the toes of her shoes stood inside the wide spread heels of his boots. She was so close he could see the tiny flecks of green and gray that gave her blue eyes the same depth as the sea, and how the darker centers had widened.

"Please," she said again, a whisper that vibrated with anger turned to excitement. He watched her swallow, saw the movement glide along her throat, beneath the red cord of the cloak. He'd come to love the line of her throat, a curve that begged for a man's lips to trace and tease its length.

Not that it should be begging for *him*, not him, not now.

Like hell not now.

With a last tug on the linen he pulled her to him, and his mouth sank down upon hers. He felt her lips flutter beneath him, the faintest syllable of surprise or maybe—better—of acceptance, and then she was opening her lips to welcome him. Desire coursed hot through his body, the heat of her mouth like a spark to the tinder of his blood. Instantly he had to fight for control and the will not to take her here, on the sand, her pale body spread for him on her red cloak. He wanted to be part of her, to find release and solace in losing himself in her. He *needed* her, viscerally and emotionally and desperately, too, more than he'd ever needed anyone else.

She dropped the gathered linen like a drifting pile of snow about their legs, and slipped her hands inside his coat. Little hands, clever hands, he thought, even when all they did was shyly circle his waist to pull him closer.

He broke his mouth away from hers to run his lips along her throat, to taste the salt on her skin and feel the pulse of her own desire beating there beneath his tongue. Lower, lower he moved, to where her stays raised her breasts high for him, the flesh so warm and soft and woman-scented that he groaned from wanting. A hundred times he'd lain awake in the loft above her and imagined this, and not once had his imagination come close to her reality.

"You're perfect, Juliette," he murmured as he came back to kiss her lips again. "Perfection."

"No," she gasped, and to his surprise she backed away from him. "No, I'm not."

He reached for her again. "Then let me prove it to you, lass."

But instead she shook her head and backed farther away, and even though her whole body seemed to radiate desire—God, how could she keep away when it was so obvious that she wanted him as much as he did her!—she was holding her hands so tightly together that it almost seemed she was punishing them for having touched him.

"And what must *I* prove to you, Daniel?"

"What in blazes are you talking about?" She couldn't abandon him like this, not now.

"About me. About us." She shook her head again, as much from confusion as denial. "About everything."

He sighed, damned confused himself. "You are not my—ah—my woman, if that's what's causing all this," he said, barely saving himself from instant disaster. "You don't have to prove anything, not to me. Hell, I was kissing you because I *thought* you'd like it."

"Don't make a jest of this, Daniel, not now." She bowed her head, hiding the truth in her face from him. "When you stopped kissing me the last time, I thought it was because you didn't—didn't want to. That you didn't care for me. Oh, not that way, not caring *for* me, because you've always done that, but that you found me—found me *wanting*."

"Oh, lass, there's nothing further from the truth," he said, appalled that she'd even consider such a thing. "From the moment you first opened your eyes to me, Juliette, I've never, ah, found you wanting. Not once. You've done that to me, and I can't deny it."

"But for us to act like this, to do these things." She gulped, fighting tears. "I cannot, Daniel, not until I know who I really am."

"I know who you are," he said, though already he

could feel the haven he'd found in her arms crumbling and crashing to ruins. "And I like what I know very much."

"But how can that be enough?" she cried with anguish. "At least now I know I'm not your—your mistress. But what if that were not the worst sin? Oh, *mon Dieu, mon Dieu*, I am so weak, Daniel, and though I know it is wrong in every way, when you kiss me I do not want to stop, not at all! But what if I didn't? What if I did lie with you, what then? Is ignorance enough of an excuse? What if somewhere I have a husband, or children of my own, that I'd unwittingly betrayed with you?"

And what if he'd had a wife, and nearly a child, and now he was empty and alone and with nothing?

Oh, aye, he knew all there was to know of such betrayal, didn't he?

When he'd lost Catherine, he'd thought his heart had died with her. But it hadn't, and if he'd any doubt he'd only to feel the raw pain he felt in his chest now. There had to be some way he could make time begin now, to begin his life all over again with this woman as his guiding star. His conscience told him Juliette was right, but his battered, aching heart didn't want her to be right, and didn't want to accept it, either. All it wanted now was the one thing he couldn't have, and that was Juliette.

He couldn't begin to explain this, his emotions too complicated for words. He didn't know what answer Juliette found on his face, but it was enough to make her turn and run back to the house, away from him and whatever it was he was trying to offer her.

As if, God help him, he had anything left to give. . . .

The sun was nearly down now, the sand growing chill

without its warmth. Carefully Daniel gathered up the two pieces of cloth from where they'd blown into the beach grass, brushing away the sand before he folded first the blue wool, then the white linen. Neat folds, the edges even, everything shipshape and smooth and tidy as it had been before.

Sachem bumped his nose against Daniel's leg, and dropped half of a dead crab on the toe of his boot. Panting with pride, the dog gazed up at Daniel, so ready for the praise he was sure he'd earned that Daniel had to smile.

"Good lad," he said softly, running his fingers through Sachem's thick fur. "Good, good lad, to know that a stinking dead crab would suit me exactly. I should have asked you what to bring to Juliette, eh?"

He sat there with Sachem until the sun had finally faded away over the dunes, thinking of all the things he could have said instead of the worthless words that he had managed to spit out. Once he'd smugly believed he'd known how to speak to women, to say exactly the sorts of flattering nonsense to make them giggle and blush. With Juliette, he couldn't say the nonsense, nor did he wish to, which made it even worse. But what the devil was he supposed to say to get back to where she'd been kissing and holding him like her dear life depended on it?

With a long, rattling sigh, he finally headed for the house. It *was* his house, blast it all, and he wasn't going to be turned out of it. But Juliette didn't look up from the hearth when he came inside, even after he made a special effort to thump the door extra loudly when he shut it. She in turn was making an extra effort of her own, fussing and banging about the kettle for supper as if she were cooking a feast for a dozen instead of warming the chowder from last night. She was, as she'd said herself, no cook, not even when it came to pretending to be one.

He lay the two folded lengths of fabric squarely in the center of the bed, where she'd have to touch them if she wished to sleep. She might have left them behind at the beach, but he wasn't about to let her forget his gifts again no matter how hard she wished it.

If it hadn't been his bed as well, he might have added Sachem's dead crab, too, to see if that might get her attention. As it was they ate together in complete silence, with neither of them lifting their gazes from their plates, and neither of them eating much to speak of, either.

And it hurt. Damnation, after all they had shared these last days, it *hurt*, and though it cost him his pride to be the first to break that stony silence, he knew he wouldn't sleep unless he'd made her speak to him again.

Not that it was easy. He drank nearly the entire pot of coffee, Sachem's chin resting on his knee, before he could find the words or the courage, and when he did finally speak, after a great rumbling throat clearing, what came out wasn't exactly the sort of reconciliatory thing he'd had in mind.

"I spoke this day with a cousin of John Robin's," he began, cringing inwardly at how pompous he sounded, like a town crier with nothing to cry. "He was new-returned from the Vineyard, and he said more flotsam—ship's wreckage, that is—had washed ashore there, on the south coast."

She looked up from her sewing, the firelight playing rosily across her cheek. "The Vineyard?"

"Martha's Vineyard, another island like Nantucket, between here and the Cape. The same red Indians—John

Robin's family—live on both." Dear God, now he was prattling on like a geography master. "Given the right tides and weather, a ship that begins breaking up in our waters may finish herself on a Vineyard beach."

She went very still, the thread from her needle stretched taut. "And this flotsam. You believe it was from my ship?"

He spread his hands and shrugged. "I'm not saying it was, or wasn't. But I thought you'd want to know."

She nodded, but her hand with the needle didn't move. "Could this cousin of John Robin's tell you any more of the ship, or its crew?"

"From the mast they're guessing it was a small vessel, most likely a sloop sailing as a packet." It *was* a guess, too, especially when scavengers would have obliterated any telltale signs on a wreck to protect what they'd claimed for their own. "You could have been bound anywhere along the coast, but not England or France."

"Were there any—any other people found?"

"It's been over a fortnight, Juliette," he said gently. "Likely you are the only lucky one."

"*Oh, mais oui,*" she said bitterly, and jabbed the needle into the fabric. "How very lucky I am, and how grateful, too."

"I am," he said gruffly. "Grateful, that is. I'm damned grateful you're alive."

She didn't look up, but the needle in her hand stilled again, enough encouragement for him to continue.

"I'm not good with words, lass. Maybe I've lived too long with only Sachem for company, and I've forgotten what's right to say to a lady like you. Maybe I never knew."

Still she didn't answer, but because she was silent, he knew she was listening. Not that he knew what to say next; he'd meant what he told her about not being good with words, and now that the words mattered so much, he didn't seem to have a single one to spare.

Uneasily he shifted in his chair, his hand grazing over the pocket on his coat. He could feel the small, heavy lump in there where he'd been keeping it as a kind of talisman, and quickly his fingers found it again, curling around the cool, smooth metal like the familiar, loyal friend it had always been. If ever he needed a bit of well-wrought good luck, then this was the moment, and carefully he drew the piece from his pocket and placed it, under his hand, on the table between them.

Curiously Juliette watched as he slid his hand flat across the table toward her, palm down, then raised it with a conjurer's flair.

At first she didn't realize the small black sun was made from iron. The center was a perfect round disc, dimpled lightly with the pattern of the hammer that had made its shape, while radiating from this center were eight rays, each curling and twisting outward with all the vitality of a living flame. It was a virtuoso piece of ironwork, as much for its miniature scale as for the sheer craftsmanship, but to Juliette its significance was so much more simply because Daniel had made it.

"This is beautiful, Daniel," she said as she touched her fingertips to one of the spiraling rays. "Truly."

Lightly he touched his own forefinger to the opposite ray, looking down at the sun and not at her.

"It was that first morning," he began, "after you'd wakened. You were standing there by the fence, and the rising sun turned your face to gold, more beautiful than any mortal woman has a right to be. After the storm and the wreck and all, that sun seemed to me a good, hopeful sign, and I knew then that you'd be better. I kept thinking about you and the sun all the way to the shop, and then I made this. For you, I mean."

She stared down at the little sun, overwhelmed. She remembered that morning, too. When she'd seen that sun, she'd felt so burdened by the bleakness of her situation, so wretchedly unhappy, that all she'd wanted was to die, while he'd seen the same sunrise as a sign of promise and hope—the same hope that he'd since given back to her.

Gently he closed her white fingers around the black iron sun, the pointed black rays jutting between them.

"You've become dear to me, lass," he said softly. "Not who you were before, but who you are now, here."

"You shouldn't speak so, Daniel," she said, breathless from the racing of her heart, "any more than you—we—should have kissed."

He looked up sharply, his pale eyes so intent upon her she nearly shivered. "Is that all you can say to me? That you regret caring for me as much as I do you?"

"I know no more of you than you do of me!"

"Aye, you do," he said, his voice rough with urgency. "Judge me for yourself, Juliette, as I am, the same as I've done with you."

Troubled, she shook her head again, roiling with indecision. She *did* care for him, though her feelings for him ran so much deeper. She was very nearly in love with him, and to her wonder she realized he was with her, too. Wasn't that what he was telling her now? Yet it wasn't that simple, not at all, and what she said next could bring her the greatest joy she'd ever known, or lead her to the most disastrous sin she could commit.

"Tell me, lass," he said. "Don't make me wait."

"Oh, Daniel," she whispered in a feverish rush. "Don't you know already? You have become everything in my life now. *Everything.*"

He didn't answer, but slowly raised her hand to kiss the inside of her wrist, there where her skin was so sensitive, where any touch would fly straight to her heart. His lips were so soft, warm, surrounded by the rough graze of his beard that she caught her breath at the tremor of raw need that raced through her. She scarcely noticed when he ran his hand along her arm to cradle her head, tangling his fingers in her hair as he rose and leaned across the table to kiss her mouth.

"Aye, everything, Juliette," he murmured against her lips. "*Everything.*"

And with a broken sob she kissed him back, praying with the same heart that loved him that everything would be enough.

The next day Juliette spent outdoors, in her now accustomed spot for sewing, sheltered from the wind by the north side of the house, there in the tiny, fenced-in yard. Although she had planned to begin Daniel's new shirt, spreading the white linen for cutting on the table before he'd left for the shop, he'd insisted she begin a gown for herself instead, arguing that while he owned plenty of shirts—albeit darned shirts—she had but one change of clothing, and that more suited for summer than the cooler weather that was clearly on its way. Not only were the days growing shorter, but the wind now had a keenness to it that promised winter, and sadly Juliette knew her days of sewing in the bright, clear sunlight out-of-doors must be numbered.

But then, perhaps, so might be her days here on Nantucket.

All morning long, her past had been coming back to her in a dizzying rush of details. As she'd deftly cut the blue wool for her gown, she'd realized that she wasn't by birth a lady, but by trade a lady's mantua-maker, a seamstress of the highest grade, meaning that in speech and manners she had had to be every bit as genteel as her customers to be able to serve them. The wide city window that she'd earlier remembered sitting beside was the front window on her shop, a most fashionable milliner's shop that she now remembered she owned and kept with her sister Amelie—oh, poor grieving Amelie!—as partner. Now, too, she understood why she'd felt such keen interest in how the Swains' humble little establishment was run, and why she continued to find such comfort in her sewing.

She remembered all the aspects of running their shop and trade, balancing ledgers and tallying accounts, cajoling this merchant and refusing that one. She even remembered the precise layout of the shop itself, where the silk threads were kept apart from the linen, and the stiff, notched cards around which the more costly ribbons were wrapped. Clearly she was a woman of property and reputation, and a woman of accomplishments and responsibilities, too.

She pulled the little iron sun Daniel had made for her from her pocket, tracing the curving rays with her fingertips and thinking of all it had meant to him, and now to her. As exciting as the new recollections were, she still didn't miss the hideous irony of their timing. Last night Daniel had told her that her past meant nothing to him; all that mattered was the present they were sharing together. It was as if once he'd given her permission to forget, she'd turned around and begun to remember.

Unhappily she wondered what troubling quirk of her head had done this, and almost against her will she thought again of how Daniel had so effortlessly managed to obscure his own past by absolving her of her own. She *wanted* to trust him. She didn't want to believe he was hiding anything from her—blacksmiths, as a rule, were not by nature sinister, even ones who'd also been sailors—but the gaps in the way he told his own life were nearly as big as her own.

She told herself with hopeful optimism that perhaps he'd told her nothing simply because he'd nothing of interest to tell, or that this very night, as they sat together at supper, he'd confide and explain the exact mysteries that were worrying her now.

She did trust Daniel, after all. Who else could she possibly trust more? And if that trust and the friendship and respect that had grown with it, grew further into love, was that such a dreadful thing, something to be avoided or rather welcomed, embraced?

But the most unsettling questions still lingered between them, begging answers she couldn't offer by herself.

What would happen when she finally remembered where she belonged, the place where she had a *place*? Of course she'd return; she owed that to Amelie, and everyone else she'd loved and left behind. But what would become of her and Daniel when she went back to the responsibilities of her fashionable shop in the city, and he remained here on this distant island in his decidedly unfashionable one?

And what would happen if one of those last missing memories included a husband, a husband who didn't smile whenever he watched her the way Daniel did, or have arms that were double the strength of most ordinary men yet gentle enough to be her haven, or could kiss no more than the inside of her wrist to have her near weep with desire for him? What would she do then?

With a groan of frustration she tucked the little sun back into her pocket and forced herself to concentrate on her stitches instead, trying to give them the tidy precision that her life lacked. A backstitch to begin a seam, then three tiny stitches forward, another back to keep the edge strong and firm. . . .

"Mistress Lacroix?" asked the woman's voice, a scolding more than a greeting. "You *are* Mistress Lacroix, aren't you?"

Startled, Juliette looked up from the work in her lap, clutching the fabric in surprise as she stood. She'd grown so accustomed to being alone during the day that the last thing she expected was a visitor, let alone the three grim-faced women standing on the other side of Daniel's low, whitewashed fence. They were so much alike that they could have been sisters, their features sharp and severe with deep, downward lines on either side of their mouths determined to prove how seldom those mouths turned up to smile. They were dressed simply, in the sober colors—gray, brown, drab red—that were favored on the island, colors that made the brilliant blue wool in Juliette's hands look as gaudy and out of place as a parrot.

As out of place as she suddenly now felt herself.

"Good day, ma'am," she said, smoothing her ruffled cap over her hair. If these were friends or perhaps the wives of customers of Daniel's, then she wished to welcome them warmly, however difficult those stern faces might make her hospitality. "Mr. Fairbourne is not here at present, but if you would wish to leave your—"

"This *is* Daniel Fairbourne's house?" the woman asked, her encompassing sniff showing how little regard she had both for Daniel and his house, and even less for Juliette. "And you are his . . . his *woman*, are you not?"

Juliette gasped, stunned and threatened, too, by such blatant rudeness. These three could not possibly be friends, not of Daniel or herself.

"No, I am not his 'woman,' " she said defensively. "I am his guest, and have been since he rescued me when I was lost at sea."

The second woman drew back with distaste, as if she'd smelled something unpleasant. "We have heard otherwise, Mistress Lacroix, which is why *we* have come this day."

"Then I venture that you have misheard, ma'am." She was still clutching the fabric, Daniel's gift, as if the cloth had the power to protect her as he would himself. At the bottom of the sandy hill she now could see the two-wheeled box cart that had brought the women, the old man that had driven them idly smoking his pipe while he waited. How had she become so lost in her thoughts and worries not to have heard them until now?

"I do not believe we have misheard anything," said the

first woman firmly. "Mrs. Greene was most clear, as were the several gentlemen with whom we discoursed."

Juliette's distrust was deepening by the moment. She hadn't forgotten Abigail Greene, or the maliciousness of her words in the Swains' shop. Whatever she'd told these women would not be good, and her first impulse was to gather her sewing and retreat inside, barring the door behind her.

But then she remembered the little sun sitting heavily in her pocket and thought of Daniel, who feared no one and nothing and didn't care a fig what anyone else thought of him. *He* wouldn't want her to scurry away like a frightened rabbit, not from these meddlers, and the more she thought about it, the more she realized she didn't want to run and hide, either.

"I am Mrs. Cushing," said the first woman, with a grandness that implied that Juliette should recognize the name, "and this is Mrs. Griggs and Mrs. Howe, and we have come here, *Miss* Lacroix, to address you regarding our concerns."

Deliberately Juliette paused to fold her sewing, taking her time before she answered as if such addresses came to her every day, as if her heart weren't racing and the house beckoning. She hated this, and she hated them, but she refused to let them cow her. "Address me, you say, ma'am? On what subject, pray?"

"On the subject of your own mortal soul," said Mrs. Griggs severely. "Our island has long been a haven of mercy to unfortunates cast away by storms, but they have been God-fearing folk, mindful of their delivery, who have been eager to follow the paths of righteousness we favor here. But you, mistress, have not."

"Most decidedly not," echoed Mrs. Howe with an emphatic twitch of her bonnet. "Obstinate, that's what you've been."

"But I have done nothing," said Juliette as firmly as she could. "Certainly nothing to merit such a visit as this from you."

" 'Nothing,' yes, exactly so," said Mrs. Griggs, the scorn in her voice withering. "God through His infinite mercy has spared you from an early death and judgment, yet you have done *nothing* to repay His faith in your redemption. Instead you have willfully chosen to become the concubine of the most wicked man on this island."

"What is willful, ma'am, is your tongue," said Juliette warmly, "for I am no more a concubine than Daniel Fairbourne is the most wicked man on this island or anyplace else."

"No?" Mrs. Griggs's eyes glittered. "Then perhaps he hasn't yet told you of how he came to us here with nothing, or how he bewitched old Master Matthews into leaving him his trade when he died."

"Daniel wouldn't 'bewitch' anyone," scoffed Juliette. "He bought the trade fairly when Master Matthews was too ill to continue. He told me so himself. The rest is stuff and nonsense."

"Is it now?" asked Mrs. Cushing archly. "Look into Fairbourne's eyes and say that. Devil's eyes, that's what he has, eyes with no human soul. He's bewitched *you*, that's clear enough, for you to be calling him 'Daniel,' so familiar, yes."

Juliette flushed, regretting that she'd been caught on such a tiny mistake, but before she could answer Mrs. Griggs excitedly pushed her way forward.

"And what of Daniel Fairbourne's past?" she demanded with such force that she practically swayed upward on her stubby toes. "No matter what lies a man tells, the Lord writes his wickedness upon his face. You've only to look at Daniel Fairbourne's eyes to see a life misspent. But I'll warrant he's shared those secrets with you, hussy, same as he's shared your body!"

"I needn't listen to any more of this," said Juliette, snatching up the basket with her thread and pins to escape.

But Mrs. Cushing grabbed her arm and held her fast. "How much longer do you intend to remain here on our island?"

"What I do and when I do it is no concern of yours," said Juliette as she jerked her arm free of the other woman's grasp. "None."

Mrs. Cushing's lips pinched together in a tight line of contempt. "Then perhaps you would concern yourself if Daniel Fairbourne's trade began to suffer on account of your willful wickedness," she said, each word like the flick of a lash. "Before you came, he was able to control his inclinations, but you have led him to choose the wrongful path of carnal temptation. *You* have corrupted him, mistress. If word of your sins were to become more common upon our island, then he might see his custom dwindle, and shift to Peter Wardell's shop instead."

Juliette gasped, furious that they'd dare consider such a vindictive act for no better reason than their own speculative gossip. "Daniel has ten times the skill of Peter Wardell!"

"Peter Wardell is a Friend, an elder in his Meeting," said Mrs. Cushing, "*and* he has a dutiful wife and five godly children."

"An *English* wife," added Mrs. Griggs.

"But for you to threaten Daniel's trade because of his kindness to me—what you are threatening is blackmail!"

"What we are doing," said Mrs. Cushing sternly, "is protecting our children and our neighbor's children from the danger of your wanton examples. But it is your choice, Mistress Lacroix."

Juliette clutched the blue cloth to her chest, fighting to control the bitterness and anger that was boiling up inside her. What she felt for Daniel was rare and special, no matter how it eventually ended, and for these meddling women to drag that through their own self-righteous filth was bad enough. But for Daniel to be forced to risk his trade because of her was unspeakably unfair.

"Your choice, mistress," repeated Mrs. Cushing ruthlessly, "and your master's future with it. When are you leaving Nantucket?"

But this time, Juliette had no ready answer, and with a cry at her own shameful indecision, she turned and ran, one more time, to the sanctuary of Daniel's house.

Chapter 8

Finally stopping work for their dinner, Daniel and John Robin sat on the old bench beside the shop, the cool breeze from the water welcome after the heat of the forge inside. Their morning had stretched well past noon, thanks to the capricious exertions of a pair of cart horses in for shoeing. Not only had both horses taken infinite amounts of coaxing and cajoling before they'd be led into the shop and close to the anvil to be fitted, they'd also turned out to be "leaners," the kind of lazy horses who'd shift more of their weight than was fair onto Daniel's back while he held their feet for shoeing. Daniel was a strong man, with a back broader than any other's on the island, but even his back was no match for a puncheon horse grown fat on summer grazing, and now he couldn't help groaning as he stretched his weary arms over his head.

"Do you think that pair makes wagers in their stalls, betting straw to corn who'll be the most troublesome?" he asked. "If I had to shoe those two more than once a year, then I'd give up farrier work altogether."

John Robin snorted. "And leave all the ponies to me to shoe? Better to let them run barefoot, the way the Maker intended."

"And watch every last horse go lame, and every carter and plowman mad. Now *that* would be enough to drive me back to the sea."

They smiled, for both knew that even a world full of ill-tempered horses and cart drivers couldn't make Daniel return to sea. Not that John Robin would be any more eager to join him there; though his ancestors had made the crossing from the mainland in canoes hacked from tree trunks, he himself had never left sight of the island since he'd been born, and never intended to before he died—one more fact that, as John Robin told Daniel often enough, the Maker clearly intended.

Now he squinted up at the sun. "Fair weather for September."

Daniel nodded. "A season without hurricanes would be welcome."

"And unknown, friend."

"But possible. It's been nearly three weeks since that last blow." Daniel smiled to himself. He knew exactly the time of the last storm, since that had been the one to bring Juliette into his life.

Everything, she'd said. He was everything in her life, and his smile broadened with unbridled joy.

"Three weeks," repeated John Robin, musing as he bit into an apple. "Hasn't been much rescuing for you, has there?"

"No," said Daniel, instantly wary. This was not the sort

of question that his friend asked without reason. "But that's no misfortune."

"Oh, no," said John Robin slyly. "Not when you've already found your fortune. Is your little castaway prospering in your keep, then?"

Daniel folded his arms across his chest. "She's well, aye."

"Well, well." John Robin chewed the apple with, thought Daniel, entirely suspicious purpose. "That little castaway's the prettiest fish you've ever pulled out of the sea. No wonder you haven't tossed her back, eh, friend? All sleek and silvery—"

"Damnation, John Robin, is there something in particular you're trying to ask before I knock you from this bench?"

John Robin grinned, and spat away a piece of peel. "No questions, no. But I am happy for you, friend, because this woman has made you happy."

Daniel scowled, wishing this conversation had never begun. What had been happening between him and Juliette was personal, private, and he wasn't about to discuss it with anyone else. "Did one of those horses step on your head as well as your foot?"

"A man needs to be happy, more than he needs gold or even food," answered John Robin with an unconcerned shrug. Clearly this was one more way that he differed from white Englishmen, who'd rather spend a week in an open boat than make such a cockamamie pronouncement. "It's good that you keep her."

"I am not keeping her, leastwise not the way you mean," muttered Daniel. "She's staying with me while she tries to remember the wreck that brought her here."

John Robin held his hand out toward the sea, making the water his witness. "May she never remember it!" he said fervently. "Since her coming, you are a better man, friend. You smile, you laugh, you see that the sky and the ocean are blue. You keep that little silver fish, if this is what she does for you."

"Damnation, stop calling her a fish! Miss Lacroix's a woman, a lady, and deserves more respect from you." Moodily Daniel kicked his heel in the sand. "Not that a rogue like you would understand."

"But I do," answered the other man easily, flicking one of his long braids back over his shoulder. "My Mary would slit my throat if I didn't."

"Mary's your wife." Which Juliette, thought Daniel, most assuredly wasn't. He cared for Juliette, cared for her very much, but he'd loved Catherine because Catherine had been his wife.

"So it's good that Mary makes me happy, yes?" John Robin chuckled in a way that said infinitely more than words ever could, and more than enough to make Daniel feel like the loneliest man on earth. "I tell you, friend, a woman is a good thing to have. You should do whatever you can to make her stay."

"Juliette's not another dog like Sachem, John Robin," said Daniel, despair creeping unconsciously into his voice. "I can't keep her if she doesn't wish to stay."

"Then you must be sure she does wish it. What have you done to make her as happy as you are?"

Daniel paused. With Catherine, assessing happiness had always begun with a litany of purchases.

"I've bought Juliette a hat," he began, "a plain hat that she's fancied up pretty as you'd ever see, and a bit of linen so she could make herself a cap and another shift, and some blue woolen that—"

"Not what you've bought her," interrupted John Robin impatiently. "I mean what have you done?"

"I've saved her life. That should account for something, shouldn't it?"

"And since then?"

"So help me, John Robin, if you don't—"

"Nay, friend, if *you* don't," countered John Robin, "if you don't treat your little fish as good as she deserves, then she'll swim away. Soon, I hear there's to be a feast out in the meadows to welcome back the whalers. Dancing, too, if the pious folk don't stop it."

Daniel had never gone to any of the local picnics, or squantums, as the island folk called them, and uneasily he wondered how Juliette would be received on his arm. Hadn't she suffered enough at the hands of that old bitch Abigail Greene? And as for dancing—why, he didn't even know if Juliette liked to dance, or if she'd be self-conscious with everyone gaping at her poor game leg. Of course he'd want to spare her more hurt of that sort.

And there was more to his reluctance, too, though it wasn't nearly as honorable. He'd acknowledged to himself that Juliette had come to mean so much to him in such a brief time that he didn't want to imagine his life after she left, but he still wasn't certain he was comfortable with appearing with her at his side at an island picnic, announcing to all the world what he'd only barely announced to her. That world would be quick to jump to every kind of assumption and misconception about them, things he hadn't begun to figure out for himself. He'd never worried overmuch what people on the island thought of him, as long as they left him alone, but Juliette changed everything.

"I don't know, John Robin," he said uneasily. "I can't say—"

"It's for her to decide, not you." John Robin pressed his palms together, the fingers slightly cupped, and wiggled his hands like a fish through water. "Else she'll swim away from you, friend, away, away, and into some better man's net."

"Better man, hell." With a grumbled oath Daniel swatted down the other man's swimming hands. "Time to work, you interfering rascal, else you'll have no place here."

Glowering, he headed back into the shop, and ignored John Robin's laughter fading behind him. The man was a trial, he fumed, offering far more advice than he'd any right to, and if there were another skilled striker to be hired on the island, he'd let John Robin go tomorrow. Tonight, even. He didn't need to hear any more suggestions about how to manage his affairs with Juliette.

Yet still the squantum that John Robin had mentioned played through Daniel's thoughts as he worked through the rest of the day. He *was* being selfish, rejecting the idea outright. He had to remember how much time Juliette was spending out at the house alone, without a soul for company, and now that she was feeling better, she'd likely enjoy such an outing. She might even have that new blue gown finished, and there was nothing a woman liked better than showing off new finery to an audience. It was easy to imagine her in it, too, laughing gaily as she danced in time to the wheezy fiddle music, her hair coming unpinned and her cheeks turning pink and her blue skirts swirling around her ankles.

Unfortunately, it was just as easy to imagine her being ogled by all those newly returned young men from the whale ships, and with an effort Daniel swallowed back his jealousy. He'd no right to it, not really; three kisses, albeit kisses that had burned hotter than the fire in his forge, didn't give him any true claim to lock her away. He had to remind himself that he and Juliette hadn't promised anything to each other, which was the way it should be. He'd offer to take her to this squantum in the same spirit he'd given her the hat, as a friend would.

Aye, that was it. As a *friend.*

But he was still rehearsing different ways of inviting her as he walked home in the late afternoon sun, worrying over the exact words as if he were asking a duke's daughter to a royal governor's ball. Maybe that's what Juliette was in her other life, he thought wryly. For his own part, he couldn't imagine any high-born lady to be any more graceful or fair, and he couldn't imagine a pleasanter way to pass his walk home than thinking of her, either, when he saw the box cart coming toward him in the distance.

He watched its approach with curiosity, for this road to the south, to his house, was seldom used any longer, now that whaling had shifted to bigger, deep-water ships instead of boats rowed from the shore. He couldn't recall the last time he'd seen a cart full of people—which this one seemed to be—come this way. Three ladies, he decided from the bobbing flat-brimmed hats and the tall-backed chairs they sat upon, plus a driver. Even from here he could recognize the man as Old Roger and his equally old hired cart, from having mended the iron-bound wheels so many times and shod the sorry old mule that was pulling it. Whoever those ladies were, they must have been on a singularly determined journey, to choose to make it in that tip cart, on those wheels, on this rutted excuse for a road.

As Sachem raced ahead to bark at the cart and the mule, Daniel climbed up the slope beside the road to let them past.

"Ahoy there, Roger," he called. "Where're you bound?"

"North by northwest to town," the old man crowed in return, waving his cocked straw hat in salute. "But I'm outbound from your own homeport."

"Mine?" Daniel frowned. The answer made no sense, until one of the ladies twisted about in her chair to peer at him.

"Mr. Fairbourne, sir!" she called, her voice shaking with the rocky lurches of the cart. "Kindly call your dog away before he unsettles our mule!"

Daniel doubted this was much of a possibility—Sachem and the mule were barking acquaintances of long standing—but still he whistled for the dog to come. Mrs. Cushing was the sort of mean-tempered woman who'd begin tossing things at poor Sachem if she thought he'd erred.

"Mrs. Cushing, ma'am," he said, touching the front of his hat as the crestfallen Sachem came slinking to his side. He could see the other women now, Mrs. Howe and Mrs. Griggs, both staring up at him sourly as the cart lumbered past him. All three were friends of Mrs. Greene, a sign of ill-will if ever there was one.

"We've been to see your woman, Mr. Fairbourne," called Mrs. Cushing. "She is an obstinate, ungrateful little strumpet, sir, and the two of you, sir, may go straight to your wicked sinners' reward together for all I now care."

"What in blazes are you talking about?" demanded Daniel, matching his stride to keep pace with the mule. "God help you if you've done anything to hurt Juliette!"

"God *will* help us, sir," said Mrs. Cushing, turning her face pointedly away from Daniel, "because *we* know the difference between sin and salvation."

"Sin and salvation?" repeated Daniel, aghast.

"Yes, yes," said Mrs. Cushing impatiently. "*We* know what is right and what is wrong. Unlike you, sir, and your little French harlot, may the good Lord show pity on your wretched sins."

"What I'll be praying, you pious old she-devil," he shouted as the wagon passed him, "is that your God isn't the same as mine!"

He ran the rest of the way home, dreading what he'd find there. The memory of how Juliette had crumpled in the face of Abigail Greene's taunts haunted him, and he cursed himself for having left her alone to face these other three harpies.

But when he reached the little house, the door was barred from the inside, the latchstring pulled in.

"Juliette!" he shouted frantically as he pounded for entrance. "Juliette, it's Daniel!"

He heard the slow scrape from inside as she raised the heavy bar, and as soon as he could he shoved the door open.

"Juliette, lass," he said, pausing while his eyes grew accustomed to the darker interior after the bright sunlight. "I came as fast as I could."

She was standing back from the door, her eyes and nose red from crying and tears streaming down her cheeks. That he'd expected. But what he hadn't, what instantly caught his attention now, was his large kitchen knife clutched tight in her hand. Had she thought it necessary to defend herself against those meddling shrews this way, or was she so distraught that she'd lost her wits?

"Juliette," he said cautiously, holding out his hand for the knife. "You don't need that now, sweetheart. Give it to me, and I'll put it away for you."

She gave a low wail that did little to reassure him. "Oh, Daniel," she cried. "Do you know what happened? Do you know what I did?"

"No," he said warily, inching closer. He didn't want to startle her into hurting either one of them; that knife was the one he used for gutting fish, and was sharp as blazes. "Tell me. Please."

"What I've done—what I didn't do—oh, oh, *oh*!" she cried with sputtering frustration, as if mere words couldn't begin to express her feelings. Shaking her head, she turned away from him with the knife still in her hand, and moved back behind the table. Then, with a suddenness that made Daniel jump, she raised her hand and whacked the knife down hard onto the table.

"I let those—those *women* talk to me like I was nothing, Daniel," she said, "worse than nothing, and I let them do it here. Oh, confound these onions, to make me bawl so like a baby!"

That was when he saw the neat pile of onions in front of her, quarters and halves and separating rings, that she'd been chopping for supper, and he felt like the biggest fool on Nantucket, or the least observant, anyway.

"You—you're not distraught?" he asked warily, wanting to be certain. "Not, ah, unsettled?"

She looked up at him without lifting her chin. "Well,

yes, of course I'm distraught," she admitted, chopping at the onions with furious vigor. "But it's worse than that, Daniel. I cannot believe I let them sweep in here and accuse me, and you, too, of such dreadful, dreadful things! They called me a—"

"I know what those old bitches called you," he said, his anger rising up fresh again, "and there's no need to repeat it, since it isn't true. I met them on the road to town, and they told me themselves."

"Vile women," she muttered. "Vile, hateful, wretched *excuses* for women!"

He thumped his fist on the table. "Damnation, I should have been here to stop them! I should never have left you alone to have to face them like that!"

"No, you shouldn't have!" she said indignantly, and to his great surprise, too. "I can't expect you to come fight my fights, at least not silly ones like this!"

"I know those women, Juliette," he said firmly. "They're the worst kind of prating she-devils, and they'd sooner eat you alive like an oyster than be civil. You needed me here this afternoon."

"I did not," she protested, the knife in her hands going *chop, chop, chop* while the onion juice wrung the tears from her eyes. "I'm not some meek little milkmaid, Daniel. I remembered more, this morning. Amelie and I own the best sort of milliner's shop, together and with no help from anyone else. I'm a tradeswoman, a woman of property, Daniel, my own property that I've earned myself, and I will *not* let myself be called foul names by a group of meddlesome old women from this backwater island!"

"No," he said slowly, "you wouldn't want that."

But what did *he* want? He'd come here to save her, not

to hear how she didn't need him anymore, and he felt something perilously close to fear curling in the pit of his stomach. If she were as successful as she said—and when he thought of how well she spoke and how skilled she was with a needle, he'd no reason to doubt her—then what could he offer her that she didn't have already? She would thank him for his trouble, perhaps grant him one more kiss as farewell, and off she'd skip, back to that fine life as a self-made woman of property.

"*Mon Dieu*, no," she said, fortunately unaware of his thoughts. "I must have stood up for myself scores of times before this, else I'd never have accomplished anything of worth in whatever fine town is my home."

"You don't remember yet?" he asked, hating himself for the note of hope that crept into his words. If he truly cared about her, then he should be happy for her sake that she'd recalled this much.

She shook her head and swiped again at her tears with the hem of her pinner apron, her bravado wilting as she scraped the onions—now so well chopped as to be nearly mashed—into a skillet filled with broth. "But I will, Daniel. I *will*. I can feel it all just on the other side of my memory, teasing me, the way the fog tries to hide things in the early morning before the sun burns it away."

She shook her head again, wearily, and now he wondered if those tears were more from her heart than the onion. "But I must remember, Daniel, I must remember everything! When I think of how Amelie must be suffering over my death, it's almost more than I can bear, knowing I can't go to her yet. But I will. I *will*."

"And when you do," he said softly, "you'll be done with Nantucket."

"Yes." She sighed deeply, her gaze still intent on the skillet and the simmering onions. "Which should make what those women said today mean even less. Why should I have let them bother me so when I might well never see them again?"

He didn't care about the three other women any longer, and it pained him that Juliette did. How could she not realize that leaving the island meant leaving him? Didn't she know that, even for her, he would not leave this place that had come to mirror his soul so perfectly?

The Daniel Fairbourne that had once flourished and shone so gloriously in the bright favor of the broader world no longer existed. Only here had he found a semblance of peace, where his life could narrow and focus on a well-turned bar of yellow-hot iron, or the shadows of the clouds as they feathered across the heather moors, or the fragrance of butter-rich chowder come to simmer on his own hearth. Aye, these meant peace to him, as much peace as his tormented conscience deserved.

But how wrong he'd been to hope that such paltry things would mean the same to Juliette as well! She would long for the amusements of town and the satisfaction of practicing her own trade, and the warm love of her family. And, worse, for the arms of that unremembered husband that seemed to loom between them with the same dark presence as did his poor, ghostly Catherine.

Everything, Juliette had claimed, *he was everything to her*, and when she'd said it she'd spoken true. He didn't doubt that, or her. His one misstep was believing so desperately that her everything would last forever.

And once again, he'd be left behind with nothing but his own sorrow and loneliness.

"You'll be missed," he said simply, still softly, low enough to hide his hurt.

"Not by that wicked Mistress Cushing, I won't," she said, her back still turned to him and her bitterness toward the women keeping her from hearing all he was saying. "Yesterday's tide wouldn't have been soon enough for her, nor those others, neither. But the worst part, Daniel, the part that made me quake with my own weakness, was what they said of you, and how they threatened to harm you."

"Of me?" he asked, surprised again. He'd gladly slay whatever dragons he needed to for her sake, but he hadn't expected any to be eager for his blood, too. "What in blazes could they do to me?"

"Oh, so much, dear Daniel, so vastly, awfully much!" With a clang she settled the heavy lid on the kettle and turned back toward him. Now he'd no doubt that her tears were real, and shed for his sake as well as her own. "They said they'd make certain everyone took their business away from you to Peter Wardell's shop to ruin you, and they will!"

"No, they can't, sweetheart," he said gently. "What can that gaggle of old biddies do to hurt me?"

"Plenty, plenty, and none of it good!" she cried, her words spilling out with her anguish. "One of our customers took a disliking to Amelie and me, and not only did she accuse us wrongly of shoddy work and refuse to pay her accounts, but she also told all her friends to do the same because we had a French name, and it was their duty as Englishwomen! Their *duty*, for all love, as if treason were bound into ribbons and silks!"

"This isn't the same, Juliette."

"Oh, yes, it is! If one woman like that nearly ruined our shop, Daniel, then consider the mischief that those three could bring you!"

"Absolutely none," he declared. "Because no matter how much mischief Mrs. Cushing and the others wish to raise, their husbands aren't about to risk their belongings or their beasts to Wardell's hands. Now come, lass, come to me and let's forget all of this."

But she didn't, instead letting those sharp, real tears flow as she struggled blindly to untie her apron behind her waist. "I should have sent them on their way directly, Daniel. I shouldn't have let them stay to say one, single, hateful lie about you, not after all you've done for me!"

"My sweet Juliette," he said, his own voice thick with emotion as he reached for her. He should be her dragon slayer, not the other way around. But how long had it been that anyone, man or woman, had ever bothered to defend him, to take his cause as their own? "Come, and be mine."

But still she hung back and shook her head, bunching the apron into a white puff before her face as she fought to control herself.

"I wasn't going to tell you any of this," she said finally, though her voice still wobbled. "I didn't want you to know how—how *cowardly* I'd been. But now—oh, Daniel, those women said I've made you sin, that I've damned your soul along with my own. That's when they said that if I didn't leave Nantucket as soon as I could, then they'd punish us both by taking away your trade. You, the kindest, dearest man in Christendom!"

Juliette knew she'd tried, genuinely tried, to speak plainly and reasonably. Yet the longer he looked at her like this, with such patience and understanding and yes, with love, too, for she couldn't pretend that wasn't there, not any longer, and with the rare, marvelling half smile that meant so much there for her, only her—it was suddenly all too much for her, and instead of being reasonable or plain speaking she dropped her bundled apron and threw herself into his arms.

"Oh, Daniel, Daniel, my own love," she whispered, her cheek pressed against his shoulder, hugging him as if she'd never let him go. "I love you too much to ever make you suffer like that, and if I must leave you and Nantucket to prove it, then I shall, even if I must pray for the strength to do it!"

"Then let me be strong enough for us both," he said, the words coming husky against her throat, "and swear you will never leave on my account, not even if a thousand times that meddlesome three asked for it."

He held her with one arm high around her waist, his other hand lower, fingers splayed over her hip, and as she eagerly turned to meet his kiss, she felt at once the change between them, the shift from simple affection, friendship, to something darker, richer, forbidden, and far beyond her experience. She'd felt it before when they'd kissed, but then she'd skittered away, fearful as much for what she'd learn of herself as of him. But now as she felt Daniel caress her hip, discovering the curves from her waist to her bottom and back again, she welcomed his touch with her heart racing in invitation, giving herself over to the pleasure he offered.

"The onions," she murmured. "I must mind the onions, Daniel."

"Let 'em stew, lass," he whispered against the corner of her lips. "Better them than us, I say."

She smiled wryly, even as he slanted his mouth over hers, for most likely he did know more about how onions behaved, just as he knew more about kisses than she seemed to.

No, he knew *infinitely* more, she decided as she parted her lips for him to deepen their kiss, quivering as his tongue found hers, and raw, unfamiliar sensations of need flooded through her. She wasn't ignorant of what would happen when she gave into that need; she'd clear memories of the revelatory conversation that she and Amelie had had soon after her sister's wedding. Her brother-in-law's name was Zach, for Zachariah—she remembered that, too, and how she'd blushed with embarrassment when she'd met him again. How odd that Zach's face now seemed to blur into Daniel's, the same black hair and blue eyes and hawkish nose, or maybe not so odd since Daniel was the one she was kissing now.

And surely if she'd a husband of her own, a man she'd loved well enough to marry, then she'd have remembered his face by now, too, wouldn't she?

Wouldn't she?

"My own dear lass," said Daniel, his voice rough with longing as he trailed his lips across her cheek and along her jaw, small, teasing kisses that made her shiver.

How could she be this much in love with Daniel if she were married to another man? Forgetting her name or her home was nothing compared to such an omission. The confusion in her head was one thing, but her heart—surely her heart would remember what her reason could not, and bravely, boldly, she pressed her lips to the hollow at the base of Daniel's throat, silently pledging herself again to the heart that beat so strongly there. They'd come this far together, and she wouldn't be the one to halt now.

Together: yes, that was the keystone wasn't it? What she and Daniel had done—what they were doing even now—was done together, two as one. She wasn't "his" whore, any more than he was "her" keeper. They belonged to each other, seamlessly, as lovers, equal and true. She had trusted Daniel with her life and now her heart. All that was left to give him was her body, and with a sweet shudder of resignation she toppled with him to the wide, low bed.

He lay half atop her as they kissed, and she sank deep, deep into the downy cloud of the feather bed as the rope springs creaked beneath them, their kisses so heady that she could well have been floating. She slipped her hands inside his coat, restlessly running her hands along the broad muscles of his back. For all that he was so much larger, she didn't feel trapped beneath his body. Instead her own body seemed to relish the weight of his upon her, and as they kissed she stretched and wriggled languorously beneath him, her movements some unconscious amplification of his mouth over hers.

"God in heaven, Juliette," he groaned, and she froze. Perhaps what she found pleasurable was not to him. Perhaps to be agreeable she shouldn't move, but lie still.

"Forgive me, Daniel," she said anxiously, "if I've acted wrongly or—"

"Nay, love, not wrong." He brushed his lips across her cheek to reassure her. "Nothing wrong, and everything right."

As if to prove it, he shifted more heavily across her, and she sighed with the *rightness* of it. He slid his hand over her breast, tugging aside the layers of linen kerchief and shift and whalebone-stiffened stays until he reached her skin. Now it was her turn to gasp as his work-roughed palm teased her nipple into a tight, hot bud of longing. Impatiently she arched against his hand, seeking more, and she felt the deep rumble of his chuckle at her eagerness. As distracted as she was by his caress, chuckling did register as better than a groan.

"Greedy lass," he murmured, his breath hot on the sensitive place beneath her ear. "That's two of us, eh?"

She wanted to say something clever back to him, but the way he was kissing her throat with his hand moving so—*so!*—over her breast made even three coherent words, let alone witty ones, impossible to conjure. Instead she sighed, wordless but blissful, and resolved to be witty later, when her body wasn't so intent on mastering her reason.

She slid her hands down Daniel's back, daring to pull his shirt free of his breeches so she could touch him, then lower her hands went, beneath the lacing at the back of his breeches to discover the shallow valley of his spine, the twin dimples on either side, more taut, unfamiliar muscles for her to explore. His skin was hot, burning, as if he'd been too long in the summer sun, her touch enough to make him groan again.

She understood. Her heart was racing, her shift clinging moistly to her body even though the hearth fire's heat could scarcely reach them. Yet still she wanted more, and more, and *more* with Daniel, with a desperation that went beyond desire.

All through her girlhood she'd been admonished to be a proper lady and keep her legs together and her ankles genteelly crossed, but now she realized that this new urgency for *more* was making her forget every ladylike warning. With another little sigh she whispered her legs apart and let Daniel's great body settle there between, and at once that little sigh changed into a startled gasp. Even though she was still protected by layers of petticoats and shift as well as his breeches, through it all she could feel the rigid heat of that most masculine part of him pressing hard against the place where she was most a woman.

But instead of retreating, her body longed to be closer still to him. She felt soft and warm and aching, her own heartbeat now concentrated in that same place between her legs, and instinctively she drew her legs up higher around his hips to draw him toward the aching, heedless of her shoes on the coverlet or how her skirts slid up past her garters and over her knees.

She might not have noticed, but Daniel did.

"Damnation, Juliette!" he rasped with a desperation of his own, his breath as labored as if he'd run from town. "You'll unman me if you keep doing that!"

"Then love me," she said in a rush, not sure of anything else. "Just—just love me."

"I love you already, lass," said Daniel, and kissed her hard, his lips demanding enough to steal her breath and maybe her soul with it. Certainly enough to make her head swirl, and to make her cling to him as if she were being tossed again in that wild, stormy sea. But now instead of the ceaseless drone of the waves, the rhythm that drove her was the thumping of her heart and Daniel's mingled with the ragged pace of their breathing.

She felt him shove her skirts higher, into a mass of crushed linen at her waist, and then he was sliding between her legs, touching her, telling her how beautiful she was, how much he wanted her, and stroking that warm, secret place at the top of her thighs, until she realized that the low, animal sound was coming from her. Her body was tightening, coiling strangely inside, and she shuddered with an odd mixture of relief and disappointment when Daniel abruptly sat back on his heels on the bed.

But only for a moment, the single moment that it had taken him to tear off his coat and open the buttons on the fall of his breeches and return to her. His palms were hot on her thighs, the soft linen of his shirt's tails brushing over her skin like another caress. Then his touch again, the same rising pleasure that made her arch and cry out for joy, and then something blunt, infinitely larger than his fingers, forcing its path into her to stop the pleasure short.

"Daniel!" she cried out, panicking, trying to scuttle backward beneath him, away from this sharp pain pushing into her. "*Daniel!*"

This wasn't anything like what Amelie had described to her. She didn't feel treasured, or blissful, or transported on the rapturous wings of angels, the way Amelie had sworn had happened to her with Zach. Instead Juliette felt crushed and stretched and filled in a way that had absolutely nothing to do with angels or rapture.

"Juliette?" whispered Daniel hoarsely, propping himself up on his elbows above her. "Juliette, love."

She didn't want to cry, not again. Better to concentrate on the one good thing she could find in this entire debacle.

"Daniel," she began bravely, "Daniel, I—I do not believe I'm married."

Gently he smoothed her damp, tangled hair back from her forehead. "I know, sweetheart," he said, "and I'm sorry."

"You're *sorry*?" That wasn't what she wanted to hear, not with him buried deep inside her poor, aching body, not with tears fighting a close battle with bravery.

"Not about the husband, lass," he said hastily, "but that I've hurt you."

"No, you haven't," she said with equal haste. "Not much."

"Liar," he said, and brushed his lips across her forehead. "But I swear, love, I'll make it better for you now."

She didn't believe that was possible, but because it was Daniel making the promise, she would try.

"Rapturous," she said with a sniffle as she reached up to kiss him. "That's how Amelie told me it would be. Rapturous, upon angel's wings."

"Hush now," he said. "Enough talk. I want you to feel instead."

Instantly she stiffened as he shifted on his knees to angle himself differently inside of her, and she breathed a tiny sigh—not quite of pleasure, perhaps, but no longer out-and-out pain, either. In fact now as he began moving again, she was surprised at how *accommodating* her body had become, and as an experiment, she tentatively tried rocking her hips to meet him, the way she had done earlier.

Amazingly accommodating, in fact.

"Little witch," muttered Daniel with a groan. "I thought I was the captain here, eh?"

"Not captain, but mate," she said, then gasped herself with startled, breathless delight as he drove more deeply into her. "Two—two mates, both equal."

"Aye, aye," he said, and when he chuckled she could feel the sound vibrate between them. "Here, lass, give me your hand."

He raised himself a bit away from her, and placed her fingers where their bodies were so intimately joined, her own flesh so wet and slick and hot as fire around his.

"There," he said hoarsely as she touched him. "That's us together, love, as close as a man and woman can be, two joined as one."

She touched, and looked, and felt, ah, such feelings! She wasn't sure that Amelie's angels' wings would have much to do with her and Daniel right now, tangled together on his bed, with their clothes half gone and what remained damp with sweat and desire and her feet in her shoes—in her high-heeled, still-buckled *shoes*—hooked high around his waist, and both of them half laughing and half weeping as they moved together, together, yes, until they'd both found the joy that would bind their love together.

And when they lay together afterwards—a long, long time afterwards, after they'd managed finally to shed their shoes and the rest of their clothes with them, after the onions had burned beyond redemption and they'd eaten bread and butter for supper, and after Sachem had been let inside to sleep grumpily on the floor beside the bed and not on it—content and exhausted, Juliette drowsily decided there was nothing better in life than to be here, now, with Daniel Fairbourne's chest against her back and his arm around her waist and his heart beating in time with hers.

"You kept your promise, Daniel," she whispered sleepily, not even sure if he was still awake, either.

"Umm," he grunted, barely proving that he was. "Promise what, love?"

"About feeling the rapture, like Amelie said."

"Oh, aye," he said, and kissed the nape of her neck. "Powerfully fine rapture it was, too, wasn't it?"

She laughed softly and snuggled closer to him, and her last thought before she fell asleep was of the angels' wings he'd promised for the morning.

Chapter 9

Daniel hauled the lobster trap into the boat and thanked his Maker that there was no other man within two miles to see him do it. Not that hauling a lobster trap was any great secret, or that he'd any mystery about the boat, either; but if even one other man on Nantucket had witnessed the great, gaping, fool of a grin that he could not keep from his face this morning, then the whole island would soon know the truth about him and Juliette.

He shook his head wryly and glanced back at the house where she slept still. Instantly he pictured her in his bed the way he'd left her, curled on her side with her hand beneath her flushed cheek, her silver hair tossed and tangled over his pillow and the sheet pulled only as high as her bare hip—well, that was enough to set him grinning like a lovesick puppy all over again.

So why should he care who knew the reason, anyway? It had been like this every morning for over a week now, every morning since the night they'd tumbled together into bed. He did love Juliette, loved her beyond any doubt or question, and she loved him the same in return. If they'd spent these last nights proving it to each other with lovemaking so hot that he'd half expected to find the sheets scorched in the morning, then whose affair was that? What he and Juliette shared and felt was between them and no one else. Now there wasn't even that phantom of a husband waiting somewhere for her. Now all that should matter in the world to him was that the woman he loved was sleeping in his bed in his house, with the kettle already off the fire and steeping with her breakfast tea.

And yet despite everything he had now with Juliette, to his despair it was Catherine he dreamed of afterwards, the old dream that never changed, just as the ending of her life could never be undone, either. They'd fought, the way they had done more and more once they'd wed, and shouted the bitter, hateful things to each other that no husbands and wives should, and then Catherine had left, her little heeled shoes drumming a furious staccato across the polished floors, her yellow skirts billowing behind her and over her rounding belly with their unborn child.

He'd let her go just as he'd done in life, but in his dream he'd watch her maid pack her trunk, watch her write the note that told him she was leaving him and traveling alone to her sister's plantation on the next island, watch her weep at the rail as the little sloop cleared their harbor, watch as the storm caught the captain by surprise and swamped the sloop, dismasted her and cracked her hull like a nutshell. All hands lost, no passengers saved, his beautiful, vibrant wife no more than a lifeless tatter of yellow silk lost forever in the blue Caribbean. Dead because he'd failed and hadn't been able to be the man she'd wanted to love.

"Daniel?" asked Juliette uncertainly. "Daniel, are you unwell?"

She was standing beside him in the sand, shading her sleepy blue eyes beneath the flat of her hand. She'd found her shift from wherever it had been tossed last night, the white linen fluttering in the breeze around her bare calves, but she hadn't bothered with anything else beyond taking the coverlet from the bed as a makeshift shawl with her long, uncombed hair tumbling over her shoulders.

He could tell her now, tell her about Catherine and lay his wife's spirit and his own conscience to rest. Now, before each minute passing would make it harder to explain.

Now.

But instead he only shook his head and shrugged restlessly, shoving the slatted wooden lobster pot deeper into the bottom of the boat. "You know I'm well, sweetheart, now that you're here."

His smile felt false, the easy gallantry so empty he hated himself for shaming her with it.

"I'm glad, love." She smiled shyly, achingly innocent of what he knew, and reached out to run her fingers along his wrist. "I knew you hadn't gone far because you'd left your boots beside the bed, but still I couldn't wait to say good morning."

There was always a giddy joy to her in the morning, as if she still didn't realize the significance of the step they'd taken and continued to take each night over and over.

But he did. Damnation, did he, and he felt that false smile of his twist around into a more truthful grimace.

Holding the coverlet around her shoulders with one

hand, she leaned toward him on tiptoe for a kiss, then giggled. "Good morning, Master Fairbourne."

"Good morning to you, mademoiselle," he answered, because he had to. "Did you find your tea?"

"I didn't look for it. I came to find you instead." She tucked her hair behind her ear, an unconsciously sinuous little gesture that nearly undid him. "What are you doing, anyway?"

"Looking after our supper." Cowardly, cowardly, to feel so grateful that he could speak now of lobsters instead of his *wife*. "I thought while you slept, I'd take this out and drop it near the rocks. You do eat lobster, don't you?"

"Oh, yes." As he'd bent over the trap, she'd come to stand behind him, linking her arms around his waist. "But I'd rather eat bread and butter again tonight if it means you'll come back inside the house with me now."

"No," he said, far more sharply than he'd intended, sharply enough that he felt her arms drop instantly from him. But damnation, he could *not* go back into that house and lose himself in the bliss and happiness that Juliette offered and that he didn't deserve, not now, not with the sting of Catherine's mocking laughter still echoing in his heart.

"No?" asked Juliette, her voice uncertain. *"Mon Dieu,* if I have offended you, Daniel, I should hope that you'd at least tell me what—"

"I never meant that, lass," he said quickly, taking her hand and bringing it to his lips. He might not deserve her, but she didn't deserve to share his bitterness, either. "Don't you know how much I love you? Doesn't that mean anything?"

God help him, how many times had he said exactly the same words to Catherine?

She glanced up at him, unconvinced and confused. "You're not making much sense, Daniel."

Blast it, he knew he wasn't, and he sighed with frustration, looking away from her and out across the water. But maybe the sea was the answer he was seeking, the same water that had stolen Catherine and had brought him Juliette. His fingers tightened around hers, drawing her to the boat.

"Here, come with me," he said. "Come out while I drop the trap."

"Out there?" She tugged back, her eyes filled with reluctance. "On the ocean? Oh, Daniel, look at me! I'm not even dressed!"

"Oh, aye, and there's so many folk here on this coast to gawk and stare." He reached over and tucked his arm beneath her knees, scooping her up and settling her onto the bench of his boat. She yelped in protest, but he was already pushing the boat forward, digging his bare feet into the sand and then the shallow water. He whistled for Sachem, and the dog came racing across the beach and into the water beside him, bouncing up and down with joyful abandon.

"Here you go, lad, up and in," he said as he boosted the wriggling dog into the stern. Though the boat rocked beneath his weight, Sachem settled instantly; if he wanted to remain a passenger, he knew here he'd have to behave.

A lesson that Juliette, however, never seemed to have learned.

"Let me out, Daniel, please!" she cried frantically, swinging one leg out of the boat as she tried to climb out backward. "I don't want to go with you!"

"Too late, lass," he called as he deftly swung himself

into the boat. "Now bring in that pretty leg before you swamp us, mind?"

She scrambled to obey, clutching the sides of the boat as she peered anxiously into the water. She still didn't seem particularly happy, but at least she'd stopped thrashing.

Daniel slipped the oars into their locks and dipped the blades into the water, enjoying how obediently the boat now fought its way up the incoming wave, hovered on the crest, then finally slid down into the trough of the next. He'd spent all his life in and out of boats and around the water, and though he'd turned his back on the endless responsibilities and headaches of being a shipmaster, he still could find peace and pleasure in the feel of the sea, the morning sun glittering on the water around him and the brisk saltiness in the air.

"I'm sorry if I startled you there, love," he said gently. Bending his back to pull the oars like this eased his thoughts as well as worked his muscles, and with each stroke he felt more like himself. "But it did seem the fastest way to get you aboard."

"I didn't want to come at all," she said without lifting her gaze from the water, her unbound hair shielding her face like a pale curtain. "I don't care if hauling me aboard like that was fast or not. I wanted to stay home, and you didn't listen. Instead you kidnapped me."

He liked the sound of that unexpected *home* from her, referring as it did to his house as hers, though the part about kidnapping wasn't nearly as pleasant, mostly because she was right. "No one's going to see you in your shift, Juliette, not out here. Except for me, that is, and I think you look most fine."

She looked more than fine, really, for the coverlet had slid off her shoulders and between the bright sun and the fine linen of her shift, he could easily, charmingly make out her breasts and the darker circles of her nipples. But still she didn't answer, making that observation, too, an unwise one to share, and he sighed again.

"I'm sorry I brought you against your wishes, Juliette," he said as contritely as he could manage, "and if it seemed like kidnapping, well, I suppose it was. But after last night and all, I didn't want to leave you behind. I wanted you with me, love, especially on so bright a morning. Where's the sin in that?"

Where was the sin, indeed? The more he considered it in the morning light, the more sense it made. By giving him Juliette and her love, the sea might also be offering him the first wobbling step toward finally accepting Catherine's death. He loved Juliette and she loved him, and loving her meant sharing his life with her, even his life in a battered old rowboat with his dog for the bo'sun. No sin in that, certainly.

Until, that is, she turned her ashy, terrified face toward him, and he realized how appallingly selfish he'd been.

To her, the ocean would bring no peace, no contentment. The last time she'd been afloat, this same water had nearly killed her, and now he'd hauled her out to sea again without a thought for how she'd suffered. Kidnapping, aye, and torture, too.

He stopped rowing and leaned across the oars toward her. "My God, Juliette," he said heavily. "How can you ever forgive me for this? Here, I'll turn round and take you back directly."

"No, don't, Daniel, please," she said, putting her

hands on his wrists to stop him. "Go onward. I'll be—I'll be fine. I'll be brave."

"But damnation, you shouldn't have to be, not when I'm the one who's the thoughtless ass." Gently he reached out to touch her pale cheek with his fingertips, wanting to find some way to comfort her. "Are you remembering the wreck, then?"

She shook her head. "It's more that I'm afraid of remembering it," she said slowly, "than the actual remembering. I know it will come back to me along with everything else, but oh, Daniel, how I dread it!"

He remembered back to the night when she'd wakened with the nightmare about the wreck, and wondered if on some level she remembered it, too. "Are you sure you don't want me to take you back ashore?"

"I'd rather you didn't," she said, though from her greenish pallor she certainly looked as if she'd wanted nothing better. "It's as you said, Daniel. I'd rather be here, with you, than anywhere else. Just—just speak to me of other things, if you please. Anything other than—than the night you found me."

"Very well," he agreed heartily as he began rowing again, then couldn't think of one blessed word to say. In desparation he glanced down at the slatted lobster trap lying in the bottom of the boat between them.

"You said you like to eat lobsters," he began, "but I'll wager you never gave half a thought to how they were caught. Lobsters are clever beasts, you know. You can't catch a lobster by waving a hook in his face. You have to tempt him with more than that, which is why some wise fellow invented a trap like this."

She nodded solemnly, and so he plunged on. "Lobster

traps have two parts, you see. The first part, there near your toes, is called the parlor, on account of it being exactly the sort of snuggery that a lobster finds agreeable for visiting. The second part, behind the parlor, is called the kitchen because that's where I've put that old piece of pork rind as bait. The lobster will sniff the bait from the parlor, just as if it were an apple pie set out to cool. He'll amble on into the kitchen to have a little taste, and that's when he'll learn he can't crawl back out again, leastways not until we come back this evening to gather him up. Ah, here's the spot, near these rocks."

Carefully he turned the boat alongside the rocks and shipped his oars. He checked the long line that connected the trap to the wooden float, then pitched it into the water. Sachem barked, as if announcing the trap's arrival, his tail thumping excitedly against the bottom of the boat, and for once Daniel didn't scold him. Juliette leaned to one side to watch the trap drift and sink through the water, until it reached bottom and the line with the float pulled taut. Watching her watch the trap, Daniel could only hope she was thinking of her supper, and not of how a shattered ship would likewise sink to the bottom of the sea.

"You'll find a lobster caught now is especially good eating," he said as he turned the boat around. He was lecturing her again, trapped as surely as any lobster in wordiness of his own making, and as helplessly, too. "Their shells are still soft from moulting the old ones in the summer. That's why—"

"I know now I was a virgin," interrupted Juliette, "but you, Daniel. You've done such things with a woman before, haven't you?"

He stared at her dumbly, struggling to make the transition from moulting lobsters to his amatory experience. It would have been the most natural time imaginable for him to tell her now how he'd been married before, that he was widowed now, that once he'd loved Catherine, too.

It would have been natural, and it was impossible.

"Aye, lass, I have," he said instead, the limit of his confession. "I'm a man, Juliette, and not a young one at that."

She smiled wistfully. "I didn't really expect you to be otherwise, especially since you seemed to know what to do when I didn't. That was most fortunate. But still it would have been rather nice if we had both been intended for one another and nobody else."

It wasn't an idea he'd ever considered, at least not since he'd lost his own virginity at fifteen to a much older rum shop serving maid in Truro. But because Juliette so clearly wished it, he nearly did himself as well, for her sake.

Which, of course, made the somber reality of his past with Catherine weigh even more heavily upon him.

"We can still have been intended for each other," he said, "excepting that we've had to tack around the world a bit by ourselves before we realized it."

"Tacking." She wrinkled her nose. "I suspect we each mean different things by that."

"There's only one meaning that I know," he said uneasily, wishing he could guess where she was headed. "To find the best use of a wind that's counter to course, a sailor must tack back and forth, not direct fashion, to make his headway."

"Ah," she said. "And to a seamstress, tacking means joining two pieces together with bold, loose stitches not meant to last."

He frowned, still not sure if she were teasing or not. "I do believe I like my meaning better, Juliette, that we've each been criss-crossing about before we've finally landed together."

"And not stitched together loosely, for the ease of ripping apart again?"

"Hell, no," he said indignantly. "I'm not the sort of man who'll bed you one night, then sail off with the tide. You've stitched yourself to me good and strong, Juliette, and I mean to keep it that way."

"You do?" she asked, the wariness still in her eyes.

"I do," he declared warmly. "And to prove it, I'll expect you to come with me to the gathering in town four days from now, to welcome back the whalers. Dancing and feasting and drinking, too, though all I'll care for is showing the world how deep those stitches run holding you to me."

The boat struck the soft, sandy bottom of the beach with a lurching thump, signal enough for Sachem to jump out and into the water with an impatient yip for Daniel to follow. But Daniel stayed where he was, and so did Juliette, facing each other in the boat.

"You are inviting me to come to this—this island *fete* with you?" she asked incredulously, holding her blowing hair back from her face with both hands on her head. "You would do that for me, Daniel?"

"For you, and for me, too," he said, realizing as he spoke how true it was, and how unlike anything he'd ever said to Catherine. "Together, sweetheart, us together. That's what I want Mrs. Griggs and Mrs. Howe and John Robin and all the rest of them to see, and to the devil with any who can't."

"Oh, and the devil *will!*" she cried delightedly, and lunged across the boat to fling her arms around his neck and topple him off the bench into the puddle in the bottom of the boat. For a long, rocking moment, Sachem barked and splashed and the oars waved upward in their locks, and Daniel took advantage of the general confusion to slip his arms around Juliette's soft, unwhaleboned body and kiss her as the boat rocked back and forth in the shallow water.

"Mind, I've one condition about this gathering," he said sternly as he swung her, wet and giggling and most undignified with her bottom in the air, over his shoulder to carry her to the house. "As much as I fancy you in this sort of undress, you'll have to cover yourself more decently for the rest of the island. Have you finished the blue gown?"

"Almost," she said, her voice coming disembodied from somewhere behind his waist. "I'll come with you to town this morning and go to the Swains' shop for the last bit of thread ribbon I'll need."

"I don't know, Juliette." Carefully he set her down on the rough slab of stone that served as his doorstep, and glanced up at the sun to guess at the time. "I won't be able to go with you like the last time."

"I won't mind," she said with a little shake of her head that sent a stray lock of hair falling beguilingly over one eye. "I'll do well enough on my own. Things are different now."

This time he knew exactly what she meant. Things *were* different now, though for the life of him he couldn't say exactly when the change had begun. But there it was, different and changed, and all because of her.

"I do love you, sweetheart," he said softly as he pushed that stray lock back from her eyes. Beautiful eyes she had, the clearest, most guileless blue imaginable.

"I love you, too." She smiled, that alone enough to weaken his knees before she crossed her arms beneath her breasts. "I'll go dress so I won't keep you waiting on my account."

He groaned. "I'm already so damned late for my work that John Robin's likely begged the constable to come hunt for my dead body."

"Then we'll meet him on the road," she said, her smile quirking wickedly crooked, "or simply let him discover your very live body here."

And that, decided Daniel with a grin to match hers as he shut the door after them, was no real choice at all.

"Betsey?" called Juliette, standing alone in the middle of the Swains' little millinery shop. "Good day, anyone?"

Someone *had* been tending shop, and not long ago, either. Steam still curled faintly from the half-full dish of tea left on the counter, a dish with a chip from the rim and so well worn that the painted pink flowers on its side were faded and faint. Definitely not the sort of dish one offered to a customer, decided Juliette primly, but a dish one would keep for one's own refreshment. Or would, if one kept shop the way she and Amelie had, and with a sigh Juliette had to remind herself that these particular ones, namely the Swains, might lean to different standards of nicety altogether.

But after her long walk with Daniel, she had to admit that the tea smelled good regardless of the state of its dish. Though she wouldn't admit it to Daniel, her scarred leg did ache after the long walk to town, especially after how little sleep she'd gotten the night before. She was tired and she was thirsty, and as she peeked through the unfastened door to the rest of the house, she hoped to see Betsey's return and, with luck, a dish of the same tea for herself.

"Betsey?" she halfheartedly called again. She wandered to the front of the shop to look from the window into the street, wondering if Betsey could have been called away from the house entirely. Juliette would wait, of course, for this was the only ladies' shop that she knew in the town, and from unconscious habit she began tidying and rearranging the ribbons and threads for embroidery that made up the small window display.

"Forgive me, mistress, for keeping you waiting!" said the woman as she bustled breathlessly into the shop. "I had to see to my—oh, Mistress Lacroix!"

As Juliette turned, the woman bowed low, far too low to be appropriate, and embarrassed, Juliette wondered how to make her rise without her sounding like a queen granting favors.

"Good day, ma'am," she ventured, and fortunately that was sufficient. The other woman bobbed back upright, her ruddy round face an older version of Betsey's, and with relief Juliette held out her hand. "You must be Mistress Swain, though you seem to have the advantage of knowing me first."

The older woman chuckled with pleasure, smoothing the front of her green apron with sweeping downward strokes. She was dressed crisply, if not fashionably, in a dark brown petticoat and a deep red bodice, her single concession to stylishness a ruffled white cap of linen so sheer that her sleek brown hair gleamed through. "Oh, aye, who doesn't know you, mistress? Mademoiselle Juliette Lacroix! Honored, I am, just having you in my little shop again!"

"Your daughter served me well, ma'am," said Juliette, "so I've returned." It wasn't only that Mrs. Swain seemed determined to treat her better than any other woman on the island. She also pronounced Juliette's last name as if it were English rather than French, sounding both the *r* and the *x*, a sure sign that Mrs. Swain had only read her name, not heard it spoken. But where, wondered Juliette uneasily, would her name have been written for Mrs. Swain to read here on Nantucket? "Is Betsey here today?"

"Not today, nor likely tomorrow, neither." Mrs. Swain glanced dramatically toward the heavens for guidance, or at least the beams in the ceiling of the shop. "Though I do thank you for asking. Betsey's young man be new returned from four months a-whaling, and I've given her leave to spend a day or two away from the shop in his company. How could I not, I ask you, when I do much the same each time Mr. Swain's ship rounds Great Point for home?"

She chuckled knowingly, shaking her head without really disapproving. "But Betsey and Eleazer Gibb are to be wed next month, so if they dally alone too long on the moors, why, there's no real harm. Not that I could stop *that* pair, anyways. Like coneys when every day's the first of May, those two."

She chuckled again, and Juliette wondered how such earthy tolerance lived side by side on the same island with Mrs. Cushing's rigidity. Betsey's young man Eleazer must be one of the whalers whose safe return they'd be celebrating, and knowing they'd also be celebrating another pair of lovers' happiness added to Juliette's anticipation.

"Then pray tell your daughter I regret not seeing her, and wish her joy from me, too," said Juliette warmly. "She was most helpful when I was here last."

"And you most helpful to her in turn, and not only about shaping hats, neither." Mrs. Swain leaned forward confidentially, even though they were the only two in the shop. "Betsey told me all about how that Abigail Greene treated her and you, and how you spoke up for my Betsey even though you needn't. And I thank you for your kindness, miss, I do."

"I don't care who Mrs. Greene thought she was," said Juliette, remembering all too clearly what had happened last time she'd been here. "No one has the right to mistreat another or fancy herself of the better sort simply because she is in the position of having more money in her pocket."

"Not that Abigail's better nor richer, not if what I has heard be true about that husband of hers." Mrs. Swain winked sagely. "But no mind. The truth is I hope you won't be judging all us islanders by them that's like that."

"Never." Juliette smiled, warmed to realize she'd made at least one ally here on Nantucket. "I've always tried to judge others by what they do rather than who they claim to be."

"Now don't that be the mark of a real lady," marveled Mrs. Swain. "Words like them show how fine you be in your heart, miss, even among us plain folk."

"I'm not so fine as all that, Mrs. Swain," protested Juliette. "I've come here today for thread and ribbon to finish my sewing, same as any other customer. We're sisters of a sort, really, for I've kept a millinery and mantua-maker's shop like this with my sister Amelie for years."

Sarah Swain's chuckle turned into a good-natured scolding cluck as she turned a chair for Juliette to sit.

"Now you do be too kind, miss, too kind by half," she said firmly. "I keep this little shop only to bring in a few shillings, while you dress all the finest ladies in New England, they say, even the royal governor's wife herself! China silks and cobweb laces, that be your stock, and there's not a woman in Boston that don't know your shop's black and gold shutters or your sign board with the plumed hat. You being the same as me! You might as well say a sparrow's sister to a peacock!"

"Boston, you say," said Juliette faintly, her head spinning as she sank into the offered chair. "My shop in Boston."

Mrs. Swain's plump chin nodded, unaware of the importance to Juliette of her words. "There in Marlborough Street, directly opposite Old South Church, where no lady would ever miss it."

"You've visited as a customer, then?"

"I, miss?" The older woman laughed merrily. "Not me, nay! But I stopped in the street to look when I sailed to Boston with my eldest boy last spring. A cat may look at a king, I says, and I wanted to look my share after reading your notices in the news sheets. 'Capuchins and heives, Paris nets and umbrilloes, trally, dott, and millinette'—you see how I remembered it, miss, for being like another language to me!"

Boston, thought Juliette in a rush of recollection that left her feeling stunned and dazed. She knew that announcement in the *Gazette* for newly arrived stock because she'd written it. The crowded street and the wide shop window and the well-dressed people parading outside her door all belonged in Boston, and so, she knew now, did she.

Boston: she could *see* the shutters painted glossy black and picked out in gold, the well-scrubbed steps that led to the door with the ribboned bouquet of fresh flowers pinned to it, changed each morning by her own hand. She remembered Marlborough Street, one of the town's most fashionable neighborhoods, just as she could picture the well-appointed front room of their shop and the clutter of scraps and threads in the sewing room to the rear, and the winding stairs that lead to the elegant private rooms above, where she'd always lived with Amelie.

Boston *was* home, her home, and had been nearly all her life. At last she could send word home to Amelie, to tell her she hadn't drowned, that she was still miraculously alive here on Nantucket. Ships and boats must clear Sherburne all the time for Boston; with luck she could be home within the week. So why, then, did she want to weep at the thought of returning to it and leaving behind the rough-hewn little one-room house by the sea where she'd spent little more than a month?

Boston. God help her, she wasn't ready to return, not yet, not when she'd only now discovered love and joy and happiness, real happiness, with Daniel.

"Do you know when next a vessel clears for Boston?" she forced herself to ask. "I wish to send a letter to my sister."

"Oh, aye, I expect you do, miss," said Mrs. Swain. "Captain Russell's packet makes the run once a fortnight, every other Monday, that is. You'll have to wait until next week."

"Thank you," murmured Juliette. Until next Monday, then; she could, in perfect conscience, remain here until then.

"Do you know that the day I came to Boston," continued Mrs. Swain with a mixture of awe and eagerness, "that very day, I saw one of those great Boston ladies come to your door in a carriage with two horses before and two serving men in laced coats riding on the box behind, just to serve her fancy. A duke's granddaughter, someone told me she was, and beautiful enough to be one, too."

Dukes' granddaughters and governors' wives! She and Amelie had worked so hard to make the shop they'd inherited from their mother the most fashionable one in New England, maybe in all the colonies. Her disappearence these last weeks must have caused anguished consternation in dozens of Boston parlors, not so much for her own sake, but for all the mantuas and petticoats, cloaks and robes she'd left unfinished whenever it was that she'd left.

And of course she must return. She wouldn't abandon them completely, her loyal ladies, any more than she would—or could—walk away from the prospering trade and reputation that had taken more than twenty years to create. She'd never do that to Amelie or her mother's memory, and she wasn't sure she could do it to herself, either. To give up the shop would be like cutting off an arm, and she'd no more expect that of herself than she'd order Daniel to give up his forge.

But what would he expect from *her?*

He'd said he wanted her with him always, even in a boat with a lobster pot. He liked her mending his shirts in his house, or curling close to him in his bed, or walking by his side across the hills to town. But what would he make of her far away in Boston, tending to her customers and hiring the seamstresses that worked for her and balancing account books by candlelight long into the night?

She felt the little iron sun Daniel had made for her, there in her pocket beneath her skirts where she always kept it now as a kind of talisman, for luck and love. Together, she and Daniel had promised each other, together was how they'd always be. But how could they possibly make one love and one life out of two that were so wildly disparate?

And what if that reckoning grew more complicated still, with one from two making three? She might have been a virgin, but she wasn't a fool. Amelie had seen to that. She'd warned that babies were as much a result of lovemaking as the rapture. These past nights Juliette had been willing enough to forget that, but now in the searing light of who she *was*, she could think of little else. Respectability was as important to a fashionable mantua-maker and milliner as silk, and she'd have precious little left if she returned to her shop with a babe soon swelling her belly.

"Forgive me for speaking bold, miss," said Mrs. Swain with concern, "but you don't look well. Might I fetch you a dish of tea, or some buttermilk?"

"I'm a bit weary, that is all," said Juliette quickly, hoping her face didn't betray her worries. Everything was happening so swiftly between her and Daniel that she longed for some time to consider it privately, before it became common gossip. "And a dish of tea would be most welcome, thank you."

The tea promptly appeared, tasting faintly of orange

from another far-off island, and Juliette sipped it gratefully.

"There now," said Mrs. Swain briskly as she bustled behind the counter for a basket of ribbons. "Better I should tend to business instead of rattling on so. Mr. Swain, he says I'd talk the ears off a donkey, and I do believe I could. Here be a card of our best sewing thread, miss, if that be sufficient. Now what color of ribbons were you wishing to go with it?"

From her pocket, Juliette drew a scrap of the blue wool cloth that she'd brought with her to compare shade. "That deep carnation silk, there," she said, pointing among the ribbons coiled in the basket, "the one that's a finger-tip wide, to lace down the front of the bodice and gather into rosettes for the cuffs. Six ells, if you please."

"A most excellent choice, miss," said Mrs. Swain with beaming approval, and Juliette smothered her own smile. Whether the customers were the wives of fishermen or royal governors, the compliments to their taste remained the same. "And I do recall Mr. Fairbourne taking this blue with you in mind. For a man, Daniel Fairbourne does have an agreeable eye for what will please a lady."

"Yes, he does," said Juliette, blushing furiously as she thought of several other far more interesting ways that Daniel knew of pleasing a woman.

Mrs. Swain smiled as she measured and cut the ribbon. "There now, miss, you've the same moony look to you that Mr. Fairbourne's had since he pulled you from the sea. The entire town's marked the change you've made in him."

Juliette's blush deepened. "Daniel's not the sort of man any woman changes."

"Not unless he wished it, nay," agreed the other woman. "But he's always seemed a good man to me, despite the foolishness that's whispered about him, and a handsome one, too. And now, because of you, he be a happy man in the bargain."

"You're too kind, ma'am." Juliette busied herself with the tea. The town could say what it wanted, but she was almost certain that Daniel wasn't going to be a happy man when he learned what she'd just learned about herself. She'd put it off as long as she could, until she could remember the wreck that had brought her here, but she'd only be buying time until she must tell him herself.

And leave.

"Oh, it's all the stuff of ballads," continued Mrs. Swain, "with him rescuing you like he did. Most wrecks on these shores don't have such pretty endings. There's more that we bury than not. How proud he must be to see what a pearl he found in the waves, you being about the grandest tradeswoman in Boston!"

"He doesn't know I'm any such thing," said Juliette softly. "He thinks I'm just—just Juliette Lacroix."

"Just Juliette Lacroix!" repeated Mrs. Swain, thunderstruck. "You, the mantua-maker to the royal governor's own lady-wife!"

Miserably Juliette stared down at her tea. Mrs. Swain was exactly the sort of warm, understanding mother that her own brittle, unhappy mother never had been able to be, the sort of mother she longed to have to talk to now. Briefly she considered, the temptation to confide her joys and her sorrows with Daniel almost unbearably strong.

But most likely Mrs. Swain's tolerance toward Betsey and her young man was based on knowing they were soon to marry, and from the way the older woman was talking now, she clearly assumed the same held true with Daniel and Juliette as well. With Daniel, Juliette knew there was no such assumption. Daniel had never mentioned marriage at all, nor had she honestly expected him to. Though she didn't doubt that he loved her, love and marriage and bedding a woman did not mean the same thing to a man; she wasn't a fool that way, either.

No. Deep down she knew there was only one other woman who'd truly understand, one woman who could sympathize with all that was twisting and turning her now, and that was her sister Amelie. Lord, Lord, how much she missed her!

With an unhappy sigh, she carefully set the empty tea dish on the counter.

"Mr. Fairbourne doesn't know anything at all about what I do, Mrs. Swain," she said, choosing her words with infinite care, "or even that I'm from Boston. And for now, ma'am, I'd be deeply obliged to you if you do not tell him."

"Of course I won't tell him, miss, if that's what you wish," said Mrs. Swain, her round face wreathed with sad concern. "But if I might speak free, miss, little good can come from keeping secrets from a man, and if—"

"Thank you, Mrs. Swain," said Juliette, rising quickly to her feet. "Now if you'll tally the sum for the thread and the ribbon, I shall be on my way."

Yet though she'd managed to escape one peril, it seemed the long walk alone back to the south shore offered no solace. With every step across the lonely moors and meadows, she recalled more about the bustling, crowded Boston that was her home, ridiculously unimportant things like the lopsided toll of the bell in the steeple of the church across the street from their shop and the one-eyed yellow tom kept by the tailor next door when she'd been a little girl.

By the time she reached Daniel's house again, exhausted in both body and spirit, she had remembered nearly everything about her past except that one last journey. No matter that she could describe every silk her shop carried, or list the names of her girlhood friends; she still couldn't explain how she'd come to land on Nantucket, what ship she'd been sailing in, or why after a lifetime spent in Boston she'd decided to sail away to be shipwrecked here at Daniel's feet.

That was the first mystery plaguing her. The second was infinitely more complicated, and with no easy answer that her memory might supply.

And that was what would become of her and Daniel.

Chapter 10

"Easy there, Bess, easy," said Daniel as he coaxed the chestnut mare along the rutted road. "Find whatever way pleases you, so long as you get me back to my Juliette."

The mare's pointed ears swiveled backward, but the real proof that she'd listened came in the way she finally picked up her pace. Daniel chuckled, imagining Juliette's reaction when he described how much power her name seemed to have over this particular horse. But then she'd probably laugh anyway—at least he hoped she would—as soon as she caught sight of him driving to the house in a box cart like this. True, the two tall spoked wheels that marked a box cart were well designed for the island's sandy roads, just as the ungainly box that gave the vehicle its name was meant for thrifty flexibility, hauling passengers in their favorite chairs or a load of salt hay with equal aplomb.

But driving one in the customary fashion, standing tall behind the horse and between those two tall wheels, always made Daniel want to laugh himself at the silliness of it. Once he'd seen a engraving of some ancient Latin nobleman, standing aloof as he drove his chariot through the streets of Rome, and that was how Daniel always thought of a box cart now, his noble Nantucket chariot lurching its way across the moors.

And noble work his chariot would do this afternoon, too. He'd borrowed the cart for the express purpose of bringing Juliette to the squantum in the high style she deserved—Nantucket high style, that is. The cart itself had been newly whitewashed, and Bess curried until she gleamed like a copper penny in the afternoon sun. He'd strung brass sleigh bells in the harness for the cheerful music they made, and he'd even made sure that the chair in which Juliette would sit sported a new red cushion plumped high with sheep's wool. Today, for her, he wanted everything as perfect as he could make it.

For what seemed like the thousandth time he patted the front pocket of his waistcoat. Tucked inside was a ring, hammered as thin and fine as iron could be. He'd defy anyone to find the joining that made it a circle, so carefully had he wrought it, with the edges rounded and smooth as black silk. He'd buy her another of purest gold when he could take her to Boston, but for now this would do. A circle without end, like the promise the ring represented. He'd made sure that was perfect, too. Now all that remained was for him to ask Juliette to marry him, and for her to say yes.

Yes.

He shook his head, practicing his proposal one more time out loud to Bess. Tonight, he decided, after the squantum, with a new moon and a sky full of stars overhead. Once and for all, he'd let go of the past, and Catherine with it. He took a deep breath. Juliette was his love, and his future, and so was the child he might already have given her. The future, aye, the future: he must keep concentrating on that. He'd already told Juliette how much he loved her, and showed her each time they'd lain together in his bed. But tonight, with a slender band of black iron, he'd tell her he meant it to last forever.

He could make out the shingled roof of his house now, and he urged Bess on, eager to see Juliette again. True, it had only been this morning that he'd kissed her good-bye, a handful of hours, but even that had come to seem like an eternity away from her.

"Juliette!" he shouted as the cart rolled to a halt outside the fence. He tore off his hat and plopped the makeshift crown of morning-glory vines on his head. "Ahoy, lass!"

As soon as he heard the door opening he struck the straight-backed pose he'd planned, mimicking that stern old Roman in his chariot with one hand holding the reins and the other over his puffed-out chest, his head turned away at a supercilious angle to best display his manly profile.

"Why, Daniel," he heard her say. "Why, ah, look at you."

He held the pose, waiting for her to laugh. She'd been serious and sad enough these last days, sometimes so patently unhappy despite her denials that he feared she'd regretted becoming his lover. His lover: the single word didn't begin to encompass all she meant to him.

Still he waited, while Bess tossed her head and nickered, the bells on her harness jingling. He couldn't remember the last time he'd done something this foolish. Not since he'd come to Nantucket, that was certain. Never with Catherine, either. Probably not since he and Sam had been terrorizing Appledore with their misguided pranks.

Hell, what if Juliette didn't realize he was doing this on purpose to amuse her? What if she'd never seen an engraving of that old pagan in his chariot? What if she thought this was just one more sorry example of what an ass Daniel Fairbourne could be?

He cleared his throat uncomfortably. "Damnation, Juliette," he said. "Don't you have a word of greeting for your Caesar, eh?"

He heard a sputtering, gasping sound, and finally turned his head to look.

She was holding both hands over her mouth to keep the laughter in, laughter that was trying so hard to escape that her cheeks were bright pink with the effort. When her gaze met his, she gave up.

"Oh, Daniel!" she gasped as the laughter burst free. "I've never seen such a—such a—"

"Noble personage?" he suggested helpfully, and was delighted to hear her practically shriek in return. "Conquering hero?"

"More a wicked personage to do that to me!" She wiped the tears away from her eyes, the kind of merry tears he'd hoped to see. "I vow, Daniel, when I saw you, I was so afraid that this was some sort of odd island custom for the squantum, and that I'd have to keep from laughing the entire *day!*"

The laughter bubbled up inside her again, and he was sure he'd never heard a lovelier sound.

"Then you won't accompany me, fair lady?" he said,

striving to sound properly, pompously wounded. "It's almost time to leave, you know. You will not be my escort?"

"Not with those weeds in your hair, I won't," she said. "Climb down here directly so I can make you decent."

He sighed mightily as he swung down from the cart. "As you wish, ma'am."

"And I do wish it, sir." She reached up to tug away his makeshift wreath, chuckling still. "Especially since the rest of you looks so fine. You weren't wearing that shirt this morning."

"I changed at the shop after I finished work." He liked having her fuss like this over him, smoothing the revers of his coat, plucking at the collar of his shirt. "I shaved again, too."

"I noticed." She grinned and quickly leaned up to kiss his well-scraped cheek, darting away before he could gather her up for more. She laughed, and twirled before him. "Not that you've noticed *me*, mighty Caesar."

But he had. She'd kept the progress of the blue gown a secret from him, never letting him see enough of it while she cut or stitched to tell much of anything. He knew she was a seamstress by trade, so he'd expected a certain degree of competence, but he certainly wasn't prepared for the effect of the finished gown, or how she looked in it, either.

Though he didn't know the proper names for all the furbelows or flourishes any more than she could name the lines and spars on a ship, he could recognize a masterful piece of craftsmanship when he saw it. No ordinary seamstress could work a length of wool into this. Somehow she'd made her waist look enticingly small while the full skirts of her petticoat swirled so gracefully around her that she seemed to be dancing even when she stood still.

And the neckline—that neckline was going to keep him fighting off other men in droves. Dipping low to frame the creamy curves of her breasts above her stays, the gown's neckline balanced the exact line between being enticing and being inappropriate. With her silver-blond hair, he'd already known she was the most beautiful woman on the island; now she'd be hands down the most fashionable one as well.

"You look grand, lass," he said. "More than grand enough for poor old Caesar."

"You're not just saying that to please me?" she asked, anxiously smoothing the ribbons that criss-crossed her bodice. "I'll look right among the other women?"

"The other women will hate you," he answered with cheerful honesty, "but I, for one, love you, and I love you in that gown, no matter what the others say."

"Good," she said breathlessly, her face glowing with a happy excitement he hadn't seen enough of in the last two days. "Not about the other women hating me, for I don't wish that at all, but about you loving me, and loving the gown. Considering how much I love you, even with weeds in your hair, that is very good indeed."

"Indeed," he murmured, and if she hadn't been looking forward to the squantum so much, he would have used the afternoon away from the forge to love her in that gown and out of it, too.

"Indeed, indeed," she said, skipping back toward the house. "Let me fetch my hat and cloak, and I'll be back directly."

"And the pies," he called after her. The apple pies dotted with cranberries, their buttery crusts dusted with cinnamon sugar, were his contribution, and their shared secret. John Robin had informed him that no island woman would dare show her face at a squantum empty handed, though a man bearing food would be a bit suspect. "Mind you bring my pies."

He filled a bucket with water for Bess, studying the sky while she drank. Weather changed quickly on the island, as variable as if they truly were at sea, and the bright blue of early morning was now patched with gray clouds, and a damp chill rippling through the wind from the north. There hadn't been a day of serious rain since the night he'd found Juliette, and while they were likely due, he hoped the clouds would hold their peace—and raindrops—until after the squantum. He'd hate to see that fine blue gown hidden away beneath a sheet of old oilcloth.

Absently he patted the horse's neck, wondering where Sachem was. Since he'd gone to the shop for only half the day, he'd left the dog home to keep Juliette company. But as much as Sachem adored her, it struck Daniel as strange that he had yet to appear since he'd returned, unless the dog was roaming after some particularly elusive rabbit in the marsh.

"Where are you, boy?" he wondered out loud, and whistled for him to come.

He heard a muffled, grumbling growl from inside the house, then Sachem came slinking through the open door, his head bowed and his tail drooping with pure canine dejection and wretchedness.

And no wonder. Around Sachem's knotted rope collar Juliette had twined another made of the same ribbons on her gown, pale blue and dark rose, tied in little bows with trailing streamers. Shamefaced, the dog came to stand before Daniel, gazing up at his master in wordless but eloquent appeal.

"Doesn't Sachem look handsome?" asked Juliette as she brought the basket with the pies to the back of the cart. "I thought if we wore our best, he should, too."

Sachem gave a baleful whimper of protest. The garland of ribbons around his neck matched the one draped around the crown of her wide-brimmed straw hat, transformed now far beyond its original untrimmed severity. Flirtatious ribbons and love-knots belonged on a hat like that; on his poor dog, they looked, well, unnatural.

"It's a handsome sort of bow, aye," began Daniel, not wanting to hurt Juliette's feelings, "and it does look most handsome on Sachem. But I expect he'll want to run with the sheepdogs out in the fields, and then—"

"I haven't forgotten you, either, Daniel," she said, and reached up to tuck an extravagant knot of the same pink and blue ribbons into the top buttonhole of his coat. She stepped back to admire it, giving a little nod of satisfaction. "There! Now you look like the very model of an elegant gentleman of the town, wearing your lady's favors."

Daniel glanced down at the knot of gay silk ribbons fluttering from the front of his plain wool coat, then farther down to poor Sachem. Never before had he been so certain that he and Sachem could communicate sympathetically without benefit of the King's English.

"Juliette, love," he began again, as kindly as he could. "Juliette. I'm not rightly what you'd call a 'gentleman of the town,' and I don't believe you can call Sherburne much of a town, either, leastways not one that supports quite this many ribbons."

The happiness fell from her face. "You don't like it."

"Well, now," he said hastily, "I didn't say that, not exactly."

"Not exactly, no." She folded her arms over her chest. "But you'd rather go traipsing about the countryside wearing *weeds* in your hair."

"Not weeds, lass. Morning glories. *Caesar's* morning glories." He sighed, acknowledging he'd been bettered. He had a great many more important things to say to her today, and he didn't want them tripped up by a bundle of ribbons. "Let's compromise, sweetheart."

He bent down and unfastened the wreath from around Sachem's neck, then tied it instead to Bess's harness. "Now Sachem can go race about with the other dogs, and Bess can be queen o' the May among the horses."

In fact from the way that Bess was tossing her head, testing the feel of the ribbons on her head, it did seem as if she approved.

"And you?" asked Juliette, the corners of her mouth twitching. "Do you wish to run about with the other dogs on the moor, too, Daniel?"

"I do not." He held his hand out to help her up into the cart. "I'd rather wear my, ah, lady's favors, to help keep the other ladies at bay."

"I don't believe a word of that," she said happily as she climbed up. "But because I love you, I shall pretend I do. Daniel, there's only one chair."

He helped Sachem, now ecstatically ribbonless, hop into the cart, then fastened the back closed. "That's for you. In a box cart, passengers sit, and the driver stands."

"How foolish." She settled the baskets with the pies, draped her cloak over the red-cushioned chair, and came to stand beside him in the front of the cart. "If you stand, so shall I."

He frowned as he untangled the reins. "It's a long drive, lass, out along the Madeket Road. I don't want you tired out before we're even there. That's why I borrowed this blasted cart and horse in the first place."

"I know, and it was most sweet of you." She smiled, and braced herself, gripping the sides of the cart as tightly as if she expected to be catapulted out. "But I'd much prefer to stand here with you, and be your Lady Caesar."

He groaned, already imagining the comments that that enchanting blue gown was going to cause, without adding the remarks about her standing proud and precarious in the front of a box cart like a figurehead beneath the bowsprit.

"Here," he said, shifting her to stand in front of him, her back to his chest and his arms protectively holding her steady. He *would* protect her, too. He'd didn't doubt for a instant that he'd give his own life to keep her from harm—which, fortunately, in a slow-as-January-molasses box cart, wasn't much of an issue. "I don't want you toppling out."

But as she leaned back against him, the broad brim of her hat bumped against his chest and down over her eyes. She muttered crossly in French and yanked it forward, off her head.

"Standing *and* hatless," she said with a sigh of impatience as she tossed the hat back onto the chair behind them. "I wonder that you'll want to be seen with me at all, Daniel."

He chuckled, and bent to kiss the nape of her neck, now conveniently exposed. "You suit me to perfection.

But mind, you'll be the only lady on this island who arrives like this, Juliette."

"Likely I'm the only lady on this island who does a great many things, Daniel," she said. "Now shall we finally commence, or must I take the reins from you as well?"

Despite its determined sweetness, her smile was one dare he didn't want to take. He snapped the reins over Bess's back, and as easily as that, they commenced.

"Oh, Daniel," said Juliette uneasily as she looked at the crowds ahead of them. "There do seem to be a great many people here."

"I told you there would be, lass," he answered, concentrating on keeping an impatient Bess from bumping into the cart ahead of them. "Though if you don't wish to stay, I'll turn about now."

"No," she said with more enthusiasm than she felt. "I don't want to have come clear out this far from home for nothing."

She wouldn't have believed that this many people lived on the island, for as long as she'd been here she'd never seen more than a handful in one place at a single time, not even in Sherburne. But the return of the small whale fleet was cause enough for celebration, especially since, as Daniel had told her, all but three of the Nantucket men had returned safely to their families. Most of the sloops had been gone for two months, first sailing south to hunt off the Carolinas and then, as the waters had grown warmer and the summer days longer, they'd followed the whales north to Casco Bay and Newfoundland, long, hard voyages filled with danger and back-breaking labor.

Now those same men and their families had journeyed out to this field used for a sheep pasture off the Eel Point Road, not far from Dionis, coming on foot and on horseback but mostly by box cart. Already a small herd of horses and mules, freed from their harnesses, were tethered and grazing together under the haphazard watch of boys more interested in stone-tossing contests among themselves. Younger children darted about, dodging horses, parents, and general disaster, while the family sheepdogs tried to herd the children with the same barking authority they used with lambs and ewes.

Beneath a well-patched mainsail that had been rigged as a makeshift tent, women of every age gossiped and laughed and unpacked the food they'd brought. Neat fingers of cornbread, crocks of honey and butter, ears of piebald Indian corn to be shucked and roasted, plates of fried chicken and potatoes, and pies of every kind, savory and sweet, molasses, pumpkin, blueberry, apple, and beach-plum, all were carefully set out on broad plank tables and covered lightly with red-and-blue checked cloths to keep away the flies. Pits had been dug and lined with beach stones earlier in the morning, filled with driftwood fires that by now had burned down to smoldering coals layered with wet seaweed and clams to steam in their shells. To one side the men gathered in smaller groups to smoke their pipes and drink rum from half-hidden bottles and jugs, bragging among themselves over which sloop had returned with the most whale oil and the greatest profits.

Yet despite all the laughter and high spirits that ruled the scene before them, Juliette still felt her palms grow damp and her mouth turn dry. True, those happy, laughing women could welcome her as warmly as Mrs. Swain, but just as many or more might turn as cold and hostile as Mrs. Greene or the three women who'd called at Daniel's house, their laughter turning into icy, hateful stares of disapproval.

Daniel guided their cart to a place among the others and unfastened Bess. Juliette reached for her hat, and wished that her fingers weren't shaking as she tied the ribbons beneath her chin. She didn't want to be the centerpiece of an ugly scene. She wanted this day to be special, and everything wonderful that Daniel had promised. She wanted to be lighthearted and laugh like the rest of the women, and to dance on the grass with her skirts flying while the fiddlers played jigs and reels. Most of all, she wanted to be like any other lass walking with her sweetheart, his hand around her waist and her head bent close to his.

"What did I tell you, love?" said Daniel gallantly as he helped her down. "You're the fairest woman here, hands down."

"Oh, Daniel," she said, letting her hands linger upon his shoulders after her feet had touched the ground. "I wish that were all that worried me. What if we see Mrs. Greene, or Mrs. Griggs, and they try—"

"Then quit your worrying right now, sweetheart, because they won't dare bother you today, not here," he said. He smiled warmly, straightening her hat for her. "And even if they did, we'd face them together this time, and send them scurrying exactly as you did before. You're no coward, Juliette. It's one of the things I love most about you."

"But if they try to slander you—"

"Then they'll have begun a bigger fight than they'd wished," he said firmly. "Most islanders are good, honest people, who'd rather wish others well than not. Including you, duck."

"I pray you're right." Her grateful smile was wobbly as she pulled the little black sun from her pocket to show him.

"Look," she said. "For luck."

He grinned and rubbed his hand over his mouth, more pleased than he could say.

"I didn't know you'd even kept that foolish little thing," he said finally. "Not that you need it, or anything else, for luck. You're already about the luckiest creature I've ever seen."

"Luckiest of all to be found by you." But as she leaned forward to kiss him, two young women pointedly slowed their sauntering pace to study both Daniel and Juliette with bold, sly-eyed interest. Self-consciously Juliette tugged at the front of her gown; perhaps she *was* too stylish, compared to everyone else, and for the first time in her life she caught herself wishing for a daub of dowdiness to fit in with the others.

"I tell you, lass, you'll outdo them all," said Daniel proudly as if he could read her thoughts—which sometimes she was quite sure he could. He took her hand and tucked it into the crook of his arm, hoisting the basket with their pies in his other hand. "It's them that's drab and plain, not you that's too fair. Why, if you wished it, you could have half of these women fair begging you to rig them out."

Juliette smiled uneasily. While dressing a whalerman's wife was a far cry from the governor's lady, she wondered again if somehow he'd guessed her life in Boston along with her own insecurities. These last two days, she'd been unable to decide whether telling Daniel the truth could possibly be worse than keeping it from him. She'd trusted him with her life and her heart. Why was it so hard to trust him with this last secret?

Because it was this last secret that could destroy their love.

"There you go, looking sad again, even after I'd stuck those damned vines in my hair. To keep you happy, I suppose I'll have to make an even greater ass of myself, capering before the fiddlers." Daniel sighed dramatically, tugging her forward. "Come, let's go try to pretend we know what we're about here."

Juliette slipped the sun back into her pocket, its weight comforting against her leg. "I'm the helpless ninny, Daniel, not you. You must have been to scores of other squantums."

"Nary a one," he confessed easily. "I'm as much a greenhorn here as you."

"You? Not once?" She stared at him skeptically. Men like Daniel Fairbourne would be regarded as rare catches anywhere, even—or especially—here on Nantucket. A gathering like this one should have had every scheming mama with an unmarried daughter panting after him. She'd already seen the women glancing his way with undisguised admiration, and with no regard for her on his arm, either.

"You have my word on it, Juliette," he said as he led her through the groups of people, forging a path for them toward the sailcloth tent with the food. "Sachem and I have kept our own company, gloomy old bachelors by the fire together, and that has been all."

"But you said you weren't—you weren't always alone," she blurted, blushing furiously at saying something so private in so public a place. "That is, I wasn't—oh, bother, you know what I'm trying to say!"

"That was long ago, Juliette," he said firmly, walking faster as if he could physically leave the subject behind him. "I'm only talking about the years that I've lived here, and even that shouldn't matter to you. I've told you before to judge me by what I am, not what I was, same as I do with you. It's the future that belongs to us together, love. Now let that be enough."

"But it isn't," she protested breathlessly, wishing he'd slow so she wouldn't feel as if he were dragging her. "What I've done, where I've been, who my people are and were, have made me who I am now with you. You can't wish away your life, Daniel, even if—"

"A sweet for the lady, cap'n?" asked a stout woman with a tray of candy before her. "Sweeten her tongue, sweeten your luck, eh, cap'n? Licorice and peppermint, horehound and butterscotch, cap'n, five for a ha'penny."

"I'm no captain, mistress," said Daniel, more sharply than Juliette thought necessary, though he dropped a coin in the woman's wooden cup and scooped a paper packet of the candies from the tray. "And my lady's tongue is already sweet enough for me."

The woman guffawed as Daniel pushed ahead through the crowd, pulling Juliette after him.

"Daniel, wait," she protested. "You cannot ignore the past simply because you didn't care for it."

"A peppermint, lass?" he asked, stopping abruptly as he tore open the brown paper. "I saw that old biddy buying her sweets from the ship that docked yesterday, so her wares should be fresh enough."

She shook her head, and he slipped the candy into his own mouth instead. He certainly still looked like her Daniel standing there, his black hair and the ribbon cockade on his coat both ruffling gently in the breeze, his thick muscled arm holding the heavy basket effortlessly, and the bulge of the peppermint showing in his clean-shaven cheek above the jaw. But something was different, something she could sense rather than see, as she grasped his arm to try to make him listen in the bustle around them.

"Daniel, love, look at me," she said, her voice low and urgent. "You've spoken like this before, and you've never yet made sense. We can't undo the past, nor would I wish to, not for either of us."

His black brows drew together in a noncommittal frown as he rolled the peppermint around inside his mouth with his tongue. "Fine words from you, Juliette, who can barely recall who you *are.*"

She sucked in her breath. "That's not fair, Daniel."

"It's not fair, no," he agreed bluntly. "But it is the truth."

That hurt; that *hurt,* and what was worse was knowing it was meant to.

Yet there was something in his expression that told her he was speaking defensively, that the pain he brought her was scant compared to what he felt himself. There was a reason for the haunted emptiness that showed so often in those pale eyes of his, the eyes that were whispered to have no soul. She thought of those odd little evasive slips and slides he'd made to her over the last weeks, his continued insistence that the past was of no importance, things that must surely fit together into an explanation. She loved him too dearly to see that suffering continue, and relentlessly she continued, hoping to find the reasons for his anguish, and the cure.

"What you did today, Daniel, playing at being Caesar to make me laugh," she said, trying another guess as she searched his face for clues, "you couldn't have done that for me without all the mischief you and your brother wrought as boys."

Behind him the sky had turned more gray than blue, the darkening clouds as unsettled as Daniel himself. "I don't see what the devil you and me or anything else has to do with Sam."

"But he does," she insisted, "the same as Amelie is a part of me. Your brothers and your sister and your parents, that little town where you were born, too—they've all had a share of making you who you are now."

She saw the indecision hovering in his eyes, the fleeting vulnerability that he'd hidden so well for so long. All around them people were still chattering and laughing, and in the distance she heard some child's shrill, rising wail of injustice.

"Please tell me, Daniel," she coaxed gently. "You wouldn't wish Sam from your life, would you?"

He bit down hard on the candy, shattering it with his teeth. "I already have," he said, "the same as Sam's done with me."

"Master Fairbourne!" Giggling, Betsey Swain bumped into Daniel, her hat slightly askew and her round cheeks gleaming like polished apples. Her fingers were locked tight in the hand of a young man with a red face to match her own, and nearly white hair that bristled out from beneath his hat like bits of pale straw. "And Mistress Juliette! Oh, my, I'd never expected to see the pair o' you here like this!"

"And why not, Betsey?" said Daniel heartily. "We've come to celebrate, same as everyone else. Eleazer Gibb, lad, you've done well in James Pease's sloop this season, haven't you?"

"Aye, aye, sir," the young man replied, if possible flushing to an even deeper shade of crimson. "Next summer cap'n says I'll be ranked mate, an' double my shares."

"But only if he signs on for longer," interrupted Betsey proudly. "cap'n Pease means to go out for five months straight next year to sail farther, on account o' the whales turning scarce near to home."

"That's a long time for you two to be apart, Betsey," said Juliette. "Especially since you'll be so newly wed."

A half an hour ago, Juliette would have judged five months to be an endless separation from Daniel. But now, while she watched him be all bluff and jolly with Betsey and Eleazer after what he'd said, or hadn't said, to her, she decided in her frustration and unhappiness that five months might not be nearly enough.

Not, of course, that Daniel seemed to be noticing.

"Finally showing the good sense to marry this pretty lass, are you?" he declared now, clapping Eleazer on the shoulder so hard he nearly knocked him over. "If any woman will know how to keep you on a straight course, Eleazer, it will be Miss Betsey here."

"I thank you for your good wishes, too, miss—I mean Juliette," said Betsey to Juliette with a jerky curtsey. "Mam told me you'd come round to say so."

"Oh, I do wish you all joy, Betsey," said Juliette in a belated rush, regretting that she'd let her own feelings shadow the younger couple's happiness. She leaned forward to hug Betsey, kissing her on both cheeks.

Betsey twitched and smiled shyly. "Do you think you might help me with a new gown for the wedding? Mam said I shouldn't bother you with such, that it was being overbold and familiar, but you being such a fine seamstress and all, I'd be hoping—"

"There's nothing I'd like better," said Juliette warmly. "Anything to help turn true love into a happy marriage."

"Amen to that," said Daniel softly behind her, his voice so uncharacteristically fervent that she turned in surprise.

Though his hand lay still on the younger man's shoulder, his expression had lost its jocularity, his gaze so intent upon her that she felt it as strongly as an actual caress. Looking at her this way, he made her feel as if she stood in the center of this crowd of people as naked as if she'd been in his bed under the coverlet with only him.

But instead of feeling shame at these wicked thoughts, her body seemed to ache and grow heavy with such longing that she wished that everyone else would vanish in an instant so that she and Daniel could find a place for loving and wantonness and bliss, here on this moor beneath the cloud-tossed skies.

"Come with me, lass," he said, his voice low as if again he read her thoughts, and shared them, too. "There's still plenty awaiting us."

Plenty, and more plenty, thought Juliette, as she linked her fingers demurely into his. His hand was rough from work, his fingers thick and strong, and even at so respectable a touch she felt her heart race as if those same hands were moving over her breasts, her bottom, her most intimate places. . . .

"Listen!" exclaimed Betsey, pulling excitedly on Eleazer's arm. "I can hear the fiddles! Oh, they must be beginning the dancing!"

The sounds of the fiddlers tuning their instruments was enough to bring a rush of excitement through the younger people. Daniel left the pie basket with the rest of the food, and together with Juliette followed the others. Because of the clouds overhead and the wisps of fog beginning to blow in from the sea, the dancing had been moved inside the large barn near the sailcloth tent. With another few weeks before harvest, the wide-planked threshing floors were open and clean, and already couples were hurrying to take their places.

The three fiddlers, two Irishmen and a Scot who more usually served as sailors, had been delighted to climb into the empty salt-hay loft as an improvised balcony, raucously calling down to their friends and crewmates below. Even with the doors thrown open, the barn was warm and growing warmer. Most men shed their coats, some their waistcoats as well, while the women contented themselves with pushing their sleeves higher over their forearms and ostentatiously fluttering the carved bone or painted chickenskin fans that had been sweethearts' gifts, newly bought with whaling wages.

"We'll dance only if you wish it, Juliette," said Daniel as he and Juliette squeezed their way inside. He had to lean close to her ear as he spoke, to be heard over the fiddles and whoops of the dancers. "I won't think less of you if you don't."

"But of course I do!" The first dance had begun, with more raucous enthusiasm than skill, and Juliette had already spotted Eleazer's white hair bobbing across from Betsey's ribbons. "I won't shame you, Daniel. I learned my steps from a dancing master who'd taught the noblemen's children at Versailles."

"Oh, aye," he scoffed, screwing up his face to show he didn't believe her. "And I learned from a mermaid who danced on the scales of her fish tail upon the sands at midnight."

"Hush," she scolded, swatting him for good measure. "At least my story's true. Monsieur Dumaire was a friend of my mother's—there weren't so very many French people in Boston that we didn't all know one another—and he taught Amelie and me as a favor."

He looked at her curiously. "That wasn't what I meant, lass. I didn't question that you knew how to dance, only if you wished to."

"Because of my limp, then," she said quickly, avoiding the other question lingering there between them. *In Boston:* what had made her say that now? The first reel had ended, and impulsively she seized both his hands, drawing him out to take a place opposite her in the twin lines of dancers. "I have always kept a wicked pace with you, Master Fairbourne, and I'm not about to lag behind you now."

"Done," he said, and she should have known from the gleam in his eye that he'd try his best to make her regret that challenge. He was too large a man to be the sort of graceful dancer that old Monsieur Dumaire had been, but, as Juliette quickly learned, stamina was far more important for a raucous country jig like "The Black Nag."

Laughing and breathless, she practically fell into Daniel's arms when the music stopped.

"Surrender?" he asked, shrugging out of his coat.

"Not by half," she declared with a grin, and untied her hat to drop it on top of his coat.

They lasted through another jig, two hornpipes, and a fandango, and when Juliette felt sure she'd have to give in and rest, the fiddlers showed mercy on the dancers, and the next tune called was "Green Sleeves & Yellow Lace." Not only was it slow enough to let Juliette catch her breath, but the sets allowed partners to meet and whisper a word or two as they followed the easier steps across the floor.

"I wish I'd wagered on how long you'd stay, sweetheart," said Daniel as he linked his arm with hers and turned. "No one would've believed a tender creature like you could dance like she'd outlast the devil himself."

"Meaning yourself?" she teased, pointedly looking down at his shoes. "You dance powerfully well for having cloven feet."

"Be careful what you say, lass," he cautioned. "Considering that you're my partner, eh?"

She smiled, letting him finish the turn before she slipped free with a graceful extra swirl of her skirts.

He nodded, waiting for the beat to step away from her. "Though perhaps," he said in the last instant, almost an aside, "perhaps such things are often said in Boston."

She gasped, but he'd already turned away, and in her agitation she misstepped badly, bumping into an older man with a pock-marked face. Somehow she mumbled her apology, her heart racing with dread as she finished out the step that would bring her back to Daniel.

Why had she made such a foolish slip? Why had she tried to hide in the first place, and made this inevitable moment so much worse?

Her hand slipped into his, her chin raised to meet his gaze. "I am from Boston, yes. I know that now."

"And so, finally, do I." His expression didn't change, his voice the same low murmur for her ears alone. "And what did you do there in Boston, I wonder?"

The truth, only the truth would do now. "I own a milliner's shop with Amelie in Marlborough Street, with mantua-making for ladies."

"In Marlborough Street," he said, and to her sorrow she saw the significance of that fashionable address register in his eyes. "Right there in the velvet lap of the gentry, eh? You must prosper, you and Amelie."

"We—we do." She gulped, the air suddenly so close she could scarcely breathe. "We work hard, and we've been fortunate."

"Fortunate," he repeated softly. "Jesus. How much else were you going to have me to guess about you, Juliette?"

"I was going to tell you, Daniel, soon, I swear it!"

"Oh, aye," he said, somehow keeping them in time to the music. "You wanted so badly for me to trust you with my secrets when you couldn't be bothered to trust me with the biggest one you knew."

"I did it because I love you, Daniel!" She heard the catch of fear in her own voice, loud enough that the man with the pock-marked face looked questioningly as the dance returned her to his side.

Turn and pause, step, turn and pause, and take Daniel's hand again.

"No wonder my sad little past was of such interest to you," he said, and she heard the pain, more pain, keening through his bitterness, "when all the time yours was beckoning you back to Boston. To goddamned *Boston.*"

"Daniel, love, please," she cried, heedless of the other dancers' hearing. "I would have come back to you!"

Men's shouts, from outside the barn and in, a horse's single nervous whinny, "Green Sleeves" disintegrating into a discordant jumble as dancers and watchers turned in unison toward the door, toward the man on the horse.

"All hands, all hands!" he roared. "There's a ship aground off Eel Point! All hands, all hands, to save her people!"

"I must go," said Daniel. "They'll need me."

And without once looking back at Juliette, he left.

Chapter 11

With Sachem at her feet, Juliette stood at the top of the beach beside Mrs. Swain and Betsey, part of a small, huddled group of women that had followed the men from the squantum. There were no children with them, for it was grimly understood that no children belonged here, not now.

With the cruel ease of the New England sea, the bright morning had disintegrated and disappeared into this cold, heavy, unforgiving evening, wet and chill on the skin. The waves were tall as a man and laced with white foam as they broke, crashed, and sputtered over and over across the sand and rocks. The clouds and fog had shrouded the sun into early darkness, and the wind that blew from the water brought with it salt and spray and biting grains of sand that made the women hold their cloaks and shawls over their faces, to their eyes, as they stared out across the beach and the water at the scene unfolding before them.

The small sloop had been blown far off its course to

have so completely missed the entry to the harbor at Sherburne. Clearly her captain had been feeling his way in the fog, searching blindly for the passage near Brant Point, when instead he'd driven the sloop aground, deep into the shallow bottom where she'd be held tight. Now the sloop canted sideways at an uneasy angle, the surf dashing into her exposed hull and washing over her deck. Her mainsail had already shredded away before her crew could take it in, and the topsail spars had snapped off like twigs, the tattered canvas trailing like wilted leaves. More ominous still were the remains of the sloop's single boat dangling from one of the davits, its hull dashed against the side of the sloop in a disastrous attempt to escape the wreck.

But what drew the gaze of everyone on the beach were the five tiny figures on that slanting deck, bracing themselves against the waves by clinging to the lifelines near the mainmast or crouched beside the hatch. They'd given up trying to save the sloop; now all they could pray for was to be saved themselves.

The Nantucket men would do their best. Someone had remembered a dory that could be dragged from a nearby beach, and Daniel had gone with them, being strongest. Someone else had run to fetch extra oars for extra hands to row through the heavy surf. Coils of heavy rope appeared from the backs of box carts, as well as old coverlets to wrap around the shoulders of both rescued and rescuers. A small, fluttering fire of driftwood was lit in a dug-out pit in the sand to shield it from the wind, as much to give a beacon of light and hope to those on the sloop as for the rescuers to warm themselves.

Though the island had no organized brigade or rescue

crew, the way some towns on the mainland were beginning to do, the Nantucket men did have the experience of having lived their lives surrounded by the sea, with most of them mariners themselves. They knew the dangers and the risks of attempting such a rescue in heavy surf, but they also knew the certain agony and death that awaited the sloop's crew if they didn't.

And so, to her growing panic, did Juliette. These were experiences she didn't want to remember, not ever, images she wanted to keep back, and yet back that awful lost night was returning, relentlessly, piece by piece.

The trip down the coast to New York had been joyous enough, accompanying the wedding party of one of her best customers. She'd dressed all the women in the family, lavishly enough to double the shop's profits for the entire year. It had been an honor to be included as a guest, but the second part of her journey was to be all pleasure. She'd booked her passage home to Boston by way of Appledore on Cape Cod, where Amelie now lived with her husband Zachariah and where Amelie had opened a second millinery shop of the famed Sisters Lacroix.

The *Lively* was newly refurbished and bright with fresh paint, Juliette's cabin spacious, the captain older, experienced, and gruffly courteous. But off the Connecticut coast the weather had turned rough and the *Lively*'s bright-painted hull began to leak and take water, gallons and gallons of water. The exhausted crew had toiled at the pumps, forgetting Juliette alone on the deck as the sinking ship had wallowed deeper and deeper into the troughs of the waves.

They'd forgotten her, but now, dear God, she remembered it all.

Of the women with her here on the dune where the wind beat back the tall grasses around their feet, only she knew the terrifying feel of a ship turned heavy and lifeless beneath her, the timbers groaning and cracking in laboring protest with the force of each wave, of being left by herself on a sinking ship.

She alone knew how slippery and treacherous that slanting deck was underfoot, how the railing that you trusted for support would splinter away in your hands, how icy cold the water was when it struck your face and filled your shoes and soaked your clothes, or the way those wet clothes would cling to your legs like a sodden shroud and try to drag you down no matter how you struggled.

She knew how any cry or wail for mercy or help would only be swallowed up by the mocking wind, how the snug sanctuary of your cabin could flood and become the coffin in which you would sink, how every effort to save yourself would be as ineffectual as a babe's against the force of the waves.

She alone among these women knew how hard it would be to survive, and how easy, how terrifyingly easy, it would be to die.

"Off-islanders, for certain," announced Mrs. Swain to no one in particular as the wind snapped her skirts tight against her legs. "And fools just as true. Driving into a sandy bottom like that in the clear light o' day, sure to be broken up and gone to pieces by morning. Makes me be wondering if the master likes his rum too well, well enough to die for it, I say."

Beside her Betsey shifted restlessly. "Why can't I go down by the fire, Mam? I'm chilled near to the bone."

"You'll be staying with us," said her mother sharply. "This be your place now, not sidling up alongsides Eleazer when he's work to do."

"He won't be going out in the boat."

Mrs. Swain snorted. "Oh, aye, isn't that a mercy!"

"But, Mam—"

"You want to be a sailor's wife," said Mrs. Swain sternly. "Well, then, you must learn the sorrow as well as the joys. Your place is here, daughter, and I won't have you going where you don't belong."

Sorrow and joys, thought Juliette, clenching her fingers into fists inside her cloak, *sorrow and joys,* the words ringing like the toll of a fine-cast meeting house bell, *sorrow and joys. . . .*

Betsey scowled impatiently, fidgeting with the clasp on her cloak. "I don't see what use I am here."

"Because your man will see you're here, waiting for his safe return," said her mother. "Because he'll carry that, like a picture carved in his heart, with him wherever he sails. Because when he's done his work here tonight, we'll be the ones to comfort them that need comforting, or tend to the bodies of them that don't."

The bodies of them that don't. . . .

Oh, Juliette knew of those, too, more than she'd ever wished to, and though she swallowed back the sob that tightened her throat she sank down to her knees to press her cheek against Sachem's back. His silky fur was beaded with salt spray, the feathers on his dewclaws and tail clumped inelegantly with sand. But the low conversational yip he made was meant to comfort her, she was sure, as was the way he tipped his head when he turned to look at her. She closed her eyes and slipped her arms around the dog, desperately needing to feel linked to something warm and alive, something that was still a part of Daniel.

She didn't want to be here. The Swains had brought her in their cart, sure she'd wish to watch Daniel—"your Mr. Fairbourne" Mrs. Swain had called him with approval—lead the rescue. But she didn't want to see him risk his life to do it, either, or any more of the wrecked sloop, or the terrified crew huddled on her deck, or what would become of them if the boat couldn't reach them in time.

What she wanted was to be home in the little house on the south shore, eating cornbread with Daniel and laughing as he licked the honey as it trickled down between her fingers and kissing him to taste the sweetness on his lips. She wanted all the ugly words they'd spoken while they danced unsaid, even unthought.

She wanted him to love her the way he had before, the way she still did him.

"So that be the boat they'll use," exclaimed Mrs. Swain with undisguised disapproval. "Look at that little cockleshell, now! They'll be making two, maybe three trips to clear everyone off in that! Oh, how I wouldn't want to be going out in them waves in a boat such as that!"

And Juliette looked, peeking over Sachem's back, unable to help herself. As Mrs. Swain had said, the boat was small, only big enough for four men at the oars, not half the size used on the big ships for blue-water whaling. But the men on the beach were still dragging it across the beach toward the water, bending their backs to move it as fast as they could through the sand.

"Juliette," said Daniel, suddenly before her.

Sachem whimpered with delight, prancing his front

paws as he whipped his tail. Crouched down beside him, Juliette's eyes were level with the pewter buckles on the outside knees of Daniel's breeches. Slowly she looked up, her heart thrumming, too unsure of what she'd find when she reached his face to hurry. He was breathing hard from helping pull the heavy boat, his broad chest rising and falling beneath his coat.

But in the top buttonhole of his coat was the love-knot of pink ribbons she'd made for him to match her gown, oh, at least a hundred years ago. The ribbons were lank and drooping, hopelessly forlorn. But he hadn't tossed the knot away. He'd kept it where she'd tucked it herself, and that was enough to make her finally dare to raise her gaze to find his.

But the welcome the drooping ribbons had promised wasn't there. Instead his face was studiously without emotion, his eyes guarded and his mouth set.

"Juliette," he said again, bending to ruffle Sachem's ears before he took her hand to lift her to her feet. His neck cloth was gone and so was his hat, either lost or set aside for safekeeping, and his black hair, like Sachem's fur, was beaded and slick with spray. "Come, lass, I haven't much time."

He glanced over his shoulder, watching the others toss the ropes and oars into the boat as he dug his fingers into the pocket of his waistcoat. He was still holding her hand in his, and she couldn't tell whose fingers were colder.

"Daniel, please," she said, the most she could manage. She was trembling, shaking so with the cold and fear and memories that she couldn't stop, and all she wanted was for him to take her into his warmth and hold her. "Daniel."

"Hush, sweetheart, and mark what I say." He'd found what he'd been seeking in his pocket, and now he raised her hand higher, nearly level to her eyes. "When this is done, I will marry you."

Numbly she watched as he pushed a narrow black ring onto her finger, holding it tight there so it wouldn't slip from her icy hand. Beside her Mrs. Swain gasped, louder than the waves.

"You'll be my wife, Juliette," he said hoarsely, as if to answer for her when she didn't. "You'll be Juliette Fairbourne."

One of the men at the water's edge shouted his name for him to come. She recognized the black, braided hair and darker face of John Robin Namis looking back for Daniel. The boat was bobbing on the waves now, the others waiting only for Daniel to join them.

"You stay and watch her, Sachem, mind?" he said, and the dog whimpered in agreement as his master patted him for the last time. "You keep Juliette safe for me."

Quickly he folded Juliette's fingers over the ring, holding her hand a moment longer, then bent forward to brush his lips over hers, too fast to be called a kiss.

"You won't forget me, will you, lass?" he asked, and for the first time he let her see the desperation in his face that was a mirror of her own. "Remember me, Juliette, and remember that I loved you."

He turned before she could answer and plunged down the dune toward the others. He splashed through the shallows and pulled himself into the boat, sliding onto the last bench beside John Robin and grabbing his oar in a single practiced motion. The prow of the boat nosed into a wave, rocking upward to hang there as the first two men struggled to pull the boat over the crest. But it was Daniel who made the difference, digging in with a strength and urgency that sent the boat shooting over the first wave and toward the wrecked sloop.

Blindly Juliette felt for the unfamiliar ring on her finger, clutching one hand over the other. She recognized the feel of iron from the little wrought sun, recognized it, too, for the metal's meaning to Daniel. No one else could have made such a ring, and he'd done it only for her. A ring glittering with diamonds or rubies could never mean more than this simple band from him. And since he'd had it in his pocket now, he must have been planning to give it to her sometime today at the squantum, before they'd danced together and everything had fallen apart.

"That be a good man, miss," said Mrs. Swain as she slipped her arm around Juliette's shoulders. "You couldn't find better than your Mr. Fairbourne, not if you searched the whole world."

"But why *now?*" asked Juliette, her voice breaking with her heart as she watched the small boat fighting through the waves. "Why did he do this *now?*"

Mrs. Swain sighed sympathetically. "Because he *is* a good man, miss, that's why. He knows you'll be looked after proper now. After you two been together so much since he found you, well, there's some who'll say things weren't as they should have been between a man and woman who weren't wed. But he's righted that for you now, hasn't he?"

"He didn't give me a chance to answer," whispered Juliette. She felt as if she were cracking inside, shattering into too many tiny, sharp-edged pieces to ever be put back together again. "I didn't tell him anything."

"Be brave now, lamb," said Mrs. Swain gently. "Be

brave, and pray. That's all he'd want from you. He's done what he could for you before he left. It's a merciful errand he's on, true enough, but that don't take away the danger. You know how the sea will be. Who lives and who dies be God's decision, not ours."

Who lives and who dies. . . .

But not Daniel, not with so much left unsaid between them. She couldn't have been spared from drowning only to lose him the same way. Not Daniel, not like this. Daniel could master a boat as readily as he could bend a bar of iron; Daniel was good and tall and strong, the strongest man she'd ever known.

But she knew how much stronger the waves could be, how cold, how they'd close over your head and steal your breath and your life and your soul.

And her love and happiness with it.

And with a muffled cry of anguish, Juliette sank to her knees on the sand.

"Jump, man!" roared Daniel. "Jump *now!*"

Still the sailor hesitated, clinging desperately to either side of the rail as he stood at the entry port of the wrecked sloop. He was an older man, the knobs of his wrists showing at his cuffs, his white-streaked hair plastered wet like a veil over his wild-eyed face.

Daniel felt the boat surge forward again toward the tall, slanting wall of the sloop's side, and he and John Robin wrenched their oars back astern to keep the boat from crashing into splinters. Careful, he warned himself silently, careful there; the last thing he wanted was to end up drowned himself, not with Juliette waiting for him on the beach.

For an instant he let himself remember the speechless bewilderment in her blue eyes as he'd clumsily slipped the iron ring onto her finger. That hadn't been anything like the proposal he'd planned, without any stars or flowers or the carefully rehearsed declarations. It wasn't the way to make her forget about Boston, that was sure. It had been terse, even abrupt, born of desperation instead of love. Love: hell, he hadn't said all he wanted to about love, and he transferred all his disappointment and despair to the man poised in the fog and mist above them.

The boat was riding too low in the water now for easy maneuvering, with two shivering seamen already pulled from the water and into the small boat. This man would be the last they could gather before they returned to shore, decided Daniel, then back here again for the rest, if the sloop held together long enough. The waves were growing stronger, driving hard against the overstressed hull and deck; he wouldn't lay a farthing that there'd be anything left at all by daybreak.

"Now, blast you!" shouted Daniel as the boat swung back, widening the open water for the man between them and the sloop. The two lifelines floated waiting on the surface, ready for him to grab. He wouldn't have a better chance, not in this life. "*Jump!*"

And at last he did, falling feetfirst into the water with his skinny arms flailing over his head. But once in the water, he knew what to do, pushing his way back to the surface far faster than the other two had done. Coughing and gasping from the shock of the water's cold, he still managed to grab one of the lifelines, and quickly the two men at the for'ard oars pulled him over the side and into the boat, carrying what seemed like half the sea with him.

"Turn short round," called Daniel, anxious to move away from the wreck. Sitting as heavily as they did in the water, his greatest fear now was that they'd broach to and capsize in the heavy surf. "We'll head back in to shore."

Obediently the others followed, all of them having pulled enough oars to understand the orders. Not one commented on how their town's blacksmith seemed as experienced as many blue-water shipmasters; what mattered was that they trusted him.

Just as he prayed Juliette could trust him still. . . .

"There be only two more left aboard her," the newly rescued sailor was saying through chattering teeth, clutching a blanket over his quaking shoulders. "Goddamned stinking excuse for a ship."

"Mind your mouth, man," warned Daniel, too weary to embroil himself in shipboard intrigue. "Tell me the name of your vessel instead."

"Sloop *Raven,* sir," he answered, instantly contrite. "Two days out of New Bedford, with a cargo of pine and tar for Sherburne town. Asa Martin, sir, seaman."

The scavengers would have a feast day tomorrow, thought Daniel, preying on a beach littered with kegs of tar and lumber. "And your captain's name?"

"Timothy Wallerson, sir," mumbled the man.

That made sense, thought Daniel, the captain being the last to leave the ship. Some masters wouldn't leave at all, preferring to go down with their vessel rather than face the shame of having lost their command.

Damnation, but he was tired. Every muscle in his body twitched and ached from rowing, mostly against the waves and in the cold bath of a mist and fog. He figured they must have spent a good hour, maybe longer, out there fetching these four. He could see the beach clearly now, with many more figures, some with lanterns, silhouetted around the low fire, and he could almost taste the hot coffee that would be steaming in the pots.

He could turn his oar over to another now, let some other man row out for the captain and the other last sailor. No one would blame him, and a fresh set of arms would make sense. He looked farther up the beach, to the somber line of women still on the dunes. One of them would be Juliette, with Sachem beside her, both of them waiting for him. For *him:* how long had it been since such a lovely thing could be said of him?

One last pull, and the boat glided into the shallows. At once they were surrounded by island men, pulling the boat in and reaching out to the shivering men who'd been rescued. More exhausted than he'd realized, Daniel let himself sag over his oar as he felt the boat settle on sand.

"Thee has done well, Daniel," said Robert Ellis as he clapped Daniel on the shoulder. "As thee always does. How many unfortunates did thee gather this time?"

"Three." Daniel stretched, wincing at how the damp cold had settled in his lower back. "You'll be offering them shelter at your house?"

"As I always do, too?" The tall Quaker flashed a rare smile beneath the wide brim of his beaver hat. "Thee knows me well, Daniel. Any lost that thee knows?"

Daniel shook his head. "There's still two more aboard, the captain and another sailor. Have you seen Miss Lacroix, Robert? She'll be with Sachem."

"The cap'n, aye, *he's* aboard, but not 'nother sailor," interrupted Asa Martin as he balanced, awkward as a wet stork, on the bench behind Daniel. "It be the cap'n, an' the cap'n's *wife.*"

"The captain's *wife?*" Daniel stared at Martin, his conscience writhing as all the old nightmares sped through his thoughts. Of all the cruel tricks that fate had tossed his way, surely this was the one guaranteed to trip him up short.

The last person on board the wreck was a woman.

A woman like Juliette, like Catherine.

"I'm going back out," he said, dropping back down on the bench. "I can't leave the lady to suffer out there."

"It's this thee cannot do, Daniel," said Ellis. Behind him stood Daniel's replacement, a tall harpooner from the whale ships named Crown, broad backed and capable, waiting self-consciously to take Daniel's seat along with the two other fresh men already at the for'ard oars. "It is gallant of thee to be concerned with the woman's welfare, but thee is too tired."

Tempted, he let himself glance one more time up to where Juliette must be standing. As much as he wanted to be with her now, he *needed* her to be proud of him.

"Let this man take thy place," urged Ellis gently. "The time is passing, Daniel, and thee could do more harm than good if thee insists on going. Thee doesn't need to prove that thee is a hero."

But he did. That had been among the last things that Catherine had said to him, wasn't it?

"I thought you were different, Daniel dear," she'd said as she'd flicked her skirts disdainfully away from his feet, the angry tears she'd first shed already dry on her cheeks. "I thought you'd be dashing, daring, my great hero from the wilderness! But you misled me, didn't you, Daniel? You're not dashing, but dull, and the only daring deed you

ever attempted was loving me. And that, Master Fairbourne, is not enough to make you anyone's hero, and certainly not mine."

If he'd dared to follow her then, if he'd been more dashing than dull, if he hadn't been a plain-spoken man from a small town on Cape Cod, then she might have loved him as much as he'd loved her. He could have saved her life, and their unborn child, and been the hero that she'd thought he'd been at first.

He didn't want to lose Juliette the same way. Now he knew he loved her far more than he'd ever loved Catherine because their love was based on more than desire alone. He loved Juliette for her spirit and her bravery and the way she laughed, for her cleverness and her charm and a thousand other little ways, her ways, that never failed to make him smile with pleasure. That was his Juliette, and before it was too late, he wanted to prove to her that he was the hero she deserved.

And if it took for him to save this unknown captain's wife from drowning the way she nearly had herself—the way that Catherine *had*—and for him to do it with most of Nantucket watching, why, then for Juliette's love he'd do it. For once, he'd make everything right.

"You're going, friend, aren't you?" asked John Robin, suddenly at his elbow. There was no question of him being too spent to continue; the Wampanoag was as eerily tireless at an oar as he was at the anvil.

"Aye," said Daniel. He took three gulps of the hot black coffee that someone offered him, then settled back on the bench without looking back at Ellis. "I am."

"As it should be, friend," answered John Robin, "because you wish it so much."

But as Daniel very soon realized, wishing was not the same as doing. His arms and back felt as if he were rowing through molasses, not water, and uphill at that, and his breath now came in short bursts that showed in the chill air before his face. He would never be warm or dry again, yet still he rowed on.

By now the foggy dusk had deepened into a disorienting mist-shrouded night. Although lanterns had been hung fore and aft from the boat, the wobbling lights penetrated the gray darkness only a few yards in any direction, and if Captain Wallerson had not managed to keep one flickering light burning onboard, it would have been possible for Daniel and the others to have rowed right past the wreck. The waves had not diminished with nightfall, the lacy spume on the crests reflecting the lantern light in constantly shifting patterns around them.

"Ahoy!" called the sloop's captain hoarsely. "Ahoy, there! Praise God you've come back!"

The sloop had sunk deeper into the grip of the sand as the tide had begun to come in, and the side of the hull that earlier had loomed so tall had shrunk pitifully, the entry port now less than ten feet from the waves. Beneath the crashing of the waves was a lower, less regular sound, the sorrowful, almost human groan of the ship's timbers pulling apart. Another quarter hour, and they'd have been too late.

"Captain Wallerson, sir?" Daniel held the stern lantern high in his hand, as did the man near the prow. The light reflected back from the ship's wet, planked sides and flickered unevenly over the water before it finally picked out two pale faces above what had once been the sloop's rail. "Ahoy. My name is Daniel Fairbourne."

"You must take my wife to safety, sir," called Wallerson. "She is most frightened of the water, sir."

And with damned good reason, thought Daniel. She wore a sailor's coat over her own clothes and a knitted cap pulled over her hair, which was why at a distance she'd been mistaken for another man. She was short and thin, even with the bulky coat, and not terribly pretty, but from the way her husband held her so tightly there was no mistaking his devotion to her, and again Daniel thought fleetingly of Juliette. She didn't like boats or water, either, and for just as good a reason.

"She'll have to jump," he shouted apologetically. "I cannot risk my men or the boat coming closer, but we'll pluck her out of the water at once."

He could see the two talking, kissing for what could be the last time. Daniel looked away, giving them their privacy as the sloop's timbers groaned and creaked more ominously.

"She's ready, Fairbourne. Aren't you, Hannah?"

The small woman nodded. In her arms she clasped a small keg to help keep her afloat, and around her waist her husband had knotted a thick line. He tossed the trailing end toward the boat, and on the third try John Robin caught it.

"Very well, Mrs. Wallerson," called Daniel, his own heart racing on her behalf. "Jump as far outward as you can toward us."

She closed her eyes, bowed her head as if in church, and jumped.

She didn't sink far, her head bobbing up as she clung to the keg, and as John Robin drew her to the boat, Daniel reached over and, by grabbing fistfuls of her skirts, pulled her up and over the side, the keg floating away forgotten in the water.

She was safe, he thought, safe here beside him, and the relief that swept over him nearly made him laugh with giddiness. He forgot how cold and tired he was. He'd done what he'd set out to do, for Juliette and Catherine and poor shivering Mrs. Wallerson herself.

"My husband," she gasped as the water streamed from her petticoats and she struggled to wriggle free of the rope around her waist. "Oh, please, you must save him! Timothy, hurry, hurry!"

Wallerson was ready, a flat tarred envelope with his log and papers tied to his chest, waiting only to see that his wife was safe before he jumped. But in that pause, the sloop rocked as her damaged hull finally split open and the waves rushed in. Caught by surprise, Wallerson pitched awkwardly forward headfirst instead of jumping, sinking fast and deep into the dark, churning water.

"Timothy!" shrieked Mrs. Wallerson as Daniel leaned out with the lantern, frantically searching the waves for a sign of the sloop's captain. "Timothy, my husband!"

The sloop shuddered again, and Daniel felt the boat being inexorably sucked toward it, and disaster.

"*Pull!*" he roared to the others as he dropped the lantern and threw his whole body into the oar. "Damnation, *pull!*"

"Timothy!" wailed Mrs. Wallerson, tearing off her cap in her despair as she realized they were rowing away from the spot where her husband had disappeared. "Oh, Timothy, you promised we wouldn't part!"

Daniel felt the shift in the boat before he realized what was happening, before he looked up to see Mrs. Wallerson standing with her hands held outstretched, pleading to the water and to her lost husband before she threw herself over the side.

"*No!*" he shouted as he lunged out over the side to try to grab her back, heedless of how the boat lurched ominously beneath him. "Damnation, *no!*"

It happened too slowly, and too fast. It seemed she was hanging there for an eternity, his hand outstretched to save her, and then she was dropping as fast as if she'd stones in her petticoat, out of his reach and into the waves. He lunged again, plunging his hand into the icy water, and felt himself being jerked backward into the boat.

"Let her go, friend," said John Robin, breathing hard as he held Daniel down on the bench. "Let her go, or you'll take us all with her."

But still Daniel searched the waves that had swallowed up the captain's wife. Through some trick of the water and light, he could see her in the wave almost as if she'd been frozen there, her hair drifting around her and her petticoats floating up like the ruffled petals of a flower. Her mouth was open and so were her eyes, staring at him, and the longer he looked the more he realized it wasn't Mrs. Wallerson he was seeing, but Catherine, her red lips laughing and mocking him, the last good-bye they'd never had.

"It is done, friend," said John Robin as he guided the oar back into Daniel's hand. "It was her fate, her desire. You couldn't change it. Now row."

And with no will left to do otherwise, Daniel rowed, through the waves, through the fog, through the darkness that matched the two deaths he'd seen. When they reached the beach, he could barely drag himself from the boat. The other two men wearily left, sympathy in their silence. No one who helped bring the boat in asked what had happened—the lack of passengers explained everything clearly enough—yet still Daniel felt compelled to tell John Robin again and again as if he hadn't been there himself.

"They died," he said raggedly as he walked unsteadily across the beach, away from those gathered around the warmth of the fire and away from where Juliette must be waiting. After tonight, he didn't deserve her comfort; he didn't deserve anything. "They *died*, John Robin, and I as good as pushed them in myself."

"Nay, you did not," said John Robin with soft-spoken urgency, following Daniel's steps as closely as he dared. "You do not have that power, friend. Better to rejoice in the four you saved, than fault yourself for the two you didn't."

But Daniel couldn't agree, not while Mrs. Wallerson's frantic wails for her lost husband still echoed in his head. They'd loved each other dearly, he'd seen that, yet what power did love have to save them from dying? And as for being a hero—Jesus, what kind of fool could believe he was any woman's idea of a hero after tonight?

The crowd that remained around the fire was growing more boisterous as they waited for dawn, when the *Raven* would have broken up completely and they could freely plunder her cargo as it spilled out into the water, a profitable opportunity that few islanders would pass. For as long as he'd helped with rescues, Daniel had accepted that. Shipowners were rich men from the mainland, with insurance against such losses, and the islanders were not.

But this night, after this wreck, the whole idea sickened him, both for its greed and its oblivion to the suffering it represented.

Would the Wallersons' bodies wash in on the waves as well? He thought of how they'd tried to comfort one another as the sloop disintegrated beneath them. The image of them as they were now, floating lifeless among the wrack and timbers and tar kegs, grieved him so much he groaned aloud with the pain.

"Come with me tonight, friend," urged John Robin, his concern giving him the courage to touch Daniel's arm among all these Englishmen. "You always have a place at my fire. My Mary will welcome you with supper, I know, and—"

"Daniel!"

Juliette was crying his name with the same desperation that Hannah Wallerson had called her husband's, her running footsteps frantic little pats on the packed sand. He told himself to keep walking, that he didn't want her to see him like this, or discover the disappointment that must surely be there in her eyes.

Then he felt her arms around his waist, and he stopped, brought to an instant halt by the strength of her love and the raw ache in his heart. He pulled her around to his chest and folded his arms around her, holding her so tightly that her feet left the sand and it still wasn't close enough. She'd lost her cap and her hair had come unpinned, a pale tangle blowing around her face. He shoved back the hood of her cloak, breathing deep of the scent of her hair and skin, the same salt of the wind and sea mixed improbably with roses, and beneath her wool cloak her body was miraculously warm and full of life.

Of *life*.

Without a word spoken, he hooked his arm beneath her knees and gathered her up, and turned away from John Robin, and the crowd of people around the fire, and the wreck and the sea itself, turning instead toward the dunes and the darkness, and no other person but the woman he loved most in this world or the next.

Chapter 12

Juliette didn't ask where Daniel was taking her. It wasn't that she didn't care, but that she couldn't think beyond this instant. As soon as she'd seen the stranded *Raven*, the memory of her own shipwreck had returned with such brutal vividness that she'd feared the price of surviving would be the loss of her sanity.

She had cowered in the sand with her arms around Sachem as her last hours on board the *Lively* had washed over her again and again, pounding her like the waves that had nearly taken her life. The longer she had watched the *Raven* and the tossing rescue boat with Daniel at the oar, the more intense the memories had become, until her fears for Daniel's life became inextricably tangled with the memory of nearly losing her own.

Each time the pinprick lights on the rescue boat vanished behind a screen of fog, she imagined the boat capsizing and Daniel thrown and pummeled and dragged by the same icy waves with such excruciating clarity that she'd trembled from the pain. When he'd returned safely with the first of the *Raven*'s survivors, she'd wept with joy, but when, to her horror, he'd gone out again, it had taken Mrs. Swain and two of her neighbors to keep Juliette from charging into the waves after Daniel. When he'd come back the second time, they hadn't been able to hold her back, and she'd run to him as fast as she could, her voice so raw with anguish as she shouted his name that the men near the fire had turned to stare.

Now they were back high among the dunes where the crash of the waves was fainter and the sandy hills were patched with beach-plums and low cedars among the marram grass and dusty miller. He lay her back on her cloak against the side of the dune, and she linked her arms around his neck to draw him down with her. The wool of his coat was wet and rough beneath her fingers, and in the darkness she could barely make out his face above hers. His breathing was ragged, harsh, and when his mouth found hers his lips were salty and tasted more like the sea than of himself.

But she'd won this time, not the waves. She'd survived, and so had he. He was *hers*, and frantically she deepened the kiss, wanting to reclaim him. She wove her fingers into the wet tangle of his hair, cradling his head as he shifted more heavily upon her. Instinctively she moved beneath him, ignoring the hard, damp sand beneath her in her desperation.

He groaned, and she felt the chill air on the bare skin above her stockings as he dragged her skirts up over her knees. She heard ripping cloth, her shift tangling and tearing as he nudged her legs apart. Instinct and urgency drove her here, too, as she arched her hips to guide him.

This wasn't lovemaking, with none of the tenderness and affection she'd come to adore with him, but a darker and more primal union that, after tonight, they both needed as much with their souls as their bodies.

She cried out when he entered her, a sharp animal cry of fulfillment as she wrapped her legs high over his hips to take him deeper, and she cried out again when her pleasure peaked and broke and carried them both away together.

"I—I remembered it all, Daniel," she whispered hoarsely afterwards. She kept her eyes closed, concentrating on the closeness they were sharing now instead of the horror of what she was telling him. "The wreck and the waves and the others drowning."

"But you're alive," he said, his voice thick. "You lived."

"Because you saved me," she answered, the simplest truth she knew, and she felt joy and contentment bloom within her.

He didn't answer at first, letting the sound of the waves and the distant voices fill the silence. "I said good-bye to her, Juliette."

She opened her eyes, confused. Over his shoulder she could see the moon, high in the night sky, where shreds of fog and cloud glided over its face. "Goodbye to who, Daniel?"

"You'll be my wife now, Juliette," he said, his words warm against her cheek. "You're the one I love best."

She ran her thumb along the inside of the narrow black band on her ring finger where he'd put it earlier. No, she hadn't dreamed that; he *had* asked her to marry him. She'd been too stunned to agree, though she had kept the ring on her finger. Then it had felt like the right thing to do, especially after listening to Mrs. Swain. But Juliette still felt dazed and dazzled by his offer—and what he'd just said wasn't doing much to reassure her, either.

"You're not making sense, Daniel," she began uneasily, not sure she could, either. "Who did you say goodbye to?"

"I did what you said, Juliette," he said. "That's what happened out there. I understand it now. I stopped pretending she wasn't a part of me, and then I could—damnation, who's that?"

The light from a lantern swept over the next dune. "Daniel Fairbourne!" called Robert Ellis. "Is thee here?"

"Blast Ellis," muttered Daniel. He rose quickly, buttoning his breeches, and held his hand out to help Juliette to her feet. "I'm sorry, love. None of this is what I'd have wanted for you."

He hadn't answered her question, she thought wretchedly as she tried to shake the sand from her crumpled skirts.

Hadn't he told her he'd never kept company with any other woman since he'd come to Nantucket? Hadn't he laughed and sworn that he and Sachem were old bachelors together? He *had*. She knew it. But then hadn't she neglected to tell him about Boston and her shop?

And in his buttonhole somehow still clung the wilted knot of pink ribbons, meant in jest to mark him as her own before the other women at the squantum.

She swayed unsteadily on her feet, and protectively he curled his arm around her waist to support her. She felt disoriented and unsettled and unhappy, her heart sore and her head aching from everything that had happened this night, and suddenly she was so tired all she wished to do was sleep and sleep until her world was back to rights again.

The lantern's beam swept over the dune again, this time catching them and stopping. Juliette squinted at the brightness, and before Daniel stepped in front of her to shield her, she glimpsed not just Robert Ellis—she remembered him from the one time she'd visited Daniel's shop—but also John Robin, holding Sachem back by his collar, and, improbably, Mrs. Swain.

"Daniel," said Ellis gently. "What is thee about here, hiding in the dunes with thy friend?"

"Why the devil are you following me?" said Daniel savagely. "Did you bring my own dog to hunt me down?"

"No one's hunting thee," said Ellis. "Thy friend John Robin feared for thee, that is all."

Daniel glared at John Robin. "Friend, hell. What kind of *friend* would chase me across the dunes?"

"Daniel, don't," said Juliette softly, resting her hand on his arm. She had never seen him like this, so defensive that he almost seemed spoiling for a fight. "I don't think they meant any harm."

"It's not us that be bringing harm, Mr. Fairbourne!" said Mrs. Swain indignantly, her hands at her waist. "Hauling your poor lady out here like she was any common strumpet! She's suffered mightily over you this night, she has, so much I feared she go daft!"

"Damnation, Juliette's not a strumpet," he growled. "She's my *wife.*"

"In some ways, maybe," said Mrs. Swain quickly, "but not in the one that matters. Though your heart be in the right place, and we can see to a wedding soon enough. Tomorrow, even."

Ellis raised his hand for quiet. "No one is saying anything ill about thy friend, Daniel. But for her sake and thy own, thee should—"

"We're not wed," interrupted Juliette, her voice scarcely above a whisper. "I love Daniel, yes, but I'm not his wife."

Daniel turned toward her. As quickly as it had appeared, his defensiveness vanished, leaving his face looking drained and haggard. Though he tried to cover it, she knew him well enough to see the indecision and regret etched across his face, and worst of all, the fear. With two sentences, she'd somehow turned the strongest man on Nantucket into the most vulnerable. How had she become so caught up in herself that she'd overlooked what had happened to him tonight?

"Oh, Daniel," she said, threading her fingers through his. "I haven't said no. I love you too much for that. It's just that everything has gone so fast for us, and I—I'd like a bit more time to consider."

His silence as he looked down at their joined hands told her how much she'd hurt him. Dear God, she'd never, ever wished to hurt Daniel!

"Time, yes," agreed Ellis, a bit too heartily. "Thee is too weary after tonight for such important decisions. Daniel, thee can come bide at my house tonight, and Juliette can stay with the Swains."

Daniel turned her hand to touch the finger with the ring. "I made it for you, you know."

"I know," she said. She heard that tonight he'd rescued four sailors, but that he'd returned too late to save the lives of the captain and his wife. While she couldn't begin to imagine how he felt after that, how exhausted he must be both in body and mind, she could understand how what he'd seen or done could have made him feel unlike himself. "That's what makes it special."

He seemed to forget the others waiting as he leaned close, near enough that his hair brushed against her forehead. "If you wish, I'll buy you one of gold instead. The kind the ladies wear in Boston."

"Oh, no," she said quickly, flushing at that mention of Boston. "I told you, it's special. Like the little sun you made for me, too. But if you wish me to give it back for now—"

"Nay." He rested his hand over hers, the same gesture he'd used when he'd first slipped the ring on her finger. "I'd never put it on another woman's hand, anyway."

He sighed. Forlornly, she thought. "Do you wish to go with Mrs. Swain, then?"

"I—it might be for the best," she said reluctantly. What she really wished was for everything to go back to how it had been, with the two of them snug and uncomplicated in the house by the water and only Sachem to judge them. "For both of us."

"Aye," he said with no conviction, only sadness. "Good night, then, Juliette."

"Good night, Daniel," she said, but he'd already turned away, his shoulders bowed as Sachem, finally let free, came bounding up to lick his hand. He joined Ellis and John Robin, the tall one in the middle as they began slowly over the dunes, the lantern swinging from John Robin's hand making their three shadows alternately wax and wane across the sand.

Juliette watched, her thumb secretly rubbing the underside of the narrow ring inside her cupped hand. It was for the best, she told herself again, the best for them both.

But why, why hadn't he kissed her good night?

"You've done the right thing, miss," soothed Mrs. Swain, lifting Juliette's hood back over her head and gently tucking her lose hair back beneath it. "It's not that your Mr. Fairbourne means to treat you badly now. I do not believe he could, not the way he looks at you."

Wistfully Juliette looked back at the fading lantern light. "He's not looking now, is he?"

"Oh, now, don't you go on like that, miss, not for one blessed moment," scolded Mrs. Swain gently. "He's asked you to wed him, didn't he? He was willing to claim you as his wife even before you took him, on account of him going out in a measly cockleshell boat on that sea. But you did right, making him wait now until a proper wedding. That's as it should be."

Perhaps as it should be, thought Juliette, but keeping herself chaste and apart from Daniel until he'd formally wed her wasn't why she'd done this. She'd never intended coyly to force him like that, a tawdry marriage by deceit, as if she feared he'd run off and abandon her and, quite possibly, their child as well.

She was too tired and numb to talk as she rode in the Swains' lurching, jolting box cart back to town, surrounded by drowsy younger children. She could only half listen to Betsey repeat every morsel of gossip she'd gleaned from her friends at the squantum and later on the beach. Not one word was spoken of either Daniel or the wreck of the *Raven*, and though Juliette suspected this was at Mrs. Swain's orders, she was thankful nonetheless. She didn't want to talk about either one, not now. With Betsey's cheerful chatter to fill in all the empty spaces, no one noticed that Juliette stayed silent.

"You'll be having Betsey's chamber, here under the eaves," explained Mrs. Swain as she led Juliette up a narrow ladder to a windowless room tucked under the roof. "It don't be a fancy sort of bedchamber, I know, but here the younger children won't be bothering you with their racketing. Nor Betsey, neither, for that matter, and I cannot say which be more of a trial."

As Mrs. Swain had said, it wasn't a fancy sort of bedchamber, or really even much of a "chamber" at all. By the candlestick in Mrs. Swain's hand, Juliette saw that the walls were unpainted rough battens below the hewn rafters, and the slope of the lean-to roof was so severe that standing upright—even kneeling on the floor upright—would be impossible in most of the narrow space. The only furnishings were a low bed, pushed close to the wall, with a thin mattress beneath a linsey-woolsey coverlet, a mended chair, and a board chest that would hold the clothes that weren't hanging from the pegs hammered into the battens.

Being under the eaves like this reminded Juliette of the loft in Daniel's house, and sadly she pictured how cheerless and empty the little shingled house must be tonight. Strange how the thought of Daniel's humble house was the one that made her homesick, and not her own comfortable home with the imported porcelain and mahogany bedstead over her shop in Boston.

"I don't wish to inconvenience Betsey," she murmured as Mrs. Swain set the candlestick on the chair and bustled about the room, turning back the coverlet on the bed and plumping the wool-stuffed bolster.

" 'Tis no hardship for Betsey, miss," said Mrs. Swain. "With Mr. Swain at sea, I'll take her into our bed. We'll have snug old times together, as if she were still a babe herself. Won't be many more like it, not with her shifting to Eleazer's keeping soon. Here now, give me your cloak."

She hung the cloak on a peg and looped the ribbons of Juliette's hat over it, then turned back expectantly. "Would you like me to undo your lacings for you, miss?"

Juliette shook her head, reluctant to undress before the other woman. She didn't want to have to answer questions about her torn shift, or any of the other evidences left from her coupling with Daniel on the dune.

"Thank you, but I'll do for myself." She sat on the edge of the low bed, the rope springs sagging beneath her, and began unbuckling her shoes. She was so tired now that if Mrs. Swain weren't here, she'd simply flop back onto the mattress without bothering to undress at all.

"Well enough," said Mrs. Swain, but making no move to leave. "Now, what following will you be preferring?"

"Following?" repeated Juliette blankly. Maybe it was only because she was so weary, but she couldn't think of what *following* had to do with unlacing her gown and stays.

"For the wedding, miss," answered Mrs. Swain patiently. "We have every sort of following here on the island. Quakers, Presbyterians, Baptists, Congregationalists, even some Philadelphians. Master Ellis could make the arrangements for you at the Friends' meeting, and he'd know who to ask with the others as well. Why, I'd warrant even that red-skinned man that your Mr. Fairbourne's been so kind to could arrange an Indian wedding for you, if that's what you fancy!"

She chuckled at so preposterous an idea. "But in all that, miss, there must be one that you'd find pleasing, to bless your marriage."

Juliette remembered the modest Huguenot church Maman had taken her and Amelie to as young girls, as well as the more fashionable Christ's Church, with its great bells and pipe organ, that her mother had joined when they were older. Somehow Juliette doubted that either one would have a counterpart here, even among so many diverse choices, and uneasily she wondered if this were another sign that perhaps she shouldn't wed Daniel.

"Do you know where Mr. Fairbourne is a member?" she asked, a question that was greeted with open-mouthed surprise by Mrs. Swain.

"None, miss," she said, though Juliette couldn't tell if her disapproval was for Daniel's lack of a church membership, or her own ignorance of such a glaring omission by the man she loved. "Not that I'm saying your Mr. Fairbourne's an out-and-out heathen, mind, not a man that does as many good deeds as he, but he does spend his Sabbath alone, doing who only knows what. But I expect he's some choice of a church or meeting that you can settle between you tomorrow. You don't want to dally about it, you know."

"No," said Juliette as she rolled her garters around her finger. "But I do not wish to rush such a grave step, either."

Pointedly Mrs. Swain studied Juliette's waist. "My guess is that these last weeks you've already had your measure of the dallying, miss, and you won't be having time to rush if your belly begins to swell. Better to wed him now, before you have to tie your apron up under your arms."

Juliette flushed at Mrs. Swain's directness. She had, of course, considered before the question of conceiving

Daniel's baby. She'd tried picturing what kind of hybrid such a child would be like: would it have her pale hair or his black, would it share her laugh or his strength, his skill in a boat or at an anvil, or hers with a needle and thread and a length of cloth?

But the image that she most usually settled upon was a sturdy, red-cheeked baby with Daniel's pale blue eyes and silky black infant curls, cooing contentedly in her arms as she sang to him in French. For some reason tonight this baby, Daniel's baby, seemed especially real, so much so that she nearly followed Mrs. Swain's gaze and stared down at her own still slender waist.

Her body didn't seem any different, as if she were growing another life inside, but then she wasn't sure exactly how that would feel, anyway. Yet it was this baby that Mrs. Swain wished so strongly to protect with a wedding that Juliette wasn't sure she wanted. Did that mean that she'd be as dismally disinclined to be a mother as her own had been?

Unconsciously she slid her hand over the front of her gown, over her belly, thinking again of that sleepy, black-curled baby, and knew in her heart she'd never be like Maman. Not with Daniel's child, not with a baby born of the kind of love that the two of them shared.

"Aye, you be thinking that way," said Mrs. Swain with approval, correctly reading most of Juliette's thoughts by her gesture. "Don't let a man as fine as your Mr. Fairbourne run free. There's plenty of other women on this island that have tried to draw him into their nets, but you're the one who's succeeded."

Juliette's first reaction was to deny that she'd ever tried to trap Daniel into anything. Her second was much less honorable, but with his curious words about saying goodbye still fresh, it was to this second impulse that she gave way.

"No other, ah, women at all?" she asked, inwardly cringing at how disingenuous she sounded. "In all the time he's been on Nantucket?"

"None," declared Mrs. Swain with a decisiveness that gladdened Juliette's heart, if not her conscience. "A comely man like that, with a good trade, and one who'll be in your bed each night, not traipsing around the oceans like so many other island men—of course he's had his chances. Oh, the widows in particular were mad for him, but he never showed a dab of interest in any of them. Until he found you, that is."

"Yes," said Juliette softly. For all she knew, Daniel might have been talking about a boat or a ship—he called them "she," too, the way sailors did—or a star overhead, or almost anything else that he might have seen out there in the lifesaving boat.

Except, it seemed, another woman. *She* was the one he loved enough to marry. He'd said so himself.

So why, then, did she still feel so unsure?

"Now, when you take your gown off," said Mrs. Swain, "you just hang it on the pegs to let out the damp. We'll touch the skirts with an iron in the morning if they need it, so you'll be looking shipshape and spruce when your Mr. Fairbourne comes to call. For now I'd best go below to make sure Betsey hasn't lost her temper and tossed the younger ones into the kettle instead of to bed."

With her hands clasped at her waist, she paused before Juliette, her smile softening. "That man will make you a fine husband, miss, and he'll make you happy as he can, just as you'll do the same for him. And that's the best any of us can ask from this mortal life, isn't it?"

To Juliette's surprise, Mrs. Swain bent and quickly kissed the top of her head. "There now, miss, sleep tight, and mind you pinch the candle before you close your eyes. The world will seem a far better place with the sunrise, I promise you."

She didn't wait for Juliette's reply, but briskly swept her skirts over one arm and backed her way down the ladder, toward the muffled din of crying and squabbling coming from her family in the kitchen below.

With a sigh that was more than halfway to a groan, Juliette snuffed the candle and swung her legs up onto the bed. Gratefully she sank back against the pillow, letting her eyes grow accustomed to the dark. She didn't care how many wrinkles set into her gown; she was simply too tired to wrestle herself out of it or her stays. As Mrs. Swain had said, in the morning an iron and a bit of steam from a kettle would remove whatever creases she happened to press in tonight.

She'd grown accustomed to sharing Daniel's bed, and this one felt chilly and lonely with only her in it. His scent still clung to her clothes and her skin, a potent reminder in this chaste little bed, and she hugged her arms around herself, pretending it was his arms instead. She missed him already, missed him more than she'd thought possible. As she lay on her back, she listened to the wind blowing against the shingles on the roof, the same wind that had brought such disaster to the *Raven* this afternoon, and then her mind raced on, inevitably, to how she'd separated from Daniel. The sleep that she'd been so sure would come vanished as, again and again, she recalled how she'd told Daniel that she loved him, loved him dearly, but how she wasn't ready to marry him yet.

Alone she lay in the dark, every muscle in her body tense, and tried to figure out why. She'd every reason in the world to accept him: she loved him, of course, and as Mrs. Swain had rightly noted, he'd do everything in his power to make her happy. He'd already done it, in fact. They'd already shared so much together, and she couldn't remember a time when she'd been more blissfully happy than in these last days with him. That had been the only reason she hadn't told him about her life in Boston: she hadn't wanted to spoil the magic of what she'd found with him.

But what was she to do with that Boston life? She'd known she'd have to make a choice, but now that she'd remembered how Amelie had married and opened another shop in Appledore, her new husband's home, that choice held more possibilities.

Without Amelie at her side, the Boston shop this year had been considerably more work and less satisfaction. She'd reached the pinnacle of her craft and trade before her twenty-fifth birthday, and she'd made a great deal of money for a woman of any age—for any woman.

Perhaps it *was* time to leave her life, as Amelie had done, to leave the hectic pace of the Marlborough Street shop and begin something different, and with tantalizing pleasure she thought again of that sweet-faced baby asleep in her arms. She'd come to like Nantucket, and to appreciate the wild, open beauty of it after the crowded, noisy streets of Boston. Perhaps she could open a smaller shop here, with Mrs. Swain to work with her. Daniel had predicted that the whaling ships would soon make the island rich, and a rich island would mean women eager to spend their husband's money, exactly as had happened in Boston.

But what, she wondered, would Daniel make of such plans? It was one thing for him to have his shop and forge, his trade, and quite another to have a wife with one, too. He was a kind man, but he was also a proud one. Would he be shocked to have his children playing with scraps of lace and ribbons behind a shop counter? Would he object to seeing her name in advertisements, printed in handbills or in news sheets? Would he approve of her speaking freely with customers and other strangers, and would he let her travel to Boston to call on the import merchants to replenish her stock?

And she'd have adjustments of her own to make, too. She'd be accountable to more than herself alone. No matter how hard she toiled or how much she earned, by law all her income and all her property would now belong to her husband, not her. If her husband died before her, his will could leave it all away from her, to another person of his choosing. Not even the lease on a shop building could be in her name without her husband's beside it. She'd no idea if Daniel would be willing to ignore such laws and let her continue to handle her own accounts and business. Or would he say she was being too bold for asking for such privileges, too independent or willful? These had all been reasons why, even though most women her age were already wives and mothers, Daniel was her first and only beau.

Yet she'd worked for herself for so long that she wasn't sure she could narrow her world to Daniel alone, no matter how much she loved him. But was her precious independence worth giving up the one man in the world she loved most?

She groaned as she struggled to make a decision, her thoughts jumping back and forth, back and forth, enough to make her toss restlessly on the narrow bed. She hated having to weigh love against trade like this, and she'd only to look to her mother to see the peril of it.

After Maman had been widowed, she'd been forced by circumstance to choose commerce over love for the sake of her daughters' welfare. Though she'd been successful, her soul and her heart had paid the price in bitterness and regrets—and constant, cautious warnings to her daughters against relying on men instead of themselves. While the shipwreck had been the worst that had befallen Juliette in her life, there were, she knew sadly, other things that she would rather have left unremembered, too.

Oh, it was all so hard to put into words, and she doubted she could, even to Daniel himself.

Especially to Daniel. Daniel's mother had been a cheerful, affectionate goodwife whose pies he still could remember, more than twenty years later, as representative of the love she'd lavished on her young family. Her Maman hadn't been anything like his mother, and neither, realized Juliette unhappily, was she. How could she make him understand so much about her, in such a short time?

For tomorrow morning—no, more likely in only a few hours now, she'd been awake for so long—he'd be sitting in the Swain's front room, waiting to plan the details of their wedding under Mrs. Swain's helpful supervision.

She couldn't do it.

All the tossing, all the turning, all the pounding of the pillow, and everything came to that. She couldn't do it.

She'd only just remembered who and what she was, and as much as she loved Daniel, she wasn't ready to run off and become someone else, even as wonderful a someone as Daniel Fairbourne's wife.

And the only one who'd understand was Amelie.

All her life, Amelie had been the one she'd turned to. She could pour her heart out to Amelie, and tell her everything about Daniel. Amelie would listen without judgment, without criticism, and she'd help her know what was right to do next. Amelie would remember their mother's warnings, and understand the confusion they'd fostered. Over and over she'd told Daniel how the past made them what they were now; Amelie was such an important part of her own past that she couldn't imagine making so grave a step without talking to her first.

To make it even easier, Amelie was in Appledore, on Cape Cod, not Boston. Daniel had told her that the Cape was only twenty-seven miles by sea from Nantucket, a day's sail with a good wind. If she left at dawn, she could be with Amelie by nightfall. One day, perhaps two, that would be all she needed, and then she'd be back with a clear head and the answer that Daniel deserved, without any hesitation or second thoughts.

But she hesitated now. This one night was the first she and Daniel had ever spent apart. When she'd added to that the next four or five that her journey to Appledore and back would take, the separation loomed like an eternity. Her stomach knotted with fear at the thought of sailing anywhere, especially across the same sea where she'd nearly drowned, and for an instant she considered asking Daniel to go with her, before her conscience told her no. This was something she had to do by herself, and for herself. Coming back to Daniel, and his love, would be her sweet reward.

In the windowless attic, with no view of the moon, she wasn't sure how much of the night remained before dawn. As kindly hospitable as Mrs. Swain had been to her, Juliette knew she should leave before the older woman woke, or she'd have no chance of leaving at all. She knew where the Sherburne docks were, not far from the Swains' house. Surely she could find a fisherman willing to take her across to Cape Cod, and for the first time she was thankful that Daniel had always insisted she keep the coins that had been in her pocket since the shipwreck. She'd use them now to buy her passage.

She leaned over the edge of the bed, groping blindly for the candlestick and the flint and striker that Mrs. Swain had left in the base. At last she made a spark that caught the wick, and the little flame flared bright, glancing over the ring on her finger. She had his ring, and the little sun, small parts of him to carry with her on her journey. With a wistful smile, she gathered her cloak but left behind her hat—for although that, too, had been a gift from Daniel, even she knew better than to wear a broad-brimmed straw hat on a boat—and, the candlestick in her hand, she carefully backed down the ladder to the hallway below.

Though she heard an assortment of wheezes, snores, and sniffles, she managed to creep past all the sleeping Swains without waking anyone. In the kitchen she paused, searching for some way to leave a message for Daniel. Though there would likely be a pen and paper in the shop for bookkeeping, she didn't see any in the kitchen, and she'd no wish to tempt her luck by noisy investigating. But on the kitchen table, she did find a slate and chalk left by one of the children, and setting her candlestick beside her, she wrote her note.

Mrs. Swain, I do thank you for yr. kindness. Please tell Mr. Fairbourne I have gone to my sister in Appledore & will come back in 3-4 days. Please tell him also that I love him much & miss him already.
Yr. Obt. svt. Juliette Lacroix

She wished she could have written more for Daniel's sake, but the slate was small and the blunt chalk clumsy, and she realized she was lucky to squeeze in as much as she could. She propped the slate against the candlestick where Mrs. Swain would be sure to see it, blew out the candle, and let herself out the door and into the lane.

The wind that she'd heard earlier had blown away yesterday's wispy fog, and a watery moon hung low in the sky to light her way. She figured there must be only another hour or so until dawn, when most of the fishermen would set out for the day, and she walked swiftly, holding her cloak tightly around her against the early morning chill.

The first boats she saw were noisily preparing to sail, the light from their lanterns spilling across the wharfs and water while the crews swore and squabbled with one another. Skittishly she kept to the shadows, for the last thing she wished as an unattached woman was to find herself alone on a boat at sea with a crew of raucous, lecherous fishermen. She hoped she'd find a more sober boat, and at last she spied one, tied to the very end of the wharf.

Cautiously she made her way toward the boat, which seemed to grow smaller the closer she came, and she thought uneasily of those twenty-seven miles of open sea between here and the mainland. The wind that had cleared away the fog was also churning the water with whitecaps, a fast day for sailing, perhaps, but undeniably a rough one.

"Good morning, sir," she called to an older man ordering his nets on the deck. "Might I please have a word with you?"

He turned and stared at her with as much open curiosity as if she'd been a six-legged calf at a fair.

"And where did you drop from, dearie?" he said as a second, younger man came to stand beside him. They shared the same broad brow bone, the same sandy hair, father and son. "You'll be finding no takers for your wares here. My boy and I be honest wedded men, with neither time nor coin to squander on harlots."

"I am not a harlot, sir," she said firmly, and, she hoped, with what sounded like ladylike and un-hussy-fied dignity. She stepped closer into the light of his lantern so he could see her better. "But I do wish to make an offer to you."

"An offer?" asked the first man suspiciously. "No good woman makes offers to men. If you're no harlot, then where be your husband, or your father? How'd they let you roam about at this hour, heh?"

She raised her chin and drew herself up especially straight with her hands folded, one atop the other, before her, a posture she'd learned from Amelie. Since it served to intimidate delinquent customers into settling their accounts, she prayed it would have the same powers of persuasion with Nantucket fishermen. "I have a great need to go to the mainland this day, sir, to Appledore on Cape Cod. I wish to hire your boat to do so."

"To the Cape, you say?" said the father, tugging at his ear lobe as he let himself be tempted. "It would cost you, dearie, to make up for what we'd take in our catch."

"You be Daniel Fairbourne's French lady!" exclaimed the younger man excitedly. "I saw you with him at the squantum at Perry's farm!"

"You be French?" The father frowned so deeply his chin seemed to melt into the collar of his shirt. "I don't much like the French."

Juliette could feel this opportunity slipping away. The horizon was just beginning to pink with dawn, and the first boats were already making their way from the harbor.

"Here," she said, digging her hand into her pocket. Her fingers sifted through the coins, then settled on one of her precious gold guineas. A guinea could well be more than the boat earned in a month, but Juliette was too desperate now to be frugal, and she held out the coin in her fingers. "Here. That, sir, should be enough for my passage, and more than enough to make you remember I am from Boston, not France."

"Aye, aye, mistress," he said, greedily reaching for the coin. "To the Cape we be bound."

Swiftly she curled her fingers back over the coin. "It's yours when we arrive safely," she said, "and as fast as you can."

"Aye, aye, mistress," the man said again, holding his hand up to help her aboard. "And being from Boston's a good deal finer than being French any day."

An hour later she was perched on a coil of rope in the middle of the deck, struggling to ignore the fishy smell of a hundred past catches that lingered in every beam of the little boat. Her stomach nearly matched the pounding of her heart as they bumped and bounced over the choppy water, and she was doubly glad now that she hadn't paused for breakfast. The sun had barely slipped above the water to the east, and the sky over Sherburne was beginning to pale to gray, the roofs of the town all sharp, black angles. Which house belonged to Robert Ellis, she wondered, under which roof would Daniel still be sleeping?

She slipped her hand inside her pocket to touch the little sun of Daniel's, and looked across to the sunrise now spreading red gold across the horizon.

Another sunrise, another new day, another new beginning.

And oh, please God, let Daniel understand why she'd left.

Chapter 13

"You can believe me or not, sir," said Mrs. Swain heatedly, unaccustomed to having her word challenged. "But there be the proof bold as day, and written in her own hand."

Daniel stared down at the child's slate that she was holding out to him. He didn't want to take it from her. Touching the slate would mean he'd accepted the message with it.

Damnation, Juliette couldn't have left him, not like this!

"One of the little ones smudged it a bit, there, not understanding," continued Mrs. Swain, "but Miss Lacroix wrote that herself before she left."

Strange how he'd never seen Juliette's handwriting before, yet he didn't doubt this was hers. Even in the rough chalk, the curves of the letters had an elegance that had to belong to her. Certainly no one in the Swain household would write like this.

But why would she have written such a message to him in the first place? What had he done to make her disappear like this, with only a scribble of chalk for farewell?

"When did she leave?" he demanded.

"Can't say for certain, sir," answered Mrs. Swain, still holding the slate out to him. "We was all asleep in our beds."

At Ellis' house, he'd been asleep, too, a sleep so deep that he'd awakened with no memory of dreaming, but also optimistic. He'd even come to see the merit in waiting, the way she'd insisted. This morning he could honor her with the proper, romantic proposal he'd rehearsed. Juliette deserved that from him, not the raving babbles of the madman he'd been last night. He'd come here to the Swains' house eagerly, on this fresh new morning so much like that first one when he'd been sure she'd live. Today, with the sun shining and a stiff, sharp breeze from the water, he was sure that Juliette would agree to marry him.

Instead she'd gone away, left, the same way that Catherine had, off across the water.

"Did she leave anything else behind?"

"Only the hat, sir," she said, beckoning to one of her small daughters, who produced the hat solemnly in both hands. "Though I can't fancy why she'd leave something so fine behind."

The hat he'd given her.

"Nothing else?" Not the ring, he prayed, please not the ring, or the little sun, either.

"Nothing, sir. But what puzzles me is the part about going to her sister in Appledore," mused Mrs. Swain. "I thought she'd be in Boston, too, with the shop and all. Why Appledore, of all places?"

He wondered why Appledore, too. Not because of her sister or their shop in Boston. He didn't give a damn about that. But because, though he'd always been careful not to say where he was from, Appledore was the place he'd been born, the place where his brothers and sister likely still lived, the place he'd decided long ago that he'd never return to again.

Except that now, inexplicably, Juliette was there as well.

"She does say she'll be back, sir," said Mrs. Swain gently. "She do be a sweet lady, and I don't believe she'd lie. She says only a few days, and she'll come back to Nantucket. If you go about your own life, why, the time will pass like nothing."

He'd tried to do that after Catherine had left him. He'd tried to forget their quarrel by throwing himself into his work, and he'd returned to the docks to oversee the loading of his ship as if nothing had happened.

By the time he'd come home that night, Catherine was dead.

He looked down at the rosette of pink ribbons in the buttonhole of his coat. Robert Ellis' wife Jane had made a great fuss over it this morning, doing something to restore the ribbons to nearly their former jauntiness when she'd brushed his coat for him. For a sober Quaker matron, Jane had been surprisingly sentimental, teasing him about how he must be sure to show his sweetheart he hadn't forgotten her overnight.

And he wouldn't forget her now, either.

"Thank you, Mrs. Swain," he said, settling his hat back upon his head. "But I'm going after my Juliette."

* * *

Juliette sat in the back of the wagon, beneath one corner of the old sail that had been rigged across the load of newly cut marsh hay to keep out the dew. She'd been given the choice of sitting on the front bench with the driver, a garrulous old man who stank of unwashed stockings and yesterday's rum, or here in the back with the hay, and this decision, at least, had been an easy one. With a sigh she settled deeper into the sweet-smelling hay, pulling her cloak around her like a coverlet.

She'd been fortunate indeed to find such a comfortable way to travel. It had been late afternoon by the time the Gearys' boat had reached the harbor at Iyanno, but it wasn't until after they'd set her on the dock, grinning and bowing and full of please and thank-you as they'd taken her guinea, that she'd discovered what they'd carefully neglected to tell her. Geography and map-reading were not exactly ready skills for milliners or mantua-makers, and to her sorrow now, Juliette was no exception.

Oh, she knew the geography that was necessary to her trade—that the best woven silks came from Spitalfields, or that the point lace from Venice was beyond compare—but outside of Boston, she had only the vaguest notions of other places in the colony. She'd known that Cape Cod hooked out far into the sea below Boston because when she'd sailed to New York it had taken the sloop nearly a week to go around it. She knew that Nantucket lay to the south of the Cape because Daniel had told her, and she knew that Appledore was situated on the Cape because Amelie had described it that way to her.

But not until she was standing alone on the dock in Iyanno, wondering which way to go next to reach Appledore while the two thieving Gearys set sail for their return, did she learn that Appledore was on the opposite side of the Cape, on Massachusetts Bay instead of Nantucket Sound, and that she'd just given away one of the precious guineas for the privilege of being stranded miles from the town she wanted to go to.

The sailor who'd told her had been kind about it, directing her to a respectable tavern nearby for better advice, but she'd still felt like the greatest fool ever born. Though she didn't like to think of herself as a helpless sort of female, this sort of misadventure had made her furious, and wonder what about being in love had turned her into such a gullible ninny. She also resolved to find the Gearys, father *and* son, the minute she returned to Nantucket (well, maybe the second minute, after she'd found Daniel) and make them give her back her money for taking such advantage of her.

But though Appledore wasn't far in actual distance, only six miles according to the tavern keep, finding someone to take her there wasn't easy. Of course no woman could make the journey unaccompanied. But there was no regular stage or post across the Cape, nor were the roads any better than they were on Nantucket. In these places where nearly every man was a sailor, she'd decided with exasperation, no one seemed to bother with travelling by land, even if it were the more direct route.

The tavern keep had offered her a room, private, clean, and with a bar across the door, until she could find an escort, but he'd also thought it might take days. She didn't want to spend days in Iyanno, and she didn't want to spend the night in this tavern, either, a barred door notwithstanding. She needed to see her sister and then return to Nantucket, and Daniel, as soon as she could.

And so last evening, with the tavern keep watching anxiously for signs of a disturbance, she had boldly stood beside the town pump, asking every man who came to water his horses if he was heading north to Appledore. She had still been so angry with the Gearys that she hadn't realized how ludicrous the scene must have been, with some men shrinking back and shaking their heads as if she had the plague, while others had tried to coax her inside the tavern for a pint of ale and other mischief.

When she thought about it now, she smiled, and wished Daniel had been there to watch. Not to act as her protector—she'd done well enough for herself in such a public place—but to laugh along with her. He would have, too, and she smiled again as she thought of how he called her the bravest woman he'd ever known.

The bravest, or maybe the least particular. When this man with the evil-smelling stockings had offered her a ride in his hay cart in exchange for a shilling, she had gladly climbed behind him. She'd bought a small bottle of cider and a bun stuffed with a slab of yellow cheese, and as she made herself a cozy little nest in the sweet-smelling hay, she wished again that Daniel were there to share it with her. The pace of the cart's oxen was stately and measured, and as the first stars peeped out in the sky, Juliette fell fast asleep, one hand curled protectively over the ring on her hand, and dreamed she was Mrs. Daniel Fairbourne, and mistress of the little shingled house by the sea.

She woke to the sounds of irate, unidentifiable honking. Groggily she rolled herself upright, and pushed back the canvas to see a straggling gaggle of geese being herded out from under the oxen and off to market by a red-headed boy who looked as sleepy as she still felt. She yawned, and lifted the canvas higher. The sky was dusky gray with the coming dawn, and to her dismay she realized she'd spent an entire day and night without reaching her destination.

Quickly she smoothed and braided her hair as neatly as she could without a comb, having long ago lost the hairpins to gather it in her customary stylish knot. She brushed the worst of the hay from her cloak, then leaned across the bench to speak to the driver.

"Good morning," she said, her voice scratchy with sleep. Over the backs of the oxen she could see the dim outlines of houses ahead of them, white smoke pluming from the chimneys of early-rising goodwives.

"Oh, aye, a good morning to you, too, missy," the driver bellowed back as if she were a half mile away instead of directly behind him. "A good morning, and a fair day."

"Indeed," she agreed, trying to shift farther away without offending him. He smelled even more powerfully of drink this morning, and she was thankful, most thankful, that the oxen had seemed to know the way with his help or without it. "Do you know how much farther to Appledore?"

"That be it right there, missy," he roared back, pointing ahead. "You see the windmills on the hill? Appledore lies below, snug along the harbor."

Impatiently she tried to make out the town ahead in the rapidly growing light. Below the five windmills, their long blades already spinning in the early morning breeze from the water, the rooftops of houses and other buildings clustered into the hillside. Already she could see that the buildings were finer, grander, than anything in Sherburne, and more prosperous, too, with tidy painted clapboarding instead of rough-hewn shingles. The source of all this prosperity sat moored in the harbor, deep-water merchant ships that brought back goods and profits from foreign ports, while around them smaller fishing boats were skimming out to the bay.

In a town as ordered as this one, Juliette wasn't surprised that Amelie's new shop was doing so well, and with growing excitement she realized she'd soon be seeing it for herself.

"I'm bound for Evans' stable on the High Street," boomed the driver. "But I 'spect you can walk wherever you needs go from there."

And abruptly her excitement thumped to a halt. She didn't know where she needs go at all. As the final quirk of her lost memory, she still could not seem to recall her sister's married name, with the strangest twist being that "Fairbourne" was the one name that kept coming to mind instead. Although Captain Zachariah Fairbourne sounded well enough, her brother-in-law couldn't possibly have the same name as Daniel, any more than his face would bear the strong resemblance that her mind was insisting.

But without Zach's last name, she could hardly ask the way to their house. At least her Amelie kept her shop under the sign of the Sisters Lacroix, with the same signboard of a plumed lady's hat that hung over the door in Marlborough Street. Juliette could ask for that, and hope that seeing Amelie would be enough to make her remember more of Zach as well.

When at last they reached the stable, her driver insisted on handing her down, much to the amusement of the grooms, and somehow she managed to keep her head high and smile as she paid the man his shilling. But as she hurried away from the guffawing men and down the street, she caught a glimpse of her reflection in a window's glass, and gasped with shame. Her once lovely blue gown was rumpled and wrinkled and stained with salt, bristling with so many bits of straw she might as well have slept in a hay loft, and with her hair in that inelegant plait, she could have been the farmer's wife who'd helped harvest that same hay. She most definitely did not present the fashionable air of the Sisters Lacroix, and from long habit as the younger sister, she could already imagine what Amelie would say.

Frantically she began brushing at the wrinkles, plucking at the straw, and then stopped. What was she doing, anyway? Amelie believed she was dead. When Juliette appeared in the shop this morning, very much alive, not even Amelie would dare complain about straw on her cloak.

She hurried down High Street, which the stable man had told her would lead her into the center of town to the market house. There'd be no mistaking *that,* the man had said proudly, and when Juliette saw it, she understood. Already bustling with farmers and other vendors, the market house was a new, elegantly proportioned building of brick whose swooping arches would have been a marvel in Boston, let alone on this little harbor on Cape Cod.

Clearly Appledore's town fathers had not only ambition, but taste to go with it, and she thought again of how shrewd Amelie had been to bring their business here. Nantucket would be a far less promising location, but as far as Juliette was concerned, it had one enormous advantage over Appledore: it had Daniel, and the thought alone of him was enough to make her smile.

"Do you know where I might find a milliner's shop here in Appledore?" she asked the woman who sold her an apple for her breakfast. "The shop at the sign of the plumed hat?"

"The newish one owned by the French lady?" asked the woman. Skeptically she let her gaze roam up and down Juliette's straw-flecked cloak, silently, pointedly, doubting that a scarecrow like Juliette had any business even inquiring about such a place. "Oh, yes, everyone in Appledore knows that shop, leastways every woman. All the captains' ladies go there."

"Then could you please tell me the way?" asked Juliette again, more insistently. It was well and good that the captains' ladies went there, but she wished to find it, too. "It can't be far, is it?"

"Nay." The woman sighed with resignation, clearly feeling she'd done her part to keep the tawdry lesser sort away from bothering their betters. "You'll find it in West Lane, there beyond the meeting house."

"Thank you, ma'am." She turned and hurried toward the meeting house's boxy whitewashed tower. Because it was market day, many of the shopkeepers had already opened their shutters to lure early customers, and she hoped Amelie had done the same. At the very least, she might be sitting in the window to take advantage of the early sunlight to sew.

She gasped with delight and anticipation when she finally saw the shop sign, a twin to the one in Boston. The shutters were fastened back, the door propped open with the familiar nosegay of ribbon-tied flowers—late daisies and roses—pinned to the door frame. She threw aside the last of her ladylike manners, gathered up her skirts, and ran.

"Amelie!" she cried as she skipped up the steps. "Amelie, I'm—oh, my, forgive me, ma'am!"

The single customer turned from the counter, her bright blue eyes wide with astonishment. One of those captains' wives, thought Juliette in a flashing instant, young and beautiful, expensively dressed in the best London style despite her obvious pregnancy, a lady she'd served in the Boston store, Anabelle, Anabelle . . . *Fairbourne?*

Merciful heavens, why could she think of no other name but Daniel's?

And then none of it mattered because she saw her sister.

Amelie was standing behind the counter, a length of curling red silk ribbon frozen between her hands. Her cheeks were as white as the linen cuffs at her elbows, her eyes wide with shocked disbelief. Her dark hair was drawn back severely beneath an unruffled cap, and she was dressed more plainly, in unadorned black silk, than Juliette had ever seen her dress before. No, she realized suddenly, not plainly, but in mourning, in mourning for *her*.

"I'm alive, Amelie," she said, her voice wobbling with tears. "I didn't drown, and now I'm here, and I—I'm alive."

"Oh—oh, *Julie!*" Amelie dropped the ribbon and bolted around the counter and grabbed Juliette, hugging her fiercely as if to reassure herself that her sister was truly here. Tears streamed down her cheeks as she laughed with joy, matched only by those on Juliette's face.

"Everyone was sure you were lost," she said in a rush, "Drowned, dead, when the wreck of your ship was found, and Zach told me I mustn't hold on to my hopes after that, but I couldn't give up on you, Julie, *ma cher* Julie, oh now, *grace à Dieu,* and here you *are,* snatched from the very grave!"

"From the very grave," said Anabelle, holding out her own lace-trimmed handkerchief to whichever of the sisters needed it most, "and from the very haystack, too, from the look of you. Come, come, my dear, you must have a vastly wondrous tale to tell us of your deliverance!"

Amelie sniffed back her tears, her smile beaming through them like a rainbow from the clouds, and though she took Anabelle's offered handkerchief, she used it to dab at Juliette's eyes instead of her own. "*Mais oui,* Julie. However did you come back to us?"

"I don't know where to begin, there is so much to tell." Juliette took a deep breath to try to compose herself. She'd imagined this moment so many ways, yet she still didn't know how to begin to explain everything that had happened between her and Daniel because, of course, everything important that had happened to her since she'd been shipwrecked *had* involved Daniel.

She glanced at Anabelle uncertainly. Though she was more than a customer to Amelie—they'd long been friends as well—Juliette was hesitant to begin before her, especially since she was quite sure she'd cry again before she was done.

"Oh, la, don't stand on ceremony with me!" said Anabelle blithely. "Tell every last morsel, or keep it all to yourself, if you prefer. I'm nothing but the poor country mouse cousin, anyway."

Anabelle was hardly anyone's idea of a poor country mouse cousin, considering she was that granddaughter of a duke who had so impressed Mrs. Swain. She was short, plump even between babies, and though she was thoroughly spoiled by her doting husband, she was also one of the most good-hearted and generous—and wickedly amusing—ladies Juliette knew.

"Go on, Julie," urged Amelie. "Anabelle has been so kind to me since you were—were missing, that in a way it seems only right that she be here to hear your story."

"Which, you know, you shall have to tell many, many, many more times," declared Anabelle as she swept her skirts under her bottom and sat on one of the shop's low cushioned stools, folding her hands over her belly. "You will be the eighth wonder of Appledore, and everyone shall wish to have you to dine so that you might entertain them with your tales."

Juliette could think of nothing worse. Her feelings must have showed on her face because Amelie gently guided her to sit on another of the stools, patting her hand.

"You tell us as much or as little as you please, Julie," she said softly as she shut the door to the shop, closing it to any other customers. "I have as much time for listening as your story will take."

Juliette smiled gratefully. *This* was exactly why it had been so important to her to come back to her sister. "It's not easy to tell. That's why I didn't come to you sooner. For the longest time, I couldn't remember anything important, as if my head didn't wish to be reminded. At least not the part about being on the *Lively*, and the storm, and the—the wreck."

"Then don't begin there, *ma chère*," said her sister gently, slipping her hand into Juliette's. "Begin at a happier place, and you can tell the other whenever you wish."

Juliette nodded, looking down at their hands together. Her sister wore two rings. One was the gold wedding ring that Zach had given her, etched with a pattern like curling waves. The other ring, on the hand that now linked with hers, had belonged to their mother, a gold band with a flower of garnets and pearls.

Lightly Juliette touched the red stones. Their mother had worn the ring until she'd died, and it was only then that Amelie and Juliette had learned of its inscription—*Love Never Dies*—and that it had been a gift from the man Maman had always loved, but had been unable to marry. Juliette had always thought that inscription tragic, but it wasn't until now, knowing both how precious her love for Daniel was and how fragile life could be, that she understood the deeper meaning of the same words.

"Tell me, Julie," murmured her sister, watching Juliette touch their mother's ring. "Does this story of yours include a man?"

Juliette looked up quickly, not really surprised that Amelie had guessed.

"Yes," she said, glorying in the confession. "His name is Daniel, and he saved my life after the wreck. He found me on the beach, and took care of me, and, oh, Amelie, he is so handsome and good and kind and brave!"

"And he loves you?"

"Yes," declared Juliette proudly. "He does, and I love him, too."

Amelie smiled, though Juliette sensed her caution. "So where is he now, your Daniel?" Her gaze flicked down to Juliette's straw-covered skirts. "He doesn't seem to have taken very good care of you lately."

"This isn't Daniel's fault," said Juliette quickly. "He's still on Nantucket—he's a blacksmith there, the best on the island—and though everyone wanted us to marry at once, I wanted to talk to you first, so I had to come here to Appledore without telling him."

Even as she spoke, she realized that, as stories went, this one did not sound particularly good, and she rushed to make it better. "That is, I didn't tell Daniel beforehand, but I did leave him a message at Mrs. Swain's on a slate to tell him I'd be back by week's end. And I do mean to. Go back to him, that is."

The two older women exchanged glances that proved her efforts to improve the story were, however truthful, not succeeding.

Anabelle spoke first, as Anabelle usually did. "Blacksmiths as a rule are vastly strong men with lovely strong arms, which must be rather nice for you, Juliette. One does want a *vigorous* man for a lover."

"Anabelle!" gasped Amelie indignantly, by which Juliette understood that Daniel's vigor as a lover was not foremost in her mind.

Anabelle sighed, not in the least contrite. "It should be a consideration, Amelie. It must be, if you wish to be happy. Isn't that so, Juliette?"

Juliette nodded happily, feeling more than a little wicked herself. "Daniel is the strongest man on Nantucket."

"Well, now," said Anabelle heartily. "Then you *do* know, you clever little minx. Your sister does, too, only she won't admit it."

"*Très bien,* Juliette," said Amelie firmly, ignoring the opportunity to admit anything. "Does this Daniel have another name, besides that as the strongest man on the entire island of Nantucket?"

"Of course he does," said Juliette, now righteously indignant herself. Just because both Amelie and Anabelle had married sea captains didn't mean that they'd any right to be grand and aloof about her blacksmith. "His name is Daniel Fairbourne."

Juliette could not have imagined a silence so complete, nor so ominous, and the looks the two others exchanged now were full of worry and even fear.

"Juliette, *ma petite,*" said her sister gently, clasping her hands in her own. "When you said your head kept you from remembering things, did you forget my husband's name?"

Juliette flushed, wondering what she'd said to give herself away. "I still can't recall it," she confessed miserably. "I suppose because I think so much of Daniel, when I try to think of your husband Zach, the only name that seems to go with it is Zach Fairbourne, and I know that can't be right."

"But it is," said Amelie slowly. "Just as Anabelle is married to Joshua Fairbourne."

Anabelle leaned forward excitedly, her palm curved over her belly. "How old is your Daniel Fairbourne, Juliette?"

"I'm not sure, Anabelle." Fairbourne was not so strange a name, she told herself desperately, nor so uncommon a one in New England, was it?

Was it?

She gulped, swallowing down her own fears. "I don't believe he's ever told me, but I would guess he's several years older than I. He could be as old as thirty years."

"And his appearance, Juliette? What does he—"

"Don't push her too hard, Anabelle, please," pleaded Amelie as she rose to stand beside Juliette, her sister's hands reassuringly warm on her shoulders. "She's been through so much!"

"I'm all right, Amelie," said Juliette, though her heart was racing and her mouth was dry with fear. She thought after witnessing the wreck of the *Raven* two nights ago that there were no more dreadful secrets hiding inside her head. She'd believed she was free of the nightmare of only knowing half, yet here it was again, staring at her in the agitation of her sister and Anabelle. "I told you Daniel is most handsome, with black hair and pale blue eyes and—"

"But does he favor my husband Joshua," demanded Anabelle, perched on the very edge of the cushion, "or Amelie's husband Zach? Do you see a likeness amongst them?"

"I—I cannot say," said Juliette miserably. "I know I've met both gentlemen, I know they are shipmasters of this town and much loved by you both, but when I try to see their faces in my mind's eye, all that will come before me is another version, another shading of my own Daniel."

"Hah!" exclaimed Anabelle, clapping her hands with unabashed glee. "It must be the same one, Amelie, it *must!*"

Amelie shook her head, unconvinced. "But on Nantucket? As a blacksmith, and not a mariner? And if he were living so close, Anabelle, why wouldn't he have returned here to Appledore?"

"Why wouldn't *who?*" cried Juliette plaintively. "What does any of this have to do with my Daniel?"

"Because, my darling Juliette, you are not the only lost soul to return from the dead!" Anabelle rose to her feet with a triumphant swish of her silk petticoat. "Now hurry, hurry, both of you, for I cannot *wait* to see the look on Joshua's face when he hears you have found his brother!"

Even as boys, Daniel had always known that his brother would do well in life. But not until now, as he stood in the street before Joshua's house fifteen years since he'd left Appledore, did he realize exactly the true definition and extent of that word *well.*

To begin with, Joshua's house was hands down the grandest in the town, perhaps the entire county, and so far beyond the small cottage where they'd been born that the difference was almost laughable. It had been pointed out to him eagerly before he'd even asked, another marvel of civic pride along with that overblown brick market and the new spire on the meeting house. But then, what else could be expected when, even in a town full of sailors and shipmasters, "the Captain" referred to only one, Captain Joshua Fairbourne?

Just as he was set apart from the others with a reverential awe, his house, too, had none of the cheerful cheek-by-jowl proximity of the other houses in Appledore. Instead his sat at the top of the town, two full stories beneath a hip roof, on the rise of the hill overlooking the harbor, on a wide piece of land to keep its neighbors from jostling too close. The distance from the whitewashed fence to the house was planted with neatly spaced apple trees, their branches now bending beneath the weight of the glossy red fruit, and a carefully raked path of crushed oyster and clam shells led straight to the front door. And unlike every other house on the Cape, this one was covered in neither shingles nor clapboarding, but in wood panels that had been skillfully grooved and painted to resemble blocks of stone, like some nobleman's house outside of London.

Yet somehow the house was not forbidding. On this warm autumn afternoon, the double row of sashed windows were thrown open to catch the breezes from the water, the curtains blowing outward like bright ragtag banners. A ladder was propped against one of the trees and a half-filled basket at the bottom showed where someone—most likely a young someone—had lost interest in the chore before it was done. A hoop lay across the raked path, with an untidy spray of shells on the grass to one side to show where the roller had skidded. From the open windows came the singsong, wordless chatter of a baby, and behind the house came the laughter and shrieks of some game in wild, glorious disarray.

Daniel stood there, listening and watching, and felt his chest tighten with longing. It wasn't his brother's position in Appledore or his grand house that Daniel coveted—he'd had enough of that sort of life with Catherine to know it wasn't for him—but the life that was going on so vividly inside and outside of that imposing facade. He wanted the children and the laughter and the happy disarray that went with a family, the things he still missed from his own distant childhood, and he wanted them with Juliette.

The fact that he didn't, that he was standing here at his brother's fence like a beggar, praying that he'd be able to steel himself to go up that path and find her, was what made him feel like a failure.

A *failure:* a wretched, blasted, cowardly, double-damned failure of a Fairbourne male.

That was what Joshua would call him, that was what Sam and Serena would think, that was what Juliette would believe, if he didn't open this gate now.

He looked down at Juliette's hat in his hand. He'd been holding the straw brim so tightly that unconsciously he'd put an extra crimp in the brim with his fingers, and left a large, wet blotch on it from his sweaty palm. Oh, aye, he thought with a grimace, she'd thank him for *that,* and who could fault her?

Beside him Sachem whined plaintively and scratched his paws at the fence, eager to join whatever fun was certainly happening behind the house without him.

"Not yet, lad," cautioned Daniel, stroking the dog's head. "We haven't even made our way past the gate, let alone been invited to the party."

It wasn't as if the gate itself were an insurmountable barrier. Made of whitewashed wood like the rest of the fence, the small iron latch was made (and made poorly at that, he noted with professional scorn) only to keep the gate from swinging, not to keep visitors away. And he wasn't a visitor; he was family. All he'd have to do was press the latch with his thumb, push the gate open, and there he'd be, on his way up that neatly raked walk to Joshua's front door.

"Do you suppose our lass is truly in there, Sachem?" he asked the dog, who probably realized as well as he did himself that he was stalling, postponing the next step by asking questions whose answers he already knew. "Do you think we'll find her inside, eh?"

Of course she was. Juliette hadn't tried to hide her trail, which, he'd concluded in a dark mood while crossing the Sound, must mean she didn't believe he cared enough to follow. He'd made a false start, sailing with two friends to the mouth of the Bass River, in Yarmouth, the easiest way to reach Appledore. When he could find no one there who'd seen a woman of Juliette's description, he'd felt the old sickening dread, imagining her boat lost, her fate the same as Catherine's.

But then in a tavern he'd overheard a man describing how, the night before, a silver-haired young woman in a red cloak had stood on the Iyanno town pump to find a ride to Appledore. His first relief was tempered by a new fear for her. Who knows what kind of rascal or rogue might have snatched her up to do her every sort of harm out among the lonely fields and marshes between Iyanno and Appledore?

But then the man in the tavern had told him she'd gone with an old man driving a hay cart, and Daniel had nearly laughed out loud as he'd paid for the man's ale. Isaiah Sawyer had been driving hay carts across the Cape as long as Daniel could remember, and the only risk he'd offer to Juliette would be from boredom.

He'd hired a horse to ride to Appledore, and at the stable there had learned the way to Amelie Lacroix's shop. As he'd walked through the streets of his old town, he wondered at the changes, the new buildings and improvements, since he'd been there last. Once or twice he'd seen a man or woman he might have once known pause and look his way, but he'd kept walking, his hat pulled low over his face and his expression determinedly unwelcoming. He wasn't here as a prodigal son; he was here to find Juliette.

But fate, it seemed, held other plans. Amelie's shop was shuttered and locked. A neighbor sweeping her steps had volunteered that Madame and a fair-haired young lady had gone off with the Captain's lady to the Captain's house. He couldn't fathom why, but he hadn't wanted to ask, even though the neighbor had clearly been bursting to tell.

And so here he now stood, standing behind this blasted gate, while the afternoon slipped away second by second, and his life with it.

"Come along, Sachem," he finally growled. "If we stand here any longer we'll grow roots."

He unlatched the gate and stepped inside, his boots crunching on the crushed shells while the long ribbons on Juliette's hat fluttered in the breeze. With a happy yip of anticipation, Sachem slipped through, too. But somehow that anticipation burgeoned into out-and-out canine joy, and before Daniel could stop him, Sachem playfully snatched the hat from his hand and raced to the front door, delighted to have his master running after him.

"Damnation, Sachem," said Daniel sharply as they reached the step. He didn't want to grab the hat and risk damaging it any more than it already had been, but he also doubted that Sachem was going to surrender it without a tussle. "Drop it, Sachem. Drop it *now.*"

Sachem cocked his head to look at him, letting the brim of the hat and the ribbons drag across the stone step and into the dirt. In desperation Daniel grabbed at the hat, and as he did he managed to strike his elbow hard against the front door, striking that special tender place that made every nerve in his forearm explode with pain, and a torrent of the foulest oaths streamed from his mouth.

And it was at this exact moment that the pink-cheeked young maidservant chose to open the door.

"Good day, sir," she chirped, as if finding a man bent, doubled with pain, and swearing a blue streak as his dog danced beside him on the step were perfectly normal occurrences. "What name shall I tell mistress, sir?"

"I haven't come to see your mistress," said Daniel through gritted teeth, still clutching his elbow. "I've come to see Miss Juliette Lacroix."

"Very well, sir." The girl bobbed a curtsey, but she shut the door without inviting him in while she went to inquire.

Daniel glared at Sachem. "You know this is all your bloody fault, don't you? I should leave you here and let my brother's brats pull your ears and tail and ride you like a pony, that's what I should do."

Contritely Sachem dropped Juliette's hat at his feet. Daniel bent to pick it up, and as he did the maidservant opened the door again.

"You may come with me, sir," she said blandly to his backside. "If you please, sir."

It didn't please Daniel, not at all, but he'd come this far, and he wasn't about to leave now. He stood upright with as much dignity as he could muster under the circumstances.

"You stay, Sachem," he ordered over his shoulder as he followed the girl inside. "Damnation, for once you *stay.*"

"The ladies are in the back parlor, sir," she explained as she led him through a hall as big as his entire house. Daniel tucked his own hat properly beneath his arm and tried to smooth his hair while holding Juliette's as well. He swallowed hard, praying his anxiety would stay down, and frantically groped about in his head for something appropriate to say to Juliette, his Juliette, before the other women.

The girl stopped before a panelled door, waiting until she heard the muffled woman's voice to enter before she began to push it open for Daniel. "I believe the Captain is with them, sir."

The Captain is with them. That was all the warning he'd have, then, an infinitesimal fraction of a second to prepare himself to see Joshua after so many years apart, and then the door was open.

They were arranged in the room as neatly as the porcelain ornaments Catherine had once favored on their mantel. Joshua stood by the window in his waistcoat and shirtsleeves, older than Daniel dreamed he'd be, heavier, his black hair streaked with white, turning toward him and away from the children playing outside, a tumbler of rum in his sun-browned hand.

The three women sat clustered around a mahogany tea table. One had dark hair and a golden complexion, an exotic elegance even in mourning dress, all mingled with an eerily distinct resemblance to Juliette: her sister Amelie. The other dark-haired young woman was round, vivacious, her eyes the color of the sapphires in her ears and her dress rich enough for an afternoon of genteel visits in Bath: of course this must be Joshua's wife.

And then there was Juliette, the centerpiece. Her pale hair was untidily braided, her nose was pink with sunburn, pieces of old Sawyer's straw still clung to her skirt, and she'd never to him looked more amazingly, dauntingly lovely.

He took one step toward her, bowed, and cleared his throat, then in desperation cleared his throat again. He looked down at his feet, as if expecting to find what to say next written on the floor, and saw the trailing, albeit now grimy, ribbons of her hat in his hand.

"Juliette, sweetheart," he said, his voice sounding gruff as a bear's. "Miss Lacroix. I have come to, ah, I've come to return your hat."

Chapter 14

"You came," said Juliette, her face blushing as pink as the ribbons on her hat. "All this way, after me."

He nodded. "Aye, I did. With the hat. And Sachem, too."

"You couldn't very well leave Sachem behind." She might have smiled; he couldn't tell for sure from the way her mouth twisted. Either she was trying to smile, or trying not to cry.

"No," he agreed. "I couldn't. Else he'd bite me on the leg next time we met."

He'd rather intended that as a jest, to help lighten the mood in the room, but no one laughed, including himself. Wretchedly he cleared his throat again, the gasping, strangled sound of a man who feels the noose tightening around his neck.

Somehow he noticed she was wearing his ring, and that her hands were trembling so that the band was tapping against the tea dish in her hand, *clink, clink, clink.* For some reason that gave him a small boost of courage, enough for him to step close enough to hand her the hat.

"Here," he said. "I thought you'd want it."

"Thank you," she whispered, setting down the rattling tea dish to take the hat. "That was—was most kind of you, Daniel. To think about me."

And most kind of her, too, not to comment on the grubby, soggy, dog-slobbery mess he'd made of it. God in heaven, he loved this woman! If the others weren't there watching, he would have pulled her into her arms and kissed her. He was half inclined to do it even with them there.

Half, but not wholly.

"Welcome, Daniel," said Joshua's wife, her smile warm and genuine, her syllables rich and full of aristocratic London. For the first time he noticed that she was with child, Joshua's child, and for some reason the realization embarrassed him horribly, as if he'd actually come across his stern older brother and his buxom little wife frolicking in bed together.

"My name is Anabelle," she continued, fortunately unaware of his thoughts, "and I cannot tell you how happy we all are to have you home. Now, might I offer you a dish of tea, or perhaps something stronger?"

What he should have said next was "thank you." He should have smiled, and bowed, and kissed the air over the back of Anabelle's offered hand. He should have accepted the tea, even though he would have preferred the rum, to make a good impression as a sober, responsible prodigal. A chair would have been found for him beside Juliette's. He would have said flattering, mildly flirtatious nonsense to Amelie and to Anabelle, and he would have shaken Joshua's hand. Then, when he'd survived all that, he would have been granted time alone with Juliette, time when he could have poured out his heart to her and begged her to come back with him to Nantucket and never return here to Appledore again.

That was what he should have done. Unfortunately, he didn't.

He couldn't.

"This isn't my home, ma'am," he said, perversely honest. "Mine is on Nantucket. This belongs to my brother."

That little hiss of alarm must have come from Juliette.

It certainly wasn't from Anabelle. If anything her smile grew wider, warmer, more coaxing, more understanding.

And still his brother had said nothing.

"This may not be your actual house, no," said Anabelle gently, unfazed. "But I hope, Daniel, that you may in time come to think of this as your home whilst you visit Appledore."

What he thought, what he felt, was that these elegant blue walls with their gold-framed looking glasses and pewter sconces were folding in upon him like a house made of playing cards. All the air seemed to be flying from the room and out those open windows, leaving him nothing to breathe except the sugared scent of Chinese tea and lemon biscuits. Trapped behind the glittering silver tea service, Juliette seemed farther away from him than she had with the twenty-seven miles of Nantucket Sound between them, as if she were a prize that was always shifting farther from his reach, a prize he'd never deserve.

He took a deep breath, struggling to control the blind panic he felt welling up inside him, sweating through the back of his shirt. This could never be his home. He didn't belong here, in this house, in this family, and he never would.

"No, ma'am," he said hoarsely. "Damnation, *no.*"

He wasn't sure how he escaped from the room, or through the hall, or even out the door without the maid-servant to open it for him. All he knew was that he was, at last, outside beneath the apple trees again, his heart and lungs laboring as hard as if he'd rowed from Nantucket. He leaned against the ladder, his palms on his thighs as he bent over to catch his breath and stop the trees from spinning around him.

And realized how, once again, he'd failed so miserably to be a hero to Juliette.

"Sachem, come!" he croaked, for of course now that he wished to leave the dog was nowhere to be seen. "Sachem, here!"

At last the dog came, loping along happily from around the house with his tongue lolling and his ears flopping. But Sachem didn't come alone. Trotting close at his heels was a small, barefoot girl, her pudgy fists pumping in determination to keep up with the dog.

"Come *here,* Master Dog," she ordered fiercely. "You come right back here *now.*"

No more obedient to the little girl than he was to Daniel, Sachem didn't stop until he'd reached Daniel, where he promptly rolled on his back to invite her into scratching his stomach.

"Shameless beast," muttered Daniel with disgust, prodding gently at Sachem with his toe. "Not a bone of pride in your worthless carcass."

"Who *are* you?" demanded the little girl, peering up at

him. Her long black curls and bright blue eyes with extravagant lashes marked her as Anabelle's daughter, with a small, stubborn chin that had come directly from her father. But this afternoon she had none of her mother's stylishness, for in addition to having lost her shoes, stockings, and garters, her gown was streaked with green grass stains, with the ripped hem dragging down over the backs of her ankles. "You look like my Papa, but you're *not* an uncle. I know all of them already."

"Do you now." Daniel sighed wearily, in no mood for discussing such niceties with Joshua's daughter. "I'm Sachem's master."

"Sachem." The dog barked obligingly, and she crouched in the grass beside him, arching her fingers into little claws to better scratch his pale pink belly. "That's a queer sort of name."

"It's a Wampanoag word," he explained, wondering how old she was. Three? Four? Living alone as he did, he hadn't much experience with children, though she did seem to be more clever than most, and a little beauty, too. He hoped Joshua appreciated her. "It means a kind of Indian king. Not that Sachem's acting kingly right now. Get up, you foolish animal."

"He's not foolish," she said, pursing her lips over Sachem's nose. "He's a good dog. I like him."

Daniel was about to say that Sachem certainly liked her in return when a shrill sound like a bo'sun's whistle came from the bottom of the path. Sachem rolled over instantly at the sound, and the little girl jumped up as well.

"Aunt Polly!" she shrieked, and ran into the arms of a young woman dressed entirely in men's clothing, complete with a brass bo'sun's whistle on a chain around her neck. But as strange a sight as the woman was, Daniel forgot her instantly as soon as he saw the tall man behind her. If he'd thought Joshua had aged, then Samson looked exactly as he remembered, still so much like Daniel himself that they could even now be the twins they'd often been mistaken for as boys.

"Danny, you rascal," he said, reaching for his brother's hand, then folding him into his arms to thump him on the back instead. "All this time we thought you were dead, then up you rise, like Lazarus himself and strong as a bull!"

"Oh, aye, and look at how you turned out, Sam!" said Daniel, pushing his brother back to do exactly that. At least he was trying to, if this odd moisture making his eyes blur would let him. "Look at you!"

"I couldn't believe Anabelle's message when it came to the ship," said Samson. "What's in the stars to reel us all in to port at once, I ask you?"

Daniel only grinned, a bit of his joy fading. Samson had been a captain for years, like Joshua, like their father, and he'd naturally assume that Daniel would have followed the family tradition. But what would Sam—and Joshua—say when he learned that Daniel had turned his back on being a shipmaster, and instead returned to the lubberly trade that he'd been apprenticed to so long ago, an orphaned ward of Barnstable County?

Samson laughed and struck his fist against Daniel's arm. "All three of us, and cousin Zach as well. You do recall him, don't you? A good lad, grown to a good sailor under my schooling, and made master, too, just last year."

Daniel's spirits were sinking faster now, plummeting like lead through river water. Four Fairbourne men in Appledore together, but only three captains. He glanced past his brother to look for Sachem, wondering how soon the two of them could slink away together.

"Aye, Zach's a captain now," continued Samson with obvious affection for the young cousin, "callow pup that he is, and taken a wife, too. A Frenchwoman named Amelie, Anabelle's old milliner from Boston, and too good for Zach by half, if you ask me."

"Amelie Lacroix?" asked Daniel slowly, though he already knew the answer. Juliette's sister married to his cousin Zach, Amelie already part of his family? It had been bad enough that Juliette had overlooked telling him about Boston, but how in blazes had she forgotten to tell him *that?*

Samson nodded. "Fortunate for me that my wife is not as taken with Amelie's wares as Anabelle is, or I'd be ruined outright. Polly, come meet my wayward brother. You've already made the acquaintance of our niece Diana, I see."

The woman in men's clothing joined them, with the giggling girl—Diana—slung over her shoulders from a piggyback ride. Polly Fairbourne was prettier than Daniel first thought, once he got past the sight of a sun-browned woman in breeches, with an impish directness that was as appealing as the freckles she didn't bother to hide.

She grinned and thrust out her hand to shake his like a man. "I've heard much about you, Daniel," she said, her voice surprisingly soft, "and not one bit of it any better than it should be, considering you're this sorry rascal's brother."

Samson laughed, and slipped his arm around her waist.

"There's no other woman like my Polly," he said fondly. "I'd even trust her to sail the *Morning Star* herself, which proves both how dearly I love her as my wife and how much I respect her as a sailor. A paragon, Daniel, a true paragon. Marrying her was the best thing that ever happened to me."

"*Someone* had to take responsibility for you, Sam," said Polly as she let Diana slide down her back to the ground. "Before the revenue men caught you and shamed us all."

Samson laughed again, and kissed her before she chased off after Diana.

"You know Serena's wed, too, of course," he continued, "must be four or five years ago now, and still living out on Cranberry Point in the old house. But where's your wife, Danny? Surely some lady's snatched up a great strapping buck like you by now."

"I'm not married," said Daniel, painfully aware of his own loneliness. Amidst all this marital bliss, wives and husbands and delightful offspring like Diana, that seemed to have showered upon his siblings, he realized that here was yet another area where he'd failed and didn't belong, first with his disastrous marriage to Catherine and now having Juliette bolt away from him as soon as he'd proposed.

"Playing the merry bachelor, then?" Samson winked slyly, and reached out to touch the knot of pink ribbons that were still tucked into Daniel's buttonhole.

"No," said Daniel curtly, and yanked the ribbons from his coat and stuffed them into his pocket. "I'm not."

Samson smiled, but with a shade too much understanding that bordered on pity. "Be careful around Anabelle, then. You've never seen a more avid matchmaker."

"I've enough trouble with her husband." Daniel shook his head; he and Sam had had more than their share of trouble in the past with their older brother, who'd always tried a bit too hard to replace the father they'd all lost. "Not one word has Joshua spoken to me yet, Sam, not one bloody word."

But instead of sharing the old misery together, Sam merely frowned, as if Daniel were the one in the wrong, not Joshua. "Likely he's just so damned surprised to see you again that you've left him speechless. You didn't give us a hell of a lot of warning, you know, Danny."

Daniel opened his mouth to tell him he hadn't come here planning to see any of them when Samson rested a hand on his shoulder to stop him before he started.

"Stay here for supper, Daniel," he urged gently. "Wait until after that to judge him, and the rest of us. Picture it: nine Fairbournes around the same table at last."

Oh, Daniel could picture it, all right. Four neat, happy pairings of Fairbournes, and him the odd one out.

He heard a rustle at the window above them, and looked up to see Juliette, resting her chin on her arms on the sill with her long blond braid dangling over one shoulder. How long had she been there, been listening, he wondered bitterly. But just the sight of her, still wearing the blue gown she'd made from *his* gift of the woolen cloth, was enough to send his heart lurching.

"Please stay, Daniel," she called softly. "For my sake. Please."

Gallantly Samson lifted his hat to her. "That's Juliette Lacroix, Amelie's little sister," he said to Daniel in a stage whisper so heavy-handed Daniel wanted to cringe. "Now she'd be one worth giving up a bachelorhood for, wouldn't she? Looks to me as if she's already taken a fancy to you anyways."

But once again, Daniel knew he had to escape.

"I have to leave now," he said, and without any more civil farewell he turned his back on them all and headed for the gate.

A fancy to him, hah, he thought as the loneliness and bitterness rose up again in his throat and his heels crunched deep into the white shells. How blasted many people were there in the Fairbourne family now, anyway? He'd lost track of all the smiling, happy faces that had come bowing and bobbing before him, pretending to be rejoicing over his return. They weren't his family, not really: they were a pack of slavering, meddlesome ingrates determined to make an even greater mess of his life than he was doing on his own.

"Daniel, love, wait," said Juliette breathlessly, catching at his arm just before he reached the gate. "Please, Daniel!"

He stopped and turned because, even now, it was impossible for him to ignore her. Swiftly he glanced past her, looking toward the house for the others who, it seemed, had interested themselves more with Diana and two more children than himself and Juliette. But to be sure he pulled her off the path to one side, where they'd be hidden from the house by a mulberry bush.

"Why did you run away like that?" she asked, still breathless from chasing after him.

"Why didn't you tell me your sister had married into my blasted family?" he demanded. "Everyone keeps telling me how surprised they are to see me. Well, I can tell you I've been damned surprised myself here today."

She stared at him, incredulous. "Do you really believe I'd keep something as important as this from you? That if I'd remembered it, I wouldn't have told you at once?"

"You didn't tell me about your shop in Boston," he said relentlessly. "Fawning over rich men's wives, growing rich yourself on their vanity."

"I didn't tell you because I didn't want to spoil what we had, Daniel. God knows it was cowardly of me, but I was afraid you'd treat me differently." She sighed unhappily, pressing her palm to her forehead. "And you do now, don't you?"

He didn't answer because, to his shame, she was right. He did think differently of her once he'd learned of her life in Boston. The fashionable shop, the wealthy friends, the excitement of living in the biggest city this side of London: how could his quiet life on Nantucket compare to that? How could *he* compare?

"Aye," he finally admitted. "Because who you are, where you've come from, makes a difference. You're the one who's always telling me that."

"But not like this!" she cried softly. "Not to pull us apart! I won't deny that my life in Boston wasn't the same as it was on Nantucket. But because I loved you, Daniel, and because Nantucket was the place we shared, I came to love it, too, in a way I never could with Boston."

"But you wouldn't have been happy for long," he said, and unwittingly his voice became sad as well. "You would have grown weary of the sameness of it, and called it dull. And then you would have left for good."

Exactly the way Catherine had disappeared forever

from his life, and dear God, he was so afraid it would happen again with Juliette.

"No!" Angrily Juliette slashed her hand into the mulberry branches, enough to shower the berries over his boots. "Those are decisions for me to have made, not you!"

"Then why the devil did you—"

"No, Daniel, I'm not through!" she said, swinging around to stand directly in front of him. She'd made her hands into tight little fists, and to his surprise she was using them now against his chest, drumming home each word as hard as she could. "How can you love me if you can't trust me enough to see I'd rather stay with you on Nantucket than anywhere else on the earth?"

He grabbed her wrists to stop her drumming, to still her hands against his chest. "Then why the devil did you come here, the one place on your blasted earth that *I* don't belong?"

She stared at him in confusion, her anger fading as she searched his face for an answer with her wide, blue eyes. "That makes no sense, Daniel. I came here to find my sister, the only family I have left, and learn to my *delight*, that she's already a part of your family, too. What could be better for us both?"

"Damnation, Juliette, why do you think I haven't been back to Appledore for fourteen years?" he asked, more despair bleeding into his voice than he realized. "I'm not like them. So help me, I tried, tried to make my way the same as they did by going to sea. God only knows what Joshua will say when he learns I gave it up."

"But you're hardly a failure," insisted Juliette. "You're a master in your own trade, you love what you do, and you're respected for it on the island. And consider all the poor shipwrecked sailors who owe their very lives to you! No one could possibly say you haven't done well for yourself, Daniel Fairbourne!"

"Not like my brothers," he said, wishing he could make her understand. "Look at all that Joshua's earned for himself: this house, that wife, hell, this whole town belongs to him now! And Sam—Sam owns that ship down there, the sleekest one in the harbor, he owns it outright, and makes a bloody fortune dodging the Spaniards. Likely even Serena will have contrived a way to marry a prince or somesuch."

"Oh, Daniel, don't—"

"Nay, sweetheart, it's true," he said, his voice sinking to a rough, bleak whisper. "We Fairbournes began the same after Mam died. We all started with nothing, and compared to them, that's what I still have. Blasted *nothing.*"

"But that's not true, Daniel," she said wistfully. "You have me."

"Oh, Juliette," he said—all he could say—while the significance of what she'd said came rolling over him like a wave. After everything else that had happened in these last few days, here she still was, offering herself as the only sure, steady rock in his life. Nothing he could say now could explain that, or what her three simple words meant to him, and so instead of trying, he kissed her with all the tenderness he could, cradling her face in his hands, striving to make the promises this way that he couldn't with words.

He *would* make her happy, he swore to himself as his mouth moved over hers, gently teasing her lips apart as he deepened the kiss. He would do that and more for her, and keep striving to be that hero she deserved. And with her beside him as his wife, anything would be possible.

"Oh, my," she murmured huskily, her eyes enormous and dark when he finally broke away. She touched her fingertips first to her own lips, then to his. "Daniel, love. Come to supper, for me, and we'll . . . we'll *talk* after that. And whatever else happens, remember that you're mine and I'm yours, and that's all that *matters*."

His head was spinning, his heart reeling. "Yes," he said hoarsely, the best he could manage. "Yes."

"So here you two are!" boomed Samson behind them, standing on the path with his legs widespread as if on his own quarterdeck. "We feared you'd vanished again for another fourteen years, Danny."

"Damnation, not yet," growled Daniel automatically, then felt Juliette's fingers gently squeeze his. Aye, she was right. With her here, he could face them all, and he forced himself to smile. "Not until after supper, anyway."

"Good!" Samson nodded with satisfaction, as if he'd planned this himself from the beginning. "Not that Anabelle was going to let you get away. She'd have tripped out here in those little red-heeled slippers of hers and driven a stake through your coattails herself rather than let you unsettle her supper table arrangements. A powerful force, that Anabelle."

Yet while Samson rambled on like this, Daniel could see how he was shrewdly taking note of the relationship between him and Juliette, how she was leaning into Daniel with such easy, familiar intimacy, how their fingers were twined together. Maybe he'd even come poking around in time to see them kiss.

Well, let Sam look, thought Daniel defiantly. He wasn't

ashamed, and neither was Juliette. Hell, she was practically another Fairbourne herself. At least this way there'd be no more crude suggestions about matchmaking, as if Daniel himself was too inept to find a woman to his own tastes.

"Are you staying here with Joshua, then?" asked Samson. "God knows they've sea-room to spare."

"No," said Daniel quickly. Even if he'd been invited to stay here—which, given Anabelle's rampaging hospitality, seemed only a matter of time—he would decline. Not even Juliette could make sleeping under Joshua's palatial roof palatable.

Though if Juliette were in the bed beside him. . . .

"You can stay with me," she suggested, as if reading his thoughts. No, definitely reading his thoughts, for she blushed when she realized what she'd said, correcting herself. "With *us*, that is. Though their house is not nearly as large, I'm sure that Amelie and Zach would welcome you."

"Thank you, Juliette," he said formally, "but I won't presume."

He wouldn't be a total fool, either. There wasn't the faintest likelihood that he and Juliette wouldn't end up in the same bed if put under the same roof. After all, it had been two entire nights since they'd been together, and he'd tasted her longing, as strong as his own, when they'd kissed. He didn't know Amelie, and he couldn't remember his cousin Zach, but either way he wasn't going to let himself be accused of debauching their house guest and younger sister.

Damnation, wouldn't Joshua love getting his teeth into a mess like that!

"Then come sling your hammock with us," said Samson warmly. "We've no house proper, but the *Morning Star* has room a-plenty, especially to ship another Fairbourne."

Daniel studied his brother's smiling face, suddenly seeing in it the impish boy he'd been when together they'd played as pirates on the rocks near their old house on Cranberry Point. They'd had good times then; perhaps they could again.

"Very well," he said slowly, and was rewarded by another gentle squeeze to his fingers from Juliette. "But mind, you must promise not to set sail while I'm aboard. I'll not be pressed into service, especially not by you."

Samson laughed, and clapped him on the shoulder. "Nay, Polly wouldn't allow it. She's most particular about our crew, and suffers no rascals on our lists. I'm afraid sometimes she thinks I'm one Fairbourne too many as it is."

Daniel made himself smile again, something he was clearly going to have to do a great deal. Dear God, after fourteen years, this wasn't going to be easy.

"Tonight, love," whispered Juliette shyly. "Tonight, after supper, we'll find a way to slip away from the others so we can talk."

And this day hadn't turned out like Catherine's last, not at all. True, Juliette had gone across the water to her sister, too, but she hadn't done it in anger or to escape him, and she hadn't drowned. He'd followed Juliette, too. He hadn't let her simply vanish. And now that he'd found her, here, she'd told him she loved him in ways he'd never forget.

He'd already said his last farewell to Catherine when she'd appeared to him that night of the Raven's *wreck. But maybe this was the real goodbye, when her hold on him was broken forever.*

He grinned, sensing that tonight would be the time when Juliette finally agreed to be his wife. They could find a quiet, dark place alone, maybe out here among the apple trees, to talk, as she'd promised, and then—then they'd likely do some other things as well.

And suddenly, smiling seemed like the easiest thing in the world.

"He doesn't say much, your dear Daniel," said Amelie as she drew the brush, crackling, through the long, fine silk of Juliette's hair. "But then, with Anabelle there, too, he doesn't need to. No one does."

"Daniel isn't a chattering man, no," admitted Juliette. "I believe that comes from living so much alone. But when he does speak, he speaks from his heart, and, oh, such lovely things he says to me!"

"Ah," said Amelie sagely, nodding at their reflections side by side, one dark, one fair, in the mirror over her dressing table, and all under the watchful, sleepy-eyed surveillance of Amelie's gray cat, Luna, curled on one corner of the table. "Lovely things from a man are, well, lovely to hear."

Juliette smiled happily. This was exactly why she'd been so determined to come to Amelie, to find again this closeness, this kind of understanding and unconditional acceptance that she'd find only with her sister. Because Maman had been so distant and Amelie eight years older than Juliette, Amelie had become in many ways a substitute mother as well as the sister who suffered with her through the same vagaries of their unusual childhoods.

Amelie knew her better than anyone, and, before she'd met Daniel, had also been the only other person that Juliette loved. No wonder it had seemed so desperately important to tell Amelie about him!

In honor of Juliette's return, Amelie had left the shop closed for the day, and after they'd finished their tea with Anabelle, they'd come back to Amelie and Zach's small, comfortable home. After washing and changing out of the travel-weary blue gown, Juliette had fallen deeply asleep, and to her chagrin had slept nearly the entire afternoon. She'd been sorry to have squandered so much of her precious time with her sister, but Amelie had only shrugged and laughed and called her a great noddy-head, and brought her into her own room so they could dress together for supper at the Fairbournes'.

And talk, of course. *That* was far more important.

"You have always had such beautiful hair, Julie," said Amelie, in the French the two had spoken together since childhood, their own language of confidences and sharing. "Do you remember how I used to call it fairy hair?"

Juliette wrinkled her nose. "What you don't remember is how it tangles for no reason at all, and how it's so fine that no matter how many pins I put into it, it always slides and slithers down in no time at all."

"I'll make it stay, my dear," said Amelie confidently. "For tonight, I want your Daniel to gaze only at you, and not because your hair is such a curiosity, either. So he has asked you to marry him, and though you love him, you have not said yes. Why is that, I wonder?"

Juliette shrugged self-consciously, unsure how to explain her misgivings, even to Amelie, and reached out to stroke Luna, who chirruped with pleasure.

In the mirror, her sister studied her slyly, her head tipped to one side with the hairbrush to her cheek. "Could it be that your Daniel isn't as—what was it Anabelle said?—as *vigorous* a man as you would wish?"

Juliette giggled and blushed. "No, no, he is quite vigorous, every bit as vigorous as I am," she said boldly. "And you were right, too, Amelie, about how *rapturous* it is, after the first."

"Rapturous vigor, or vigorous rapture," mused Amelie as she began twisting and pinning Juliette's hair into upswept curls. "Ah, these Fairbourne men! But if that isn't what's wanting, then what is? Is it his trade? Does that shame you?"

"Oh, no!" exclaimed Juliette, and proudly held out her hand with the little ring. "He is an exceptional smith, Amelie, and besides doing the usual sorts of blacksmith tasks—shoeing horses and fashioning things for ships—he makes little fancies out of his head, like an artist. He made me this ring, and I have a little sun, too, in my pocket that I must show you, it's so beautifully wrought!"

Amelie nodded thoughtfully. "Then the problem isn't with him, but with you. And I'd guess it's the shop in Marlborough Street."

Miserably Juliette bowed her head, for this, too, was the reason she'd come to Amelie. "He will not leave Nantucket, Amelie, nor would I ask him to. But I don't want to leave it, either. At first I thought it was an awful, empty place, but now everywhere I look I see more beauty, a wild beauty, true, yet enough that I can't imagine returning to Boston, where the sky is only a tiny square of blue to glimpse among the chimneys."

"You love Nantucket," said Amelie softly, "because you love Daniel."

"But how can I leave the shop?" cried Juliette unhappily. "I can't remember living anywhere else. It's our home, our livelihood, and Maman's dream for us!"

"It's only an old building of brick and timbers," said Amelie firmly, "stuffed full with a great deal of silk and lace foolishness. How can that compare to what you feel for your Daniel?"

"But, Amelie," protested Juliette, struggling with a lifelong responsibility. "The shop and our mantua-making and all the customers—it's all who we *are!*"

"It's who we've *been*, Julie," said her sister, gently twisting another lock of hair. "And it still can be part of us now, or in the future. But it doesn't have to be everything, the way it was with Maman."

"But Amelie—"

"Hush," ordered Amelie, "and listen. Look at me, here in Appledore. My shop is a tiny closet of a place, a quarter the size of the one in Boston, and Anabelle is the only customer I have who'll spend more than five pounds on a single gown. Five *pounds*, Julie, which means I must sell a dreadful lot of cheap Nankeen. But it's business enough for me, more than enough, because I have Zach. And it would be enough for you, too, I think, with Daniel."

"I don't wish to quit, Amelie," said Juliette quickly. "I don't think I could give up sewing entirely. But Nantucket is changing, growing, and I think a small shop, modest to begin with, would do quite well in time."

Amelie nodded, slipping in the last hairpin. "Just as the Boston shop does well without us. When I thought you were—you were gone, I hired Marianna Dupris to run things, and she's succeeding admirably. You remember Marianna, a charming, clever girl with a good head for account books. I don't see why she can't continue, and leave you free to marry your Daniel."

Juliette stared at her in wonder. "You are sure of this, Amelie?"

"Would I have suggested it if I wasn't?" said Amelie gently. "Maman did so much for us when we were young, but I also don't want either of us to repeat her mistakes, either. Now come, I want to see you in this blue satin."

But before Juliette let her sister lace her into the blue satin gown, she hugged her tightly, both of them weeping a bit with happiness and relief, too. As she stepped into the cloud of rustling satin, she laughed with sheer joy. Tonight, she'd explain all of this to Daniel, convince him how she could make a shop, a small shop, on Nantucket work without taking away from them, and then she'd say yes.

Yes, yes, *yes*, and she laughed again, imagining his face. Whatever bad feelings he'd had in the past for Appledore would be forgotten now; she'd make sure, extra sure, of that.

"Hold your breath in, Julie," ordered Amelie, frowning as she tugged on the yellow cords that zigzagged down the front of the bodice. "We've always worn the same size before, and this fits me to perfection. I thought we'd laced your stays tightly enough, but sweet Mary, look at the gap over your breasts!"

"I think my stays shrank in the sea water when I was shipwrecked," suggested Juliette. "They do seem a bit snug."

Amelie's frown deepened. "If they'd shrunk, they

wouldn't still fit in your waist and across the shoulders. Here, lean over, and perhaps we can make do that way."

Juliette obliged, though doing so made her light-headed enough that she had to sit back down to keep from fainting.

"There," she said, taking a deep breath as the room stopped spinning. "I knew you could do it, Amelie."

Amelie's frown was now directed entirely toward Juliette's *décolléte*. She'd never been more than pleasingly endowed in that area, but now her breasts rose dramatically beyond the top of the gown, full and round and, to Juliette, so astoundingly lush that they must have belonged to another woman.

"You know something else, too, that you haven't told me," said Amelie, accusingly. "Come, come, you know a lady's mantua-maker recognizes the signs long before the poor father. When were your last courses?"

"I'm not sure," murmured Juliette. "I suppose when I was still in New York."

How had she been so preoccupied with Daniel and her addled head after the wreck that she'd forgotten *this?* No wonder she'd been thinking so much of babies! With stunned fascination, she stared down at her newly fertile breasts and rested her hands gently over her belly, over Daniel's child.

Amelie sighed, draping a large, fine lawn scarf around Juliette's shoulders and modestly across her breasts, tucking the ends into the front of the bodice.

"It won't be your hair that fascinates him tonight, Julie," she said with brisk resignation. "Not Daniel, nor any other man at that table, either. You must marry soon, of course. Anabelle and I will tend to all of that, and do our best to stave off the gossip, too."

Juliette's smile wobbled. "You are not happy for me, Amelie? Not even a little bit?"

"Of course I am, you silly goose," Amelie said warmly, kissing her on the cheek as she gave her shoulders an affectionate squeeze. "I'm immensely happy for you. But, oh, Juliette! Why couldn't Daniel have kept his *vigor* to himself until after you were wed?"

Chapter 15

There were so many of them at supper that night that the long mahogany dining table was made longer still with every extra leaf in place, and angled across the room to make it fit.

For a simple family meal—at least by her definition—Anabelle was nearly delirious with the pleasure of making so many choices: which porcelain dinnerware to use (the creamware won by virtue of there being enough plates), which linens to take from the press (the second-best damask), how many silver candlesticks to light so long a table (four), whether to put sweetmeats or nuts in the crystal pyramid (the sugared sweetmeats won), which children might possibly behave well enough to earn a seat with their parents instead of in the nursery (an unequivocal none), and of course, the menu itself, highlighted by a roast turkey, an oyster stew, and rabbits Florentine.

It was left to Joshua to decide the wines and brandies,

and mix the rum punch in his favorite blue-figured punch bowl—a highly secret, nearly lethal concoction of rum, sugar, arrack, water, lemons, and oranges that he'd had imported from the Caribbean and hoarded especially for this purpose. Joshua was also the one who waggishly calculated that there'd be nearly twenty-five feet of Fairbourne men seated around his table, the fortuitous result of four tall men being born into one family, the shortest of whom still stood over six feet in his stockings.

That shortest man was Daniel, who'd always believed that he'd been well enough compensated for that extra inch or two by being the brother with the strongest arms and the broadest chest. Not that he cared much for Joshua's well-measured braggery, anyway; it might serve to increase the awe that the people in Appledore already felt toward the Fairbournes, but personally Daniel thought the figure made them all sound like the prize bulls at a county fair.

No, the ciphering he liked best was even easier to calculate, and that was the number of chairs around that long table in the front parlor. A tall-backed armchair at one end for Joshua, another opposite it for Anabelle, then four others marching evenly down each side. Not nine, or eleven, or any other odd number made odder still by his presence, but an even ten, two by two, as if old Noah himself were waiting in the harbor with his ark tied to the Fairbourne dock.

An even ten. Because to his infinite joy, he'd been paired with Juliette.

He watched her now, across the table from him, the way he'd done through the entire meal. He'd hardly tasted the meal Anabelle's cook had toiled so upon, and he'd scarcely heard a word of the conversation swirling around him.

All he'd need to feast upon, he'd decided poetically, was the sight of his Juliette dressed in silk satin the exact color of a robin's egg, her pale hair shining silver-gold in the light of so many candles. By that same light, too, he couldn't tell if she was truly pale or not, and with some concern he noted how she only picked at her food, too, sending much of it away untouched. Then she'd smile his way and he'd forget his worries, and think only of how much longer before they could reasonably slip away.

He idly dipped his spoon in the cranberry jelly that he prayed was the last sweet before the ladies retired, and wondered if Joshua ate this lavishly every day. It was more food and ceremony than he'd want for himself and Juliette, but Anabelle did seem to know how to please his older brother.

Granted, everyone changed over time, but Joshua was undeniably happier now than when he'd seen him last, more at ease and patient with himself and his world, than Daniel would ever have thought possible. Joshua still hadn't addressed Daniel in any but the most general terms that any host would use with a guest, but considering the pitched battles they'd often fought before, Daniel would gladly accept the benign host instead.

A bell rang, and as the conversation stopped, Daniel looked toward the doorway. There stood Joshua and Anabelle's two oldest children, Diana, who he'd met earlier, and her older brother, Alexander, a tall, black-haired model Fairbourne male even at age seven. All traces of grass stain and grime had been scrubbed away, with both children ready for bed in a clean white shift and shirt.

"We've come to say good night," announced Diana, giving the bell in her hand an extra ring for good measure.

"Then do so, my dears, then off to bed," said Anabelle, and solemnly the two children made their rounds, Alexander bowing to the gentlemen and enduring kisses from the ladies, while his sister offered sloppy kisses of her own.

When they came to Daniel, Alexander bowed as he'd done before the others, but Diana hesitated uncertainly before him.

"You don't have to kiss me, lass," said Daniel, keeping his voice low and gentle so as not to frighten her. She didn't frighten him, either, the way most small children did, perhaps because he'd seen how well she did with Sachem. If Sachem could trust her, then so could he. "I don't ever force ladies to kiss me if they don't wish it."

"I'm not afraid," she said quickly, though one small pink foot was sliding uneasily up and down the opposite ankle. "I'm only wishing Sachem were here with you, too."

"Sachem wasn't invited," answered Daniel solemnly. "His manners aren't equal to your mam's table. But I'm sure he'd like to see you tomorrow."

"I would like that, too. Good night, uncle." She stood up on her toes and Daniel bent dutifully so she could reach his cheek. "And I like you, too, and not just because you brought Sachem, either."

"Diana," said her mother, warning enough in that single word to make the girl bob a quick, appeasing curtsey.

"Good night, uncle," she said again, and shuffled on beside her brother to her Aunt Serena.

Daniel's smile lingered, painfully bittersweet as he

watched the children repeat their ritual, finally climbing onto Joshua's lap for an exuberant, noisy hug to go with the kiss. Though Joshua laughed and scolded her with mock severity, the look of purest love on his stern face as his daughter's chubby arms linked around his neck was enough to make Daniel's own heart twist with regret.

Diana must be close to the age of the child he'd lost with Catherine, and though he'd never know if that baby had been a boy or a girl, seeing Diana with her damp black curls bouncing down the back of her shift, one plump little shoulder wriggling free of her shift, made him grieve for what he hadn't had the chance to have.

Until now, he reminded himself fiercely, and looked again to Juliette. She, too, was watching the pair of children, her expression misty eyed, her smile doting. She'd be a good mother, he decided, an excellent mother, and it was wonderfully appealing to imagine their own little house on Nantucket overrun with the same childish disarray that persisted even in Joshua's grand house.

Their house, he thought again, relishing the sound of such companionship. Not his, but theirs.

God help him if she didn't accept him tonight.

"Ladies," announced Anabelle as she stood from her chair at the head of the table. "High time we left these gentleman to their rum and pipes, and retreated to our tea."

With a rustle of petticoats—for in honor of supper, even Samson's wife Polly had put aside her breeches for more ladylike attire—the women followed Anabelle. Before Juliette left, she flashed a quick conspirator's wink to Daniel, blushing with anticipation that he shared.

Before he took his seat again, he pulled his watch from

his pocket and checked the time. He and Juliette had agreed to make their respective excuses ten minutes after the ladies withdrew, and meet beneath the third apple tree in front of the house.

Ten minutes, he thought with satisfaction as the punch began making its first round of the table. Though it would stretch like an eternity, he could survive ten minutes, and use it to dream of the heaven ahead.

"Daniel," said Joshua, and for the first time Daniel realized his brother hadn't resumed his seat when the ladies had left the room. "I'm sorry you won't have the chance to sample my punch—a devilish brew it is tonight, isn't it, Sam?—but I've a few words that need speaking to you alone. Come, we'll go back to my office, and leave these rogues to guzzle our shares."

"A few words, Joshua?" Daniel asked with unreasonable hope as he followed his brother. Expecting Joshua to limit himself to a "few" words was as vain an expectation as looking for rosebuds in the middle of a Massachusetts February.

Joshua grunted as he pushed open the door to his office. Obviously this was no spontaneous conversation, for the servants had recently lit the candles in the brass chandelier overhead on their master's orders. Though Joshua kept a more formal office in a warehouse near the docks, the tall desk here and surrounding shelves were still piled high with papers and ledger books, and a large map on the wall had colored pins scattered across the seas and countries to mark the passages of ships with Fairbourne interests.

"Don't tell me you can't stomach a handful of words from me after, oh, what has it been—eight years? nine?—

since I saw you last on St. Bartholomew?" Joshua waved his hand at one of the leather-covered chairs for Daniel to sit, then went to pour two glasses full of the Newport rum he still favored. "Go on now, sit."

As he dropped into the offered chair, Daniel's hopes for that ten-minute rendezvous sank even further. Joshua wouldn't squander his best Newport rum on just any handful of words. He had something serious planned, something that was bound to take longer than ten minutes. He stared glumly at the tall case clock, ticking away the seconds instead of Joshua's words.

Nine minutes now.

"Here." Joshua handed him the tumbler of rum, and as he sat in the opposite chair, he raised his own glass. "Here's to your return, Danny. I don't know why the hell you've made yourself gone so long, but we're glad you're back, and that's an end to it."

"Thank you," said Daniel stiffly, uncomfortable with this un-Joshua display of sentiment, and sipped at the rum. He'd have to down it completely before he could leave, even if Joshua had finished whatever he planned to say. "It's, ah, good to be back."

"Aye." Joshua drank more deeply than Daniel did, pretending to mull over what he'd say next. Joshua mulling was a dangerous portent, and Daniel braced himself for what could come next.

Eight minutes.

"I congratulate you on your wife, Joshua," Daniel said awkwardly, hoping perhaps to deflect Daniel's real purpose. "She's a charming woman, and very beautiful."

"Nan is the love of my life," said Joshua, and from the smile that lit his face there was clearly no mulling now, just fact. He looked younger when he smiled, or maybe it was simply thinking of Anabelle. "Every day with her is a joy. Her grandfather's a duke, a peer of the realm. Did you know that?"

Daniel shook his head. Joshua would have married a blue-blood wife, he thought cynically, then felt the mean-spirited cynicism turn to guilt. Anabelle hadn't earned that from him, and neither, really, had Joshua.

"I had to steal her right out from under her family's high-and-mighty noses," his brother continued, chuckling fondly at the memory. Joshua had been a privateer in the last war, where he'd made a good beginning on his fortune and acquired a profitably predatory outlook toward trade that had carried over into peacetime smuggling and, apparently, his love life as well. "Nothing like a challenge to make the prize all the sweeter, eh?"

Again Daniel shook his head, stole another glance at the clock, and gulped more of the rum.

Seven minutes. What the hell would Juliette think if he left her standing alone among the apple trees?

"But that's part of what I wanted to say, Danny," said Joshua, turning serious. "I was sorry to hear what happened to your wife, damned sorry. Lost in a storm like that, all hands gone—that's no way for a woman to die, especially a pretty little creature like I heard your wife was."

Daniel felt as if the floor had just dropped from beneath his chair. He'd disappeared himself as soon as he'd learned Catherine's fate, and kept it so thoroughly to himself that, in all the years since, this was the first time he'd heard a single word of sympathy or shared grief.

And to hear it now, from Joshua, was almost unbelievable. He would have laughed out loud if he hadn't been so damned close to crying.

"Drink, drink up," said Joshua, splashing more rum into Daniel's tumbler. " 'Tis no mystery how I knew, Danny. I'm no mountebank conjurer. But in those first years I looked after you, from a distance, mind, but close enough to see how well you were doing for yourself. I was proud enough to burst when I'd heard you'd made captain, and without a lick of help from me, either. A regular run in the islands, a name for yourself as a steady master, then marrying that planter's daughter, the fine house, the place among her people—oh, aye, you did well, Danny. Then your poor lady drowns, and—"

"Catherine," said Daniel softly. "Her name was Catherine."

"Aye, it was," agreed Joshua. "And didn't Catherine Fairbourne have a pretty sound to it!"

"Almost as pretty as she was herself."

He remembered that about Catherine, how she'd been such a great beauty that men in the street would turn to stare. But strange how, beyond that, he no longer could recall the details of her face or features. Poor Catherine, indeed.

For the real tragedy had been that neither one of them had deserved the other.

"I've never seen a man vanish so completely, Danny," said Joshua, shaking his head as he turned to reach in a chest behind him. "I was sure you'd gone mad with missing her, and tossed yourself into the sea. We gave you up for dead, and who could blame us? But here. This should help ease your burden."

Proudly he thumped a heavy cloth bag on the table beside Daniel, a heft and muted clink that could only belong to coins.

"Go on, look inside," urged Joshua. "That's your master's share from your last voyage. You earned it, whether you collected it or not, and I made sure to get what was due you—for safekeeping, mind. But it's all yours now, and I'll wager that gold will be mightily useful since you're planning to wed again."

Juliette. Swearing, he looked up at the clock: seven minutes past the time they'd agreed to meet.

"I must go, Joshua," he said, jumping to his feet, hurriedly. "I must—"

"Hold now," rumbled Joshua as he seized his arm. "You're not going anywhere yet. And do you think Nan would let that lass go traipsing about alone in the dark?"

"How the devil did you—"

"We're not blind, Danny, and we're not fools," said his brother. "Besides, there's no trickery you can try that Nan and I didn't do first. Miss Lacroix's safe in our parlor with Nan, sipping tea and gossiping while she waits for you. And you're not leaving here until we decide which ship you'll be sailing under the Fairbourne name."

So this was it, thought Daniel, the real reason for everything else. Joshua didn't have to explain any more. They both understood what he was offering, and how generous an offer it was. Any of Joshua's ships, with any cargo bound for any port he pleased, as long as he'd agree to be the captain. Once again he'd be a welcome member of his family, proudly sailing under a flag that bore the Fairbourne name.

If he agreed, he could build Juliette her own grand house here on the hill in Appledore, and let her fill it with whatever treasures she wished. She could see her sister Amelie whenever she pleased, and stroll here to take tea with Anabelle. Their children would be born here, and grow up playing with their cousins, in a town where everyone would know and respect their name. Instantly he and Juliette would be as close to gentry as anyone born in New England.

And they'd both be miserable.

"I've given it up, Joshua," he said. "I'm a blacksmith now."

Joshua scowled derisively. "That's what Nan told me, but damnation, I don't believe it. You're a Fairbourne, Daniel. The sea's in your blood." He grabbed the bag full of coins and shook it. "Do you make that kind of gold tapping away in some dark, dirty little shop, eh? Do you have men fear you and respect you, and wish their sons would grow to be like you? Do you remember what it's like to run fast and true with the wind on your back and the spray on your face, and know that you've mastered the sea itself?"

Oh, aye, Daniel remembered the exhilaration of days like that, but he also remembered the darker ones when the sea was the master, and all anyone, master or sailor or lowest ship's boy, could do was shorten sail and pray for mercy. He remembered the tedium and the cold and the hunger and the utter loneliness of being away from home for months at a time, and he remembered how commonplace, even expected, death and injury became.

And he remembered why he'd never gone back.

"You won't change my mind, Joshua," he said, surprising himself by how, finally, he could stand up to his brother. "Nantucket, and my shop, suit me fine. As soon as Juliette's done visiting her sister, we'll go back together."

"But damnation, man, what about Juliette?" demanded Joshua. "You can't expect her to be content with nothing. Women want to marry heroes, men they can look up to. How can you be that to her covered with soot?"

A hero. That was the one word that nearly tripped Daniel, the one argument that almost made him falter. He *had* tried to be a hero for her, hadn't he? He thought again of the wreck of the *Raven*, how he'd help save four lives only to lose two more.

Yet still Juliette loved him, and he loved her. She'd fallen in love with him as a blacksmith, not as a sea captain, and she wore the ring and treasured the sunburst that he'd made for her. And soon, very soon, he hoped, she'd be his wife.

"Don't refuse me outright, Danny," urged Joshua. "Think of it for a day or two, and I'm willing to wager you'll come around."

"I'll think of it," said Daniel. "But I won't change my mind."

Joshua made a disgruntled noise deep in his chest. "You always were a stubborn little bastard, Daniel."

"That's because I learned from a big one." He grinned and held the tumbler with the last of the rum up toward Joshua in silent salute before he drank it. Who would have thought when he'd followed his brother into this room, that he'd be leaving now making jests instead of dodging fists, and sounding almost like friends?

He shook his head, marvelling at the change as he tucked the bag with the coins into his pocket. "Now I'd better go learn if Juliette's still speaking to me."

"Oh, she'll be happy enough when she discovers you have gold in your pocket," said Joshua dryly as he emptied his glass as well. "Leastways Anabelle always is. But one other thing, Danny, before you go."

Daniel turned back, expecting another joke, but his brother's face was now serious. "This is meddling, Daniel, pure and simple, and you can tell me to shove off and I'll mind. But tell me: does Juliette Lacroix know you've been wed before?"

Daniel looked down, away from his brother, and frowned. "Not yet, no. But I intend to tell her, Joshua, and soon."

"Make sure you do," said his brother earnestly as he opened the door. "I know it won't be easy, but you must speak to her. That's the kind of thing that will hurt a woman faster than a knife. Now come, let's see if those ladies of ours have floated away on a sea of tea."

But when Daniel hurried ahead to Anabelle's small back parlor, to his great disappointment neither of the Lacroix sisters was there.

"I'm sorry, Daniel," said Anabelle, patting his arm gently. "But Juliette wasn't feeling well, and Amelie decided to take her home."

"Juliette's ill?" demanded Daniel with immediate concern. "What's wrong?"

"Oh, I'd venture nothing that sleep won't cure," said Anabelle quickly, though Daniel didn't miss the meaningful glance that passed between her and Joshua, sufficiently meaningful that behind him Joshua grunted with wordless surprise. "She's had a difficult time of it lately, you know, and the poor lass hardly ate more than two bites at supper. But I expect if you call on her tomorrow morning, you'll find her vastly improved, and vastly ready, too, to give you the answer you wish to hear most."

"You know?" asked Daniel, surprised that this secret, too, seemed no secret at all.

"Oh, la, I know everything," said Anabelle blithely. "And a good thing, too, since Amelie and I have already begun planning the wedding."

"Be careful with Nan, Danny," cautioned Joshua, "else she'll be planning your funeral, too."

Anabelle poked him with her fan. "Hush, captain, or I'll plan worse than that for you. But please, Daniel, do not worry about your own ladylove. I promise you by morning—not early morning, please, please, but later, at a civil and sociable hour for ladies—she'll be overjoyed to have you call."

But Daniel had waited for days for Juliette's answer, he'd waited for hours, and then, finally, his appointed ten minutes. And as he said his farewells, he resolved to wait no more.

Juliette lay in the middle of the bed, counting the pleats along the tops of the bed hangings to try to make herself drowsy enough to fall asleep. She very nearly had in Anabelle's parlor, and also very nearly toppled off her chair in the process, startling Anabelle and her sister so that they were convinced she'd fainted, not fallen asleep.

No matter how much she'd protested, Amelie had insisted on bringing her home, undressing her like a child, and putting a hot brick wrapped in flannel at the bottom of the sheets to warm them. She'd rather liked the hot brick, but still she certainly hoped she wasn't going to spend the next eight or so months being treated like a baby simply because she was going to give birth to one.

And now, of course, with the rest of the house and the street and the whole wretched town excruciatingly quiet, *she* was wide, wide awake. Restlessly she wondered if Daniel were asleep, too, and what they'd told him when she'd been swept off so early after supper. She'd begged Amelie and Anabelle both to let her tell him about the baby, which they'd agreed was proper, but who could guess what tale they'd told him in its place. Even the truth—that she'd fallen face first off her own chair—was sufficiently humiliating. And tonight should have been so memorable for much better reasons!

With a mournful sigh, she flopped her arms out on either side of her head and began counting the pleats again, this time in French.

"*Une, deux, trois, quatre, cinq, six, sept—*"

"Juliette!"

She stopped counting, sure she'd imagined it. Who would be calling her name at this time of the night, in that odd raspy half whisper, half shout?

"Damnation, Juliette, are you awake or not?"

"*Daniel!*" In an instant she was out of bed and across the room to the window, grimacing at the screeching squeak of the sash as she eased it upward and jammed the wooden prop in place to keep it open.

Eagerly she leaned out, searching the empty street for him. "Daniel?"

"Over here, sweetheart."

She leaned out a little farther, and saw him in the shadow of the tall wooden fence that ran between Amelie's house and the next one.

"I cannot believe you're here!" she whispered as

loudly as she dared. "Can't you see it's the middle of the night?"

He pulled out his battered pewter pocket watch and held it up for her to see. "It's half past one exactly, which isn't *exactly* the middle of the night."

She laughed, not so much because this foolishness with the watch was so amusing and exciting, but because she was so pleased to see him again. They'd lived together in one room for weeks, and they'd shared a bed as lovers, but somehow she found this odd enforced separation, especially having Daniel standing below the window of her bedchamber, his upturned face washed with moonlight, the most wildly romantic situation imaginable. Once, long ago, she'd read a story about a lady calling down to her lover from her balcony, almost like this. She didn't remember much else about the story, except that the lady had had her name—Juliette—which seemed most appropriate for this evening.

"Anabelle said you were ill," he said, "and that's why you left. Are you better now, sweetheart?"

"Oh, yes," she said, resting her head on her hand. "Much."

"That's good to—*oww!* Clear off, you infernal animal!"

She leaned farther out the window and saw her sister's cat sitting on the top of the fence, one paw leisurely swiping down at the top of Daniel's head while he swatted his hat toward her.

"That's Luna," she said. "She belongs to my sister, and she's not very fond of men. She tolerates Zach now because he threatened to toss her overboard, but he could tell you how long she picked on *him*."

Two houses away, another window slammed down in speechless, but hardly silent, protest.

"Oh, my, Daniel," said Juliette, lowering her whisper. "I suppose we've been too loud."

"Hell," he grumbled, still rubbing the side of his head where Luna had clawed him. "Why don't you just come downstairs to open the door and let me in?"

"Amelie would be furious if I did that, and she's already cross enough with you for—for not bringing me to see her before this," she finished lamely, almost announcing her special secret to all of Appledore. "You should probably go soon anyway, before you wake her and Zach."

"Not before I have my answer," he said. He swept his hat in front of his waist and bowed grandly over his leg before he looked back up at her. "My dearest, dearest Juliette. Will you honor me forever by becoming my wife?"

She pressed her hands together over her mouth, wishing there was some way she could capture this forever. She didn't know how she could be this happy and survive, it was all so blissfully, wondrously *perfect*.

"Oh, yes, Daniel!" she shouted, spreading her arms and not caring if the entire town did hear her now. "Yes, Daniel Fairbourne, I *will* be your wife!"

He grinned up at her, his joy an obvious match for hers, and flung her an extravagant kiss through the air in lieu of a real one on her lips.

"You must come back tomorrow, Daniel," she said. "I have something very important to tell you."

"As if you could keep me away." She thought his expression darkened, the joy fading, but it could have been a shift in the moonlight as well. "I have something very important to tell you, too, love."

The window between them squeaked open, and

Amelie's head in a ruffled nightcap poked out to look down at Daniel, then up at her. "Good *night,* Juliette."

"Good night, Amelie," she answered contritely. "And good night to you, too, Daniel, my dearest husband!"

"Good night, little wife," he said, his whisper so low and suggestive she shivered. "Good night, and sleep well."

And when she crawled back under the coverlet to sleep, this time it wasn't curtain pleats that she counted, but how many times, and in how many ways, Daniel Fairbourne had told her he loved her.

He was waiting for her in Amelie's parlor when she came down the stairs in the morning. He had, she knew from Amelie, been there waiting for her a good long while, but as eager as she'd been to see him again, this morning she hadn't been equally eager to leave her bed. She had not actually been ill, but there had been some dreadfully long moments earlier when she'd pulled the chamberpot out from beneath the bed and prayed fervently for her lurching stomach to settle. Though with Amelie's help she'd finally dressed and managed to nibble at a piece of dry toast, she'd still crept down the stairs as if she were a thousand years old, and Daniel's greeting kiss had turned into one more battle of wills with her churning innards.

"Maybe I am too early," he said with concern as he guided her to a chair. "Damnation, I should never have kept you up so late, yowling at your window like an old tom cat."

She smiled weakly, remembering how Luna had treated—or mistreated—him.

"I don't regret it for a moment," she said, "because

now we're formally promised to be wed, and now I can tell you my secret."

"Ah, aye." He looked down at her hand, obviously troubled. "Juliette, maybe it would be better if I told you mine first."

"Mine is a happy secret," she said, his mood making her uneasy. "Wouldn't you rather have that first?"

He sighed, resigned. "Go on, then, love. What's your secret?"

"I don't know if it can be properly be called a secret or not," she confessed, trying to smile, "considering how many other people seem to have known it before we did. At least before I did, anyway."

He waited patiently, clearly not guessing, and she noticed how he'd borrowed a coat from Samson to come calling, a coat that was too tight in the sleeves and too long at the hem, with the buttons pulling all the way down the front. Maybe that coat was why he looked different this morning. Maybe there wasn't anything else about him that had changed.

She looked down at her hands in her lap, at the thin black ring he'd made for her. "I thought for sure you'd figured it out last night when Diana and Alexander came to the table to say good night, and you looked across at me, and I—I—oh, Daniel, I do hope this first one is a girl, like little Diana!"

He stared at her, the truth beginning to dawn. "You're with child? My child? *Ours?*"

She nodded, blinking and trying hard not to cry. This wasn't happening the way she'd imagined last night at all, not at all. "I told you it was a happy secret."

"And it is, lass, it is," he said firmly, though the emptiness in his pale eyes said otherwise. "The best secret I've ever heard."

She wished he'd ask how she felt, or said if he'd hoped for a boy or girl, or told her something else to show her he really was pleased. But he didn't. All he did was sit there, in a plain wooden chair, and stare at the floorboards between his feet.

"Very well, then, Daniel," she asked at last. "What is your great secret?"

"Aye, my secret." He took a deep breath, but didn't raise his gaze. "When I marry you, Juliette—if you marry me—you won't be my first wife."

Chapter 16

"Daniel," she said, her voice echoing distant and odd in her own ears. "Oh, Daniel, please. What are you telling me?"

Still he didn't look at her. "That you won't be my first wife," he said raggedly. "What I told you before. It's true, Juliette."

"Very well," said Juliette slowly, trying to cling to whatever was left of her world. "This—this first wife of yours. Where is she now?"

"Catherine," he said. "Her name was Catherine. Joshua told me I must tell you about her, and now—now I have."

"But you haven't told me anything!" cried Juliette. "Where is she—where is Catherine—now?"

"I don't know," he said, his voice so low she could scarcely hear it. "They never found her."

"Oh, Daniel." Trembling, she rose to her feet, not because she wanted to leave, but because standing somehow made it easier to bear. "Is she still alive, then? Is that what you're telling me, that we cannot marry because you're already wed to another?"

"No," he said, finally looking up. When he saw she was standing, he rose, too. He didn't try to touch her, or make any other effort to comfort either her or himself. He simply stood there, his expression as empty as a man's could be.

"No," he said again. "There's no doubt that she's dead. Everyone else died, too. It was a long time ago now, five years, four months, and—and I used to know, Juliette. I used to know exactly how long it had been, and now I don't, not since I found you."

Five years ago, then, he'd been widowed. Five years he'd lived alone, counting the days and likely the nights as well. Mrs. Swain had said that all the time he'd been on Nantucket, he'd never kept company with any woman, but in a way, he had. He'd been keeping company with the memory of his dead wife, Catherine.

"I'm sorry, Daniel," she said, quavering. She knew she should be relieved that they could still marry, that her child would have a name, but it was impossible for her to feel any real happiness over someone else's death. "I'm sorry that you lost her. Lost Catherine, I mean."

"I didn't lose her," he said, his voice rising sharply. "She died, and it was my fault, and *damnation*, I don't know why Joshua says you must know this!"

His vehemence frightened her, and she clasped her hands together so he wouldn't see how they were shaking. She had always wondered what had happened in his life between the time he'd left Appledore and when he'd come to Nantucket, but she didn't want to know *this*.

But Joshua was right. If she truly loved Daniel, then she must take the bad as well as the good. Their life together wasn't always going to be throwing kisses in the moonlight. But she knew that already, didn't she? Hadn't he saved her life when he'd found her on the beach, and hadn't he given her hope when all she'd wished was to die? Now it was her turn to help him, to listen, however he needed her.

But oh, dear God, she didn't know where to begin.

"I love you, Daniel," she said, returning to the only truth she had left, "and you love me, and that's all that matters now, isn't it? Isn't it?"

"I don't know," he said, finally meeting her gaze, and for the first time she glimpsed in his eyes the pain and confusion that were roiling inside of him. "I don't know anything. She was young, Juliette, like you, and beautiful like you, too, and when we married, I did love her, and I hope she loved me. But then she didn't, and she left me to go to her sister on the next island, just like you did, and I let her go. I didn't try to stop her, Juliette. I let her go."

"And the boat she was in sank, didn't it?" whispered Juliette, suddenly understanding. "That's what you meant when you said everyone died."

She could see by how his features twisted that he was reliving it again as they spoke, his own nightmare so uncannily mirroring her own.

"After the storm, some of the bodies washed ashore," he said, the words almost torn from him. "Most never did. There are sharks among those islands, you know, and they feed on wrecks."

She hadn't had to face sharks, and just the little he said sickened her. All she'd had to face was the icy grip of the water around her, the way it pulled and tugged and tried to draw her down, and suddenly she was remembering it all too clearly, too keenly, fighting the terror of knowing she was going to drown.

She closed her eyes, struggling with her own memories. She had *not* drowned. She had *not* died. She'd survived and she was alive, and Daniel was the reason.

But he hadn't been able to do the same for Catherine, Catherine who'd been his first wife, Catherine who hadn't loved him the way he'd loved her.

"That's why you walk the beach after storms in Nantucket, isn't it, Daniel?" she said, her words tumbling over one another. "And why you're always the first one in the boats whenever there's a shipwreck. You're looking for *her*, to save her the way you couldn't before."

"I can't help it, Juliette," he said with despair. "She said I'd never be a hero, but I kept trying. Damnation, I've kept *trying!*"

"You, Daniel?" she asked in wonder, and anger, too, at this heartless Catherine. "How could she say you weren't a hero?"

"For her I wasn't, was I?" he said, shaking his shoulders as if he could free himself that way from the weight of his guilt and grief. "But then when I went looking for her, instead I found you."

"And you saved me," she whispered, her heart racing as she remembered again that awful night.

But which now was the greater fear? To feel the icy, dark waters lapping at her again, or the awful possibility that Daniel only loved her as a substitute for his lost Catherine?

He reached out to her then, and she stared at him,

standing there, needing her with the same raw urgency they'd shared that night on the dunes. Yet still she held back. His embrace had become the one place she always found peace from her fears. But what if it wasn't her haven to have, and never had been? Where would she go now for solace, for comfort?

Where would she go without Daniel's love?

"Oh, sweetheart," he said desperately, seeing how she had begun backing away from him. "Don't leave me now."

"I'm not leaving," she said automatically, willing herself to stay for the sake of them both, forcing herself to stay where she was and stop inching backward. "And Daniel, I'm not—I'm not Catherine, either. I'm Juliette."

"Juliette, my own love, if you'll still have me." He smiled wearily, and something shifted subtly in his eyes and he suddenly was again the Daniel she knew, the Daniel who loved *her,* Juliette Lacroix. Now when he reached to touch her, she welcomed it, shivering as he gently ran the backs of his fingers up and down her forearm. "My sweet lass. And our child, too."

He lowered his glance along her body, as if he could somehow see the tiny baby growing within her, and the tenderness of it made her want to weep with happiness.

"You are happy, then?" she asked shyly. "About the babe?"

"Oh, aye, love. Seeing Joshua's children put me in that mind, too," he said softly. "I looked at little Diana, and thought of how the babe that I lost with Catherine would have been her age now."

Juliette's smile froze, her hand instinctively covering her belly. "She—Catherine—was with child, your child, when she died?"

With great gentleness he laid his hand over hers, over their child. "I lost them both, together, and if I—"

"No, Daniel!" she cried, whipping away from him, "no *more!*"

She saw the fear in his face, but she didn't care. "Juliette, please, I didn't—"

"No, Daniel, not like this," she said as she backed away from him, her whole body so taut with anguish that she felt if he touched her again she'd shatter. She snatched a shawl from the back of a chair, wrapping it tightly over her shoulders and around her arms. "Not like this."

"Juliette, please," he said again, and she knew with awful certainty that as he watched her now, he was remembering Catherine leaving. "Sweetheart, please, don't go."

"I have to," she said, the tears stinging in her eyes. "I need time alone with my—my thoughts, Daniel, and so do you. I know that she—Catherine—is a part of you, and always will be. I accept that. But I'm the one who's here now, and our child, and I'm the one who loves you, oh, so much, and—and—oh, Daniel, I don't know anything any longer, I don't *know!*"

And before he could argue with her, she fled the house. Down an alley, across one street, through another passage between two houses, her steps quickening until she was nearly running. It didn't matter where she was going, as long as she kept moving, always moving, as if her feet must match the breakneck pace of her own emotions.

"Aunt Juliette!" called Diana shrilly, and abruptly Juliette stopped. "Aunt Juliette, ahoy!"

Somehow she had walked clear to Front Street, near

the wharfs and warehouses, with the bright morning sun glittering off the water and the street full of people beginning their day. If she'd wanted solitude, Front Street had not been the right choice, but she was here now, and now Diana and Samson's wife, Polly, carrying a wicker hamper between them, were dodging a fish cart to come speak to her. She took a deep breath to calm herself, smoothing her shawl over her arms.

"Ahoy, ahoy," said Diana cheerfully. "That's how sailors say 'good day,' you know."

She was dressed the same as Polly, in her brother's outgrown and well-worn breeches and checkered shirt, with a knitted sailor's cap pulled low over her hair. No one except Juliette seemed to find this unusual, proving again, she supposed, the power of the Fairbourne name in Appledore.

"Ahoy, then, to you, too," said Juliette. "And good day as well, since I'm not a sailor."

"But *we* are, and *we* are going sailing," announced Diana importantly. "That's why we're dressed like real sailors, Aunt Polly and me, and not like ladies."

"Upstart little minnow," teased Polly, tugging Diana's hat lower over her brow, nearly over her eyes, to make her giggle. "It takes a great deal more than the proper clothes to make a proper sailor."

She smiled warmly at Juliette. "We're only sailing to the mouth of the harbor and back. We'll be glad to ship another crew member if you'd like to come, too."

"Sail with us, Aunt Juliette!" Diana hopped up and down with excitement. "It's a bee-ooo-tiful day, and maybe we'll see turtles, even seals!"

Juliette couldn't help but smile at that, thinking wistfully of how she'd told Daniel she'd like their first child to be a girl like this one, albeit one that she could dress more stylishly.

"I don't know if you should be calling me your aunt just yet," she said. "I'm not married to your Uncle Daniel."

"But you will be," said Diana with considerably more confidence than Juliette herself felt this morning. "Mama told me you would. She said to be vastly kind to you, too, since you'll be a Fairbourne woman, and we Fairbourne women must all stand up for each other."

"Now that *is* true," said Polly with amusement, "especially for the hapless women who marry Fairbourne men. But I'd wager you don't need us to tell you so, do you, Juliette?"

Juliette didn't, not in the least, and she thought sadly again of the dismal scene with Daniel that she'd just fled. But Polly's smile was so warm and sunny, her confidence so engagingly uncomplicated, that impulsively Juliette decided that shipping on with these two for the morning might be exactly what she needed.

"I don't know fore from aft," she said, "and I'm not dressed at all properly, but if you still wish to offer me passage, I'd like very much to join you."

Though Juliette truthfully did know next to nothing about boats or sailing, she could tell as soon as they walked down the wharf that Polly knew a great deal indeed. She called to sailors and wharf men she knew, bantering and trading raucous insults, and swinging herself down the ladder and into the small sailboat with all the ease of a long-time topman. Diana, too, scrambled down like a blue-eyed monkey. Only Juliette fumbled awkwardly, bunching her billowing skirts with one hand as she tentatively felt her way backward, rung by rung, until she reached the boat.

"Just keep low," advised Polly as the boat rocked and Juliette grabbed at the side. "Here, come sit beside me."

"Yes, Aunt Juliette," chimed Diana. "You must keep your bottom down. That's what Papa always says, too."

Deciding she'd much rather hear such advice from Diana rather than Joshua, Juliette gratefully took Polly's hand and let herself be seated in the stern sheets, beside the tiller, feeling as unsteady as someone's aged grandmother. The boat was smaller than any she'd been in before, with a single sail made for one person to sail with a passenger or two and used for short sails from one town to the next or to carry provisions out to the largest ships moored in the deeper water. Diana scrambled to the front of the boat with the dinner hamper, as close to the bow as she could, obviously anticipating the feel of the wind and spray on her face. Juliette watched with awe as Polly deftly untied the lines, pushed the boat free, and set the sail for exactly the right angle to catch the breeze and sail away to the open water.

"I've no notion at all of how you do this," she marvelled as Polly came to sit beside her, leaning into the tiller to steer even as she was trimming the sail to catch a better wind. In a strange way she felt less afraid and more relaxed in a smaller boat like this, gliding over the swells like it was a part of the water, than in a bigger ship that seemed to fight through the water instead. "It's nothing but a complete mystery to me."

"Oh, 'tis not so very hard," said Polly modestly. "It's whatever you're accustomed to, that's all. I've sailed since

I was younger than Diana, and think nothing of it. But take me into a fancy shop like yours, and I become the worst sort of dull-witted noddy, unable to choose my own petticoats, let alone gloves or ribbons or fans."

"But that's fun!" protested Juliette. "That is simply a matter of guiding one's taste with an eye to the new fashions."

"And this is what's fun for me," said Polly cheerfully, "guiding this boat with an eye to steering clear of all the fools pretending to be sailors. All we women have our own talents, you know. The hard part is discovering them, then finding a man that is willing to let us keep doing what we enjoy."

"Samson doesn't mind you sailing?" she asked curiously.

"Oh, in the beginning Sam refused to believe I could know anything at all," said Polly, laughing at the memory. "But now he even lets me steer the *Morning Star* if I've mind to, and says he trusts my eyes in the lookout more than any man on the crew. Is that what you and Daniel were quarrelling about this morning, then?"

Juliette flushed, wishing her emotions were not quite so easy to read. "I wish it were that simple."

"Nothing is simple with the Fairbournes," said Polly firmly. "You must have realized that by now. I don't know why it is, but they feel things more deeply than other men seem to. They care so much about making things *right*, in a world that doesn't care much at all one way or another. It's what makes them so loyal and lovable, of course, and such admirable men, but it's what also makes them such a trial to live with, day in and out."

She glanced at Juliette shrewdly. "But I expect you've likely figured that out for yourself, too, haven't you?"

"Yes," said Juliette slowly, "I do believe I have."

And the more she considered what Polly had said, the more sense it made. She couldn't undo Daniel's first marriage, or pretend it had never happened, nor, really did she wish to. He did feel things more deeply than most men, and for him to have kept Catherine's fate locked up inside of him for so long must have been torturous for him, and the fact that he'd chosen her to share it with proved how much he trusted her, and loved her. When she thought of it that way, it made heartbreaking sense. If he hadn't cared so much about Catherine and her baby, then he wouldn't be able to care as much about Juliette and hers now. In a way, Daniel likely valued life, and love—her life and her love—all the more for having lost them once before.

"Are you ready to go back to shore and make up with Daniel now?" asked Polly wryly. "I'd promised Diana we'd sail to the point and back, but if you wish we can turn about now."

"No, no," said Juliette quickly, glancing forward to the little girl in the bow. "I don't want to disappoint her. But when we do return—oh, Polly, thank you so much!"

They sailed to the sandy point at the mouth of the harbor, where they ate slices of ham and golden cheese stuffed into buns and drank lemonade and collected dozens of tiny sand dollars. But while Juliette danced barefoot on the sand with Diana and taught her a song in French, Polly kept an uneasy eye on the tide and the weather.

"Time to shove off," she finally announced. "The wind's freshening, and I don't like the look of those clouds."

To Juliette the sky still seemed every bit as sunny as it had earlier, with only a few downy tufts of clouds to mar the endless blue, but as soon as they put out into the water, even she could feel the difference in how the boat responded.

The wind was fighting them now, changing direction without warning, the swells chopping into whitecaps, and instead of the smooth, easy sail they'd had before, now Polly was laboriously tacking back and forth in a slow zigzag across the harbor, fighting for every inch of headway they gained. The tide was turning, too, contriving with the wind to push them back out to sea. Polly had long ago stopped talking, concentrating instead completely on the sky and the wind, and even Diana sensed the change, abandoning her post in the bow and coming to curl up in Juliette's lap.

"How much longer, Aunt Polly?" she whined mournfully. "I want to go home."

"Not much longer," said Polly as cheerfully as she could, though it was clear to all three of them that this was unabashedly optimistic, if not an out-and-out lie. They were closer to the moored ships now, including the *Morning Star*, but still far from the safety of the wharf and shore.

"I'm sure Aunt Polly is doing everything she can," said Juliette gently, smoothing the little girl's black curls back from her forehead. "You know she's a first-rate sailor. Your parents wouldn't let you be here now if she weren't."

Diana sniffed, unconvinced, and wriggled closer to Juliette. "I miss my mama."

Juliette understood. The rougher the water became, the harder the wind blew into the single sail, the more uneasy she became, and the more her old fears began to return. She hugged Diana close, as much to comfort herself as the child, and fervently wished she were safe on shore with Daniel.

"Oh, hell, now what?" grumbled Polly, pulling with all her weight on the line to try to bring the boat about on a fresh tack. As hard as she pulled, the mainsheet wouldn't budge, fouled somehow inside the block. "Here, Juliette, hold the tiller and don't let go. Focus on a point on shore—I've been using the meeting house tower—and keep aiming at that to keep us steady."

Reluctantly Juliette leaned on the tiller the same way Polly had, surprised by the force of the water against the rudder. It was harder than she'd expected to hold it steady, and she had to reach over Diana to use both hands to keep the tiller from moving. Polly shifted forward, tied the line to a small cleat, then turned to the fouled block, yanking on the wooden oval to free the tangled lines. The knot gave way easily, but as Polly trimmed the sail, a gust of wind from the opposite direction swept the boom across the deck to catch her against the chest, knocking her hard flat upon the deck.

"Oh, dear God, no!" gasped Juliette. "Polly, are you all right? *Polly?*"

But Polly wasn't all right. She was lying on her back on the deck, her eyes closed and her mouth open, her skin already turning ashy beneath her tan, and she wasn't moving, not even to groan.

Without thinking Juliette released the tiller to go to her, and immediately the little boat lurched to one side. She grabbed it back, trying to return it to the place it had been by focusing on the meeting house tower, the way

Polly had said. But the boat wouldn't settle, and began to lean so far over she feared they'd all be thrown overboard.

"I'm scared, Aunt Juliette!" wailed Diana, her arms tight around Juliette's waist. "I'm *scared!*"

And Juliette knew exactly what she meant.

For a long time after Juliette had left, Daniel stood alone in Amelie's front room, looking at nothing, thinking of everything. He'd known that telling Juliette about Catherine had to be done, and that it wouldn't be easy, not for either of them. He hadn't needed Joshua to tell him that.

Yet somehow, though he'd tried to speak honestly, from his heart, he'd managed to make such a mess of it that he doubted Juliette wished ever to see him again, let alone marry him. He'd wanted her to know how Catherine had died, so that Juliette understand how doubly much finding her on the beach that night had meant to him. She was the second chance that most people would never have to set their lives straight, and every morning he thanked fate for giving her to him.

If Catherine had been his first love, then Juliette was the deeper one, the one to last the rest of their lives together. And while her news of the coming baby had shocked him, he'd no doubt that this, too, was a sign that their union was already blessed.

That was what he'd tried to tell Juliette, what he'd come here this morning determined to explain. Until, that is, he'd opened his mouth and every last wrong word had come out instead. With a groan he swept up his hat from the table in the hall and jammed it onto his head as he headed out into the street, whistling for Sachem.

"I thought this was your dog," said Samson, following Sachem as he bounded up to Daniel. "I saw him as I passed by. He's too good a dog to leave here in the street, Danny. Someone like me will take him away from you. Isn't that right, boy?"

Sachem ran to Samson, snuffling happily at his legs, then bounced back to Daniel, whose greeting was more distracted.

"Good Sachem, good lad," he said, scratching the dog behind the ears. "I couldn't take him inside, not with Amelie's blasted cat."

Samson twisted his face to show exactly how little regard he had for Amelie's cat. "But how is the fair Juliette this morning?"

"Mad as blazes with me," confessed Daniel grimly as they began walking. "Last night 'twas all moonlight and smiles and aye to my proposal, but this morning she'd rather see me flayed alive."

"Ah. I'm sorry my coat brought you no luck, most likely because you forgot this with it." Samson handed Daniel the bedraggled ribbon knot that Juliette had made for him for the squantum. "Polly found this in the cabin, and was damned put out with me for not making you wear it."

"I needed more help than that this morning." Daniel fingered the sad little ribbon knot, an unavoidable reminder of happier days, and tucked it back into his buttonhole. At least he could have that much of Juliette nearby. "At our wise older brother's suggestion, I told her I'd been married before."

Samson stopped, and whistled low. "You surprise me, too, brother. You're right, no scrap of ribbon's going to set that back to rights. I'd say you need a tankard of ale to loosen your tongue, and tell me what other trouble we can spare poor Juliette."

Much later, in a dark corner of a tavern near the water, and after much coaxing from Samson, Daniel finally reached the end of his story.

"I'm sure Juliette's back with Amelie now," he finished glumly, "telling her about how cruel and deceitful I've been."

"And I doubt she's saying anything of the sort," said Samson as he pushed away his now empty platter from supper. "You've tested her sorely, aye, but it's clear she loves you enough that she'll forgive you, if you're willing to do it right."

"Right, ha," said Daniel, who'd neither eaten nor drunk much of anything, instead emptying his plate by slipping the food to Sachem, gobbling contentedly under the table. "Everything I've done is wrong."

"All you must do is tell her you love her," advised Samson. "A woman never tires of hearing it, and it's the best cure-all I know after a quarrel."

"But it's true," protested Daniel. "I do love her, more than anything or anyone else in the world. What I felt for Catherine is nothing compared to how I feel for Juliette."

"Then it should be easy enough, shouldn't it?" said Samson as he motioned for the keep to pay their reckoning. "Tell her you love her, and the rest will follow."

Tell her you love her, and the rest will follow: it sounded both wise and easy, and the more that Daniel considered it, he knew it was the best advice in the world. After keeping to himself for so long, he felt an almost overwhelming sense of relief at having shared his past—and his present—with his brother. In some convoluted way, this had been his real return to his family, and it could not have come at a better time.

In the doorway they paused, blinking as their eyes grew accustomed to the sunlight.

"Tell me, Sam," said Daniel. "Do you think if we'd become pirate kings, the way we'd planned, that we'd have had an easier time with women?"

"Hell, yes," said Samson as they began walking toward the wharf. "How else do you think old Blackbeard kept peace with seven wives, eh?"

Daniel laughed, but Samson's attention had instantly focused on the *Morning Star*.

"There's something amiss on board," he said, striding quickly to the end of the wharf as he reached inside his coat for his spyglass. "They're all scurrying about on deck like a flock of headless hens."

"Look over there, Sam," said Daniel, pointing into the harbor beyond the bigger ship. "That smaller boat, there. I'll wager that's what's got their attention. What's happened to her sail, I wonder?"

Samson shifted the glass. "Jesus," he said. "That's Polly's boat, but she's not aboard. Hold, there's Diana, though, and another woman. Blast it, where's my lass?"

"Why doesn't the *Morning Star* lower her boat to help them?" demanded Daniel. Not sweet little Diana, he thought with despair, and not Sam's wife, too.

"Because the damned boat's *here,*" said Samson, shoving the glass back into his coat.

Daniel grabbed him by the arm. "Then we'll go ourselves. Damnation, Sam, hurry!"

Samson pulled three more men from the gathering crowd, and the five of them, along with Sachem, dropped into the *Morning Star*'s boat. From habit Daniel claimed the starboard after-oar, and from habit, too, he set the same brutal pace for the others he used for rescues on Nantucket. Though the sun still shone bright overhead, this wind would have been against a small boat with a single sail, and even an experienced sailor like Polly would have had difficulty returning to shore. Relentlessly Daniel pulled at the oar, determined to reach the boat before it foundered.

Samson had handed the spyglass to the man at the tiller, to help keep them in sight of the boat and to tell him, too, if he caught sight of Polly. The man shouted something to Samson, who turned enough to look over his shoulder at Daniel.

"Danny," he shouted into the wind. "The other woman—it's Juliette."

Without thinking, Daniel broke stroke, turning to look at the boat. They were near enough now that even without the glass he could see the unmistakable bright blue of her gown, the blue that had been his gift to her.

Not Diana, not Polly, oh, dear God, not Juliette and her babe, not now. . . .

With a roar of desperation he threw himself against the oar, pulling so hard he could feel the boat lift beneath them. From the corner of his eye he saw the tall, dark hull of the *Morning Star* as they shot past her, and the ragged cheers of her harbor-watch urging them onward. They must be close now, but he didn't want to break stroke again to look.

"Give way starboard!" bawled the man at the tiller, and swiftly the others at the oars obeyed, slowing and bringing the boat around. Breathing hard, at last Daniel looked for Juliette.

The sailboat was nearly upon them now. The waves were tossing the boat up and down, and the hull was nearly keel up; they were in very real danger of capsizing. But what terrified him the most was the sight of Juliette and Diana huddled together beside the tiller, clinging to it for dear life.

"Hold on, Juliette!" he roared. "Hold on!"

"Are we near enough?" asked Samson, breathing hard from rowing, and Daniel nodded, gathering up one of the coiled lines from the bottom of the boat.

Swiftly he wrapped one end around the bench, then took the other, tied to a heavy, clawlike hook, and swung it over his head. As soon as he felt the line spinning fast enough, he hurled the hook at the sailboat. The first throw missed, the hook falling short into the sea, but the second one caught the side and held fast, the line snapping taut between the two boats. The second hook caught on the first try, and at once the men began slowly pulling the two boats together.

"Where's Polly?" shouted Samson. "Is she there?"

"She's here," called Juliette, "but she's hurt. She's unconscious."

As Samson swore, the sailboat suddenly jerked and twisted, bucking against the force of the other boat's ropes.

"We can't pull closer without sending her over, Samson," said Daniel, pulling off first his boots, then his coat. "I'm going across."

Samson's mouth was a tight, tense slash across his

face. "Don't get caught between," he said, "or the boat will crush you."

Daniel nodded, the too-real possibility already in his thoughts. Grabbing hold of the line, he slipped over the side. The water was cold, cold enough that he gasped and swore as a swell washed against the side of the boat and back over his head.

"Daniel!" shouted Samson, leaning over the side as he held Sachem's collar. "Take care, mind?"

Daniel grinned, or at least grimaced, and began moving along the rope, hand over hand, dragging his body through the rough water to reach the sailboat. He went slowly, making sure of each grip, gasping for air after each wave washed over his head, more spent than he'd realized after the long, fast row from shore. But Juliette was waiting; he couldn't fail her, and hand over hand over hand, he would reach her.

He was nearly there, the sailboat only a few feet away, close enough that when he blinked he could see Juliette's frightened face watching over the side. Suddenly the rope in his hands sagged, plunging him deeper into the water, and the next wave slammed his head hard against the side of the boat, so hard that he saw a million tiny stars before his eyes with Juliette in the middle. His fingers flew open and the rope slid from his grasp, and he felt himself drifting down without the will to stop.

Catherine and Juliette and Polly and Diana, he thought dully, and now me.

But another hand was clawing at his, pulling him through the water, refusing to let him go. His head rose clear of the water and he swore as the air found the cut on his forehead.

"Daniel, love," gasped Juliette, her fingers still wrapped tight around his wrist. "Can you pull yourself up?"

He nodded, knowing for her he could do anything, and by following the line hooked over the side he was finally able to pull himself over the side.

"Oh, Daniel," cried Juliette, hanging to the side. "Your head—you're bleeding."

"Not much, lass," he said, his voice thick, and smiled at her as best he could. The deck sloped so steeply toward the water that he didn't dare try to stand. Across from them huddled Polly, pale and shaken with one arm cradled in the other and Juliette's shawl tucked over her like a blanket, and Diana crouched beside her.

And there, swinging free like a whip, was the line he needed. Carefully he inched forward until he reached the rope, bracing his feet against the side. He untied the line from the cleat and paid it out so that the boat could turn up into the wind and stop. The little boat rocked once, twice, then righted itself as if it had meant to do it all along.

Then Juliette was there, holding him, hugging him, dabbing at his forehead with her handkerchief as the tears streamed down her cheeks. The other boat pulled close and Samson jumped aboard, rushing to Polly, and the sight of them together reminded him of Sam's advice.

"I love you, Juliette," he said, loudly, so she'd be sure to hear, and everyone else as well. "I love you, sweetheart, and I always will."

"Oh, Daniel," she whispered, her dear face wreathed in joy. "I love you, too."

"So do I, Uncle Daniel," said Diana, climbing onto his legs to kiss one cheek, while Sachem licked the other. "You're a hero."

He thought of how Juliette had been the one to keep him from sinking, and tried to shake his head. "Nay, I don't think I'm—"

"You've always been my hero, Daniel," said Juliette firmly. "You *are*, and don't ever forget it."

Epilogue

Nantucket Island
July 1728

Juliette lay in the hammock, drowsily watching the sun slide low over the moors. Daniel had rigged the hammock outside for her, here beneath the porch, when in the last month of her pregnancy the house had seemed too hot for sleeping, and their bed too uncomfortable. But out here, swaying in the breeze with the sound of the waves to lull her, she'd been blissfully content, the ocean on one side of her and the moors on the other.

Two gulls danced in the sky overhead, mewing to one another, and at the sound little Sarah stirred, stretching her tiny fists in her sleep as she snuggled closer to her mother. Juliette smiled, and lightly traced the pattern of a heart on her daughter's cheek. Daniel would be home soon, and he'd tease her if he found her asleep in the hammock again. That made her smile, too, and she let her eyes drift shut. Another minute would cause no harm, she decided as she cradled Sarah in her arms, another minute, maybe two.

"My two sleepyheads," said Daniel softly as he leaned over the hammock and kissed Juliette. She smiled as she woke, and reached up to draw him closer for a better, more wide awake kiss.

"Your daughter has behaved quite well today," said Juliette, reaching out to pet Sachem as Daniel carefully lifted the baby and settled her against his shoulder. "I don't think she's cried more than twice since you left."

"What can she possibly have to cry about, when you spoil her so wickedly?" He held his daughter securely in one broad arm, her head cradled in his hand as he kissed her, too. "Isn't that so, pretty Sarah?"

It was a sight that Juliette loved, her great strong blacksmith husband holding little Sarah as gently as if she were made of porcelain, her long white embroidered baby robe, a gift from her godparents Anabelle and Joshua, drifting over his arms.

"Tomorrow, if you two ladies wish," said Daniel softly, letting Sarah sleep, "I'll take you to Sherburne so you can see the progress on your milliner's shop. I believe you'll be pleased, Madame Fairbourne. Everything is exactly as you ordered."

"I cannot wait to see it!" said Juliette excitedly. Though the Sherburne shop would be small to begin with, she'd still wanted it to be as beautiful as the one she'd left behind in Boston, a place where women would wish to come and linger. She'd already hired Mrs. Swain to be her assistant, and John Robin's wife, Mary, to help with stitching.

But to her great wonder, Daniel had paid for the building and the goods to go inside it, using the windfall money from his last voyage as a shipmaster to fund her dream.

She'd been as overwhelmed by his support and understanding as she was by the gift, and she'd thought often of her conversation with Polly. Truly the Fairbourne men *were* special, in all the ways that mattered most.

"You have ladies already peeking in the windows," continued Daniel. "I had to chase away three of them today, telling them you wouldn't be open until the first of September."

"The first of September, and not one day before," said Juliette firmly. "This summer belongs to Sarah, and you."

He leaned over to kiss her. "I do love you, Juliette," he whispered. "For everything."

She grinned, and pulled him back to kiss her again. "Then make me the happiest woman in the world," she whispered back, "and let me love you for everything else."

And forever after, she did.

Return to a time of romance...

SONNET BOOKS

Where today's

hottest romance authors

bring you vibrant

and vivid love stories

with a dash of history.

PUBLISHED BY POCKET BOOKS

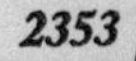
2353

Delight in every romance title from

MIRANDA JARRETT

Wishing

Moonlight

Under the Boardwalk

Cranberry Point

The Captain's Bride

All available wherever books are sold

SONNET BOOKS

2380